WRITING IN SPIRIT

Jeanne's Story

A NOVEL BY

RUTH LEE

Spirit
Wind
BOOKS

For more information about Ruth Lee and her books go to
www.ruthlee-scribe.com

Spirit Wind Books, an imprint of Love Your Life Publishing
427 N Tatnall St # 90946
Wilmington, DE 19801-2230

ISBN: 978-1-934509-74-6

Library of Congress Control Number:
Printed in the United States of America
First Printing 2014

Cover and design: www.Cyanotype.ca
Internal design: David Redondo

Others Books by
Ruth Lee

Novels

Angel of The Maya

Within the Veil: *An Adventure in Time*

The Books of Wisdom From
The Teachers of the Higher Planes

We Are Here

The Work Begins

The Art of Life ~ *Living Together in Harmony*

Now is The Time

The World of Tomorrow

Bliss is It!

Other Works

The Word of The Maya

The Making of a Scribe
How to Achieve a Life You Can Write About

Can You Pray?
We Are All Here to Seek the Way

Dedicated to Lynne Klippel, *a scribe and writer in her own right, who generously supports other's work as if her own.*

Table of Contents

Katherine Hepburn reportedly said:

"If you want to sacrifice the admiration of many men for the criticism of one—go ahead, get married."

Chapter One

Passing Time

The other day, while visiting an old friend, I saw her as she is—not as she wished to be seen. She hoped to project success *and* happiness, and all I saw was misery. Thinking back… It started as I stood outside her high-rise condo, not moving even though she had buzzed me through the security gate. A dread started spreading through me like fog, but there was no turning back. She knew how long it took to get to her floor. Once there, Sue threw open the double doors and pulled me in, crushing me to her chest, but like the welcome mat, the hug was for display purposes only.

For all the show, I sensed anger, anxiety, and tension as Sue pecked one cheek and then the other, but what to say? So I lied. "You look great!"

Beaming as she pushed me away, Sue said, "So do you!"

I thought she looked terrible, but what to say? So I lied again.

"Your dress is very becoming." Meanwhile wondering if she was about to announce an unplanned pregnancy, but then Sue would never let things get that far.

Her smile disappeared as she said, "Your pants remind me of my trip last year to India. They're so pretty and dainty—the way they balloon around your legs—like a harem girl."

A harem girl in India? Ignoring the clash of cultures, I said, "Show me your pictures. I have to see them all. I haven't been out of the country in ages, and miss so many vacations flying here there and everywhere on business. It's exhausting!"

When Sue said nothing, I added, "It's a bother, and so much work, but a gal's got to do what a gal's got to do to keep it together."

Keep in mind that I am recalling all this, trying not to edit so as to make myself look better, but try it sometime. It isn't easy to achieve a balanced memory.

We kept pecking at each other until I got tired—about two minutes after saying 'Hello'. I tried to figure out why Sue wanted me there, while she avoided the issue. It turned out she didn't want to see me per se, but no one else would listen to her brag and complain at the same time, so I had to do.

Once upon a time we lived together, but never good friends. To be honest, I wanted to get married and have 2.5 kids while Sue wanted to make out with my boyfriends behind my back. I did try going out and doing things with her, but she always made me mad—so I took to hiding when she wanted a friend. Back then it seemed we sat around and stared into air a lot— ignoring each other whenever together. We eventually grew older and wiser, talking more about who we were and less about who we aspired to be.

Life became more tolerable then, but obviously something was very wrong now. I dreaded hearing about it, but made no move to leave as Sue fluffed her longish blond hair and looked at herself in the mirror over the mantle. She carefully arranged her features to project long-suffering and grave concern before turning to launch into her latest venture.

"I have a house near you that needs repaired and was wondering if you knew anyone who could look at it and tell me what needs taken out or put in—what needs redone. You're always so mechanically minded, Jeanne—so very crafty."

Why ask me? My place could use a paint job for starters and the To Do List goes on endlessly after that. Could this be why she *had* to see me? I couldn't buy into it, but what to say? So I was honest and said, "You can send out for bids. If it's too much from the standpoint of making money, figure out what needs done and what can wait."

"But you have such a good eye for construction, Jeanne!"

I almost blurted out what I was thinking: What a laugh! You have the Decorator of the Year on retainer.

I was wondering what to say when Sue said, "Although my income is great, I'm trying to stem cash outflow—to insure my early retirement. I'm not like you. I have to have security. You do know how business is now, don't you?"

As Sue said this, she reached over and pulled at a thread on my blouse and snapped it off. That is when I knew what was going on. She was about to be axed, but what to say? So I strung her along. "Is there anything new going on at your place? I heard there's a merger in the wind. Will it affect you?"

She spoke too quickly and too loudly. "No!"

She stalled, but I knew she would tell me more than I wanted to know before I left, and I also knew what would follow.

"There's nothing much going on in my area, but others are scared of losing their jobs. I'd be scared, too, if I had cut and axed my way to the top like they did."

It had to be bad, but what to say? So I purred, "You don't have to worry, Sue. You never cut up anyone or did anything evil to get where you are. If that *is* what is going on, you can rest assured *your* career is safe. But what about that guy who always gave you a hard time—and all his work?"

"Oh, you mean, John. John's great! He isn't going to be let go. He's too smart to let that happen to him, and he's not as nasty as he was. He has to be nice to me now, because I know where all the bodies are buried—and I know all about him and how he works. I'm the only one who does."

Oh, Oh! Big time trouble ahead, but what to say? So I laughed and said, "That's a relief! You can sit back and watch others go flying out the door."

Sue is a neglectful hostess at best, but we finally entered the kitchen so I could serve drinks. I poured two tall glasses of Southern-style sweet tea while waiting for her to decide what she would tell me about her job.

Twisting her hair, about to put it in her mouth, Sue realized I was watching, so she snapped, "Well, I can't sit back and relax—not just yet. I have to cut back my department, but not as far as others. There are at least six or seven departments above me who have to cut back, too, but they're all waiting for me to take the lead."

Surprised, I couldn't help thinking 'six or seven above me' meant she had slid down their corporate totem pole and had to be in bad shape.

With a little pout she said, "You should see what they did for the big boss on his birthday. They got together and bought him a car—not a real one. After all, he has two Company cars—both Jaguars! This was a toy MG, because he always wanted one when he was in college—but couldn't afford it. He got a big kick out of it, especially when they said they all chipped in and bought it with *their own money!*"

Thinking back over years of Sue's tales that were even more evasive than this one, I managed to say, "Wow, the last of the big spenders!"

Her eyes grew misty as she rewarded me with possibly her biggest, toothy grin ever. Shaking her head, she said, "You don't get the picture, Jeanne. You never do! Nobody buys the boss anything—ever! And definitely not with their own money!!"

Fully aware of how many lovely days I had wasted in the past listening to Sue cry about work, I snapped. "Oh, yes, I forgot. Corporate types never pay their own way. It's just we peons who buy gifts and pay for travel. We who are self-employed don't have *bosses*, per se, but we have customers who expect to be treated—at a ridiculously low tax deduction, I might add."

With a loud sniff, Sue said, "Oh, I didn't mean to rub it in. I'm just trying to show you how desperate *they* are!"

Almost choking on my iced tea I barely managed to not shout. "Yes, yes, I see. You aren't desperate at all—and that's great—really great!"

I swear Sue turned murderous then, but I felt anything was better than sitting around listening to her blubber about money wasted and no one benefitting but *them*—and how *they* all hate each other.

Without looking at me, Sue said, "Let's change the subject! You can't imagine what it's like at the top! It's terrible—but I love it!"

If she had wiped her brow I would have laughed out loud, but she looked pathetic, so I agreed. "Yes, you're right, Sue.

We don't have much in common if we talk only about money and jobs." I couldn't go on without getting too upset to work later. It's Sue's style to continually cuss out those who pay her bills, so why would she be loyal to me? I realized that kind of thinking always ruined our times together. Furthermore, Sue looked like she might explode any second, so I sat quietly waiting to hear what she wanted to talk about—other than her career.

Suddenly she said, "What do you want to eat, Jeanne? I thought about making lunch, like I said, but it was so late when I got in last night—and the cats were hungry, so I fed them the tuna."

Tuna! Sue was going to feed me canned tuna again, after bragging about her expensive meals at every fancy restaurant within a 50-mile radius. I decided if I had to put up with her whining, she would pay! "It's your treat, but why not try that new restaurant you told me about last time?"

Knowing she could not make me pick up the check again, Sue changed tactics. "What new restaurant? I can't remember. They come and go so quickly, but I was at a cute little Italian place last week. I think it will be perfect—since you love pasta."

Ignoring her comment, I smiled and said, "I remember the name of the place, Chez Paree. You know how much I love French cuisine! You said it was simply divine—and lunch was very reasonable for French."

Sue's pout disappeared and her fidget started as I forced her to eat her words. Barely audible, she said, "Oh that place! You wouldn't like it. It's really not that great."

She grew more nervous as I talked of spending her money— not mine. I knew then she was broke and her cards maxed out again, but I had no intention of buying a meal she invited me to, even if we never left her place. I was not treating—or retreating this time.

"I'm sure you love Chez Paree, Sue! It's the talk of the town. But if you want pasta, that's okay. I'd treat again, but I need to deposit a check and get money from the ATM. I use plastic only for business expenses—not food. There's no percentage in it. Besides, the IRS has made treating clients too expensive— let alone friends and relatives."

Frantically flipping her hair, trying to act nonchalant, Sue said, "Oh, I don't worry about tax stuff. Our accountants take care of all that. I go in and dump my receipts and let them figure it out. It's their job! One bookkeeper hates my guts, because she's jealous of what I make. She gets paid well for doing it, otherwise, why did she become a CPA?"

Determined not to be sidetracked, I mumbled, "Must be nice," and stood to indicate I was ready to leave.

Ignoring me, Sue sat until she could keep quiet no longer. "What? Oh, yes, we were talking about lunch and you hadn't made up your mind. You know me, I've always been decisive. Now what do you want to eat—pasta or Mexican?"

So typical, Sue never decides anything without wasting an hour—but how to make her pay? "It's your treat, Sue. You decide! If you can't swing French, either is okay with me."

Her gaze shifted to the front of my white blouse, as if checking for stains. She looked so sad, I relented—as usual. "Why don't we go for pasta?"

Her expression immediately brightened as she said, "That's exactly what I mean about being decisive. I always know what you like—and what is best!"

Once on the elevator—almost to the first floor, she attempted another coup. Rummaging through her huge handbag, she said, "Oh, I forgot my keys. Can we take your car? You can keep an eye on your car better there than here."

Sue either didn't have a company car anymore or didn't have gas money—again, but what to say? I struggled to speak nicely. "Is there a problem with your parking lot? Don't tell me cars aren't safe here."

Admittedly a low blow, but I didn't want to spend any more time parrying and thrusting, knowing I could quickly finish Sue off and would—but later.

Her cheeks were quite pink by now, but I had not yet agreed to drive, so her voice softened to a sweet trickle. "Of course there's no problem! I've just begun worrying about crime—everywhere. It's even starting to move this way."

Interested, but unconvinced, I decided to flush out whatever she was hiding. "Thinking about moving, Sue?"

"Well, no, but if it gets bad, I'll have to."

What she meant was: If she gets fired. So I proceeded to unsheathe my rapier—or what was left of it after years of futile duels and said, "I thought you bought your place out right—paid cash."

"I did, I mean I have a mortgage like everyone else—except you, but I didn't put down as much as they wanted originally when my raise went through. They gave me a lot of credit then, so I don't have any real equity to speak of now." Then she smiled as if she had received some kind of divine inspiration and said, "I can walk away from this place any time I want and only be out the amount of rent I'd have had to pay for an apartment like it."

Dumbfounded as usual when confronted with Sue's reasoning and sense of logic, I said, "Won't that adversely affect your credit?"

She looked at me strangely and said, "Oh, I see what you mean. Yes, it could prove to be troublesome to some folks, but I don't have to worry about such things. I'm not about to go into business for myself."

As usual, her ignorance got a rise out of me. I almost screamed. "Everyone has to worry about their credit standing! It's part of living in this world. If we all decide to cash in and demand our money back, where will we live? You're either part of the community and care about the housing needs of others or building a castle with a moat to keep the world out—and in the end that won't work."

She sniffed, before saying, "You were smart, Jeanne. You bought a little two-bedroom and paid it off right away. But having to maintain my executive position—I encounter financial drains you don't have. If an Assistant Vice President at Grant doesn't live up to the standards they set, they'll look you in the eye and tell you to move on. I have to keep up appearances! I can't let myself go."

Wowee, wow! Claws and fangs in abundance, but I couldn't stop myself from saying: "Yes, I keep forgetting about corporate cattle calls. I was once a poor little heifer myself—until I stopped taking their bull and built my own ranch. True, it's small, but it's all mine! You might think about doing the same—soon. It's a lot better for your health. Believe me!"

That's when I realized Sue had maneuvered me over to my car and was waiting for me to unlock the doors. How does she do it?

"I know it was better for you to get out, but my health isn't a problem. I give people heart attacks—I don't have them! Oh, yes, I forgot to tell you I bought a membership in City Spa, and my membership is being processed at the country club this month—a social membership —no golf."

"No gold?" It was a Freudian slip of sorts, but I let it hang there.

Sue looked perplexed, but bounced back with, "What? Oh, yes, I see. Golf does cost a lot, but that's not why I didn't apply. I don't like to play that much—and we can't take customers out like we used to. If a customer insists on it, I can put the cost of a few rounds on my expense account and be reimbursed more easily."

Trying to sound impressed, I said, "Sounds like you have it made!"

Obviously, she had to disagree. "Oh, no, I have to be seen. I don't need to do it, you understand, but with times as they are women have to compete with men on their turf."

Teasing, but not really into it, I asked, "Why?"

"Why? You must be crazy. We all have to do it to succeed!"

Stamping her Prada-clad feet so hard she rocked my Mini with the impact, I chose to ignore the intent and quietly said, "I don't."

"What do you mean—you don't? Of course, you do! I know you're supposed to be some kind of eccentric—down on men, with no intention of marrying again, but what are you saying? You ignore men?"

Now what? "There's nothing wrong with men."

She appeared stunned, barely able to control herself as she yelled, "What?"

"You heard me. They have their style and we have ours, but everything's the same as it was. You either feel secure or you don't. An insecure male is more treacherous and nasty than the average female could ever be. You know that. So why do I have to repeat myself—constantly?"

"No, you're wrong. Women are terrible in business. They don't make good bosses!"

No luck in restraining myself, I spoke too loudly. "Shame on you, Sue! You're in business. I'm in business. All our friends are in business. Name all these terrible businesswomen!"

Her mouth kept opening and closing, making little O's. She was stymied, didn't know which ship to jump off or which side of the argument she was on and gave up. "Well, you know—women can't handle power."

"They're really getting to you at the office, aren't they? You better figure out real quick how to get your money together, get out of debt, and get the hell out of there!"

Forgetting our agreed upon destination during our bitter exchange, I found myself turning into Chez Paree's parking lot just as Sue started crying. Totally out of control, she grabbed my arm and jerked it off the wheel. Even though it was her fault, I had to say something, but what to say?

"Sue, don't cry. What is so wrong that it can't be fixed? You have money invested in real estate and IRA's, and a good job that's secure. Right? So, what is causing you so much grief?" I sat quietly a minute or so before I got out of the car.

Apparently my lack of attention got through to her. She wailed, "I don't have a man!"

Stunned, I said, "W-h-a-a-t? How will that help? You don't have a man? Aren't you lucky? This way you can do whatever you want and never have to look back or worry about how your decisions affect *his* life. When you have a man around, your options are automatically reduced. You have to boost his ego, even if yours is sagging—and think about all the other games men play. You're lucky you're single!"

Immediately Sue became her manic self and said, "Yes, I guess I am lucky! I knew when I chose career over marriage that I was on the winning track, but every once in a while I envy divorced people like you. I want to be married, divorced, or whatever, to show the world someone wanted me."

Good grief! Things had fallen to our old lows of communication. Managing a smile, I said, "Sounds intriguing, but I hear it all the time. Where do women pick up that crap? It's not logical—sounds weird, but I heard it last week—at an outside meeting."

Arranging her hair, Sue said, "You've had it all, Jeanne, so you don't know how hard it is when all you can do is wonder about lasting relationships. I never married. I never quit. I just work, work, work and help other people who never help me."

I couldn't help thinking, when did you ever help anyone who didn't pay you, but what to say without preaching a sermon? Inspired, I said, "You have no problem! The universe repays in the same coinage those who help others—ten times the amount given in love by them—even more if you don't tell others about it. So don't worry! If you've accrued a lot of credit, you'll get a lot of help when you need it. It's like money in the bank, only better."

As I waited for her next move, Sue's eyes shifted to the entrance, so I gave her The Look! She knew then that if she didn't stop whining, I was going to order the most expensive entree plus dessert—if we ever made it into Chez Paree.

Apparently my message got through, because she jerked open the car door, but didn't move. Managing to smile, she said, "Jeanne, do you have an extra twenty? I just remembered I didn't put enough money in my wallet this morning."

"No, Sue, I don't. You can always use plastic. They take Visa. See the sign?"

Her smile vanished as she hoisted herself up and out of the car. Staring at me over the roof, she said, "Oh, I forgot. Normally I don't charge food."

I silenced my grumblings, but couldn't stop thinking, Hah! She charges groceries, notions, whatever every day! She hasn't used cash since she started climbing the corporate ladder and became a big-time spender. She's so lost she doesn't know what day it is.

Sue's incessant whining brought me back in time to hear her say, "I don't know what it is about our luncheon engagements anymore, but they depress me. You used to always be so upbeat—lots of fun."

My reaction was knee-jerk, but I was wise enough not to say, I used to let you bleed me dry—but no more. That Jeanne has given up playing games—especially with you. No more tapping into my energy, depleting me—then not calling until you're half-dead or totally depressed again. I'm not a booster cable or AAA waiting to jump-start your engine whenever you're depressed. Do it yourself! That's what I thought, but all I said was, "What do you mean, Sue?"

"Oh, nothing." The pout back in place, she tried pushing the guilt button again, but I was determined to put it out of commission forever, even if it meant we would no longer be 'best friends' as she liked to tell her clients and strangers. Everyone else knew better.

As if lost in thought, Sue said, "You seem different today, Jeanne, unhappy, upset—or something."

Another battle about to be launched and me with no lunch, so I said, "I'm feeling great! Too bad about your career, though."

Appearing stunned, Sue said, "What do you mean?"

Oh, oh, too deep a thrust. Not wanting to precipitate another bleeding heart episode, I decided to retreat—appear to grovel, so I said, "Oh, nothing. As you always say, you have so little time for yourself, because you always have to work, work, work—yet never get done."

Brightening for a moment, Sue simpered for the benefit of Chez Paree's waiting hostess, "Oh, yes, that's true. I have so very much!"

As we moved toward a table, our waitress rolled large, gray cat eyes at me as if we were part of a conspiracy. As we sat I felt as if someone else's face was moving—not mine. With right eyebrow arched, I said, "Ever wonder why?"

Obviously offended, Sue said, "What do you mean?"

Had to change my approach, after all Sue has to live with herself, I don't. I reminded myself of the drain she has always been on my resources. Removing her from my life required the cut be deep, quick and clean, if it was to last.

Before I could speak, Sue changed the subject again. "You know, Jeanne, you really should do something about your car."

Good intentions seldom last. Snapping back as usual when Sue went over the top, I said, "It's paid for. Is yours?"

"What?" She looked aghast.

Was my thrust unexpected? Moving behind the large menu I said loud enough for all following our conversation, "It's paid for. Is yours?" I enunciated every word. Rapier wit, ha!

Sue sat and looked out the window before speaking to me as if talking to a child. "You don't have to get nasty, Jeanne. I don't know what's wrong with you anymore. At times you act like such a moron. Anyone in their right mind would think my taking you out to lunch would cheer you up, but no, you get angry and hostile—like always. Can I help it if God has given me so much more than you?"

Much too loudly, I said, "God gives to those who can't make it on their own—so don't be so pleased with yourself!"

A sneer highlighted Sue's too-white teeth, pushing off-center her green contacts that never quite covered her brown eyes, as she spoke, even louder than before. "You really are a creep, Jeanne! You know that? You're like all the other women I know. You're all so jealous you can't stand to be around me at times."

After pausing long enough to gulp for air like a snapping turtle, Sue tore into me again. "Get used to it! I'm not about to change. Maybe we should call this whole shopping thing off? You don't need anything anyway—so why bother?"

Aha, another ploy not to pay for lunch. What a relief to end this masquerade! Preparing to leave, I said, "You're absolutely right, Sue! I don't need anything. Why shop—or eat?"

She appeared to be looking for a couple of dollars to tip the waitress for putting up with our display, while I hoped our scene had made her day. Sighing, Sue put away her wallet and started scanning the menu. What was with that?

As I rose from the table, Sue lowered her voice as if offended and said, "All I meant was, you don't look like you used to look.

Anymore, you're so—casual. You don't seem to care about your looks or anything."

"I don't."

"What will that get you—a trip to the welfare office?" Obviously desperate to maintain control of the conversation, Sue forgot which buttons belonged to me and instead hit on another woman she used to micromanage, too.

Having hesitated too long, I barely managed to say, "I'll let you know if it ever comes to that. In the meantime, I don't have any bills. I don't have any worries, and I don't have any spare time. So do you want to eat lunch or would you rather pass on it now?"

Her smile, blinking like a light on a battery charger, revealed that whatever calculations she was making did not elate her. "I don't know how we got so far off-track, Jeanne. I'm famished. Let's eat. You can even have shrimp cocktail. How about that?"

I wanted to pass on lunch and move on, but it appeared my life lesson in such relationships wasn't over, so like a bona fide weenie, I said, "Yeah, sure. Why not? We can split dessert."

Chapter Two

Eventide

The only day of the week I really relax is Saturday when everybody else is out running around hoping to see who else is out and about. Unfortunately, my Saturdays have become hectic lately. All I wanted to do was sit around, read a mystery, and sip tea, but I couldn't shake off my outing with Sue. Her moods soared and plunged so often, I felt like a therapist working with a lunatic all day without pay.

Sue called a little bit ago to say she's all keyed up, but I had nothing to give. It bothers me—a lot, because once I was where Sue is now. That is why I know she won't listen. She has to figure it out for herself. I wish her luck, but I'm tired of it!

Running around with Sue nagging at my mind doesn't help get my notes together for tomorrow's seminar. I have to put her out of my mind and get on with my life. If I don't get a grip, I'll be frazzled and bore everyone with tedious references to women who aren't really friends—but how to get to the point quickly?

When your life is in order, you seldom think about when it was crazy. You can't remember why you were out of line. So why bother trying? Back then you were the same person you are now, but didn't believe you could ever be happy or serene.

In fact, I doubted anyone who wasn't unhappy. I didn't really believe in God or man, nor did I care if I ever made a difference. What is truly weird to realize is that just being here—*makes a difference!*

Recently a critic said I don't let others into my past. She questioned the wisdom of doing that. Would opening up more about me help others? Wouldn't it instead encourage therapists to needlessly wander about trying to figure out why women listen to me or buy my books, rather than consult *them?* I guess I'll never know unless I try—but how to begin?

Thinking about it doesn't get it down on paper. Maybe I should leave well enough alone and continue doing what I always do? But if I don't explain myself to the public, someone else will do me no favors, preferring to gossip instead.

With pencil in hand, idly beginning to take inventory of my past, I felt myself float away into time, as if on a boat headed for the far horizon...

Once you know yourself and who you are, it is important to remember who you were when you were a child and file it away for another day.

I better explain that...

When I was a baby I was perfect, so were you when you arrived, but we had to mess things up by being petulant and ignorant of the facts of this life. We had to assert our brand of individuality. We cursed those who would not obey our commands or cave-in to our demands. We fought and won. We fought and lost. We fought and fought and fought until somewhere around age six we learned we had to conform or be caged. Kindergarten is when you can sense if you will make it or not. You either conform and adjust or contend with a lifetime of maladjustment and struggling to assert your will.

Who were you when you reached first grade? As for me, I was a kindergarten drop-out!

After the first few months of kindergarten, I would not go. I wanted to work and they expected me to play. I thought it was dumb and a waste of time, so I didn't go back. My mother gave up once I devised a fail-safe system to stay home.

Upon demand I could produce a raw, virulent, inflamed throat. It looked like diseased tonsils then, but I still have them now. My body provided a good alibi. The truant officer tried to coerce me into conforming to the system. I was reprimanded and my mother severely criticized, but she stood by me and afterward tried again to get me to return to kindergarten.

This petty bureaucrat played an important role in my life. He predicted I was doomed and would be a truant and poor student. He had to be proved wrong and my mother's faith kept intact, so I never played hooky or missed school, and always got great grades, but did not go to school until it was compulsory. I showed him!

I found myself in first grade. I loved to read, even though my teacher ignored my passion and forced me to sit in the back of the class. Why? Maybe she knew about my kindergarten transgressions or remembered the sibling she failed years before—or she remembered Mama? She did her best, but could not suppress my love of books. In time my abilities forced her to grudgingly move me up—to the Blue Birds Table to roost among her pets. Imagine me nesting beside the wealthy dairyman's heir and a beautiful Shirley Temple wannabe. They sat at Miss Albright's right and left side.

Then we moved to the country so my mother could regain her health. I went to a one-room school with 27 students from first to eighth grade. The teacher was nice, but not at first. I sat and listened to her teach other classes, instead of practicing my *spelling and arithmetic. Since I was the only one in second grade, Mrs. Allender let me read every book within her domain and introduced me to the best of public education. I never forgot the stories she told the older kids during the course of a day. From there on out I was ahead of my peers over the years, simply because text books were seldom updated—About then is when I noticed I was ahead of time.*

Now what else might be of interest to people who judge children—and me?

Halfway through third grade we relocated and I went to a big consolidated school. Mrs. Ferguson told me to memorize the multiplication tables and many, many words for vocabulary and spelling. With great difficulty I learned the tables and decided to never memorize anything else. Through repetition and tests I became a decent speller, but I can still look at a word and doubt I spelled it right. Recently someone told me I was probably dyslexic, but what did we know about that back then?

I don't dwell on the past well. Oh, yes, the mother thing! Must not forget to include that or *they* will claim I was maladjusted and whatever.

At home I was fascinated by the way my mother kept busy. She worked constantly, yet read much more than I ever have. She would sneak a peek at books while stirring bubbly strawberry preserves, even while ironing. She never listened to soap operas and such—warning me they encouraged unrealistic romantic ideas and provided bad information on how to handle men. She never mentioned sex—only later did I realize she was talking about it then.

At that stage I was a calculator—had to compute everything. I drove my menopausal mother crazy in those days. I once asked her how many books she read in a week. She said she didn't know and wondered why it mattered. A few weeks later she said she read about eight books a week—not counting the Bible and Concordia, of course.

My mother studied—not just read—the Bible and daily meditations as a continuance of her four-year degree from a Midwest Bible college. She never gave up her love of Christian philosophy or her dislike of modern psychology. Many years later when I studied psychology and sociology I discovered my mother was a brilliant social psychologist—not a sociologist as stated on her diploma.

Sitting lost in childhood memories, attempting to encapsulate my life, I thought of what it was like to be sixteen. I worked hard at building and respecting my sense of self—not to expect much from others. I wouldn't want to repeat those lessons. But when I see friends ruining relationships, because they didn't do their homework, I'm glad I learned my lessons well and passed the tests when young. It was no fun, so I don't remember much of my teens.

My father died when I turned 16, but is still with me. It took me ten years to figure that out—another lesson once learned promotes you in life.

Whenever I mention him, I tear up. I used to think it was caused by grief, but discovered the truth. It happens when his spirit gets too close to my core being—crowding me a bit. The years pass and condense into tears. I ask him to back off, give me space, and the past disappears as my eyes clear.

When you know your father is on a cloud nearby and can pop in on you at any moment, you don't live like a fool. Your father is around and you know it—and others can believe it or not.

Should I care if others don't believe what I know to be? I say 'too many care too much about other people's opinions and not enough about what makes sense to them,' but what can I say about emotional common sense that might help children under the control of such men and women?

The love of your life isn't going to leave you if you let the phone ring a few times, but you could lose love by being too possessive.

We want to own others, but refuse to be owned. We attack others, but hate to be chastised. We want others to do their part, while we sit and talk. God is divine, and we are always insecure, but somehow it all works out. In the end, we're lucky we don't get what we deserve.

What to do about the times in-between when you can't remember who you are and why you came to be here? If I sit a bit, it will appear in dreams. I'll live it that night or the next, but probably not remember it the next day. Why?

You retrieved a file from memory, but have to print it out and read it over to understand what it means. Your mind computes, but it is your spirit that knows how to use it. After a bit of relaxation, tune into Spirit through meditation or contemplation and you will do better work.

What is so difficult to understand about all this? I don't get why everyone isn't on the same page and on the same line once they know how life works.

Work teaches you to compute what goes on around you in your world. Deviant sex, mayhem, jealousy, greed, and such vices thrive in a world based on anxiety and fear. There is some good to be found in anxiety, since it makes you try harder, but it can be a waste of your mind when it confesses to things it never did or works out problems you don't have. Anxiety isn't what it was.

Devised by the mind, it helps you cope with the necessity of living with others.

No one wants to fail. When you see others fail, you grow anxious and nervous—may even feel sorry while shrinking away from them. Why? You don't want to lose, too. Regardless of your placement in life, you want to associate with winners. If you're low-bred and remain that way, you may have many unmet needs, yet aspire to be recognized as higher placed this life than you are. If you are highly placed at birth, you may want to keep the less entitled around you—to boost your ego. If so, you have difficulty believing anything, and your Spiritual Guides have a hard time getting through to you.

I know. When I meditate, I sometimes see the glowing outline of a being I assume is Divine—and my Spiritual Guides are often in my dreams. They appear as three old men dressed in casual work clothes.

Everyone has Guides, but may not see faces and bodies well enough to identify them. After all, they are spiritual entities, not human beings.

When I speak of Guides during the course of seminars, I emphasize they're different from guides you hire when traveling to assist you in getting from one place to another, but they are similar. I now have to get across to the unsuspecting that they have Spiritual Guides who came with them at birth to Earth and know why they chose to arrive or return—even if they never heard of them before.

Slipping in and out of my everyday mind during dress rehearsals helps me decide what God is to me and why I exist, but I do wonder if anyone is listening.

We all traveled to Earth together. For me that is a fact. But for some it conflicts with what they have been taught—and even thinking such thoughts is construed to be a sin. I write and talk about my experiences here on Earth, staying away from theology and philosophy, because I am my mother's daughter. She could not tolerate conducting discussions about God or who we are this life. You either believe—or you don't! If you don't, see you later and let's compare notes then.

Speaking of notes, I better get more cards. I need to move, if I intend to deliver this 'sermon' tomorrow.

After so many years of working on the big lessons, I see myself beginning to grow intolerant of those who believe in nothing. I think it's a sham meant to gain attention—rather than a plea to maintain sanity. Many psychologists maintain the balance of sanity lies in the hands of those who can believe in a superior being as all-knowing, all-achieving, and responsible for everything you will ever be. I don't.

Long ago I realized I don't believe in Christ the way my mother did. I know she is in the next life while I'm here, so it can't be bad to segregate your beliefs while on Earth into one system and exclude others—demanding everyone believe as you do. However, I think a line is drawn when you're intolerant of all others' relationships to God.

I have a tough time being a Christian, because I was raised in that tradition and totally believed what was taught. As an adult I found I was intolerant of other religions, yet could not find answers to my most pressing problems within my own. I remain grateful for the lessons and basic teachings provided by my family and original religion, because humans need an ethical structure and belief system to struggle against and build a strong life based on it. Fortunately, no one sees things like I do, thus I have to tolerate other faiths.

What you do now and then won't change you, but if you do something monthly or religiously, you become addicted to it. Imagine what happens if you practice one religion diligently every day? Having said that, I think it's obvious why I don't teach or compare religions—especially for my readers and audiences.

'What you do in your life is your business—until you tell me how to live my life' was an American credo taught in the past, but nonexistent today. No one willingly tolerates all others now. It's an ideal many strive to comprehend, even approve, but too biased to separate one's own feelings from unfounded fears.

While in school I believed in speaking nothing but the truth and lost a friend because of it. That taught me to scam—to lie bit-by-bit, or have very few friends. Does anyone exist who has not lied or misapplied the truth to make someone else happy?

I could analyze lies that appear in my work or stay at home trying to figure out what I did wrong then or in the past, but I would not be living in this world now if I did.

Knowing all this, the audience or reader accepts me as is or gives up trying and leaves. Life is an adventure—and you either follow or lead. Not being a follower by nature, I live in order to learn how to lead. Readers can unsubscribe and students can study with others, but this is how I teach.

Do I sound *holier than thou?* I hope not. I'm human and make mistakes while striving to return to the perfect state I was in when I arrived on Earth—which can never happen. Can it?

Chapter Three

Three Years Later

*T*ime slips by ever faster as I enter yet another social whirl and plan for the future rather than look back at the past. I haven't done much journaling lately and wonder why.

That struck me as funny—I can't hold back a laugh. The truth is, the last time I wrote anything meaningful in my diary was almost two years ago! Scanning those pages I search to see when I changed—how everything became as it is now. How did I become famous—with a child totally dependent on me? Many people don't see how beautiful he is, but I guess that is normal.

Once you arrive, how can any biographer discover enough about you to possibly understand why you took that path rather than another? As I look back, trying to be objective, if anything changed, it's the way I write. Checking past entries it's obvious I write differently now, yet the old style agrees with what I say today—maybe slanted differently. Anyway I can't figure it out quickly.

The day of the week that suits me best is the day I'm at home and no one calls or visits, but that seldom happens anymore. I have an enviable life, if it is my life. I feel it's not real—yet gladly accept it as if it is. Does that make sense?

It makes sense now, although not in line with a busy mother who never takes a holiday. It's weird to see me so idle. Back then I thought I was working hard, so maybe I have to go back further to start this piece.

When I left the business world a few years ago, I left a world of intrigue and deceit to enter a realm—not a world—where people do their own thing—usually behind the scenes. This new world's culture was so different from the corporate structure that it took me almost a year to adjust my focus enough to see this other reality. Up until then I never noticed them, as though they existed in a different time or place—yet in my space.

Whatever you do, and wherever you go, first you see those who are like you, then those who are very different. You miss the shades between the extremes. They slip through the cracks of our mind all the time....

Hmmm, I wonder what I was leading up to. Maybe if I skip ahead I can pick up clues? I see a beginning where I was starting to channel, but unaware of it. I wonder when I stopped thinking and started Writing in Spirit full-time.

If you are immature, most of your friends are your age or younger. If you seek out mature, wiser individuals hoping to learn from them, you probably have more work than those who came before you—and are wiser and richer than they are now. Why? You use work provided, as well as people around you, or you pursue avenues others advise are better—even when you're initially confused.

That sounds boring. Not something I would want to save. Maybe the desire to analyze is a journey back to the wilderness of the past? I'll keep to the chase and erase what isn't needed now, as well as whatever tracks past adventures and routine tasks, so I can live better than I ever lived before.

I want to exist in this special niche and work with these people I never knew existed, so I teach, lecture, counsel, and write—a lot. What else would you have me do?

This reference puzzles me. Reference to 'these people', whoever they may be, and how I organize my thinking to become one of them—or so it seems. Ahhh, this looks like I've struck the mother lode—where it all began—how I began channeling and what led me to adopt my little man.

Within a year or so of doing many new things and seeing strange beings, I agreed to create a work entitled: "Relationships at Work". Without any idea it would come to define my life. From the very beginning things came to me intuitively or happened serendipitously.

I wonder what will become of me if I continue to Write in Spirit every day?

Having decided to go with the flow, I can see where it's taking me. I find myself light years away—totally new in every way. Now I can accomplish work in a wink that used to take me a week. Really!

Wandering through these thoughts, I wonder if I should go into detail and specifically identify the turning point—as I saw it then. I think it may have come together during a lecture I gave graduating students at Yale.

Ahhh, here it is—the entry that describes what happened then:

As I stood in front of the class, several students looked dead—more than just hung-over. One slept as I felt myself rise, detach, and drift into another time and another place.

How it transpired was very strange—much harder to explain! If I rewind the frames and go back to that day, maybe I can illustrate what happened.

To help others you need to think of life as a movie constantly being filmed, then filed away for review—to be edited later. It's easier than that, but it helps to go back and bring forward renewed thoughts about the old you....

To teach this concept I'd ask the class to focus on me standing comfortably at the front of the room. Behind me stands a blackboard covered with triangles, squares, and all kinds of diagrams.

...I stretched to imagine myself as an intelligent, well-dressed woman of a certain age, smiling as often as my material allowed.

I remember how clipped my speech was then. I talked too fast! Even now I have to remember to talk slower and let the momentum take over.

It's always best to note on paper any inspiration you receive, rather than let it go into the ether to be forgotten...Whenever I pick up a pen I sense someone else is about to write, instead of me.

Can it be I'm no longer able to write on my own—using only this mind—that being a spiritual scribe I'm now condemned to take dictation and transcribe others' work—without adding my own thoughts?

I can remember saying: "When you realize you're wise— which hopefully happens more often as you age, you find it difficult to cultivate fools as friends. Fools don't recognize wisdom. If you succeed in thinking as fools do, you will not retain wisdom either."

I felt weird, so I reoriented my talk and moved closer to the class—speaking louder and slower for whatever reason. Where are the notes for what came next?

The business of fools is of no use to the wise. The wise must mend the fences of today's business again and again—continually performing miracles to keep them all afloat. Why? The world of big business is floundering—about to capsize and sink with a lot of hoopla. Regardless of what is said, it will sink—just as Atlantis did....

It is said: When you are drowning you hear waves crashing over your head. Today many hear waves overhead. They struggle to find a place to plant their feet in shifting sand, hoping to build financial security in a land of opportunity—but more and more find no place to land or expand. They continually hope business will turn around, but it never does. They did that in Atlantis, too.

As I recall, a few students opened their eyes and looked around, but according to my journal, I spoke so loudly they awoke with a start.

I have this theory about ancient Egyptians and am surprised to discover how many others think the same as I do. We covertly introduce ourselves by saying something like, 'I have this thing about Egyptians.' That's our secret code! We don't know why we're fascinated by Egyptian artifacts and spend time and money, as well as risking our lives, visiting their ancient tombs.

Here's my theory: I think we arrive on Earth as a tribe from time-to-time—prepared to transplant the best societies, cultures, or knowledge from past lives into a grand new world here. We gather to do what others will not or cannot do. We begin by dismantling the status quo—with the intent of rebuilding on the ruins.

To transplant a Tree of Life it's necessary to gently pull up the roots so Earth crumbles away and releases it. All the while, protect and support the tree's trunk. Once transported and replanted, hopefully the roots grow deep into Earth again so you can safely lop off the top. Toppling the tree or lopping too much from the top can result in a total loss of whatever society achieved or could have become....

People are more like plants than trees. We need to sway enough to survive storms, as well as the process of connecting and adjusting to Earth changes as they occur—while somewhat aware we're being pulled from one world and trance-planted in another. I believe that is about to happen again!

I don't know who was speaking through me as I presided over students who demonstrated no interest in ancient Egypt or Atlantis, let alone establishing new societies. Did anything like that ever happen to you? Think twice before you judge what you think happened to me that day in class.

I remember continuing to lecture as though *today* was past history. I said something like: "If you ever lived and participated in *another world*, even for a moment, you *know* it's a world unlike any other—and has its own place in history. To me it's like Camelot. It existed, but is gone for now—seldom remembered except in legend or song. It was not an artistic forum, rather a brief opportunity to favor those with military minds—letting them make war in peace. We can still learn much in time."

By then everyone was alert, eyes wide open—watching me. Never before had every student's mind opened at the same time! For a brief instant we connected and I was fully accepted as their teacher. I held the stage and continued to fill that space with pronouncements that amazed even me! According to my notes, I taught:

In our age the military mind of civilians has been tamed and permitted to run organizations, many as huge as great armies of the past. Initially the United States produced steel for cars and tin cans, but moved on to producing arms. When guns were finally turned into plow shears, bread and butter flowed for millions. Everyone prospered as never before—yet war games never really end.

When you make time to study such games, you see they have all the earmarks of elementary school behavior. The playground bully grew into a tyrant during the times of 'big business.' There was always one who reported others' indiscretions in hopes of gaining points. Plotting to win whatever game by fair means or foul.

Scholars studied and worried about success in the marketplace, as well as workers who managed with increasing difficulty to pass from one class to the next. They labored and eventually perished like good soldiers do. All who once existed in the workforce worldwide—still exist—but today's industrialized societies are considered 'undeveloped' or 'third world' by sophisticates...If bullies arrive where you labor and demand you bow down and kiss their feet, will you?

My voice rose and I remember sounding like a man mimicking a woman. "You say you must obey and comply or you won't work very long—and it teaches you to be humble." I remember shifting back to my normal voice then. "What god are you kneeling before now?"

Looking back, I recall one coed was so deeply disturbed that I had to smile and change my tone before saying this:

"When life ends, you discover why you worked as you did in this world—and why you didn't work on your own for you alone. Here are a few clues: You didn't want responsibility—just authority. You didn't know how to inspire others to work, so you did the work rather than seek teachers who could demonstrate the best way to lead.

When you are mature you know why you hated your elders, but until then you may think of a million ways to countermand such conclusions. It ends the same anyway, so why bother arguing—ever?

According to my notes, at this point I was perched on a high stool behind the podium hugging myself as I said:

Among those who ignored that work ethic—even though others looked askance at them, were local grocers and small home-based business owners. They were called 'homies' by those who considered them to be second-rate wage earners. Perhaps called that because they seldom extolled their virtues outside the local Chamber of Commerce and Kiwanis? I suspect they didn't brag in order to discourage competition. After all, they had it made! Today we know why they preferred to live in the shade beside the busy highways of trade rather than create garish displays for everyone passing by to notice.

The bigger a company grows, the more government gets involved. The smaller the business, the fewer employees to report discrepancies or taxes owed. Many 'homies' can't display their wealth. They maintain low profiles in order to avoid taxation. Such businesses thrive in your town, too. Check them out and think, 'Are they paying their fair share to maintain the nation's infrastructure?' Probably not!

Many pay cash for everything, yet are still in debt like everyone else—a lesson we all need to learn. When big city boys merged and overthrew the old order, they let third and fourth class whomevers run their businesses—and 'homies' lost out. It had to happen—in order to destroy the old order more quickly. The old order was not unlike today's local merchants, but wealthier.

How did they get wealthy? Too much to go into today, but remaining unnoticed was the fastest way to get rich then. The old order amassed money within their own pension plans and ruled *them to be tax-free. Small merchants couldn't do that. The rich created laws to preserve wealth and provide wages for taxpayers. They put in place legislators who worked for huge pensions, too. It's easy to understand. Wages are for those who earn their daily bread as well as dividends for corporate owners....*

The wealthy had no pain or sorrow related to life. That's a fact you may be unaware of, but it's true. The wealthy know pain and sorrow, but not of this world. Their pain and sorrow resides in spirit and mind—not the poverty of life.

You have to know the rules of life to avoid penalties. Today, almost all the players have no clue about how to win The Game of Life. Why? The rules have been confiscated and returned to a primitive state so as to confuse those playing the game now.

The old ball game is no longer in effect, but the shuffle continues. You either know how to shuffle paper to get the best deal or you lose. There is no best way to beat the shuffle. You can pitch and play and see who stays, because some are allowed to win in order to determine how far the foe can go. You must discover how vicious your enemy is to determine the degree of payment to extract later when he is punished....

Admit it, you don't have a clue about what I'm saying. Do you? Don't worry, the game isn't over. You'll have your turn at bat."

Looking back, the students who woke up half-way through the lecture appeared perplexed—probably wondering when the subject changed. They watched me watching them, as I changed into someone very different from my usual persona. I talked with grave authority. I remember saying: "What if Earth suddenly spun off its axis and headed straight toward a major planet like Jupiter? Would you be able to stop it? No, but God of All can!"

My notes confirm my memory and add more:

You believe you can't stop the major collision about to occur when this world collides with the new one—and you don't even try! God isn't going to help, because this world is man's creation. Man must take responsibility and do what is necessary to save his world or be lost.

When you sit and ignore all you gained without labor on your part—perhaps complaining and wanting more—you have time to study the inner world and design a better one than we have now.

Can anyone design a better world? You working alone can do it!

This world isn't 'just another' world. It's the only world you have—now! Either you accept ownership of it—or you share and divide what others give you daily. You may have a lot of practice doing that—developed a habit, but why not try a new way and start living today by giving?"

I remember my voice dropping as I said: "I can see you're getting upset—with me. So what? I don't care if you like me or not. Your thoughts are of no consequence to me. If you want to hurt me for disturbing your peace, then bite me."

Right then one fellow jumped up and said, "Hey, take it easy man, no need to get upset. We didn't do anything."

I ignored him and raised my voice. "Which day of the week suits you best? I like today. In fact, it's always my favorite. I don't remember yesterday while living today, but I can remember the past—if I stop living now to do so. You stop, go back and review what you do, or sit idly in the present, or move into the future! You decide why—I already know."

At this point the movie clip broke. Now I have to return to what I was doing when it started. My mind is flipping through time until I hear myself saying: "Three years ago today I missed corporate life—and never missed it again. If you're lost and start wishing the past was back, stop and forgive everyone—including you—then it will fade. You have only today to live and enjoy! Why bother with people, places, and circumstances that bear no relationship to who you are now? I've done it and know it takes time to learn to live—but you have enough time."

Something in my back snapped as I returned suddenly to that class and saw myself lecturing those same students. In my journal I saved what I said and can now hear myself talking. It's coming through garbled, but I'm saying, "When you're locked into labor, you can't wait for the jailer to unlock the door, which usually happens when you least expect it. You retire, are fired, die, or leave on your own one day, but you leave. It's the same with life, only you never know when it's time to pass from this world into another."

I'm having trouble organizing my thoughts, but I know I spoke more softly as I said: "What if you have a small ego? In the world of business they'll work on it. They take you to task for too much ego or not enough, so learn to laugh!"

I don't have to refer to my notes, because I know what I said next. "You learn, you develop, and you identify with the organization or leave it, but you learn—which is why you came to Earth in the first birth. You should thank every big corporation world-wide for teaching so many how to work cooperatively to produce a common product they then taught mankind to need. It's still like that. You either live together cooperatively or flounder on your separatist egos.

"When laws are enacted, who is represented? Think about it. The wealthy influence the law, but average people enforce laws and keep legislation in place or not. If everyone refuses to obey, how can The Law be enforced? If you doubt me, make a study of all the weird laws on the books that have never been enforced. Why not erase them? Because it's easier to make a name for yourself by adding more rules and laws."

I stuck to the subject even if it doesn't sound like it now. "No one wants to clean up or eliminate what doesn't work. No one wants to do the housekeeping necessary for a company or country to grow like good, strong families grow. Families cooperate or fail! All around us destabilizing forces are at work in our homes as well as the work place. The game is changing and families are adapting or perishing. When no one wants a large work force or wants to assume responsibility for maintaining stability, they sell out. Too many believe they don't have to work—or at least not as hard as their forebears worked. When you sell off your share of a business, you need not worry about it later. However, a family is a different kind of business! When you or others renege and no longer cooperate for the good of all, you split and never get over it. Your family is your ticket to the future. When you punch your time card at the end of this life, you'll be fined if *your* family isn't in good working order. You may have to return. You're responsible for what you produce—and there is work involved in delivering children into this world. You must do the required work or pay over and over in surreal ways—which is where we are today as a nation."

Right then I snapped back to this space and time—talking to no one present. "I'm a single Mom! Never had a child, but now I'm a Mom."

I feel panicky—unable to calm my thoughts. I'm letting fly whatever flows through my mind. My voice is echoing loudly through the otherwise silent room.

"Let's see if I can make sense of where I've been—and where I am. I just adopted a little boy unlike all other children. He was incorrectly labeled. *They* said he was 'Mongoloid', what rot! Too many adults glance away when he approaches—until he gives them a smile that pierces their plastic armor and hits their heart center. Brian is a lover of life—and he's mine forever! He won't be taken away from me, because he wasn't and isn't wanted by his birth parents. He doesn't know what happened and never will! He is mine and I carry him in my soul. One day we'll work together. We'll get his life in order—and he'll be a success! I know it's his life to live, but he wants to succeed—and with me at his side, he will win at life!"

Enjoying this track so much, I want to relive how I converted from corporate climber to work-at-home mom. Flipping through my journal again, my finger stops at something I wrote long ago.

Everyone said I had a bright future in business, but I knew the end was near and jumped off before the merry-go-round stopped. As a company slows—about to stop, some think they can keep it going by dumping assets. Too late for that—even I had worked too long at that venerable Dow Jones utility. It was tragic what went down the drain—especially the brains.

Every day Americans pay corporations to sell back to them what belongs to us—never checking to insure such firms remain honest stewards of our natural resources. As I see it, utilities do very little to deserve this trust, but the public doesn't care—and now I don't either. I'm through, are you?

When your life is full of life or love, you're excited—seldom settling down—living inside your head. Once you get off the merry-go-round of money and esteem, you sit and stare at the money saved for such a day—having no real idea how to live the rest of your life without money in abundance. You know you have gifts and talents that you never applied or appreciated, but which one to develop when you have time and need money?

Flipping ahead several pages, my thoughts stayed pretty close to this track for quite some time.

You can become rich and famous if you have great talent and specialize in one area...You can become well-off and fairly famous if you do one thing very, very well—or care a lot about others, but you have to really care. That is the key! Obviously, you must do whatever very, very well, but it's easy when you're talented or gifted.

Why 'gifted' as opposed to 'talented'?

Many gifts arrive suddenly and by chance—or so it appears, but not talent. Talent is developed and has to be practiced—a lot, to gain recognition. Do what you have to do, but use your gifts first. They display your work in a totally different light.

No gifts? Then talent will serve you well—but you have to work at it! Talent is not the gift of fame and fortune, but it can produce both, if you apply yourself daily.

At the end of the journal are more scrawled notes. When did my hand start writing—without stopping—saying things I never thought about?

When I bought this house, I had no real need for three bedrooms, except for resale value. I seem to always think ahead—don't know why, but I do. I figured if I lived here only a few years, I could more easily move into a nicer place. Now my life is here and I use the second bedroom for Brian and the third for my office.

The last page stands out...

Brian is my baby! He is everyone's baby, but not for long. He will not be on Society's tab. He will be able to sustain and maintain his own life and be of use to all—unlike so many able-bodied people who have damaged their minds by being unkind.

You must welcome all creatures of Earth willing to help you, but this one is such a loving, gentle soul you have to wonder why anyone would prefer a dog to a loving human being. There are people around here who ply their animals with caviar and fine food and never eat so fine themselves. They appear to love animals more than God, and maybe even refuse that love for themselves. That can't be wise.

Animals are at a lower vibrational level and cannot be human at this time, but eventually will be. Animals watch us based on our characteristics and may or may not decide to become humans based on how we treat them, or they may elect to take some other form in the ascendancy.

You made such a choice, but think you are human because you always were. You have so much to learn...If you can't figure out who you are, who can?

...I have this thing about not being bothered about lost loves and past lives, but others are trapped in it and can't understand why I feel this way.

In order to figure out why you chose this path, you have to see into the past a bit; but once you have a grip on it, why cling to it?

When your love isn't around, you think of all the people who are, then wonder why they are here and he is not—but you know.

You have to have time for yourself. If others are in your life, you cater to them and put together your life in a different pattern—upholding and defending them to everyone. That takes time, patience, and energy, which isn't necessary when you live on your own.

Once you admit another into your life, the time to be alone is over. With Brian in my life, I *have* to live outside myself, and

I *have* to be patient. I *have* to sit and figuratively mend socks at times, too. It's those times when you're darning or sewing or knitting that you stumble upon the great ideas of the past and figure out the old ways—and put them down on paper again.

I remember the day I was sitting and darning a table runner where the fringe had been ripped away. As I stitched, I felt a tug at my heart. I felt an annoying being within me, maybe an imp or cupid or something—nice, but naughty. I suddenly realized I had to buy new fringe or replace the runner, which meant I had to go shopping—and I didn't feel like it. I went anyway.

I entered a shop selling dry goods and saw a Down syndrome child with an old mother and thought how nice they looked together. Yes, it's nice to see a Madonna and child in real life, but my heart felt strangely sore. I hate to think about all the mothers who upon discovering they are carrying a so-called 'mongoloid' child, immediately abort it. I prefer to imagine mothers taking gifts God gives them and building a life of love around them. I wondered if the woman had mixed emotions about her child, but saw no evidence of it. Time has a way of erasing misgivings, especially where children are involved, and mothers are the most self-less of all human beings.

As I studied the mother, I felt the child's eyes search mine to see if I meant his mother any harm. I know that is what he thought—and I knew it instantly. As he looked into my eyes, I saw eternity. I really did! My eyes filled with tears as I peered into deep pools of emotion and oceans of understanding. I felt longing—like an orphan seeing her mother for the last time. All of this happened by really looking into a small boy's eyes. When I couldn't maintain his stare, he looked away. He was more mature than me.

What you recognize in another must first be present within you, but you may not realize it at first. You may think others have a lot of time to develop and learn about God, love, and life, but maybe they don't. We never know.

With a child considered to be inadequate by the world's standards of perfection, you never doubt they will have problems adjusting—unlikely to 'have it all'. You accept it. Some say the world can't benefit from such monsters, yet the world needs more loving hearts and able minds. Does it not?

I thought if I could find another child like that little boy, I would enable him to do what he came to Earth to do—because I knew it would be far more important than anything I was doing then.

Chapter Four

If We Quit, We Lose!

*W*hat *if you decide to quit breathing? You can't! God inspires and respires you, thus keeping you here until such time as Spirit is ready to leave. Others may believe they keep you alive, but they can't! They are merely playing at being gods....*

Rain streaming down a pane blurs your view of what lies on the other side, while tears focus your attention on what lies within. The secret is to let water flow when and where it will, but man tries to divert it with dams and canals—playing at being gods until the day God steps in and sweeps all away in a storm. Is it because we want to be gods that we interfere so much, or just a way to pass the time until we arrive again on the other side?

I stand watching Brian play with toys, wondering what he is thinking, but I have no right to do so. You can't intrude into another's thoughts without disturbing them in profound ways—or perhaps I imagine we have more power to interfere than we have? Being a mother doesn't make you a god, but the fact remains, mothers coerce others to act like them.

The other day while making a list of things we needed from the store, Brian asked for water. I realized only then that he doesn't prefer soda pop and other sweet drinks! Why do we then teach kids to seek artificial stimulants?

What if we sat and watched water running down the drain without stopping the flow?

I can't know what you're thinking, only what I think—until I see your reaction. If you make no move—say nothing, I assume we think alike and thus act according to my beliefs or tag along with you.

Where does it say you have to be like everyone else? I try to be different, but whatever I do, others copy. At times I get tired of being original and almost wish I was stupid or young enough to dress outrageously—but in truth, the young cling to what others do more than adults ever would. Everyone may look the same outwardly, but inwardly we differ—or do we?

Weather patterns supposedly aren't difficult to predict, but meteorologists are often wrong. Yet we listen to them on a regular basis. Why? An educated guess is better than not knowing—or is it?

Maybe if we sat quietly without looking at each other for a few minutes—in a blissful state, we could communicate more easily and decide more quickly whether or not to do something, rather than talk non-stop and accomplish little.

I know Brian is brilliant. We don't talk a lot because it's difficult for him, but communicate intuitively all the time. I think we now have to start talking aloud to be sure we are thinking alike—or not.

Since you want to play outside without me, you need to tell others what is yours, why you want something, and what you won't give up. If not, you'll have to fight to keep what is yours, and that is too slow and angry a way to grow up.

"Okay!"

Brian said, okay—just like that!

"Brian, you just said Okay—just like that! I thought you couldn't talk, so I tried to learn your internal language—now I discover you've been hiding things from me!"

"No, Mummy, I not hide. I love you."

Water streaming down a window is nothing compared to a mother's tears when her child says for the first time, "I love you."

I was going to go out, but the rain put a damper on my plans. Then I was going to go next door and visit Charlene, but she was out. It meant only one thing. I had to do housework. My, how I hate housework!

"You do stairs, Mummy. I run sweeper."

"Oh, Sweetheart, that is so nice of you. You do such a good job, too, but I better wash clothes first. Maybe later we can clean the steps—inside and out."

His natural glow dimmed, but then he grinned and said, "I help you wash."

"Wonderful! You sort the clothes and I'll set the machine. Then we'll both watch it work. How's that?"

"I work."

"Yes, Honey, you work, but the machine washes the clothes and the other machine dries them."

"I work!"

"Okay, but first roll up your sleeves like I'm doing. Then we'll separate all the whites—blouses and underwear that get bleach and stuff. Then we'll pull out pastels and light colors that have white in them, which leaves us with a small pile of dark clothes to wash by themselves."

Brian's hands immediately went to work as his eyes searched the dirty clothes. Painstakingly he picked up one shirt and one sock from the pile, but seemed puzzled by a shirt still in the hamper.

"The shirt is striped and has some white, so it goes in this pile." I demonstrated by adding it to its pile. "The sock is black, so it goes where?"

He placed the sock in the pile of dark clothes, and looked up hesitantly.

"Wonderful!" Not too effusive—just right. Look at that smile.

"Mummy work. I play."

"Good, that's enough laundry for today. You work when you play, and I want you to learn to play by yourself and have a good time—and not get into trouble. Okay?"

"I do dat!"

"Wonderful."

Brian played nearby with Batman and other action figures while I did the laundry. I enjoyed my chores as never before, because he shared the world of a three-year-old about to be four with me. He may not be able to do what most four-year-olds do, but how many four-year-olds around here work with their parents?

Why deny a child the opportunity to learn how to work beside you? I think it may have something to do with pride; but if you're a great mother and housekeeper, why wouldn't you teach your children how to take care of themselves? Kids don't need more self-esteem! They need to develop confidence, and confidence comes from competence, and competence comes from practice—lots of practice!

When Brian is 13 or 14, or whenever he asks about sex and such things, I guess I'll have to start letting him visit other kids more like him in order to figure it out. My mother never told me anything, and I didn't do such a bad job figuring it out. She *just knew*, and her mother before her *just knew*—so I *just knew*—and Brian will *just know*. No big deal!

There is something about a child with an easily perceived disability that brings out the best of the worst and the worst of those who think they are better. With Brian you can see a bit deeper into his personality, but not enough to really know him.

After the laundry lesson, I went over to Charlene's place to hold a conference about sharing baby-sitting tasks. I discovered she wants no part of watching Brian. However, she wants to unload Daphne on me every other day. She doesn't want me to ever leave Brian with her over-night, because she fears he might do something to Daphne. Obviously, Charlene is making up excuses to exile Brian, and so it goes.

When you are self-employed and work at home, you get to the point where you have no distinct home or office. It all blurs together and ends up more one than the other. For a few months I had to let the house and my work sit while I concentrated on Brian, but that ended when the bills stacked up. The world doesn't respect heroines much—nevertheless, Brian is my hero!

When you are the only one to pay household bills, you might think you're in charge, but you're not. Definitely not when you take in Siamese kittens! We recently adopted twins who are now in charge of everything and everyone.

Brian thinks they're the most important beings on Earth—beside us. He now dreams of being a cat doctor, even though he doesn't like doctors. I think it's his fear of the kittens getting sick that makes him want to be a doctor—but what do I know?

Weather patterns and Siamese cats are unpredictable, but the weather doesn't stop cats—only from getting wet and dirty. You either know what I mean or you don't, but Brian is easier to raise than pandering to two bums in cat's pajamas. The only work they do all day is boss us around. Mostly they sleep, eat, or chase one another all over the house. No consideration whatsoever is given to either of us.

Brian loves watching them play, but at first they scared him. He thought they were mad—as in angry, when he saw fur fly as they wrestled and rolled around. When they quit rough-housing and start licking one another, he always feels better. Brian never asks anything about them, he *just knows*.

Within a week of Brian moving in with me, I had adjusted to him; but it was painfully slow for Brian to understand he was here to stay and would not be moved to another home again. He was sure he would be taken away, but is finally getting used to this place—just when we have to move. We both need to break it off here and go where he can play outside and have more friends nearby.

My plan was to bring up the subject a week before moving, but now I think it's unwise to wait that long. Brian can read me and knows something is up. I know he senses we are moving, but 'why' we need to move is beyond him. He doesn't really have to know why, but I hope he does. Perhaps that's just me playing God?

You don't have to tell kids everything. Usually they know enough, but you may want to unload your worries on someone else—and they're handy. You may even tell them things you wouldn't want others to talk about in front of kids. Do we mean to enlighten them? Church or temple may enlighten them, but gossip usually dims another's light.

Open your heart and look inside—my boy is there. His name is Brian. He exists. If you care about him, you *just know* he will grow into a fine man. Regardless of what anyone else says or does, you want his life to be easy, too. Don't you? We both believe Brian needs to be challenged and to overcome adversity to learn and accomplish much—but why?

We don't want our children to experience conflict, especially pain and suffering caused by others, so some don't send their children to public schools. They end up in the world sooner or later anyway, unless they enter a convent or monastery—or form a cult. If your entry into the world is delayed, you have a lot more to learn due to inexperience in meeting strangers and working out problems in outside groups. I say, let children find out early in life what it's all about.

You can train kids in their teens to adjust to financial obligations as befits your resources, but I wouldn't talk much about your money before then. They'll become snobs soon enough if they have no sense of their own worth when apprised of your status in life. Snobs are continually surprised that others are as smart or smarter than they are and *not* favored by others.

I can tell you a lot about Brian, but this isn't about Brian. It's about me, you, and a few characters who will show us the path to the next world. We're going to move forward and take Brian with us! His Guides are okay with this line of study about time, are you?

Chapter Five

Two Are More!

*N*othing exists within a place except you and whomever you live with. You fill such places with all you are. Can it be so simple that we are who we are now, and we are what we love?

I never thought of it that way until I set out to move from a small town near the border of Oregon and Washington to a city far, far away. I looked at a map, circled an area of green and simply finger-walked across the states and decided it wasn't that big a jump. I had lived there before, but left to find work—and *find myself,* as we used to say. I never lived anywhere but these two places, yet it seems like I lived in a small town all my life.

When working for a few people, you feel confident you can do whatever needs done, and probably make it easily on your own, but when you work for a giant corporation, the ego struggles to survive. Few are wise enough to build a business on the side to provide for termination of employment, yet most are let go sooner or later with no idea where or how to begin again.

After years of specialization and following orders you can't believe you know enough to make it big on your own. You're sure it takes millions of dollars to start a business, thus you have to work for others. Get over it! Your premise is flawed—basically incorrect, and certainly unworthy of you.

You don't have to work for anyone else! You can create your own business and work from home, but don't follow the teachings of your mentors from big business—that road quickly leads to bankruptcy. You need to think big and plan small to build a small business? Big ideas crowd your mind and cramp your purse. You don't need an MBA to succeed as an entrepreneur.

Several types of employees do well on their own, but some abandoned corporate types are too dependent to thrive and enjoy being their own boss. We want our lives to be free of care and worry—assuming worriers never enjoy life because they fuss and fume over little things and usually miss the big events. But it's the worriers who usually do best—when it comes to creating a successful business. They assume nothing and double check facts and figures until they make dollars and sense.

When the time came to put my exit strategy in place, as happens to one and all, I planned to become some kind of consultant. It turned out my severance package wasn't large enough to subsidize such an enterprise very long. I had to find work that paid at least as much as monthly unemployment—and find it fast, because I was a long, long way from being eligible to draw Social Security and pension benefits.

Whatever your work, it isn't really *you* if you can easily leave it. Every job shapes your persona *and* concept of self. A career isn't a job made up of small tasks anyone can master with practice—tasks designed with efficiency in mind, in order to cut up a big job—to get it done quicker or eliminate being dependent on one person who might leave when needed. Employees may stay occupied for years and be satisfied doing tasks others don't like, but it's not a career. A career challenges your mind or spirit. The best careers do both!

Our Spirit seeks challenge and action, while our minds store memories of slights, hurts, and bits of junk—lots of useless detail. It's not a place to visit when new work needs to be done or you want to quickly move forward. Instead, visit Spirit and erase bad memories before they depress you.

Moving away from where you lived a long time quickly erases the past, but usually it's not practical. How to achieve the same benefit without moving? I find cleaning out closets and drawers clears the house of whatever lingers there. Once your inner life is shorn of hairiness, you can enter other areas and cut back what no longer benefits you. Getting rid of *stuff* is difficult for many, but if you don't need it you pay too much to keep it.

I welcome the effort it takes to get rid of *stuff*. It frees me of much worry, because the mind catalogs and juggles all we keep, as well as obsolete beliefs. Let this be our mantra: *Keep things simple. Don't litter your mind (or house). Move on and leave your worries behind!*

If you have a lot of time, deciding what to take and what to leave is tough. If pressed for time, you start tossing whatever is in your way or doesn't fit in a box. When you do the packing, you're careful; but if packing takes too long, you may end up throwing the last bits and pieces together with little thought. That tells us something—we don't need what we ignore until the last minute.

Keeping all of this in mind, I sat for a minute before I started packing and entered Spirit. This is what happened: I picked up two big boxes and said, "These are for clothes." I repeated this as I labeled boxes 'Books' and so on. Eventually I had boxes lined up two-by-two down the hall—like Noah's ark, but not as congested.

When you question everything, like 'where do I get boxes', carefully reconsider what to pack. Constantly seeing obstacles usually indicates you don't want to do whatever. Accept the consequences and do it quickly!

It's easy to decide if large furniture is worth the expense of moving. The really old and really new are probably too expensive to replace, so get rid of what falls between these extremes.

In my dreams, moving on seemed easy, but when it came to doing it—with another person involved, it was a lot harder than when I moved in alone. This time I had to consider what Brian likes and doesn't yet realize he wants to keep—which is tough. But what mother doesn't feel like that?

If you walk quickly through the house—not loitering, it's easier to throw out stuff. You'll probably regret throwing out something—but that comes later. So Brian and I walked through the living room picking out two things I dearly love but he didn't. I removed nothing from the dining room, since it held nothing that can't be replaced at any mall, and the master bedroom had nothing of interest to either of us, so we quickly moved upstairs to my office. It's arranged somewhat efficiently, but not much of an office. I put computer stuff in a box, added a few gadgets, and felt I would be ready to go into business as soon as we relocated.

When we got to Brian's room, however, he went into a frenzy sorting everything by color. He didn't notice many toys had disappeared. Obviously, he wasn't attached to them, but what he did notice and loves much was packed. Brian has rights, too.

Why is it so difficult to decide which clothes to take? Thinking about who you used to be, you wonder if *she* still exists—and will you ever need to fill that role again? Being practical, I always believe I'll save money by revamping what I have, but if you never wear it, is it waste to pitch it? Some things I never tire of wearing, but worn clothes must go.

Originally I thought Brian and I couldn't make this move alone, so I talked about it constantly with everyone I know. Why did I do that?

Three people are in my home now, because I want them here. The rest showed up to help me throw away what I don't want. In a situation like this, you can't help if you never moved or don't like those moving on—especially if related. Stay away if you don't intend to help!

There is no way to thank people who help you move away from them. It's ridiculous to believe you can adequately show your gratitude then. At some other time and place you'll repay the karmic debt. You can be sure of that. Karma is so misunderstood! Many think they will escape payback in this life—maybe repay in another life—what dreamers! You balance your books before you close the door.

I'm the oldest woman in the house, because I've out-aged all my old friends. I left many behind in my hometown to make friends here who were very old or quite young. Since then all the old, new friends died. I think that's weird!

When you meet certain people, I think you know immediately you won't be together long—thus the relationship is more intense—perhaps a hot, passionate break from reality. That is how it is for me anyway.

I think everyone deserves a few flings in life, but continually seeking them is a waste of passion. We need passion to reside within us—not in others. It's not for others to use or abuse. They can drop us when they've had enough—but why go into that again?

Thinking back to relationships that began with much passion and died quite suddenly makes me think about my thighs. Ridiculous you say? Well, my first thought when I think of Doug is about the fat dimples on my thighs. Cellulite comes to mind, because all he ever talked about was my weight. How dumb can a man be?

Since Brian arrived I seldom think about such trivialities— or about the past. I thought it must have disappeared, but then out of the blue it came back and I thought: Why not work hard and fry the lard? But forget the gym!

I kept at it—heaving boxes and helping people load my old things into their new SUVs and pick-up trucks—until the last day when the only friends left to say good-bye to were Brian's two *Mongoloid girlfriends*, as Charlene always describes them. Brian is sweet and honest—and happy, but they aren't. They show signs of jealousy and envy already.

Being the only male, they compete to be with him. Poor Brian! He shares whatever, which surprises them. Perhaps they can't recognize his innate goodness? He doesn't care much for either, and it appears they use him to irritate each other.

Invariably, Brian chooses the high road and the middle path—but his access to friends is limited. When it comes to loving others, he has no incapacity. He loves far deeper than most adults—yet is looked down on by too many. Makes me wonder, but I have to get moving instead of brooding!

Three of my neighbors are the source of much joy, but the rest no longer exist. You know what I mean. Hectic lives become blurred images in the rearview mirror. Too many are confined to suburban prisons they call home. Those who don't mow grass or work outside are considered to be blights on the community's social life. Apparently, no one trusts those who live in self-imposed isolation.

Studying my soon-to-be-forgotten neighbors, I wonder if you can ever be a family if you live alone. Families are described as a relationship between several related people. When you have a family, you can unite with your tribe for additional protection and support. If no one accepts you, you move on until you find more hospitable camping grounds.

Tribes provide greater access to spiritual blessings, thus the expression: *When two or more are gathered together there is love.* If you check out all the lives you live now and have lived in the past, you can see yourself as a tribe, but too many are unaware of the many lives they live in this one small speck of time and space. I once believed I lived only one life—until I split from corporate and found I could fit into smaller, more intimate work places. I easily fit into a lot of niches representing lives I lived then or live now.

You decide which lives you'll take along with you. Some lives don't take up material space, but cling to whatever you take. If you retain work material, a career is ready to appear. If you take art supplies, your creative life will open more. You decide what is important and wrap it up now to use later.

Throwing on some bubble wrap and wrapping in paper isn't good enough for fragile wares, but suffices for what is durable and bounces easily. The latter describes me and Brian. We bounce back from all sorts of things that would crack or break more fragile egos. God made us resilient and able to lead many lives!

Keep reminding yourself that Brian is a special being who elected at birth to take this misshapen body and do something great with it. He is determined to be as normal as you and me—and he is, but being more experienced actors, we think we are superior.

Brian has everything you and I have, but he 'knows' and 'sees' things we miss or can't comprehend. We decide what is wise or necessary to discipline and train him, and he watches and imitates us. We may not like his impressions, because we are seldom as honest as he is. Brian never lies or is mean.

Finally the only thing left undone was a trip to the library to research climate changes. It takes Brian a while to fully grasp new concepts, so using books on tape isn't practical—unless there are lots of jingles and rhymes. He needs repetition to do his best work.

Work isn't difficult, except for the inept, and children are inept until work is explored and explained. The child who knows what to do and when to do it is doing adult work. If you teach a child one task a day, you will have an adult by the time he is through puberty. Why doubt it—try it!

Some count teen years as childhood, but thirteen-year-olds are on the last leg of childhood. By that time you have them in line and able to support their needs—or you missed the best time to socialize them. Children either know how to get along with others by then—or don't care. If you're the one who taught your kids and ever failed them as teens, they'll strive to show you up. Whereas kids taught by others seldom remember teachers who weren't there for them in high school.

The Law, Society, and Neighbors don't let parents off the hook. You're still seen as the parent, if your kid is 38 and does dumb things to draw attention to himself. Either you did passable work along the path—graduating to a peaceful state of mind when free of labor, or you live the past over and over again in your mind. Which makes the most sense?

Whoa! I really got lost in thought! I was telling myself we had to move and suddenly I was going for the jugular. All because one lazy neighbor refused to help me move a few things. Todd is 18 and strong, but inept and talks with contempt about anyone he perceives to be different. He can't even be bribed to help others—and is mean to Brian. So why did I invite him to The Moving Extravaganza? I needed a strong body, but forgot it's of no use if controlled by an immature, undisciplined mind.

A lot of work took care of itself. I said I wasn't taking this or that, or it no longer needs to be maintained—and poof, it disappeared! The three-ring circus that was once Brian's bedroom has been reduced to one big box. We don't need all the diversion and part-time baby sitter supplies any more. Thank God for that! We'll be so much better off without people coming and going through the house all day.

However much the media might like to believe Today's Women don't need to work for pay. I do. I didn't take on Brian as a community project or a Band-Aid meant to ease emotional pain—or to call attention to me. I merely decided to end my eternal youth and take on more responsibility in order to help a young man I instantly knew would be my best friend forever.

It took some time to end the misery of Brian's having been bounced around strange families for years, but I did it without any help from Family Services and others paid to do such things. Brian was so mistreated by *kind* people that he is still nervous when a stranger talks too sweetly or tries to hug him too soon.

For a few years children overrun every area of your life and need lots of attention. Thinking of yourself as having an inner child doesn't equip you for parenthood. Adults need to always be present and visible, if children are to learn what they need to grow beyond selfish interests, as well as how to live comfortably with others who hopefully will help them excel.

"Until today, Brian, I couldn't see why you wanted to take so much with you. We argued about it, but I can see now what you saw then. You're not upset, you just want privacy—and you want to keep a few favorite things."

"Yeth, I want my dog and GI Joe. I don't want that and that."

How simple life can be when you live with a mature being. Brian is an adult, if only for brief moments. Eventually he will be adult most of the time and a child seldom. Aren't we all that way? What is normal?

Well, here we are at the end of the trail with two boxes for me and two boxes for Brian, and we have it all. Yes, after packing everything we need or want, it fits into two boxes!

Chapter Six

Timely Waves

*W*aves of the future crash so loud and clear I think I'm already there, yet haven't done much. I wonder why so few think about the future like I do? What do you think, Greg, I mean, Jeff? You appear to be clever, earnest—intelligent. What do you think about the future?"

The mountain of a man remained motionless, but finally said, "I don't."

Staring at the huge lump lounging on her couch, Jeanne said, "You don't what?"

"I don't think about the future, never have. I live—and live. And it never comes to be, so I don't."

"I see. That *is* clever." Jeanne marveled at his inability to realize she wasn't impressed with his conversational skills.

"Not really, but probably the most intelligent thing I do."

Jeanne smiled ever so slightly while he continued to stare at the dark TV. Although she had difficulty making sense of his studied responses, she said, "What is the difference?"

Speaking from the side of his mouth, as he puffed out his chest, Jeff said, "You have your basic intelligence, which many never use. But if you use it a lot, like I do, you're clever."

"That is clever!" Rolling her eyes, Jeanne forgot to not laugh. Jeff didn't notice and said, "Exactly."

At this point Jeanne drifted off into thought: When talking with Jeff, I think back to when I was alone and wonder if I shouldn't stay that way. But the fear of being old and decrepit with no one around drives me to seek men again.

As if reading her thoughts, Jeff said, "Jeanne, you need a man!"

No longer smiling, she said, "How nice of you to say that."

Her mood grew darker—thinking about men who sell themselves well in the beginning, but quickly degenerate into a 'you're lucky I even look at you' attitude. The pasty-faced man blushed and sputtered until Jeanne realized he was either reading her mind or she had spoken her thoughts aloud.

"What? Can't I compare you to other women? You admitted yourself that I'm clever."

Deciding to cut to the chase, rather than prolong the nonsense, Jeanne said, "Yes, I'll grant you that, Jeff, but you're not clever in the ways of women."

Smiling as if nothing was amiss, he said, "What a terrible blow to the male ego! I've been married, divorced, and around the block a couple of times and now you're telling me I don't understand women. Ha!"

Surveying Jeff's immense chest as if measuring him for a straightjacket, Jeanne said, "Strange, how young you look. You could pass for 35—maybe even 33."

He had hoped to make a good impression on the fashionable woman seated opposite, but could not keep up the act. Raising his voice, he said, "Stop it! You've gone too far! I am 35!"

With a look of amazement, Jeanne said, "No, you can't be 35!"

Leaping to his feet, Jeff countered with, "Look at you! All red and blushing from ear-to-ear—upset with me for being younger than you! So what? I get a bit testy, but I'm not vain! I don't mind if you're older than me."

When Jeanne remained silent, he added, "I can't help wondering why everyone tries to make me older than I am."

"That's because you're so desirable—a real catch—and so young." Jeanne's mouth suddenly went dry. Why did she say that? What is to be gained from such an exchange? She decided to rest and talk just enough to get him out the backdoor and into his waiting limousine.

"Right, older men desire young girls, but older women don't desire young men. Is that what you're saying? It's discrimination—and I'm going to leave, if you don't stop staring at me that way. You're looking at me like I died."

Sighing dramatically, Jeanne said, "Yes, you were a glint in my eye for a moment, but the gods have had their way yet another day. *We* are just not to be!"

Blinking rapidly, he said, "Let me interrupt you for a second, lady. Why can't we be partners? We can go places and have lots of fun. You're not too old for me—so how can I be too young for you?"

While looking up at the man hovering over her, Jeanne lowered her voice to a whisper. "Men are always too young. And it's even worse when they *are* young—younger than you, that is."

"I'm sorry, but you don't make sense."

With catlike grace Jeanne moved her hands across her face as if executing a dance with veils. "Don't worry, Greg. You're only five-to-ten years away from chasing little girls—so be patient."

"I resent that! Not every man is stupid. I have a great life and don't need a wife, but I want a suitable companion to go out with and do things—to be with, but I don't have to own her—and my name's Jeff!"

Jeanne purred, "Oh, dear! You sound so good! But, no, you're much too young."

"Then I'm leaving!" Jeff turned on his heel and headed toward the backdoor.

With another wave of her imaginary scarf, Jeanne said, "That's too bad, but it's better if you leave. You say you're not into marriage, but I am. Yet I don't see myself changing diapers or doing things a younger man might expect of his wife. Can you see where I'm going with this?"

Putting on his trench coat, Jeff said, "NO!"

Remaining seated, Jeanne smiled and said with a flourish, "Then, go."

Unwilling to leave without having the last word, Jeff shouted, "I'm leaving, but first I have to say you're a desirable woman who has a very weird attitude! I have a yacht, and a hundred shares of every major corporation in the world—and you, you have next to zip in the bank. You could have had a great time with me, but 'NO,' you want an older man. Bah!"

"Don't be such a sore loser, Greg." Jeanne spoke to the room at large, because she thought someone was peeping through the shades.

Rearing back as if to strike her, Jeff said, "Every loser gets sore, but some lose so often they forget they're losers. I never lose, but it has to hurt. Too bad! See you later, JOAN."

Certainly not exhausted from scintillating banter exchanged with the big man, Jeanne yawned and said, "Yeah, yeah, take it easy and all that."

Without a thought as to whether or not the man's car had pulled out of the driveway, Jeanne slipped into reverie. *What a relief! I almost lost my mind—and control over my life. But right at the crucial moment my spirit asserted itself and I returned to me—the one I truly am—this me. I'm so glad I had the sense to end something that wouldn't have lasted a year— if that long, but maybe Jeff and I can still be friends for life?*

Pulling out a journal she kept beside her reading chair for moments when she was in the right frame of mind, Jeanne searched for a few gems she could include in an upcoming lecture. She seldom borrowed from her journals now when writing books and preparing classes, instead preferring to let Spirit take over.

Her hand lay still a few moments, then began to slowly glide across the page. Her journaling was not automatic writing. When preparing students to work the same way, she described it as *Writing in Spirit*. If writing in a diary, rather than a journal, it would be a rehash of events, but Jeanne's journaling seldom demonstrated concern or interest in relationships of a personal nature.

Slipping into a deep muse, she thought: *When women and men converse or whatever—and think of something funny, they wait to share it—meanwhile losing the thread of what was said—and probably forget the joke, too.*

With a smile, Jeanne wrote:

The classic art of conversation isn't limited to brilliant repartee. To master the art you have to listen carefully, absorb the full intent—then respond when the other completes his or her thought.

But how is that possible when communication, as opposed to conversation, is conducted at a mile-a-minute or faster? We all work so hard at multi-talking! Thinking fast—nothing makes sense then or is remembered later. What is really going on between us now? She watched as her hand wrote:

You have it made when you enjoy your own company.

Watching Sir Charlie Rose on PBS at his round table, I imagine what I would say if he rolled his big, tired eyes at me, searching for any sign of intellectual life. When I stall, that usually gets me started again. My mind seems to swell as I watch Charlie, but what do I know about him or other men? Nothing, so I'll stick to my own philosophy for now.

Sitting still, Jeanne could feel a voice more than hear it. It was as if someone she used to know years ago was talking to her now. This voice usually introduced subjects she normally never thought about, let alone would write about. She heard:

'What you and I have in common—being one and the same being, is this body that conveys us where you want to go and keeps us grounded for now. Once I figure things out, I leave my mind, then my body. It's not going to be easy, but let's see what we can do to move more quickly.'

Right then Jeanne seemed to lift out of the chair, yet her body remained still and quiet. *The voice* spoke louder than before:

'There is a full life out there—You have a job, a child, a mate, and nothing in your background to disprove who you say you are, yet you don't know You. Why? You can't do it all without this entity fracturing and becoming scattered. To be scattered is the worst possible future for all you are.'

Jeanne immediately became defensive and mumbled, "Who isn't scattered? I know perhaps one or two people who aren't smattered over several arts, but most people under 50—maybe 60—are so scattered they accomplish very little. On the other hand, why do women appear more poised as they age—unlike when younger?"

Feeling slightly uncomfortable listening and not writing, Jeanne decided to concentrate on her journal until the words grew less and less distinct.

The work of the world is to keep this world as is. If you don't like it this way or it doesn't fit your needs, why work on keeping it as is? I wanted a better job, but it wasn't available, so I dropped the search. I never think back about that career—because it disappeared! Can the world disappear as easily?

When I was in school it was the only world I knew. It seemed to be the most important place on Earth, but now I can't remember much about it—and certainly have no desire to return. I don't even go to class reunions.

She stopped to read what she wrote, intending to think about it, but her hand continued to do its own thing.

When you live up to the highest degree feasible for you to achieve, you don't feel a need to do it over again. Why not develop your personal life instead? You can, we can, so why recreate high school, college, jobs, etc.?

Etc. covers a lot of territory! You can recreate aptitude, I think, but I'm not sure. If you can recreate a memory, you should be able to recreate past events.

What if after years of hiring others you decide to file your own taxes? Sit, go within and examine what accountants did in the past. You may discover their contributions were quite insignificant.

Don't tell everyone, but tax forms aren't that tough to fill out.

The IRS creates that impression so you will take seriously the filing of your tax returns—and pay taxes at the highest level—all the while benefiting the economy by providing jobs for others.

We all created a world full of taxes. We turned it into a big deal, because we want our country to have enough revenue to do all the things we think someone else should do. Local governments either don't do enough or can't do much when it comes to major disasters—so it falls to the Feds to do it. Everyone chips in and pays and it seems cheaper that way.

So, a bow to how our world works now—and don't forget CPA's need work, too. Who would pay to retrain them? This world doesn't provide everything, but it does provide a lot we would all miss.

If I ask ahead, usually I get what I need when I need it. Just sitting around, waiting because I need money, clothes or whatever, I fall behind. So I write out my bills and enter them in my check book as debits, waiting for the money to arrive. When it does, I tear out the check and mail it in. I pay for necessities first, never failing to get what I need. I'm not sure what happens if you blow the gas money on a red satin dress, but you probably could get away with it once or twice.

When I had a lot of dental work done, my insurance company refused to pay for most of it. I told my dentist he was charging too much and he knocked off 20 percent. That taught me a lot about those who overcharge. Get over thinking you're rude to negotiate!

The older women around me aren't very old, but compared to the young and restless I once worked with in corporate America, they're wise and well-endowed with common sense and talent. What I'd like to know now is: Why are there so few older women in major corporations?

No one is interested in saving that world.

Huh? What if you were in my shoes? Would you panic and say, 'I can't move or work away from home because I have a son who attends special classes, has special needs, etc., etc.?'

We do not panic, but we are no wiser in the ways of the world than you are. When one of your own goes too far, do you create an alibi?

I bet everyone does.

Today, most women and men deny and create alibis—covering terrible things their children do, yet no one labels it 'disbelief'.

So it appears, everyone lies in order to preserve their way of life. How long can it last?

Not much of the world is left within you now.

Before I moved I did a lot of soul searching. I kept grinding away at my life—trying to polish it before I left.

Memories of that life are becoming dusty and dim.

Why?

You do not have to redo the past—so why remember it? You have to be yourself. You, your Higher Self, is more important than you, yet for most of this life You seldom gets a chance to speak.

When home, I want to always be me, but when I go out it gets to be quite a strain. I assume a mood of nonchalance and bravado which fools no one but Brian.

You really are brave and nonchalant today! You must be all you can be before others accept you for being half of what you are. That is one way of analyzing life, but some see it in other dimensions.

Before you criticize why I'm like I am, be sure you know who you are! What if my life isn't a story, merely a tragic or comic episode in an ongoing soap opera?

Yes, it could be.

This sounds worse as we go on.

If you don't recognize yourself as a comedienne, you are doomed to be a tragic heroine and relive the role over and over again—

81

always ending up dead at the end. Why not choose to have a ball this time?

What if my life is wonderful! I'm having a ball, but everyone sees me as weird, wild, or whatever? Who cares, as long as I don't harm others? Maybe someone in my future is complaining, but no one here cares.

Having a ball without considering your future could cause you to careen around a blind bend in the road so rapidly you couldn't stop or slow down, but it is your life! Do whatever turns you on, but don't turn on us when it ends different than you expected.

I think I'll surrender this life to the IRS. Trying to calculate my corporate taxes correctly is too confusing. When I did calculate what remained after expenses and whatever else ate up all my money, I couldn't decide if I owed or not. Using my head for once, I'm going to sleep on it.

Sleeping on a problem uses your mind and usually produces the right answers.

Last night I was so tired when I created ten pages for a client that it made no sense, but this morning I wrote glorious prose—still can't believe what I wrote! Here it is:

What you do about your being and your life isn't a problem unless it conflicts with my life or my being. If it does, who gets the best? I do. I'll take care of me, and you take care of you, but you should not ask me to take care of you, too.

Working around the house is a breeze since I opened it to the outside world. It's nice to go upstairs and look out over trees instead of streets crowded with cars belching fumes and men honking horns—at girls or whatever—everyone seeking to be noticed. I'm alone now—but feel at home here.

When I was a girl earning a large income—compared to others in the neighborhood, a local girl who didn't work after school constantly begged for change. I felt sorry for her and thought money would help. Today she is married and her husband demands she stay at home. I believe I somehow contributed to how things turned out for her. I wasn't a friend then. I should have urged her to do without or go out and work. Instead, I felt embarrassed for her—maybe I was on an ego trip? Anyway, I didn't help her then and today we never speak. Actually, it's an ego trip to think about it!

As a friend you either give or take. Power wavers back and forth over time—not steadily one way or the other. If a relationship's energy runs from one to the other too long, it will end with one or both burnt out.

I know all about friendship. I love it! But marriage is too confining for we martyrs.

You try to be all things to a spouse and give away everything you have, which does not work.

I want nothing so much as a wonderful love in my life, but I'm too afraid to do anything about it. Besides, it would change everything about our lives! If I got married again— or worse, I didn't. I would still be me, but my life experiences afterwards would be very different.

I need to realize where I'm weak and where I'm strong— then tackle one thing at a time, correcting what is wrong by borrowing from what I do right. I excel at friendship—and marriage is a type of friendship, right? But I can't imagine marrying any of my friends. It doesn't compute!

Friends do not impose—making demands—and remain friends, but mates do and will and can't be neglected—not if you're to learn your lessons well enough to ascend and never do them again.

I intended to re-enter the world and take up where I left off when I got out of school, but the world didn't wait for me. I had to backup several steps before I could start over, and that made me mad, but now I know it was fair. The world isn't here for me alone—but in a way it is.

What a world! Thinking I had a lot of time left to live, I returned to college to take psychology and other *social* studies— not history or whatever. I needed to know more about men before jumping back into the matrimonial whirlpool—and that is when I decided I couldn't marry again.

It was my decision to add Brian to my single life and forget about becoming some man's wife, but it ignited a slew of problems I didn't expect. People constantly ask Brian about his father, which puzzles him. He thinks he has none. He doesn't understand what they mean. He doesn't know about the games women play, but I do—and I hate them!

The women or the games?

I don't really know. I'd have to guess.

Your guess is as good as it gets.

What if I relax and let myself go back to my relationship with Jeff?

Nothing happened that can't be undone, but all your work here would end. You have to end one life and live another to be sure you are true to your inner self.

If you take on someone who isn't your ideal as a mate, are you tempting fate?

You create ideals to help you do what you want to do and do it well.

If there is a next marriage, it has to closely resemble my ideal—no more experimenting. Jeanne could feel her energy fade as she wrote a few last lines:

I was going to help other women explore men and relationships with them, as well as relationships with other women and found it very confusing. My advice lacks credibility. Why share me with them?

With that Jeanne lay down her pen and put away her journal.

Chapter Seven
Thursday Doldrums

*W*eekdays seem to fly by, but never Thursdays. I don't know why, but I never accomplish much on Thursday. Come Thursday, I'm either ahead or behind schedule. If ahead, I slack off and do little—if behind, I panic and do less.

Today is Thursday and once again I intend to change my ways. Today I'm going to get a lot done! But first, I need to catch up with my journal—maybe work on the next book. If I don't, that voice in my head will override everything and drive me crazy.

I can't stop thinking that the man of my life, although not apparent, is out there beyond the fog. I can feel his presence and just know he is there, yet not quite visible. Oh, well, nothing a nice cup of tea and a few cookies can't fix while I jot down a few thoughts about recent events.

Brian and I were going to begin a nice, quiet life here—then EZ came along. Our relationship, if there ever was one, was so disruptive to my career that I had to end it as soon as it began. He is so spoiled he makes Brian look like a man. I don't intend to rush Brian to grow up so this overgrown boy can remain an adolescent.

'What a way to celebrate your birthday!'

Who said that? As a writer I'm used to hearing words as I work—like taking dictation, but anymore I feel like there is someone within me trying to guide and help me decide things more quickly. Wonder why—and why now?

I saw a movie yesterday that I can't remember now. After that I went to the little chapel behind the store where I buy honey, but can't remember what happened at the chapel. Am I going crazy— or am I already there?

Then I went to a little beauty shop and had a manicure—my first. What a grand and glorious day! Body, mind, and spirit all pampered and the synergy was wonderful. I forgot to think about EZ, but it all came back later. I have to work on it now!

'How can you be sure you're not throwing away something good?'

Yeah, that bothers me a lot—but what to do?

'Put whatever on a shelf for a week or two. If it still looks good then, use it. If not, drop it!'

I put EZ on the shelf weeks ago. He still looks good to me—but is he? When I'm with him I always feel someone else's presence around us. At first I thought it was another woman and attacked. I told him it was best to end it. I don't want a man who claims to love me only, but isn't loyal. I don't want anyone who cheats while saying he's only thinking of me and Brian—and wants to get married. It may be in style to be disloyal—but it's not for me. I am who I am and I intend to stay that way!

'What if your life is affected adversely by this decision? What do you intend to do then?'

My life is affected by what others say and believe—and some things don't matter that much—but EZ? I think I'll work it all out on the treadmill.

'Go out and walk. See who else is around.'

But I might see EZ.

'He lost you—Keep it that way.'

What if we had matched up and cleared the most obvious hurdles, would he have gone for the brass ring—on my finger?

'It has to be gold—not brass, or it will tarnish quickly and crumble in time.'

I know I would have to be three-mothers-in-one: My own, Brian's, and EZ's.

'Men are not maternal enough—most not even paternal. Women make them who they are.'

I believe women can change things! If we can't, another generation or three will be cast aside and of little use to mankind. What would happen if we threw men out of our lives?

'They'll find women—no problem.'

If all women refuse to accept bad behavior, will there be any men left?

'Not if you continue throwing boys away. Why not recycle and salvage your old flames and pass them on to younger women?'

If we don't recycle and/or get them into rehab, what will happen?

'They will die in the streets—fighting, feuding, locked in isolation, homeless, alone at computers with nothing but drugs and porn for company. It won't be good!'

Why would it come to that?

'Women create monsters when they let men become their masters!'

Where do such ideas come from? Do other women worry about the future as much as I do? Are American women more worried about men than they are?

'Let's pretend we are!'

I've been sitting for a few minutes without anything further coming through, but if I pick up a pen I bet I'll start *Writing in Spirit* again...

When I started analyzing my deficiencies, I didn't check out what men were doing. When I did, I discovered they don't worry and analyze themselves nearly as much as women do—maybe not at all.

In the past women joined groups to talk—mostly to compare and check out their relationships and soon discovered few if any were happy with changes they had made to escape single lives.

Men thought women wasted time overthinking things, when all you need do is live the good life—like they do. Old boys said they had it made, other than women expecting too much. Maybe they were right? They claimed whenever women get what they say they want, it's never what they thought it would be.

Sitting here with pen in hand, my mind ranging over time, I feel strange, but happy. Now has to be the best time to go back and see if there is anything worth saving—something I can salvage from my marriage.

I married a flashy salesman. He was so sure of himself while courting that I, too, believed he was going somewhere. But once I was sold, he started selling someone else the same goods. We weren't together long, but flesh wounds go deep enough that you don't want to duel with men until those scars disappear.

Comparing EZ to Bachelor Number One, EZ was a knight in shining armor—but the romance only lasted a day and a half. All my friends said EZ was a bum trying to appear bright and shiny—and his finish would wear off quickly. I let my friends talk about him—never said much, just listened. Bad sign! Now I was disloyal, too. Hard to believe, but I had fallen for another salesman!

I went over and over everything EZ said. Not hard since he said less than Jesus is recorded as saying in the Bible. He wasn't dishonest. I just heard what I thought he said. He didn't think much, but reacted quickly. He slowly answered any questions with my own words. Since I didn't talk much, it came down to building a lifetime commitment on a few truths and a lot of false premises. Obviously, I really wanted him to be The One! But such foolishness led directly to more aloneness.

'Where does it say you have to live alone if not married?'

Nowhere! But everyone pushes marriage and kids—in that order, if you're ever going to be happy.

'You have to know by now that you are always alone. Your heart seeks to unite with You—your Higher Self. It is your mind alone that searches for others like you. And you, hoping they will accept you, try to be like them. Your heart aches for home and You alone.'

I don't know when I stopped writing and entered the deepest meditation of my life, but it happened without any effort on my part. I remember thinking back to when Brian entered my life. I had to send out a lot of energy while he released his past, but he doesn't need that kind of help anymore.

Brian meditates and prays all day without knowing it. I pray aloud and he follows—repeating his version of what he thinks I say. He does spiritual work in his own special way.

At times we talk quietly about darkness and night, and what happens when our eyes close. In the morning I ask what he saw in his dreams and he tells me what he remembers. We sort through his thoughts and discuss his dreams, so I know where he was and is. I can tell immediately if he is okay or not, based on his dreams, but he reveals less and less about them as he matures.

Brian is becoming his own person. I like that because it frees me to find someone to share my dreams—not another child or pet, but a man traveling through life at the same pace as me. I thought EZ was that man. Apparently he got lost in adolescence—maybe forever.

Oh, EZ! Now you have time to be all you can be—nothing to regret, since you haven't done much. While I sat still, you moved. While I meditated, you put on an act. We could have been great! We both take action, but not together. Maybe some women and men aren't meant to marry? I think we all are—but then I'm still hoping to form one lasting partnership.

Suddenly I remembered when I used to visit an old friend's store in the mall. I would sort through her junk and rearrange it so the usual browsers would think it was new—and it usually worked. As an artist, she claimed to have no sense of the practical, but even she knew that rearranging her assets made them look better to bored people ambling through her shop. I decided to take a page out of her book—editing it lightly to suit my needs.

First, I made an appointment to get my hair colored a more vibrant shade than its usual tired, dusty blonde. It definitely changed my appearance and how others saw me. I was still the same old me, but with a few superficial changes my life appeared better. Would it last? Would it change my mind and how I viewed the world? I doubted it, but had to begin somewhere. After all, nothing says 'looking for love' louder than bleached hair and bright red nails.

I wanted a new look, but wasn't out to fool anyone—a lot. I can't change too much or clients won't recognize me. How can I expect audiences to quickly adjust and trust a new me? After all, I'm the one who always nags everyone to accept themselves as they are. Too many women think remodeling and making over their life means altering their face and body. If I claim that I've changed dramatically and want my outer appearance to reflect this new me, they may never get the point, but is that my problem—or not?

After imagining what might happen if I bleached my hair, I decided to leave well enough alone and get a new, hip hairstyle instead. Same old hair—just rearranged—like re-shelving old merchandise to fool bored shoppers.

Thinking back, in all honesty, I had to change my hair style because I started out cutting my bangs and ended up ruining my hair, which resulted in needing it professionally styled. Amazingly, right after that EZ appeared on the scene!

Where I used to live I ran around with a girl I trusted a lot. I didn't mind her continually flirting with every man we met, while supposedly carrying a torch for some guy who never called her. Why? Because I thought I understood her.

When we went out to dinner back then, we were approached by guys in blue jeans and corduroy jackets—until she bleached her hair and made a few wardrobe changes. Suddenly older men crowded around. They obviously wanted sex with no strings attached—anyone knows that means they're married! I worried for her, but turned out that was all *she* wanted! I never knew that until she advertised it in living color.

'You imagine yourself to be an alchemist turning brass into gold.'

Huh? Well, that is why I'm analyzing the sudden need to cut and color my hair. I don't want any hidden agendas resurfacing.

Thinking about hair, I went to dinner last night with a friend and found a hair in my soup—a blond hair. I think it's significant—an omen, but my sister's old neighbor who now lives down the street said it was *just a hair.* She's probably right, but she sees nothing in everything, while I see something in everything. If we could merge our talents, we might have a great friendship, but that's highly unlikely. She slurped her soup and ever so discreetly burped. That was enough for me. Most men wouldn't give up so easily. She has large breasts. Aaahh, I'm letting my mind run away with me tonight. I have much to do—much to write!

One generality I tend to accept is that men are greedy and women jealous. If a man is jealous, it's usually because he thinks another man is stealing his lover. Men honestly believe they can be whatever—thus more assured and less inclined to envy others. Their enhanced egos protect them from doubts that worry women. Greed is the average guy's Achilles heel while few women are greedy. Jealousy among women causes most of their broken friendships. Jealousy is based on fear and envy—usually because another woman is doing better or is judged to be prettier. It's seldom about the love of another.

An entire day doing little except talking to myself—and journaling, produced a few good ideas for my next program, so all I have to do now is set it up and go with the flow. Compared to today's inner conversations, there is no profit to be made sitting around on an average Thursday chatting with neighbors and friends. These ideas can easily lead to seminars—maybe even a book or two!

To write a book, I take journaling a step further—super size it! Lots of seemingly random ideas are really thoughts out of rotation, out-of-order. Later when you rewrite and edit, they fit in like pieces of a jigsaw puzzle.

One time I was sitting in front of my old computer staring at a blank screen when suddenly my fingers moved rapidly over the keyboard. Words mysteriously appeared—which my ego still refuses to believe I wrote. Was I writing in my right mind? Could there be another *me*? I read the words then, as easily as I can see them now:

When you combine your life with anyone—male, female, child, parent—you never see them change, nor how you blend with them to absorb such changes, but it happens. To avoid becoming a drab shade of beige, change before you blend into another personality. To others it appears they are changing and you are merely blending in with them. Ergo: If I change, I think I made it happen—but others feel the same way!

Within seconds of writing such lines, I remember my mind spun out and I thought about things I previously could not understand. I only channel to a very deep level like this after meditating an hour or so, otherwise I might as well pull out the Ouija Board and act as a medium, risking strange beings entering my thoughts.

Usually I let my mind write questions, then sit and wait for answers to come through spiritual channels. I am definitely the one writing these messages, but they seem to come from someone who is very wise—definitely not me! The 'answers' appear almost instantly.

To teach this, I have students write out on a separate sheet questions they want answered, then wait to see if anything comes through the veil. For example:

I just wrote: *What if I let EZ go and never say another word about him?* I then free my mind of all conscious thought and sit quietly. With eyes closed, I visualize a white screen in the area of my third eye. I'm watching to see what appears on the screen now.

Wow, this is what just appeared: *No one else cares about EZ, but some may wonder why you never talk about him anymore.*

Thinking of all the things that happen in life and marriage, I now realize I loved and trusted men too much, but would like greater clarification on that point. I'm going to ask questions and see if anything happens.

Q: What if I never cared about others, never pushed myself to do more with or for them?

A: You would not have moved ahead—gotten it together to become the one you are now. You would have been scattered here and there—never happy—unable to develop spiritually.

Q: Why?

A: In this sphere we know about things designed to help you grow and progress in the material world. At some point you have to prove you learned the lessons taught along the way, but the best way to pass the final test is to demonstrate what you did and how you shared it with other human beings. Marriage is a great way to demonstrate sharing, but you can also do it through various other relationships.

Q: How?

A: Women must expel offensive males from their lives. These men can be recycled and refitted for women with less refined tastes. They will marry again. It is not easy to weed out what will not flourish. Women need to conduct refresher courses or finishing schools before demanding men act like men again; but how many women remember how great men can be?

Thinking back, I remember in elementary school I had a male teacher who was extremely arrogant. He made fun of me every time he sent me to the blackboard to work math problems. He stooped to ridiculing how I made numbers. He said I was a 'backward, dumb Dutchman' because I made 4s and 8s different from others. What I remember most about him was he never apologized—ever. My mother said he was a legend in his own mind, but she was being kind. He was the sort of man who works out his hatred of women on children. Why am I thinking of him now?

'When you see a man in a suit, you think he is refined, well educated, and has a great job.'

Ridiculous, the rudest men I know wear suits to work and go out afterwards to see what is available—free, since yuppies are notoriously cheap. Cutting off the classy freeloaders would be a start. We could quickly eliminate men most inclined to offend women, but it won't work unless every woman changes and is willing to recycle unwanted men.

If you see yourself as 'only a woman,' you imagine you are of little value. The truth is women are priceless and have much to offer! Why see yourself as priceless? It isn't practical to think otherwise. When you live alone—why eat leftovers and sleep on cheap sheets? Why not use your good things all the time?

Men will continue to reign unchallenged until women learn to work, live, love, and like themselves full-time—not only when very young or having reached a certain age. According to friends, when you stop listening and start talking to your husband about your work or what interests you, they feign ignorance or speak condescendingly about it. That is, if they talk at all. If that is true, why bother with such men?

Would you talk shop to a dog and expect it to tell you what to do? Women who consent to putting everyone before themselves struggle to maintain peace of mind. Interestingly enough, these same women emphatically agree their husbands are responsible for how they live—that it is men's fault they are upset, afraid, or unhappy. Are men aware of it or living in blissful ignorance?

That reminds me of some teenagers who came over to watch Brian work around the house last week. They were part of a 'Y' thing studying, believe it or not, 'Mongoloids' and children with similar *disabilities,* in order to earn community service points for college entrance and scholarships. Not Down syndrome or Special Needs, mind you, but 'Mongoloids'!! They came to check Brian out, but they couldn't wash or dry dishes or put them away. Brian had to show them! They didn't do anything better than Brian, but all firmly believed *he has serious life adjustment problems!*

I guess it does bear repeating whenever motherhood comes up: "Your sons are what you teach them to be. If you hate being a woman, wish you were a man, you're creating a problem for other women—a man who disrespects women—just like you!"

Thinking back, that is where blame—if any, needs to be placed. But I'm hedging around it, because I have no *natural* son. I don't like to talk about what isn't my life experience.

'You need to write and talk about it—a lot.'

Work is hard if you never prepared your mind for it. But when the mind can skim off the dross and filter the dust, you create pure, refined work you can love. Clouding every issue with prejudice and emotion leads to distrust, maybe even hatred. Good work helps clear away depressive clouds so you can soar.

I remember when I started working I didn't have a clue about what was expected of me specifically or the labor force in general. Now I know there is no force—just individuals pulling together to accomplish something or not. It is management's job to make sure a team gets the message and works collectively—and when they don't work in sync, look to the boss not the workers.

If an organization is greedy from top-to-bottom, the net result amounts to nothing, even though they pulled together and worked hard. It's too materialistic to rise above the vision of what is important to individuals.

Accountants don't produce a product. They create a concept of organization. Their work is greed-oriented, yet they must deal well with emotions to succeed—because greed is an emotional thing.

Enough already! I'm tired of writing about greed. Something new is headed this way, but I don't feel like discussing it now. Maybe it's a book about greed, but not now, in the future— please. It's time to put aside my musings and research what others have to say on the subject. Let's start with our new friend's latest book about love. That should change the flow of ideas rather gracefully. Oh, dear, I'm having trouble already with this:

> *You will find your love is either alive or inanimate. You may transform another living organism into a human who suits you, but it will not reflect complete love, because it cannot share with you or respect you.*

According to this new guru,

> *During this life you must transform through love to achieve the next life—or remain here forever.*

She may be an average woman, but she knows more than I do, and is a decent writer. Thus I, too, label her guru.

> *In your teens it's natural to admire elders with a lot of style or because they are famous, but how many kids admire their teachers? Every kid has heroes, but how many are women?*

"Not enough!" According to my friend:

> If girls admire the woman parenting them, they are wise beyond their years...Everyone is part of the universe and must develop spiritually to learn why they came to be; but those who spend their formative years seeking gurus of the opposite sex, gain little.

Why?

> To become fully integrated, you have to assimilate all you think and believe about others. Without a good model, you have little to work with. When transferring love from an image or idol of the same sex to others, it gets easier over time. This is what guides you when you operate in automatic pilot mode.

This woman has taught me so much about *the after-life!* She isn't weird or sensational in appearance or demeanor, nor rich and famous, but she could be. She urges us to be ready to do something great, but can't say what it is. She is emphatic about not being a *seer,* says she merely analyzes who we are and what we do, then sifts through what isn't practical or likely to produce success.

We're expected to sort out what we hate to do, then what we love to do and why. It turns out the work we want to do is part of our being—thus it thrills us. We get so excited about these discoveries we cry and laugh. Unfortunately, friends outside our group are becoming envious of the way of life we're attempting to create—before we've done anything! They believe we will succeed and have it all—and already envy that we'll become 'all WE can be'—even though they don't want what we seek. Amazing!

I love going over to her place and talking about me. I get to be the student and listen to her rather than rephrasing others' questions so the audience stays tuned for the answers. She has problems, I'm sure—or does she? I never hear her talk about herself unless it is to teach something. She sort of points out *evils* in each of us or others, but doesn't explain much. For her, *evil* is whatever causes you to become someone other than who you are. She describes that as self-abuse.

She seems to be in a trance most of the time we're in session! If we act weird or talk about strange behavior, she lets us run on and on and appears to listen—but seldom says anything. She doesn't get involved in our weirdness, so that is how we know it was a dream—not reality. She never cuts us up for what we say, either.

One time our guru traveled to another part of the country and after a week some of the women in her study group got angry. They said they hated her, because she reminded them of their mothers or whatever. They called others and said she abandoned her classes, even though she never said she was moving away or changing direction. They just imagined it—or did they?

Some even claimed to have inherited her *powers*, insinuating she was evil—in the traditional sense. Some claim to be gurus, even though no one else agrees. Upon returning home she *excommunicated* all of them from her study group, so now they act like orphans. They don't study with anyone nor follow her wisdom.

Everyone is an orphan, but some can assimilate the world's news, disperse ugly rumors, remove sin, and get to the heart of life itself.

Love that lesson! I want to make my living doing that kind of work! But right now I have to practice what I intend to teach.

Today I applied at The Daily News, but they said there wasn't room on staff for another 'by-liner', so I agreed to be a stringer. After we had a couple cups of tea and talked about a few articles I brought with me, they decided a by-line would be given if and when my work merited it. Sometimes by-lines lead to syndication, so I AM VERY HAPPY!!! They are, too. I believe in me and so do they—for now.

Sitting here I remember the ideas I got from my guru the other day just as I left her place. The gist was life either flourishes or wilts and decays. She said something like, "If you don't want to do something, withdraw your energy. It will soon decline and die. If you want to prosper and flower, enter into meditation. Give your life love and light."

I asked, "What if your love is fading?"

After a couple of seconds, she said, "Let it fade. It will emerge strong and bright in another form—it never disappears. Shadows may emerge from time-to-time, impinging upon the degree we can love. If no love emerges, the day may end in complete darkness—but you control the light! Love is the light of day *and* night."

Right then I heard: *'Where is day now?'*

Instead of trying to answer, I went into a trance-like state of meditation. I discovered a lot of love within me that had no outlet—wasn't being used.

I was confused and not in control then, but I'm in control now—so watch out!

Chapter Eight

Year of the Pig

*W*hy would Chinese astrologers choose a pig to denote prosperity? You could Google it, and do other 'quick-and-dirty' research, but why not settle for reading the placemat under your beef lo mein?

Which branch of astrology came first? Every culture seems to have one of its own, so some must overlap. The Japanese reportedly take what the Chinese create and develop—streamline it and call it their own—like many Christian churches in America. Wonder if Japanese restaurants provide similar placemats?

With a plate of lo mein blocking my research on the 12-year Chinese astrological cycle, my attention eventually wandered back to the book I'm reading. Even shuffling through my friend's book doesn't stop me from thinking about pigs. Such thoughts drag me down and I don't want to go there. I need to move away from the past by thinking of something other than men. Oh dear, I think I saw a man turn into a pig!

There is something about animals influencing the affairs of men that harks back to mankind's beginnings. Why is it that most references to pigs are negative—being sloppy or greedy. Pigs are funny, smart, full-figured—but hogs are different. To me, hogs describe greed. They trample you, gobbling up your money, time, and love. Interesting that whenever we compare animals to humans we insult *them?*

'It may have happened before or just now, but every thought gives you an insight into life—or not, but reading can end all thought when you become involved within the writer's life and lose your mind for a time.'

Who said that? I'm definitely losing it! I used to hear my thoughts, or a voice, when I was home alone, but I'm at Mr. Chan's Rice Museum and hearing it here!

'This life on Earth is not your best, but it is the best life for Brian.'

I agree about the Brian part. Brian can't do many things easily, but what he learns, he does very, very well. In fact, he is teaching his new boyfriend how to cook. He taught him how to microwave mac'n'cheese. It thrills Brian to share everything he knows, but until this happened, he wasn't aware he was superior in any way to another.

Once you find someone less developed, intelligent, or whatever than you are, you have the foundation for greater self-love. If no one commends you, you may never realize what you do better than others. That could be a good thing.

Growing up among strangers—alien beings totally unlike me, I discovered via a sibling who continually whined she didn't have enough, because of me, that I wasn't wanted from the beginning. She hated sharing, thus was constantly told to share. The lesson she never learned took root with me and was the means by which I won my way in the world.

I had to fight to be a part of the family. If you think it was easy, you have no concept of sisterhood in the 60s. I learned to endure icy reserve and nasty tirades. As a bonus,

I learned early how to handle such women—and totally enjoy solitude.

Never actually saying much about our mutual lack of love and respect, no one in her 'normal' family said a word to me about adopting Brian—not a word! No parties, no signs on the lawn, no calls—just one hasty note. "We all hope you enjoy this attempt at motherhood—but are you sure?" Sure about what?

Nasty mail from people you know might drive some up the wall, but I knew what to do. I called my sister's home and the first person to grunt 'hello' got the full brunt of my gushiness. I said, "Just this minute I got your card! Thanks so much for your support—your timing is great! It's just what I needed! Please tell everyone I loved it! Got to run—tata!" Radiating happiness and charm, I hung up.

With passive aggressives, I recommend reacting differently than what others teach. That type seldom bothers to analyze others, assuming everyone is like them, so it's kind of easy to know what they intend, if you know them better than they do.

I was taught that over time you can induce sneaky people to behave sanely and say what they mean—but all my attempts to change familial behavior failed. No one believes anyone who arrived after them knows half as much as they do, and their offspring believe no one older than they are knows anything. By the way, I'm not laughing. Up until I hit 14, I was slightly depressed or upset by someone at home every other day—until one weekend!

Sort of sleeping while gazing at the sky, I became a *walk-out!* Left them behind and never returned! After two or three days in space I emerged as an adult who took what was offered and reciprocated in kind, unless I felt like giving more. Never again did my parents find my behavior offensive. I no longer played games at home, but have retained my hard-earned insights from family feuds to this day.

Life is strange! I sit here sipping won ton soup, thinking about pigs and crazy people, then glance at my book and notice:

> *If you play games, you play to feel alive.*

When I stopped playing games, I felt more alive than ever before! Knowing I could never win, why play at family ties? Since I wasn't wanted from the start and had learned to make my own way, I discovered I could live with anyone—I had it made! Others can't sting or bully me easily. I offer no resistance. I know I can win, so game players intuitively know to find another stooge.

During high school I met a kid in art class who was funny and feeble. In a way, that is why I liked being around him—I thought I made him happy. I was his superior in academics and social graces—but thought it didn't matter. Looking back, it may have been the 'soul' attraction that hooked me. Teachers took me aside and told me to drop him, which made me resolve to stick. I felt so sorry for him that I made me unhappy!

When you love someone, you don't fear them—but you should. They take you as you are and you gradually become someone else. At the end of a long courtship I reluctantly entered an unwanted marriage that was never consummated. It changed me as I was then, but mostly it changed how I view me now. Something I can't explain. Funny, as I turn the page—staring at me are the following lines:

> *Consummation is seen as sexual achievement by most people,*
> *but it is not. Sex is not a game that ends in matrimony or*

living together, no matter how many women want to believe it to be true. Most men can engage in sex with disinterested women who may be neither enticing nor alluring...

Being honest, I was never interested in what he said or did. I didn't care, so no communion or consummation was possible. I lost interest in the boy-never-to-be-a-man, but was into being a martyr—and I reveled in the role.

About then is when I began playing games within my mind. I pictured myself at the stove or sink working busily at chores he would neither appreciate nor recognize—while believing angels or whoever were watching and applauding me for being the perfect wife. I was self-sacrificing—just as they taught in church. I strived endlessly to please St. Paul. But in the end I was unable to turn the other cheek again and again, as Buddha preached. I finally admitted I should not have married him, but I didn't leave then.

As years passed I wanted more and more from life, but it never changed. As he took more and more, I got less and less. Pretty soon everyone believed he was my superior. I had traded places with him. He seemed unable to do much work at home, but always took full credit. Surprise! Surprise!

I wasn't recognized as a leader—even a team player. I was a slave deserving no recognition for work done daily to support him and the lifestyle he had grown accustomed to enjoying at my expense. For years I created the drama in which I played a miserable woman. How much crazier can you get?

As the waiter removed dishes, a few tears ran down my cheeks. Attempting to gain self-control, I flipped pages until I spotted:

What if your life is full of holes from self-induced delusions? Never feel sorry for what you did. You will emerge a winner. You move and gear up for the big time and go places because you learned to love without giving away yourself. This gives you more life...

Remember to save time for people who are not upset by your being yourself, but bear in mind they will not care if you are not yourself.

...Acknowledge your family after a fashion all your life.

Why? My parents are dead and my siblings are interested only in themselves. I gave them all so much time, effort, and love when young, because I really thought they would always love me, but I was obviously wrong.

The world views a family as those who raised you, thus deserving your respect. It's been my experience that once you stop providing money and providing treats they ignore and easily forget you. The remnants of my family don't worry about me—or is it the reverse?

Keeping in mind that no one else cares, you have to create your own life and live it well...

I learned that lesson when I broke up with the last Casanova. Not a bad guy, just spoiled by too many women before me. Confident he could satisfy me as well as a few other women on the side, I never told him I loved him. If I had trusted and loved him, I would not have lingered in limbo wondering if I should reveal what I felt or not.

When you linger and dawdle over a lover, you aren't sold and should move on as soon as possible. If you are sold, believing 'this is the one', don't compel the other to love you. It will end badly if you do.

I could write a book about this last guy. He was a real test of ego—the one who crossed the final frontier. I caught him in his own lies time and again, but let them go unchallenged—making allowances for him, but not me. Why?

I had to get beyond love and lust. Discover if I could love someone—and now I know I can. Now I want to move up to a better life—not social climbing, but greater self-acceptance. If you spend a lot of time in the past looking back, you either move up or drop out. Unbelievable, but I just spotted this on another page:

> *You either do the work yourself or end up rechecking everything someone else did to repair, mend, eliminate, edit, whatever. It is easier to do it yourself. Live your life easily and completely—never look back!*

Now that I've done it all, I want to move up and out into a better life while here on Earth, but that dream isn't easily achieved. I'm not talking about money! Why seek riches if not poverty-stricken? You either understand money doesn't create peace of mind or believe you need money to be happy, but peace is priceless!

Why not study wealthy people's personalities rather than dream about being rich? Get right to the point and discover why 'The Rich' aren't wealthy due to great personalities. Realize if your goal is to accumulate money you will take a lot of punishment. To accumulate billions you will abase yourself—or your family did it before you. Is it worth it?

After my divorce I attracted a wealthy man who quickly decided I was after his money. I was never so fully cross-examined by anyone! As I aced his tests, I discovered I didn't want him, but it was nice to know I passed before I walked away.

If you do better on tests than others, you feel superior—and because I test well, I love tests. I admit it! I don't live any better, but test even better as I age. Many other students of life forget to study, fail to pay attention, or don't follow instructions. Not bragging, but at 40 I scored as high in scholastic tests as students 19 or 20, and didn't struggle to do it. I just read what is assigned and listen to the wise.

If you do only what is assigned, you're not outstanding—no matter what your grades imply. Average students do only enough to pass. They're not educated in the classical sense, but hopefully trained well enough to successfully pursue a vocation or trade.

At university I took on extra work. I thought it proved I was there for all the right reasons, but younger students didn't get it. They bought term papers, stole exams, and hi-jacked class assignments—but who were they cheating? Me! I was denied the benefit of experiencing many minds fully engaged at the same time working on the same subject.

When I brought Brian home I thought he wouldn't do well in school, so I denied him much TV. I treated him as if a fragile doll, so he never sang letters and numbers with a purple robot. He learned to count using his piggies and tried reading along with me—memorizing a few lines here and there—just enough to prove he wanted to be educated at a higher level than experts expected.

French educators propose that childhood is a magical time and should not be rushed because mothers must work elsewhere during the day. Whereas Americans strive to cram facts and figures into the minds of the very young, in the guise of being early childhood daycare, assuming their children will be smarter than those who play outside school much longer. Does it work? American children pushed to grow up too quickly often burn out as early as fifth grade.

Compared to French students, via any international testing, American college students trail French counterparts by a long distance.

I've decided Sesame parents are as bad as the show's producers. They want to believe it's good for kids to sit in isolation and watch cartoon characters all day. It just isn't true! It's been proven such learning doesn't increase a child's willingness to learn later on. Results abound that conclude too many kids are failing at mastering life skills and are socially inept, because they don't play enough with other children.

I don't want to contend with a 'kindergarten burnout', but what to do? I set my sites on helping Brian learn at his pace, while protecting him from those who might ruin his love of discovering things for himself.

A very loose interpretation of a French saying: "Let a child be a child and you will have less trouble later." Their methods continue to be ignored by Americans who remain socially isolated from the world due to inability to communicate in languages other than their own. Many children are no longer taught English at home, thus they resort to slang and irrational idioms in an attempt to bridge gaps and gaffs when trying to communicate with peers outside.

Reminds me of that old joke, "How do you describe a person who speaks two languages?" The answer: "Bilingual." Next question: "What do you call a person who speaks only one language?" Answer: "American."

English was the only language taught in my schools, so I learned it along with a little bit of Latin, and they served me well—even in France. In Paris I was never told to 'talk French', nor was I treated more rudely than in New York or some other large city. Why do so many Americans complain that Parisians are rude? Perhaps if you're unaware you are rude or crude, it takes someone mirroring your behavior to expose you? Aliens see you as you are, while friends and family may excuse bad behavior because they act the same.

'You can't blame others, including the French, for being rude if you are.'

Somehow this lunch is unlike any I have ever had. I can hear my inner voice clearly and believe I'm thinking clearly and ideas are popping up out of nowhere. I wonder if I've been drugged and am hallucinating.

I checked out my friend's book again, because it's weird how it answers my questions. I ask, then haphazardly open the book and point to a paragraph—and there is the answer. I must say this has been a truly moving experience!

'You asked to move up—quickly.'

Yes, I did, but this is ridiculous! I glance at a page and suddenly I'm lost in space—or maybe it's time.

> You have to believe in yourself and accept this as your life. If you cannot locate where you left your life's path to search for another person, return to your first meeting and remember what you did together then.

I left my life path when I got involved with the manic depressive lad in high school, but going back shows me nothing. It's as if it didn't happen. I didn't care that much about boys back then—not like my school friends. I was wise beyond my years about life, but maybe got off-track when I broke off contact with my first love—never again available to him. Don't know.

After working a few years, I met a very affectionate and caring man. He was sweet and funny and made me laugh in spite of my sad life. I thought I wasn't happy then, but it turned out to be the most carefree time of my life—so far anyway. Don't know why I know it, but it was his happiest time, too.

As happens all too often, he was married and I was unaware until too late to continue as *just friends.* We went out once on a kind of date, but he was afraid to be seen with me—which made *me* feel strange about being me. He was nothing like he seemed to be. Surprise! He was serious and stiff—mumbled and grumbled. No resemblance to the carefree man who called several times a day at work and at home.

I was crushed, as they say. I tried to shake it off, but it hurt—a lot. I can see now that I never got over that affair, even though it too was never consummated. I was left trying to figure out why he did what he did and couldn't shed tears to rid myself of it.

He was just another selfish man seeking excitement outside marriage, with young kids and wife blissfully unaware of his roving mind. As it turned out, all he wanted was sex—and not just from me. Although conservative and introverted, he was fairly adept socially. I agreed with him then that he was witty, intelligent, and handsome. He talked about silly, funny, weird people we worked with—not too unkind, but snide and cynical. I loved him anyway.

An old friend told me to lie low and not go out of my way to see him as much. He was unlike my friends, so they disliked him for me. I continued to care about him until he offended my sense of self or dignity. It took something like that to wrap up the loose ends and get going again. He should have done the manly thing, had the decency to tell me it was over, but he wasn't much of a man. Was he?

'Few men do the decent thing when it comes to getting what they want.'

You might judge others by one set of standards and yourself by another, but a true measurement isn't worth your time if you don't stand up for your own beliefs and face the music—or get lost. I was lost—and immediately found his clone! Believe it or not!

Analyzing my past over a plate of Chinese is so therapeutic I might ask for dessert. It's hard to imagine why anyone would sit and reminisce about lost lives. I mean last loves—lost loves—whatever.

I feel like I'm 17 again—maybe because the man after Jack was much older and more cultured than all the loves before him. At first he annoyed me—a lot. He started riding my bus, flirting with a young, bold woman/child who chattered about a boyfriend, whom he called a prize jerk. He looked so delighted I figured he was getting it on with her, until he sat beside me and quickly started telling me about his work. No introduction— just started talking as if we were old buddies. I didn't like his approach, but did agree work could be interesting.

Now I realize he was a major player. Not too many successful people ride buses, but in the days of carpools you never knew who might sit beside you. He was a throwback to those days.

His conversation never amounted to much, but I sat and listened attentively since I was unsure about his motives, especially the weird thing with the young woman. I didn't like that, because too many men who encourage children and childish women are predators and unworthy of respect. I don't approve, so I ignore them—until then. I wanted to know why he was interested in someone far from mature.

Later I discovered he was married and forced to live far from his pampered family in order to earn the money they seized upon so readily. He missed his teenage daughter so much he unconsciously sought a substitute in the young girl on the bus. Hard to believe, but I bought the idea that his thoughts of this silly girl were strictly paternal.

What happened next was the biggest mistake of my life! I settled into a relationship similar to what I had just abandoned. As I seemingly or seamlessly picked up the dropped threads of the previous affair, I remember thinking, 'If I didn't know better, I'd think this is Jack.' Nevertheless, I proceeded to follow my nose to explore another pile of—.

When you aren't busy—and bored best describes your mood—you forget your dreams. Mine stopped! Nights spent in dreamtime ceased to be. I became consumed with wonder about this man and what it would be like to be married to him. Fully aware he was not husband-material—good husbands don't flirt and carry on with other women. Still, I thought he was better than anyone who had 'loved' me in the past.

Before these two bores, there were many men around me. I paid little attention, because I was consumed by grief. For too many years I had participated in my mother's agonizing struggle to live. Memories of her last few years remain painful and unresolved in my mind even now.

During that time we became inseparable to the point my mother didn't want to leave me for her *home in the sky,* as she described death. I was deeply attached to her needs as much as her personality. I truly loved her, but she never loved me as much. She was a fair woman with several other children to love, while I had only one mother.

I never regret loving my parents. I was never abused or accused of any wrong doing by either, but frequently chastised for not being tidy and neat like my sister and others. She used to tease that I wasn't exactly what they wanted, but would do. I may not have been the son they wanted, but I did okay and benefitted from being trained in the traditional, practical German way of life.

I guess that is how I look at men even now. They're not exactly what I want, but they're easier to relate to than many women. Why are so many women difficult to get along with?

'Jealousy rules their day.'

The day I went off the track and accepted the advances of the man-about-town is where I must return now, if I'm to pick up the pattern and weave a good life out of all these broken threads. It's necessary to go back and pick up the original pattern—I can see him smiling at the girl on the bus now....

The other day I met a recently-divorced friend who is having a bad time adjusting to his change of fate—as he sees it. He's doing things now he never did once he settled into marriage. He claims he was not emotionally involved with his wife and describes his marriage certificate as confirmation he was owned by another, and his wedding ring was proof of his bondage. He joked he should have worn it in his nose rather than on his hand. He admits he wasn't much of a husband, so without too much acrimony he paid off his wife to be free again. Now she seems to be satisfied with him. I used to think those who fell once will fall again, but feel sure he will be fine when he marries again—and be happier than he was or is now.

The book my friend wrote was good, but ended without resolving my issues. More than ever before I call on my Spiritual Guides to help me discern what is wise and what I can achieve, but now when I think of *her*, messages come through time to my mind, too.

Now what did I do with my journal? My belief system is so limited I have no idea where the words come from, but discovering my journal always brings amazing revelations. Now where is my pen?

What if a fallen man doesn't get back up—or walks away unscathed? What if he is crippled mentally and blames others, using his disabilities as an excuse for bad behavior? What if he has a stroke due to internal injuries suffered when his marriage abruptly ended? Health is a concern when anyone ages prematurely due to immaturity. Do you care?

I do, but I spent too much of my life nursing my parents and other family members to want to do it again. I learned whatever lessons and wanted to move on once I realized no one cares enough about me to nurse me through old age.

What if I go out and find a new man—dropping all past associations? Would this be wise and safe? There is such a plague upon the land you don't know what is wise or safe if you want to be a wife.

Yes, I know. I love being a wife or in relationships with caring adults, but I don't want to be controlled and smothered by jealousy or rage when things don't go as planned.

When I was very young and taken in by the world, I believed others were perfect. I believed I was good, because I did what others expected—plus. I couldn't understand why no one noticed that. I wanted to be perfect because movie stars were perfect and thought everyone could be perfect if they worked hard enough.

I was always sincere, honest, and hard working. Hoping to be worthy of admiration, only to discover celebs were not. The pain of this realization left me without anyone to love and idolize—for a couple of months. When I discovered the pursuit of wisdom, I dumped them all.

Throughout childhood and adolescence, I went to the movies. Sitting there—looking up, watching glamorous people living in beautiful homes say the most amazing things. I thought they created the lines, always dressed beautifully, and lived with style and grace—never angry or stupid. I believed in what they appeared to be until it dawned on me anyone could deliver clever speeches somebody else wrote. What takes a lot of work and luck is living the good life as you are.

Movie magazines regularly reported this actor and that actress did nothing to attain stardom. Simply being in the right place at the right time, looking beautiful or tough was enough to get noticed in Hollywood. Being ready to be spotted had to be more important than anything else. Right? I think it was then I started thinking seriously about fate. It took much longer to register that we produce the scenes that make up the movies of our lives.

You are not born to a place. You are not required to always live there. You gravitate to a soul ready for you. You go to that soul when accepted, but you may reject one like it later.

Very interesting—not what I expected would come out of nowhere.

During what was your mother's last painful pregnancy, she attended two Christian women's conventions where they laid hands on her and prayed for her baby. Each time they prayed to The Holy Spirit to deliver her from pain and the sorrow of another miscarriage. She felt poor, because your father was out of work and they could not afford another mouth. She firmly believed her in-laws hated her, and she had no close relatives to lend her support. Unwell due to losing three babies before concrete absorption of their souls occurred, she could not understand why it happened and secretly believed your promised arrival would end badly, too. Thus she ignored family to attend assemblies of Godly women.

You never thought twice about accepting your father's request for an angel. She asked for you, too, but didn't remember it later. Your mother was a teacher of the highest order, thus able to teach you about Earth and how to assist in preparing for upcoming world changes.

You were not a baby when you entered this world, but you never saw her before you arrived. In lives past you gravitated toward monks or being a priestess or oracle. You always love sailing the seas! Most of your many lives were spent here on Earth. You avoided evil, and never married in past lives, but you did raise many children—none were your own.

What I needed then and now was a woman like my mother, someone who taught the child I seemed to be, helping me develop a life that would lead to wealth and fame—while remaining unconscious of the quest. My soul recognized her as the mother I needed this life—a warm, wonderful woman who opened doors for me. I have been truly blessed!

At the convention where she prayed for a child who would love and help others, achieving things she could never aspire to do, we responded. She had to wait until the second convention before your spirit entered this world again. Praying women laid their hands on her as your soul quickened. They all marveled at it, but she felt nothing!

I believe if you don't know who you are, you can find out. I enter into deep meditation or trance and witness it all. I remember my mother talking about this event from her perspective, but my view differs from hers; however, I think it agrees with what she believed.

'Remember, if female and well-adjusted, men are mothers to you, too.'

I loved my father and respect men like him, but I was never a 'Daddy's Girl.' To me, 'Daddy's Girls' don't become well-adjusted women. Too often they seek older men to replace doting fathers, even though such ideals never existed. Their shadow blights the daughter's love of others. I love men who aren't like my father, but don't get that involved. Maybe I love me too much? What to do with *my* love?

Going back in time, I've found many places where I went wrong by pursuing my own ideas. I'm going to head out now and find a man not at all like me—but on the way up. If I can seek spiritual growth and follow that path—anyone can. If a man can't live up to my ideals, I will leave—I don't have time for that.

You must know by now what is really bothering me! Why I'm going on like this. I don't want Brian to be fatherless. It isn't exactly his idea that I remarry, but he wants someone else to love and trust beside me. Since I live alone with few males around, he loves them all. I don't, but he does—so they get grand ideas.

I want a steady man who is here for me and will help if needed. I don't want leftovers or crumbs from another woman's table. I want my own man and vow to keep his love forever. If I don't find anyone worth the effort soon—a man who is loyal and wise, I'll give up, knowing I tried—I really tried!

Chapter Nine

Titles Are Not Proper Names

*I*t's so much easier now to get answers to problems that once bothered my mind for days at a time. Now I sit and write letters to Hirman, my spiritual guide. Thoughts I *never* had before come pouring onto the paper. Sometimes as I write I hear a voice that sounds like a man, but it's probably all in my mind. I imagine Hirman lives inside my diary—because it's amazing how clear-headed I feel after journaling.

Dear Hiram,

Since I last wrote to you about life, I did a lot of work on this old house. What a wreck! Nothing of value left inside, but they did leave a lot of salvageable junk in the basement and garage. Why leave stuff for others to pass judgment on and pitch—things you valued enough to save?

Being curious about the previous owners, I spent weekends working through their things, doing little with mine. You can't work on others stuff without sidetracking your life, but I discovered a lot by examining what they left. I've become a modern-day archeologist.

Thrifty person that I am, I was shocked at how much 'trash' turned out to be valuable. If broken, it took only a minute or a few dollars to fix. I redid or sanitized everything and am holding a garage sale next week. No one will believe it is all discards.

As for me, I have this thing about old stuff—I don't like mucking about in it. When I see heaps of dingy stuff at flea markets or thrift shops, it makes me sad, even a bit sick. I dislike antiques and old-fashioned clothes, especially Victorian clutter, yet love ancient artifacts from Egypt, Greece, and the Roman Empire. I thought maybe I lived then, but you said I'm attracted because I didn't live then and want to know more about them. Which version is true—mine or yours?

'The bottom line is you are allergic to dust. Working with old clothes makes you sick—physically. The thrust of work with us is that you do not have to think as much. You can accept what we say, because we see much more than you could ever imagine before you began to channel.'

Hmmm, that sounds reasonable to me. When you think about it, why would you care much about places, people, and events if you had been there and done that?

'You would not be as drawn to their history and philosophies or fine art and furnishings as that of people you never knew. You would take it for granted—maybe even a bit boring.'

I believe I lived in Egypt long ago, and it was not a good life. Maybe I was a slave or adventurer who sailed the Nile? Definitely not a noble, so now I want to learn about the first Pharaohs, as well as life in their upper classes. At first I thought all that remained behind are relics of the rich, because that is what intrigued me—maybe because it represents a different life style than I led, or it explains more about those who then controlled my fate?

'What if you were rich and famous and could have everything you ever wanted?'

I would buy two houses—one for me and one for Brian. Obviously, his house would be governed and maintained by me, but his in title and design. My house would be imprinted with Brian, but not his to rule over day and night. This house is not his enough to suit him, and not mine enough to suit me, but we get along.

Constantly working over the gingerbread on an old Victorian is neither easy nor fun, but Brian loves it. Maybe he was poor and miserable in the Gay Nineties and I wasn't? I remember nothing of that era, but feel something stir when I clean the eaves or wipe down the stairs to the second floor. If I had been a maid in such a house back then, wouldn't I hate doing such work now? To me, it's a big house that constantly needs maintenance. Even though it has many rooms, I still can't find places to display my collections to the best effect.

Visitors rave about the high ceilings, always asking how I heat the place without going into debt. Of all the unlikely comments made while entertaining 'my public', that one amazes me most. What cold? When we were kids my fingertips got frost bite while waiting for the school bus—now that was cold! I don't feel cold inside—just tired of cleaning up after people who don't pitch their rubbish.

What if we traveled this summer to another area? I've been thinking about taking Brian on a car trip to the fords of a river upstate to look at the falls—maybe tumble over them. We liked to do that when I was young, but Brian is a handful and could fall and get seriously injured. When he climbs a firm hand is required, but other than that, outdoor life is wonderful with our new Scout.

Sitting in reverie rereading my diary, thinking about today's worries, I see a similar collection of things written in the past—

and similar words playing in my mind today. Is that normal or am I the only woman who talks to her Guides?

'There are many others who are wise. You must make greater efforts to find and support them.'

Hmmm, not to change the subject, but I was going to talk out my thoughts in an effort to force you to respond with more than your usual, "Uh, huh," but I take it all back. You don't have to call or write, because now I know what you think.

'I know.'

"You're still inside my mind, but I feel like I have this vast ocean of love and contentment passing through a veil from you to me—even if you don't feel it. This morning I was positive your waves of love would be waiting—as always, but they weren't there and I missed them. Why couldn't I feel your presence and love then?"

'Are you in love?'

"I feel something is missing from my life. Are you giving up and moving on to another plane or another person instead of helping me?"

'You must not think we will not approve of whomever you turn your attention to now. I believe you can tell me what is happening without my having to watch and wait all day to see what you are doing. We all want to be a part of your happy times, but you never call upon God then! As your Guide, I want to be part of the life you live daily, but if you never call or write, how can any of us know your plans and what you need to advance—and perhaps we can provide? Remember, we are a part of 'You' and your old friends, too.'

"Just the other day while throwing out stacks of old newspapers and magazines I realized I couldn't throw out your messages, Hirman. I reread every letter and couldn't throw out any old manuscripts, either. After a while, though, I held the manuscripts up to the light and began pitching them into the fireplace. I burned them without prayers, incantations, or anything. Just threw them on the fire and watched them go up in smoke. It really was too warm for a big fire, but I felt I had to do it."

I just realized I was talking out loud to you, Hirman! You are the only guide I know, and I love talking to you, but no one else knows you exist. It's weird enough to journal with you, but talking aloud is really far out! So forgive me for preferring to write in Spirit in my diary and journal most of the time. I have a problem with walking around talking to 'myself' when others might hear me. Can I mumble instead?

'Muttering would be very hard to understand.'

What if I chant?

'Chanting is great!'

Okay, I'll let it rip! I'll sing out whatever I'm thinking and hope it sounds like Phil Collins composing something—rather than me droning a strange, weird dirge.

'Begin now.'

"Oh, Hirman, you should see how the cat looked at me! I think I scared her. My voice is out-of-tune, screeching like an old Stradivarius. She is as sweet as any cat can be and I hope we can keep her. I used to be allergic to cats, but I can stand her now. No sneezing, wheezing, or itching—but how long will it last? Will I have to pass her on to someone else? She likes to creep under the covers, and Brian loves her much…Maybe that is what happens in marriage? You can tolerate loving a man as long as you don't get too stressed—but if the match isn't good, you over-react, acting out rage and fear in strange ways—until one of you has to move along."

I was bitten by love once. It left me immune to its effects—sort of like a homeopathic cure.

'Or so you thought.'

What if I chase after this movie star? And what if he flirted back—and it turns out he is ready to settle down and do the work necessary to cement a lasting relationship?

Never mind, why would he want me anyway? I get only so far with daydreams before they fall apart. I don't know how to dream about love anymore. If I tried to attract a man like Him, where would it take us? I would gain power and prestige by association with a star—but what would He get from it?

'Maybe he would find peace.'

And I would have to give up mine.

'He might find a calm harbor where both of you could rest in peace.'

I would have to give up my life.

'He may be able to let down his guard and feel free to be who he is with you.'

But I won't be able to let down my guard. I'll have to watch for poachers and stalkers wherever we go. If I were to be loved in return by such a man, I would lose too much. I better forget following through on that dream.

'Why not at least try?'

It is possible I could do much more for the world if I moved in higher, more powerful circles.

'If in a powerful position, we could do more for you. However, positions gained through another—not earned by you—are not very comfortable—at first.'

I used to get upset easily. In fact, I'm upset just thinking about it! I get too intense when my life centers around a man. My mind takes over, instead of my heart. It talks me out of love before we even go out. Why bother thinking about men like him? He could be an ax murderer for all I know.

'You cannot tell until you give him an ax and a motive, but cutting up people is not what this man does. He is above such ideas of power and strength. He has no need to gain everyone's attention. He does not have much passion anymore.'

That's it! He isn't passionate!

'As an actor he learned to control and channel his passions in order to be creative.'

I dig that. I'm that way, too, but if two creative people marry or whatever, would either create as well as when they were separate entities? I think not, but how do I know?

'You did it before!'

Wow, I'm on a roll today! I can feel your thoughts within my mind and soul. I feel like I can finally remember past lives and figure out why I do so much that doesn't really matter.

I was sure love would happen naturally along the way, but it never did. Perhaps this is it? I never loved or felt like this before—yet others say they fall in love on a regular basis. If this is love, why am I so late finding it? Am I so difficult to please, yet can please others easily with only a moment's notice? Apparently it's my life to figure out who I am, because no one else cares enough about me to add knowledge to my thoughts.

'Align your spine and sink back in time.'

What do you see?

'What will you believe?'

Let me see. I know I was in the world at least once as a slave. Funny, as in strange, I sense it wasn't always that bad—being a slave—even though I hate those who enslave others to gain wealth and power, and disrespect those who submit to the yoke when it's easily discarded. Actually, that is why I avoid bridge clubs, country clubs, and places where women sit and gossip behind each other's back. I despise the mentality that enables some to usurp their men's power in order to look down on others.

'Some whom you think of as slaves are actually missionaries sent to change women of today and help men left without friends due to jealousy among women.'

Really? I'll have to think about that. What if you were a slave working beside me in another time, Hirman? I bet if we met today, we'd laugh, then walk away not knowing we had worked together in another life. What a day we would have—and it happened because we happened to bump into one another here.

Now that I can see better, I don't want to remember the mundane, stupid things I worked through, only what is weird. Like I've always wanted to know why I settled for such a mundane life.

One idea appears brighter than others—that I was born into wealth in the Gay Nineties, but didn't live long. That could explain why I bought this big house for the two of us, and why we surround ourselves with older people who do little more than check out how we live—never saying anything you would repeat to a sane person. It could also explain why I like to stand at the top of the stairs on the third floor and watch others swarm over the house, trooping up and down the front steps like they did at the House and Garden Tour last month.

What if I once lived *'upstairs'* as a wealthy man's wife or daughter? Would I enjoy slaving over the running of this house now? I don't! Whenever I dwell on little bitty details, I get confused. Speaking of confusion, I was so addled I actually called up a guy and asked him for a date.

'You should not do that.'

I was sure he was a really great guy, but when he saw I was interested enough to chase him, he turned into an ego-driven machine. I was horrified to see what I'd started. I couldn't get off the phone fast enough.

'What do men want?'

I was a man several lives here on Earth—a good man, but today's men are lazy. They don't try to do great things. Most of the great ideas of this world are old—and merely being copied now. I've never been impressed by 'national pride', but it was better than this apathy that invites anarchy.

'You either take pride in your country or it isn't your country long. You either think you do things well or you don't.'

What to do about a country too big to manage?

'Let it fall apart—but why?'

When men roamed the mountains—never living in them, I was a mountain man. When the mountains became home to those who waste millions, killing birds and animals for no good reason, I fled in horror. Now I don't want anything to do with hunters! Fishermen don't bother me—even though some are gluttons, too, maybe because they meditate more than prey. Those who buy guns with scopes to aim at big bucks shout, "I'm great! I can kill these suckers whenever I want," I don't want them anywhere near my son! One day they might have me where they want me and kill me, too.

That is how I see Great White Hunters! They apparently see themselves quite differently. They would not be so offensive if they used Indian-style bows and arrows and wore moccasins—and ate what they kill, but spending thousands to load up and traipse around in outlandish clothes in search of baby deer scares me—But no one listens!

Why not reintroduce wolves into the mountains and let them thin the wild herds instead of using helicopters and urging paramilitary types to shoot them? No money in that! We sell hunting licenses to produce millions in revenue and use the opportunity to train younger generations to kill.

'You think. I'll write.'

What would it take to clear up the Earth's pollution?

No response, so I'll write what comes to me in Spirit now.

It could be done by these same hunters. Let them dress in expensive clothes and walk into the hills with shovels to retrench and plant trees, instead of carrying guns with the intent of killing anything with four feet. They may want to walk about in the woods to lower their stress levels.

But I'm a dreamer—always was.

'You see things first—then prepare.'

By the time I see them, they're knocking at my door. The other day I was looking at a magazine spread on homes and gardens of the rich and famous and in walked you know who.

'Tell me about it.'

What a day! I was exhausted from all the visitors we entertained in the name of charity during the House and Garden Party. I had just put Brian to bed. He was overly tired from all the excitement. I didn't want him to regress into baby talk, so I sat with my feet propped on the coffee table, sipping sweet tea when the biggest surprise of my life popped up. I never expected Him to come walking down the garden path and into the front parlor, but he did—and now He is gone. I doubt he will ever come back.

'Stop thinking about him! Be yourself! Live the good life—for you and Brian.'

The only time I stop thinking about HIM is when I'm not thinking, so I've been meditating and dreaming as much as I can. I always thought he was some kind of god—instead he's a man of great intentions and healthy appetites—not at all like he appears on the screen. I thought he was some kind of Casanova or Latin lover—sweeping women off their feet. But then, men can't work that line anymore. Can they?

'It's a dead way.'

I think you mean, 'It's a dead giveaway.' Who is into macho men now? But women continue to fall in love with the sincere—and the weak. Anyway, when he strode into the kitchen to check how I had fixed it up, he started crying. It was so unexpected that I became passionate. I fondled his hair and began to rub his back.

'Really?'

Really! I was in a passionate position when Brian entered the pantry and saw a usurper in his territory. He became a tyrant. He was jealous and got very upset. I had created another monster, but HE calmed down when he saw how upset Brian was. Grabbing his little hand in his very large paw, we stood there in the pantry like a family. It hurts to remember, but that's when I fell in love with Him. Now what to do?

'When you fall in love, you do not see others as they are but as you wish them to be. You want your life to be bigger and better, and you do not want anyone to speak ill of your relationship.'

You want to say 'I love you' so he will respond passionately. Only then are you assured you're loved—but are you?

'What if you stunned the universe and married a big star?'

First, I want to know if it hurts. I think so, because it's happening already. Now I know what it's like to be star-struck. I'm like a spaced-out teenager! I obviously have to experience this to attain mature love or return to living happily alone, but want to get over it fast! Maybe you and my other guides can help me get over it in a month or so?

What a month! I haven't written or talked to you, Hirman, for so long that I'm embarrassed to write without first making excuses.

'They better be good.'

I was sure Steve would drop me if he visited again, so I tried to make it happen—but he resisted. A man has to be crazy to want a woman around him who can't laugh when he is near her.

When we first met I was funny and witty, but no longer. I hope he is willing to wait until that woman returns! Which is unlikely, based on how I've been acting this past week.

I was so sure of myself when we first met. In fact, I was positive I could keep my integrity and sanity—never give in to pettiness or jealousy, regardless of what happened with him, but that confident woman is gone. This new me is a burden to bear. I can't stand me anymore!

I stop to do something, then stand there doing nothing. I even stopped writing my book to spend more time staring at the phone, trying to make it ring—just like some stupid teenage crush. What a nightmare!

'What if you had never met him?'

Brian and I would be living out a peaceful life in the Burgh. Everyone would be nice, and we would be happy to see visitors. That is impossible now! Everyone on the street—sometimes even at home, is sickening sweet, rearranging memories to demonstrate how much they love me—but the message is clear: It's not about me! It's all about him—and it's maddening how people take it out on Brian.

'Keep working with people as you did in the past.'

I tried to do something for the public library, but the librarian said it wasn't the season to introduce new programs. What a laugh! Since when does the library have too many writers willing to help others?

'We wonder about the librarian. She does not grasp that as she writes, so she exists and will be. For that reason she may be unable to publish her work.'

I was lucky to get published—or was I?

'If you had not published and made a big success of your works, you would not be agonizing over love now.'

I'm not agonizing, just not meditating as much—or praying. I get upset and scattered when I don't get enough rest.

When Steve and his posse first approached me at the end of a long day of signing autographs at Borders, I wasn't ready for their camaraderie. I was annoyed that this blond, brazen man had so many friends and I was all alone—not even one hanger-on nearby.

'They were there to entertain Him. He laughed to relax.'

Well, I had no intention of joining in their antics. So I started signing my name and out came a funny, sarcastic bio of Steve instead. It was fun, because it wasn't really coming from me. I had no idea how it would end. He laughed until tears rolled down his cheeks, even though it wasn't that funny. He acted as though it was about someone else! I wonder why?

'*You can't hurt some people, but everyone hurts.*'

I wasn't trying to hurt him. It just flowed onto the flyleaf. So if he was hurt, why would he come by my home later—alone? We have nothing in common. I'm plain old me and he's a man of the world. I must be so different from everyone in Hollywood that he's curious and wants to make sure I'm who I seemed to be when we met—or a raving lunatic. After all, I keep telling him to stay away.

What does he see in me? I don't sit and primp and practice new faces to see if this look or that pose is sexy or cool. In fact, my face has lots of fine lines and wrinkles, because I move all my face all the time. My dimples aren't from God, but from leaning on my pencil while writing. Otherwise, I'm much the same as when I landed on Earth—just a bit more ragged around the edges—and a lot happier since Brian came into my life.

Looking back, Steve must not have checked me out at the book signing—or maybe it was the lighting. I remember he sort of glanced at me, then looked away and laughed. I was sure he wasn't paying attention to me—just entertaining his friends at my expense. Maybe that is why I whipped him into paying attention.

Steve says he was interested before I attacked. Apparently, my 'wit' made him laugh enough to relax and he wanted to see if it would happen again. It has never been the same, but he calls and stops by whenever he can get away from his entourage.

We really aren't that different, if you study social psychology, but at a glance we look so different we could never end up together—like Woody Allen and—just about any woman. Our facades are so different—nothing suggests we could be compatible enough to marry—but we are. Steve's veneer is shiny and hard—according to the tabloids; but I know he's deep where I'm shallow—and the reverse is true of me.

We may have met to fill a part of our lives that was vacant and unsuited to cohabitation, but I think we now know better why 'we' came to be—and it has little to do with loneliness or finding your bliss.

It took a while to adjust our schedules and daily habits, but we got into the rhythm of a relationship without Brian getting even slightly jealous—or annoyed at how much I grieve when Steve leaves. If given a chance, Brian accepts everything. He's even more of a lover—and he needs Steve. He really does—and that will hurt most when Steve leaves.

Leaving will be Steve's decision, because I don't leave—at least not easily. I'll stay until I'm run over, dragged out, flogged in the middle of the street and left to bleed. Only then will I analyze the breakup, wondering if I upset him doing this or that. I won't leave, but will know it's over before it is. How? I instinctively start rearranging my nest.

Right now my home looks like it did when Steve visited the first time, but I find myself looking at house and garden magazines in order to avoid reading the scandal sheets at check-out counters.

"Hirman, I want to know for sure if he is just cooling his heels here while waiting for another role or is using us to add another dimension to his acting. He doesn't say why he stays on or when he'll leave, but I heard him talking on the phone the other day to his agent. He said he was in limbo. He said it kindly. No actually, he was quite regal."

Steve is a Leo! I never wanted to get involved with a Leo, but it's sort of nice to meet him in the den. He is endowed with sunlight, and the sun follows him wherever he goes. The glow is enough to tan everyone around him. He doesn't seem to notice, but he does protect his domain—like a lion.

Steve will not be taken for granted or second-guessed! Otherwise, he lets whatever happens happen while he sits and watches from his elevated status. He is very proud, like any Leo, but not conceited. He is very popular, but not arrogant as some Leos can be—and he is very loving with us—not like an old lion with its pride.

"Years ago I was told by an astrologer that I would marry a man who was an Aquarian at heart, but ruled by Leo. I never thought of a man with a mane, but Steve has long, flowing hair. Up close his great mass of hair tickles me. At first I wondered why he would want such long hair, but now know it's to attract women. Women scream whenever he walks into a crowd with his hair streaming in his wake."

'To be noticed by women is obvious, but not his idea.'

"He really is wild, but doesn't believe in doing things in order to be noticed. In that way he's like me. He gets his hair trimmed every other month or so, lets it grow its own way, relying on his hairdressers to keep it in check. He intended to get his hair cut after making a safari movie, but it needed so little work that he never got around to cutting it back.

"I hope you don't mind, Hirman, but I'm so nervous I have to write in my journal now. Is that still allowed?"

'Your words will always be read, but to be allowed to think or talk out loud and have someone on the other side accept it and respond to it immediately is a gift.'

"Wow! I never knew that! I'll write and listen to what you say, and definitely honor your advice and live it as best I can."

No reply, but my hand is writing furiously—so quickly I can't speak.

If you went out with a man dressed in African safari clothes— better looking than Adonis, you'd be nervous, too. It is very difficult to be calm when crowds rush forward—totally ignoring you—or worse, loudly criticizing your looks as they flirt and act incredibly adorable or lascivious toward the man walking beside you. Their eyes invade my privacy, too, and their hatred is so intense at times that I feel like I'm being stabbed with icicles. I hate it! I hate this side of our life. It's not what I ever wanted, but have to take. It comes with the package—I guess.

When I get old, and famous people are no longer important to me, (Will that ever happen?) I want to sing and dance like I did before I met Steve. (Is that time coming soon?)

I'm aging with him as never before. Maybe it's because he is so much older than me. My face is wrinkling more and more as I dry up inside. My mind is dry as a bone!

Nothing new appears when I sit down to write. My lips let the stupidest remarks slip out. If you knew me, you would know I'm not myself now, yet most think this is me. I hate that more than anything, but it'll pass.

"I'm going to meditate now."

Chapter Ten

The Ways of the World Are Weird

*T*he other day, while sitting on the window seat watching Brian playing on the swing with the little boy next door, I felt pleased and proud.

'Of what?'

The swing. I made it! I didn't make Brian, and I didn't create his friendship with the little guy who follows him around, but I made that swing—and it's darn good.

'You can't be proud of another, but mothers try. You cannot live another's life, either, but everybody tries that at least once. You cannot make anyone else happy, but many think you should try.'

I love my work, I really do! It doesn't make me that happy very often, but I love it anyway. People I meet infrequently often suggest I do something new or try whatever they're selling then. Why should I have to defend my ways and explain that if I needed advice I'd ask an expert—not them?

'What if you sit and muse about all you are and what you do? Would you come up with someone like me?'

Probably not.

'Now that I've brought it up, you may see more.'

That would be great! On Earth we learn by watching others. We seek out models. We think that is the easiest and best way to learn how to behave, even live. We follow their lead until they fall or do something stupid. That is how we get along—and learn, but it's not a good way to move ahead in times such as these.

'What if you are surrounded by bigots and other terrible people?'

You would think as they do. If not, their hatred surrounds you and makes you sick. The way it is now, it's impossible to be yourself if no one else is like you. You change to become what you believe will succeed or leave you in peace.

When you want to change, I was told to seek it with others first, but it isn't that easy. When I tried to lose a few pounds, only a few people I knew had done it successfully, so I asked them how they did it. Each did it differently, and when I tried their ways—nothing helped. I had to lose it my way.

'Forgive me, but that sounds like meditation.'

My soul's meditation is different from my mind and heart meditations. I try to learn from others how to go deeper, but it isn't happening. I get only so far before something brings me back to Earth. I can't lose the world like they do—at least not doing it their way.

"Mommy, can I play with Justin?"

Jostled back to the present or perhaps jettisoned into my present future, Brian tugged on my sleeve and smiled up at me as if trying to awaken me from a deep sleep. I have to admit I feel sluggish, but have enough sense to smile and say, "Sure, but be back in time for lunch."

The blessing of friendship has added a new aspect of masculinity to Brian's sturdy body. Watching him I can see the man he will be one day. Having a little man around the house certainly is educational. Now when I look at men, I often see them as the eight-year-old boys they once were.

"Mommy, can I bring Justin home for lunch?"

"Sure, if his Mommy will let him."

"Okay-Dokay."

"That's Okeydokey."

"That's right, Mommy. We play outside 'til lunch."

As he runs out the door, trundling past the kitchen window toward Justin's house, I feel a surge of maternal bliss—or whatever. We've bonded, but it's quite obvious some of the kids at his school haven't bonded with their mothers. Why let expectations of physical perfection cloud your love for a child? Their obvious dissatisfaction with outward imperfections prevents them from enjoying the beauty of a child's inner being. Such people can't teach me anything about living with Down syndrome. I sometimes wonder if those types even love children?

'Maybe that is why you are here.'

Well, Hirman, if you and I knew all the answers, we would be on another plane—out of here. It depresses or represses me to think about it, perhaps a side-effect of 'intended motherhood'. If you take on a full-time job like Brian, you know it's long-term and will require all you can give—maybe your entire life—not just a few years. Natural parents expect 'normal' birth and little who's it popping out with all systems go. They live together for 18-20 years then return to pursuing their own lives. That won't happen to me. Brian is mine as long as I live.

'It is possible he will return to a state where he can tolerate all others and work every day.'

Will he ever be able to make it totally on his own? Maybe that is too much to expect? But if it's possible, I'm all for it. I don't want him to be proud, weird, or scared, but people get that way when they socialize only with people who look or act like they do.

'When the only ones who like you are like you, it's hard not to congregate and develop group think.'

Wishing to see what else is out there, Brian and I reach out to the world. Even so, I project indifference! It's worked so far, but will it always work?

'Why not?'

This lover of mine isn't much of a lover, but he's mine. I have him, but don't want to imprison him. He's such a wonderful man! Just as nice and down-to-earth as everyone says he is, but no one else really believes it. Who believes anything in the papers? The power of the written word has been eaten away one page at a time.

How can I make an indelible impression on the public with my next book? It's impossible to dig into the serious aspects of life and make it interesting or witty enough to keep 'average people' reading. If you write about loving someone, most expect sex—and the more explicit and gratuitous it is—the better! If you write *passion* most think it means the same thing—maybe a bit hotter—perhaps immoral. If you skip the sex, readers assume nothing is going on between the sheets.

So what are you supposed to say when you want to tell someone you really care and want him to stay with you always? How can you evoke deep emotion *and* write about it?

'Open your mind and scribe what your Guides prescribe.'

I don't want to write about me now. I want to talk to my friends about Steve, but all they want is celebrity gossip—sound bites. Anymore I can't carry on a simple, honest conversation with people around here. Women I just met ask about his performance in bed or wherever. Ugh, so distasteful! But what to say? Why would anyone ask such personal questions—especially someone they just met?

'Lives are intertwined so you can figure out why they are here, too.'

Maybe, but too many people are crude and rude. Too few are interested in anyone but themselves. So why am I shocked when old friends are bent, too?

Back in Psych 101 the definition of mental illness was total involvement with self. That includes refusal to accept others into one's life and lack of interest or concern in what affects others. That pretty much describes our nation. We're all too much like that! The majority are self-involved and don't want to be bothered with others, some label it apathy caused by success, but I see it differently. No wonder enemies label us isolationists, yet in private say we're acting out individual self-centered agendas on a national stage.

Earlier this morning while sitting on the front porch, I spotted an envelope sticking in the door. It had to be from a neighbor since no one approaches the house now without an invitation. The note rankles because it wasn't signed. It said Brian was a nuisance and should be kept at home.

'What has Brian done?'

Nothing! I keep thinking about it and wondering who is offended by Brian's inability to walk and talk fast. He communicates easily now and takes care of his personal needs without help, but apparently some neighbor hates him or expects him to be perfect.

'*Compared to what?*'

If Brian was perfect, his parents most likely wouldn't have abandoned him. Could they love him as much as I do? I doubt it, but it's possible. If they loved others, they could not have given him away. But that is too prideful to write about—I can't judge others like that.

'*Why not?*'

I'm being judged now—and Brian is condemned, and I hate it! How can people be so mean? Why not instead condemn those determined to harm others?

When I see kids in wheelchairs and on crutches clutching each other, it always makes me tear up.

'*Why?*'

Their greetings are so sincere. You can see and feel their love for each other. It's like warm air rising from a stand of evergreens in Spring—all piney and squirrely and fresh.

Yesterday, while sitting in the park waiting for Brian to finish playtime school, I was watching some 'normal kids' playing around the swings when all of a sudden a bigger—but not older boy started pushing smaller boys around. It was nasty—a real fight scene. Mothers grabbed their kids, clucking like angry hens as they pushed them under their arms, ever mindful of the hawk in their midst. Smiling slightly, as if impressed with his prowess, the boy's mother apparently perceived him to be a leader rather than a bully. When one of the boys eventually turned as if to take him on she finally told her son to stop before he got hurt.

I was thinking, some kids are short and some tall, but tall kids usually stoop to talk to friends, while short guys usually don't stretch much. It's an analogy of life.

'If so, it is not a very good one.'

Anyway, it seems to me life is short and guides are tall—so when we stretch, maybe you could stoop a bit to get the message across to us.

'It makes more sense to stand tall and make others look up.'

Now I'm confused. What do we have to do to see into the future?

'Times to come are not revealed until they arrive.'

If I know anything about anything, this is the only time there is, because we can't remain in yesterday—and tomorrow never arrives. So today is tomorrow—and life here and now is and will be my life as it exists—unless I change. But why would I change what works great?

'Because people are weird! They change whenever things are exactly as they prayed and asked for them to be. When it is most difficult to see what is ahead, they stay put—afraid of getting sidetracked or hi-jacked by others' plans. But as soon as the road ahead becomes straight and smooth, they willingly take big risks.'

What if I stayed like I am today?

'You would age and Brian would age along with you. Think about what will happen to your world if you never produce new views of what you can do while here?'

Sometimes I get silly and laugh non-stop, because all this life is about me. I laugh or get mad at others, but it's really all about me! I don't cry if I can't relate to a story, and I don't sit and ponder the worth of lives unrelated to me. But if it comes close to me, I get giddy, sad, or introspective—sometimes all at the same time.

'Hysteria frequently visits those who are lonely.'

When Brian comes home for lunch, I'm going to ask him where he goes while playing. Maybe I can find out what goes on in his mind that way?

"You're home early, Brian. Where's Justin? Is he coming over for lunch?"

Brian's eyes become cloudy and gray when he tears up. He crunches them closed to stop tears from flowing. Suddenly I don't feel great. My son is unhappy and can't comprehend the nuances of his friendship.

"He not allowed to come over. His mother say he too tired, but she say to other lady she drink coffee with she is who's tired of me."

My heart leapt out of my chest and crashed to the floor. What could possess this supposed friend to deny her son and mine such fun? She may think she is hurting us, but she is hurting her son more. After all, Justin models her behavior—and chasing away friends can cripple him over time as much as it hurts Brain now. What a stupid thing to do! It's lame, but forgive and forget is the name of this game.

"It's okay Brian, I was going to call and ask you to come home—alone, because I got this urge to go to the movies and see 'Lion King' again. No one else but you likes to go with me to see old movies and eat greasy popcorn."

All woe was immediately forgotten. Brian glowed with smiles and laughter. Love erases hate, they say, but with Brian hate doesn't really register.

"Oh, Mommy, I'll go with you. I take you. I have money."

"Okay, you pay for the movie and I'll pay for lunch. We'll go to McDonald's and eat Happy Meals and go to the show. How does that sound?"

"Oh, Mommy, that's just what I wanted to do. Can I take Justin, too?"

Without waiting, Brian was out the door and on his way to invite Justin. His heart was overflowing with love and he needed to share it. What does he know of wickedness? Why would Cheryl act so nice to my face and then go behind my back and attack my poor, little defenseless boy?

'She is afraid of you!'

Why? How can the love of my life cause her such trouble?

'To attack the child of another is evil—in no way comparable to an animal protecting its young or its territory.'

I can understand when women attack because they think you're after their lovers, but to attack a child because you're jealous of someone else's lover is bizarre—or is it? Maybe Cheryl isn't happily married?

'Why think that?'

I don't know. Cheryl has everything the world advertises as necessary to be happy—a lovely house, a passionate husband, and a lovely son. She is healthy, but has been acting sort of weird. Maybe she misses working—but why?

When I left Corporate America, or whatever they call it now, I went into hiding. After a year I started writing articles and began what I now laughingly call my career. I love this work. It's fun, but it keeps me constantly running, trying to keep up the pace I set before Brian.

By contrast, Cheryl sits around reading romance novels and watching TV all day when she isn't on the phone. She now has a cleaning lady she calls a maid and doesn't do anything around the house. Doing nothing useful all day every day would drive me crazy, but it's her life. Some mothers are ignoring her because they see her actions on play days as inconsiderate—and now I'm inclined to agree.

'Look to her mother and dreams she promoted. Cheryl may be trying to live them. Remember, misery is usually self-induced and has to be nurtured to last.'

Not sure about her mother's imprint on Cheryl, but I think the media ignites some of her misguided, selfish fantasies. Wow! Just thought of a great story idea: "*The Dangers of Using Reel Women for Role Models Rather than Real Women with Cellulite Thighs.*"

'You do obsess about cellulite and thighs. Don't you?'

Doesn't everyone? Just kidding! When Brian gets back, I'll let him wear his new jacket and we'll take the big car.

Thinking about the scene we would create, I failed to hear the phone until the third ring. Who is calling on that line? Only a few know about it—maybe it's Steve? My pulse rose as I said hello, but my wishful thoughts crashed to earth.

"Oh, Cheryl. How nice of you to call...."

"Yes, Brian and I are going to McDonalds and the movies...."

"He's not allowed to ask? I don't understand what you...."

"You thought he just made it up? Oh, no, Brian is an innocent. He doesn't make up stories—not yet, anyway, but he might start copying playmates..."

"If he is annoying you..."

"He's not annoying you? You didn't happen to put a note on my front door..."

"Oh, no, I don't mind taking Justin to the movies with us. You go ahead and enjoy yourself at the spa. We'll be gone all afternoon."

Poor Justin! His mother would rather run around with her girlfriend than spend time with him. Once I asked who sent the note, it didn't take long for God to expose her. I now know for sure Cheryl wrote it!

'It seems weird to American human beings, but the closer you are to God, the faster your prayers are heard, answered, or whatever.'

It's ridiculous how fast I'm finding out stuff now. I'm not sure I can handle it. What with talking in my head, writing words I never thought, and a TV show every week, what is a girl to think?

While I was talking to Cheryl on the phone, I could hear what she was thinking as easily as what she said out loud— sort of stereo. It was really weird—and the phone amplified what I was feeling! She was intent on being nasty, but couldn't get through to me. I blocked all attempts to contaminate my day or my child, and ruin my work. She can sit and fume, worrying about me, but I'm through thinking about her. We won't be bothered by her much longer, but poor Justin. If he ever escapes, we'll welcome him. No time to dally—need to do a few things before the boys burst through the door.

Too late, they're here! Justin arrived wearing a shirt with a designer logo sewn over his heart and a twitch in his left eye. How can you not cry over this little guy? I felt sick, but with a happy face said, "Wow, Justin, you look cute today. You have such a nice smile—and what do you have in your hand? A dandelion! How beautiful! I'll put it in water, so we can all admire it."

"It's for you, Mommy, from both of us."

"Oh, thank you, Brian. You're both so thoughtful. I love dandelions! Yellow reminds me of the sun."

The boys didn't notice my tears threatening to erupt. Their eyes were riveted on the flower in Justin's fist. I put the dandelion in a small vase and we stopped the world to examine its beauty. That is the scene I framed and froze in my brain to remember this time and place.

As Justin stared at the flower, Brian said, "God makes dandelions for us, Justin." When he got no response, Brian spoke louder. "God makes dandelions just for us!" This time the toddler nodded his head as if a wise, old man.

Not wishing to break their concentration, I said, "Sit and stare at the dandelion, see if you can count how many petals it has. I have to change clothes."

Without looking up, Brian said, "Okay, but we already know."

That stopped me in mid-step. I had to know what he meant. "You do? How?"

"I just asked God."

So simple, but I had to know more. "What did you say?"

"I asked God, and he told me."

That certain look on Brian's face, and Justin's serious demeanor, convinced me they knew—but how?

"You just have to ask, Mommy. God knows everything."

Awestruck that he could read my mind and answer immediately, I managed to say, "You're right, Brian. When you become an adult, you forget to ask."

I regretted having to leave that magical moment behind, recognizing the privilege of being present in the company of such great souls. So sad that Justin's mother was tuned into TV rather than him. Too immature to realize the mysteries of life are being solved in front of her. Instead, she seeks others to tell her about life or watches TV gurus instead of living her own life and making up her own mind.

Am I ever lucky! If I hadn't met Brian at the Orphan's Ball, I would never have had this moment. Life is a series of happy accidents, but we usually don't know it until too late. What a break to be able to see what is happening as it comes through the door. Will this knowledge end all grief—or add more? No matter how sublime the moment, life rushes back in as you remember why you left the room.

Looking in the mirror I realize I need something warmer to wear. Who is that woman who makes my decisions? Where does she go when I meditate or rove the globe talking to people about their comparative needs and what I see to be possible solutions? This version of me arrives when I have time to indulge in pursuits of a physical nature, but isn't that weird?

So it is agreed, this woman will wear her cashmere sweater set—ready for whatever happens next.

'Why cashmere?'

Need to dress up, because this is the day we show up Cheryl—and gloat! If that sounds vindictive, I say, 'too bad.' I'm not happy with her attempts to hurt my child, so I choose cashmere as my armor. Cheryl is about to be taught a lesson, and if she's wise she will learn it the first time—or we'll do it again and again until she learns to never attack me or intentionally harm my little man!

Chapter Eleven

Running Requires Legs

I went out and about all day yesterday and found only a few things I was looking for, but what a grand and glorious time! So what if I didn't find a new pair of jeans for Brian? So what if his wardrobe is diminished because he lost his one pair of jeans? There are still nineteen pairs of pants left, but we have to replace the lost.

Buried in such mundane thoughts, I pulled out my journal and started scribbling notes as they popped up.

I got side-tracked trying to help Brian fit into the crowd, but he's finally in. What makes me dress Brian in fashionable clothes? Am I competing with other mothers?

'Why make children self-conscious?'

Hi Hirman! Just musing about things. I was sure Brian was well-suited for a new class, but they said he wasn't ready. I argued, but know the truth—they aren't ready for him, so I best wait.

When you realize your son isn't going to be a great athlete, scholar, or whatever, you can choose to feel disappointed. It's absurd, but anyone can turn a perfectly good kid into someone no one is happy to be around.

'Remember, you didn't create this child. God created Brian and God is not complaining—you are.'

Which leads us to the next dilemma…

'You have no choice but to ridicule your belief in God if you think you know who or what God is.'

In my opinion, trying to figure out why God exists—and other things theologians wrestle with, defeats God's plan by stymieing efforts to create a practical ethical system that works for all concerned.

'If theologians ever figure out who is a saint and who is not; and why Martin Luther did what he did; and why John Calvin is wrong or right, you and I will be long gone and on the way to glory. Where will they be then?'

I wonder about people who don't work. Did they get a special dispensation? How did they get a free pass?

'You say you want to know, but you do not.'

I was going to take Brian to the new school and give him a change of scenery from always being with me, but the new school is so drab and ugly inside I decided not to impeach him. I'm going to take some classes on home schooling and find out why they can't teach kids like Brian—unless the school admits they can and welcomes him.

'What time is the best time for humans to enter school?'

I went when I was almost six-and-a-half. Being older, I easily got ahead. According to scholars, if Brian is seven when he starts school, he should advance quickly to his potential by the end of his first year.

'So why do Americans go to school from age two and up?'

I don't know.

Parents want to be free of childcare or want their children to win in some undefined competition that may elevate family status— seldom because a child wants to learn more than the parents can teach at home.

Whenever I contemplated leaving Brian at child care centers in the past, I asked myself, 'If you can't take care of him every day, why did you adopt him?'

I heard something to the effect that ego is too involved in decisions about mating and interferes with raising kids, so I rethought each day's plan—until I found a way to not worry about strangers and other kids possibly hurting Brian's mind—or body.

I read a study that kids raised in daycare are more aggressive than kids trained at home. If you examine how aggressive our society has grown since it became the norm to farm out children to daycare, you might agree and come to the same conclusion.

It took time for me to adjust to having someone around all the time, but now it's hard to imagine being apart. Brian is ready to go to school, but they say he will be better off waiting another year. The real problem is it hurts my ego that he can't enter school as he is now—not his.

'When you get too involved with the child you were, adopt a new mindset and cross-examine yourself to determine if you are on an ego trip.'

I admit it! At first I was on an ego trip—liked the attention I got when I took Brian to the drugstore where we used to live. I relished their blunt questions—even their pity and scorn. Now I see such people as idiots or delights, and I don't bother converting or educating them. It isn't necessary for others to believe Brian will be a great star.

You can see I still have a faint yearning to be a missionary, but Lutherans back then forbade girls mission work—except as the wife of a missionary. I had been raised in the traditional German way, not as a Presbyterian—with a rich father, so mission programs were closed to me. Today I see that as a blessing.

Years ago some girls were so concerned about conditions in Africa they decided to make a strange suicidal attempt to change it. Can you imagine their ego? What would you do if placed in charge of a church in the Congo, watching employees file out and solemnly face children and elders praying in a strange, alien language? What are they really doing? Who told them they should do it? Why would God send a narrow-minded minister and his hapless wife and kids to transform a village of perfectly respectable, Godly people into a tribe of rebels? God did not send them!

You're now warned that my thoughts can be weird and totally aimless, so read my journal at your own risk!

I'm five feet two and one-half inches tall, but lately I feel very tall. I feel growth, but it can't be measured on the chart in Brian's room. I could ask, 'How did this happen?' But I already know.

God isn't a physical being and never lived as a human. God is more of a feeling or sensation. God is the wind is the best explanation I can come up with. Like I said, I can get radical and weird.

'Nevertheless, your mind is a very useful tool.'

Tools are to be used or abandoned, updated or thrown away— but lend them to others and you may never get them back.

'Ever think you do that with your mind?

No, but I bet I left my mind at the door when I talked to a neighbor and agreed to run the block party, because it sounded like a good idea at the time. It was her idea, but I let her take over and use me to finish a job she wanted done.

'*We all do it—all the time.*'

I guess this is payback for all the times others helped me by buying my books and working with me.

Until yesterday I was hidden from the neighbors by a high hedge and wall around the west side, plus a six-foot tall fence behind the house, exposed only to the worst of 'friendly' neighbors on the east. I've enjoyed my self-styled convent and un-conventional life, but today I'm Ms. Personality—personally-appointed diplomat of the co-op for our so-called block party.

Actually, this neighborhood is notoriously cold—often described as frigid, but I will prevail and evoke the spirit hidden from sight, but obviously alive—provided they're ready to party.

'*Normally, who would want to head up a block party?*'

No clue! I'm supposed to get everyone together to decide what to do, but I'm not. I'm going to write up a list and circulate it around the block to see who wants to do what. Anyone who dallies or isn't home will do what is left.

'*That is how God runs the universe, so it will work for Sunnyside.*'

How ironic! Sunnyside isn't displayed at the head of the road leading into our little development, but it sounds a lot better than Beecher's Woods. Only a man would describe this place as a woods—and then name it after himself. Tim Beecher is such a beast, but his wife and son are beauties.

Can you tell I'm not thrilled with the developer? That is because he didn't do a good job. He wanted to box in the community, so no one could see into another's yard.

Apparently I was the only one to spot this design flaw. When I pointed it out to other concerned parents, we opted to create a central spot where the kids can safely play. It isn't going over well with childless couples—even some parents, but we intend to confiscate the cul-de-sac at the end of the street for the block party and as the party ends propose it become community property. That could go off like a bomb, but if they're oiled with enough liquor, they may give up without a fight.

'Drunks do not fight about important issues.'

You have to plan your approach if you intend to encroach on a property and reduce the rights of others, even though the government's minions do it daily. The circus in the park bragged about how many pay-offs were made before it could take place. City Hall is the real circus!

City Park isn't a park anymore, more like a municipal dump. Every member of council's family is on the payroll or parole, and we let them sit around—even gamble or sleep, instead of working for us. No one cares as long as tax-paying adults can jog and bike on well-maintained paths near their homes. It irritates me that there isn't a place for the little ones to run, too. They are definitely not welcome on the bike paths! Why are runners and bikers given more consideration than everyone else?

'Are you alone in this? Does anyone else see a problem?'

Brian does. He wants to run! Watching boys running everywhere, he has decided running fast has to be the greatest achievement in the world.

'That doesn't sound like much of a problem.'

It is, because I hate it! Brian can't run alone, so I have to run with him. And when I run, I feel my shins tighten, my feet flatten, and my tail jiggle. I don't know how much punishment my lungs can take. I'd love having sleek thighs like women who run, but I don't want to work that hard.

We started out walking together and he would run down hills. I'd catch up to him, but within three weeks he outdistanced me, so I had to run when he ran. Now I'm trying to keep up with him period—that's how much he has improved.

There I go again, can't seem to stop bragging about Brian.

'It's the American way to raise kids!'

Pop-psychology books and daytime TV shows preach that kids need to be constantly praised and stroked from crib-to-grave or they won't love themselves and respect others. Certainly mothers must know that is nonsense! What does it take to correct a mistake?

The average working mother and father may not know how to raise children of affluence, having been raised by working class families. Many became individual success stories, as they see it, without benefit of parental discipline or love. They did it all themselves and like to shout: Look at me!

Mothers of my generation didn't work outside the home and didn't feel guilty about making kids do chores. Back then, mothers who drove their kids to soccer, dance, and music lessons were scoffed at behind their backs. The only exception was the one-in-a-million kid who was gifted and needed special lessons.

Women race around town now as if demonstrating how much they care for their children—but maybe it's to feel needed? Many stay-at-home parents say they can't do enough for their kids—not me.

'That is because Brian is adjusting better than if enrolled in public school.'

We go to the library every other day to see what is going on there, then shop. We add up expenses to practice everyday math; but before shopping for groceries, we usually visit the cellar of the village market to peek at old merchandise displayed in a kind of household museum. We talk about local history with the elders who collect there, to learn a little bit about modern civics—no need to make the boy sick.

After we take our stuff home, maybe eat lunch, depending on my schedule, we walk around the park and run a bit for our gym class. As it turns out, geography is simple. Brian runs into the woods and has to find his way home. We usually pretend he is visiting Asia or Africa or Canada during these jaunts. I quiz him about what animals he saw, what mountains he climbed, and what the natives looked like. He really likes that game.

'Artemis is the goddess of the hunt and forests. She rules the moon.'

Brian isn't like me. I was a tomboy and loved exploring for the sake of adventure, but Brian runs in the woods and announces, 'I'm home.' That's all. He feels the woods are his home. It makes me feel good to experience his contentment.

Strange, Artemis just popped into my mind. I wonder why?

'Many Americans talk a lot about the old ways. Why?'

The other day, while waiting for Brian at the library, I was joking about being a goddess and six or seven females of various descriptions started telling me how they are like this or that goddess. When I asked them who the goddesses were and what they did, they were uncertain and walked away. Maybe they imagine themselves to be mythological archetypes rather than face the fact they are women of today—women with important lives to live now?

I intended to take Brian and Justin for a walk, but with all this journaling the day got away from me. Now it's raining and Brian is home coloring in his cowboy book. He has such an eye for color!

Moan, groan, whoa, there it is again—the All-American boast. Sorry, Hirman!

'Would it matter if Brian couldn't hold a crayon and had no eye for color?'

No, but it's nice to see him create beauty. I enjoy watching him color and paint, but painting requires too much cleanup afterwards, and I'm too lazy today to do it. When he recognizes the power of color and can blend them, I'll teach him how to draw forms. For now, Brian's an all-star with crayon and paper.

He does a lot of marvelous improvisations in color—not space. He still can't figure out what to do with a lot of space. He either blocks out a big picture, filling only a tenth of the page, or he puts a teeny little figure in the corner, using even less space.

'No one seems to realize that when you understand spatial concepts, you have it made.'

I never figured it as a major accomplishment until I learned to parallel-park. My girlfriend had a lot of trouble with it, but I didn't. In fact, she still drives blocks so she can pull into a parking space rather than parallel park.

'It was the concept of space that caused the problem—still does.'

When young I didn't see many things like my school friends. I'm probably not like most women even now, but I get things done.

Hirman, when you and I are old and gray—not quite white, I want to sit down and evaluate everything I wrote in these journals—but not today. Today I want to write and keep on writing, letting words flow as my fingers fly across the paper. What comes up isn't exactly what I'm thinking—in fact it's about things that normally don't interest me enough to talk about it with others. If it's not me in this ego existence writing this, as well as most of my books, who is? Who is doing the thinking, if I'm not?

'If you allow anyone else to decide what you should do with your present being, your thoughts are not your own, but at times you must listen to others to know who is wise or practices things you need to know. It takes time to develop an ear for wisdom and an eye for beauty.'

When you and I were young, Hirman, we often sat in the sun and got tanned, but now the sun is so strong even I get burned. I want to do something about it, but to devote your life to a big idea no one will give you any credit for when it's resolved seems too great a price to pay.

You can take a fight only so far before men see a profit and go for the greed. They dump you and take over in order to rule without opposition from idealists. It happens in every revolution.

'Not this time.'

Yes, I can see women aren't as docile as in the past.

I was watching a TV show and the women got so angry they told off the emcee—forced her to call for backup—a man with many degrees. The audience made up almost entirely of women stared round-eyed! They totally capitulated as he repeated everything she had said—but not as well put. Why do women listen in awe to men with a couple of degrees and not women?

'How many women in America are well-educated?'

I know the answer to that. Before the 50's, few women went to college. Those who did believed they were elite—usually held themselves up to be better than other women, but still kowtowed to men. Some wealthy men encouraged a favored daughter to do whatever, even provided a good education, but too few to be more than an anomaly.

'How odd!'

You remember the 50's don't you? You and I were kids then.

'May I remind you that you never had time to meditate and study during your early days on Earth—once you left the home of your birth? I was not assigned to you until you changed your daily work.'

How interesting, but my hand itches to write....

During the 50s many middle-class American family men decided they could educate not only their sons, but their daughters as well—but only for a short time. It was intended that daughters sent to college were to meet men suitable to marry. Such girls said they were majoring in a MRS degree—and if they were pretty enough, they married the first year and dropped out.

'How bizarre! In communist countries women of the same age were tested and, based on their scores, educated and advanced to positions of prestige.'

I've met women who escaped the Iron Curtain and came here to work for better wages and living conditions. They said women in their countries were not granted the prestige and money men got for the same professions. That is why they revolted or bolted and came here—only to find it wasn't much better.

'Young women are foolish not to obey their own inner wisdom and pursue education for its own sake.'

Women have great opportunities today, but too many fail to know what they do best. They're lost in the system! Meanwhile their male counterparts capitalize on education and experience—using both to make a good living—then find women who suit their vision.

'You often say women admire women with brains.'

Forget it! Women don't want another woman telling them what to do. When women perform to gain attention or be noticed, they'll be attacked—not by men, but by women.

'*Why?*'

Minority paranoia! All minorities react that way—just fill in the blanks. Start with any group that sees itself as having little or no power and check it out.

The 'powerless' become angry when the powers that be recognize one of their own, especially if those in power bestow an honor on him or her. Such distinctions create jealousy among peers. It works to control women all over the world, but in America it's an art form.

'*I did wonder why you wanted to write about women. Now I see it is because you are a woman this time and need to know more before you ascend and leave Earth behind for others to develop or not.*'

I was a woman once or twice before, Hirman, but I've been a man far more often. I feel an infinite need to be by the sea and know it's because I sailed the oceans in times past. I just know it!

A few years ago an old crew of mine visited me while working intuitively with a client. We were experimenting with Distant Viewing when it happened. I was sitting on her porch when it suddenly started raining in the middle of an otherwise sunny day. Just as suddenly tears welled up and a fog descended over me. As if at a great distance I heard the voices of men screaming. They were on a sinking ship—I felt it!

I saw little during the storm, but knew what had happened. The crew came back that day to thank me for saving them when our whaler went down on a reef. I held the ship as steady as possible until all the long boats got safely away. I told them I would wait with the ship—so salvagers couldn't take over the cargo. I left them, but they never left me. They claimed to be guides of a type now, but not mine.

I don't know anything more about it. Hirman...

I have to read to Brian now. If he doesn't nap, he'll be fussy and not his usual sunny self. Although he needs a nap every day, he protests he is too old for them now, so I put him to sleep by reading my poetry to him.

Chapter Twelve

Interest Does Not Equal Work

*A*t the block party I realized everyone expected my 'Main Man' to escort me—probably why they chose me to take over the event. Instead, Brian escorted me and helped out a lot. He was a burden to no one, but still made some nervous.

Usually I write to underscore my commitments or what I think needs work, but sometimes the conversation going on in my mind can't be transcribed. I have to get ready for a seminar now, but my mind keeps running in circles or steering me to write about the party while it's still fresh. Which is it to be?

'Keep writing.'

I'll try. Brian did grow from the experience and enjoyed the group, but he never saw what was really going on.

'You have to stand apart to see the impact of energy.'

Among those present were a few easily described as conceited and totally disinterested in all others. They hung around whomever or whatever was the center of attention—contributing nothing! Hard to remember who they were. When you're the center of attention it's hard to partake of what is going on around you.

'Center is the perfect place for a loner.'

Whenever someone's energy exceeded their space, others felt pressure, but it faded quickly—so no one left early. Ever feel a balloon deflate rather than burst? If so, you know what I mean about the party. It held together, but never got off the ground. Whenever we got something going, it fizzled out. The festive mood disappeared too quickly to have a really great time and lasting memories.

At the party-before-the-party, we laughed at everything— eager to hear the details about anything and anyone. Wit wasn't required. When stupid and inane things popped up, we laughed every time!

We were eager to party because everyone got enough attention and fun working together. At the actual party everyone worked too hard at being witty, urbane, sophisticated—trying to fit in with whatever they thought others expected. As it turned out, we all got enough neighborly camaraderie to last a year. Would our relationships improve if we saw each other more than once a year?

The night before the party neighbors filled my kitchen and wouldn't go home, but I haven't seen anyone since the party. I wasn't very hospitable to two who didn't work, but they were too self-involved to notice.

'You are in a bad mood. Aren't you?'

Hosting parties leaves me exhausted—what made this one worse was having no one to talk to later about what we did or didn't do well. That is why I let go of such thoughts and fears by journaling. I won't lose friends or make enemies this way. Anyway, I have a seminar today and can't give way to fatigue or discussing social issues relative to urban living. I'm on a short leash today. I've got to get going on my speech!

"Working together works or doesn't—It fails when two or more avoid labor."

Interesting premise, but it puts me out front talking about something I didn't intend to mention. Why am I so upset when people don't do their share—or act irresponsibly in front of children? Why do I dislike the actions of so many neighbors? I want to build bridges and create harmony, but instead sense so much discontentment and dishonesty that I want to scream and not talk to those who have paid to listen to whatever I have to say. Help me!

"I had my share of Yuppies playing at work when I was part of 'corporate America' and I've avoided them ever since." Until the party, that is. The aura of such fragile personalities continues to linger in the air. How can I help anyone stuck within such dense egoism?

"It's too recent to regain my usual demeanor! I orchestrated a great party with the help of people I barely know. As usual, the majority pitched in and did whatever was necessary—laughing and creating a kind of family circus that bodes well for future events. However, in any garden there is always a snake and its mate."

Right? I think this approach makes me a bit crazy. I don't like mixing metaphors about personal experiences with psychology, philosophy, and spiritual work done by others. Help me pick up the best channel available now!

"Snakes slithered among the flowers—hissing and sneering—disapproving everything. They whispered to each other and giggled on cue when asked to pitch in and help. Sipping wine, eating treats set out for workers—contributing nothing, not even words of praise or thanks."

Earlier my speech sounded okay, but grew weird as I delivered it, until a smiling woman seated front and center nodded and said, "Same old women, same old ways of discrediting those who do all the work."

As she spoke a shock ran down my right arm. I felt a pin prick in my left index finger. At last I was channeling—and it was registering in my memory and their minds!

God alone was within me. I was used as never before. Some of what I said came from my journal, but most of it was new to me, too.

My voice rang out across the hall. At times it was as if urging women to take up arms—but it wasn't me talking!

"You have few friends, if you think they only care about your home. Most people think a neat, tidy house indicates an organized, great worker, but it doesn't. It's easy to get confused by outward, orderly appearance, as well as stylish ways of controlling people and space...Fung shui isn't about space. It's about faith within the human race...Everything seemingly under control does not signify people are working to clear the Earth of debris or improve the world—or enjoying peace while here. In fact, it may only mean they can afford to employ others to keep their external world looking pretty and neat...."

Previously *My Guides* helped me work on the premise of work, but I was still surprised when I almost shouted: "You may think of work as labor, and labor as something done to improve appearance or whatever, but before you can do either correctly, it's necessary to differentiate between them."

At that moment I realized this seminar had been pre-arranged by Spirit. These people were not students waiting for me to explain how I write. I was the student! Everyone present was my teacher or tutor, helping me understand why I resided in this far-away stretch of mind so much of the time.

Hearing myself talk, I watched as I addressed the women seated nearest the stage. "I wasn't going to talk about this, but too many seem to think I live a sheltered life hidden away deep within suburbia and don't get around much anymore—which is true, but false."

This switch to a folksy, chatty conversational tone was something I had never done before—and it felt weird!

"Today, at this point in my life, I'm tired of my suburban woman image. However, hope springs eternal—and tomorrow I'll rise and have fewer opinions about my status than I have now. Right now you're here to discover why I write and how I write—both very easy to explain, in my opinion."

I tried to smile, but could not.

"My life, and yours, is all about living alone and living with others. You can't write fairy tales unless you live within your dreams most of the time, and I don't! I'm pragmatic and don't indulge my imagination much, so my prose is sometimes blunt, but always concise. You have to be who you are, and know why you're important—even though you're not. I can see many wondering about that last remark. It's as true as anything you've accepted so far."

Pausing to pour a drink, I let my words sink in. Fully conscious that this is not how I normally address an audience, I felt repercussions from some as they wondered if they should demand their money back or not.

"To become a better writer, you need to sit and talk to your neighbor right now—have a few laughs. And when you're done, we'll reconvene to discuss the merits of writing about people in your present life, knowing they will leave once you write about them."

Everyone was surprised by my announcement—even me, but it was perfect timing. All who were lost or oblivious to why they were here or what they expected to hear had an opportunity to catch their breath and ask others what to think. Some asked others to condense the material covered—and a few repeated and restated it beautifully, while the rest sat and claimed to be meditating.

What makes me think that? Perhaps I'm being too harsh? Anyway, the seminar so far created a lot of spin!

Things really took off when I asked everyone to take out their notebooks and quickly write whatever they were thinking right then. It quickly aborted individual exit strategies, causing many to center on what was taught. To conclude my presentation, I said, "Work on getting your social calendars filled. I'll be here, but you'll be somewhere else." When everyone realized they were free to socialize and go to lunch, the group quickly dissipated, leaving behind only snippets of their small talk.

As Jeanne headed toward the coffee shop next door to the old theater where she was conducting the seminar, an extremely thin woman waved a newspaper at her, hoping to catch her attention. Unnoticed, Jeanne quickly chose a booth and sat down. The woman quickly followed and sat down beside her. As though invited, she immediately launched into a tirade.

It was a one-way conversation until Jeanne smiled and said, "What a day to do nothing!"

Speaking through up-turned lips, the woman strived to sound sincere, but her cold eyes stayed unfriendly. "Oh, Jeanne, you do too much. You over-produce! Everyone admires your style of writing, but some of it is a bit much. Don't you think? Like, you talk about men in such militant terms—then praise them and say it's our fault they act the way they do toward us."

Smiling at the distraught woman, Jeanne said, "Look who sounds militant. You! You're the one rolling onto my side of the bed complaining I'm crowding you. These are your ideas—not mine. We all have to do what we have to do, and it starts by believing in our own ideas. I'm not trying to be everywoman's sage."

"Oh, Jeanne, you laugh, but this isn't funny. I mean it! I get so upset with obnoxious men, but I take it. I don't even— please stop smiling!"

Trying to ignore the other woman as she ordered lunch, Jeanne sipped sweet iced tea. After taking several deep breaths, letting each one out softly, Jeanne said, "Trained to be good— much like dogs are trained to obey—how can you disobey when your lord and master speaks?"

Too loudly, the woman said, "Now that's unfair! Just because you got away from here, you think you can tell me I can't be true to myself, too."

As the intruder raved, Jeanne shook out her long, loose mane as if about to gallop off into the sunset. As she ran her fingers through curls, as if combing out snarls, Jeanne envisioned Medusa, but let it fade. Seemingly without emotion, she coiled and struck out at the pest. "I never said that, Sandy. You do what you do, and you see yourself as no one else can. I left this place in order to see it more clearly—especially how this environment impacted my thinking. You stayed and learned to live through it. We don't see the same things the same way now, if we ever did."

Much too loud to be friendly, Sandy said, "Now you're trying to make me feel better, but it doesn't work anymore."

No longer willing to sit back and humor a woman who appeared to be tired of being whoever she pretended to be, Jeanne said, "That's too bad, Sandy. I wasn't trying to make you feel better—you are. I don't care enough to try to make you feel better about whoever you are. It happens or it doesn't, but has nothing to do with me. It's too tiring to bribe people to like me or you—so I don't."

Raising her hand languidly to cover her mouth, Sandy yawned. When Jeanne remained silent, she said, "You're too deep for me, Jeanne Beck. I don't get it—and I don't get you!"

With a sweeping gesture, Jeanne began clearing the table. "Keep saying this mantra to make it happen: 'I'm not shallow!' As for me, I've got to go! I have much to do."

Making no move to leave, Sandy said: "You look so pretty, Jeanne, and I love your earrings."

Fortunately, she could not read the thoughts running through Jeanne's mind along the lines of: 'I dare speak of dense clouds gathering above us—and she likes my earrings!'

The program resumed where Jeanne had initially expected to begin the seminar. "This is just a sample of what will happen tomorrow, but you have the power to stop listening to what you don't approve, or want to do, or have already done. Never again can you say you have no power! That belief system is no longer acceptable here or believed anywhere else in our world. "

Pausing for emphasis, Jeanne then said: "When you write, you won't always get published. In fact, you seldom get published by others nowadays, but it helps everyone understand what is going on in your universe. How? Whatever we write enters the universal stream of consciousness—eternally flowing upward and outward. If we want something, but can't talk about it for whatever reason, we can write about it! As we write and think, it brings change—in a weird and wonderful way only God may see…Oh, yes, whenever I use the word *God*, some women claim to be offended. They believe the word *God* represents male-dominant societies that have imprisoned women far too long, thus turning men into gods. As for me, I use the three-letter word 'God' to represent *all that is*—and because it saves time and is easy to spell."

Pausing just long enough to see if others agreed, Jeanne dropped a bomb. More often than not, some didn't appear to get it. At such times her mind unwound and let her talk without thought—open to receiving teachings available to all seeking such wisdom. Since the afternoon went well, Jeanne was unaware of what happened—until the final day.

Following her usual protocol, Jeanne did whatever felt right. Everyone laughed a lot and many women and some men who had not shown up the first day were attending regularly by the final workshop. Glowing with peace and happiness, Jeanne announced, "I want this conference to end on a very up-beat, positive note, so I'm not going to drink of the fountain of wisdom too long."

Men laughed loudly, but no women smiled, so Jeanne added, "I want everyone to have fun and enjoy life, so I'm not going to bore you with details about living in a world we hate—yet refuse to change. I won't do anything weird or infamous either, because I intend to write what I think later. But keep in mind that writing weird and infamous things tells the world you're starved for attention and don't want to work to earn respect…."

As the audience accepted her message, Jeanne ventured to share more about her life. "I have six or seven books at home that may be published one day and put before you to judge, but probably not. They're filled with the wisdom of beings not present. They're not in this world, but they still exist. You, too, must acknowledge Spirit within your work—or it won't demonstrate what you believe and wish to achieve." Jeanne saw puzzlement in most faces, thus surprised when a few nodded as if they knew what she meant.

"If you ever stand where I am now, share with writers the fear of the unknown, but also share the joy. The mere pleasure of writing is nothing compared to residing in the same universe as another who is wiser, or prettier, or more exceptional than you. However, *you* have to move into *their* world. Such beings don't enter ours! That is why we're talking about meditation— not writing, per se. If this change of agenda upsets you, you can leave or go to sleep, meanwhile everyone else will meditate with me."

No one left the room! In fact, an air of expectation descended over the crowd, as when a great event is about to take place. All eyes were on center stage so as not to miss a thing. Closing her eyes and smiling, Jeanne spoke slowly and softly.

"There is a message for everyone in this meditation…Some minds will close, while most of us will relax deeply enough to clear our minds of all thoughts and slip into a state of non-being we call meditation…The ever-vigilant mind seeks stimulation, remaining ever alert, in order to spot possible threats, but you are safe. You don't have to worry about anything. I'll let you know if you have to leave…Sit back and relax and don't worry about a thing.…"

Perhaps a minute passed before Jeanne said, "I'm going to give your mind something to do—so your spirit can rise and enter infinity for a time. I'm going to read a list of words designed to help your mind collapse into time: Wilted lettuce…Dead, dried flowers in a vase…Foreign words on a page…Glue on an envelope…Sticky buns in a pan…Nothing.…"

The room seemed to expand and become a sacred space in a strange and wondrous way. Speaking in hushed tones, Jeanne said, "Do you feel anything?"

When no one responded, she murmured, "Good."

Some time passed before Jeanne prompted them again. "Relax and breathe more deeply—quietly. I have nothing thrilling or weird to say. Feel yourself gliding across the surface of a frozen lake…Relax…Now let's fly to the top of the mountain…You're writing a best-seller now. It's a novel, but it's all true. No one, but us, knows it's all about you…Place your attention on the page in front of you…Write!"

After five minutes or so, Jeanne said, "Stop writing and let your mind fly away…Elongate your spine—stretch your body from the inside out. Sit so tall your head reaches the clouds— stretch higher and higher…That is all you need do…Now sit and stare at your mind—as if it belongs to someone else.…Your mind isn't deep within your head. Its right behind your eyes… Stare into your mind and let the light of God, and all that is, enter you and erase all that bothers you about you or others… No need to work clearing your mind…All the debris and trash is being erased…You can breeze through life, collecting only what you need or wish to keep."

After several minutes of silence, Jeanne intoned: "House, garden, garage, flute, cello, fireplace, oboe, clarinet, the rest of your life."

As if in deep trance she whispered into the microphone: "Now you're inside your inner mind...Don't worry...You're alone...No one can see what you do there... Only *You* lives there—the real you! You want to be perfect...Use what you know, let others use their minds, too...Let everything and everyone flow and grow..."

Pausing to clear her throat, Jeanne said, "The band has arrived and is playing your song...You are writing music, but think it is poetry...Use every instrument, even though you excel at only one... Prose comes from the mind...Poetry comes from the heart. Fiction is prose not true to you. Go more deeply within now...Select the instrument you play best...Begin playing...Can you hear a flute? Deliver a message to the flutist: 'Think love. See beauty in everything. Do your best.' The magic flute is all you hear. Tell those playing your song to do their best...Speak to them one-by-one...Direct everyone to reach higher than ever before. Your music grows louder. Everyone is jamming. "

Jeanne began to sway gently and smile as if listening to a heavenly choir. "Now your sounds become blissful music rising far beyond our present lives...Those above interpret our music and help us produce harmony in our world...Let the muse of poetry, prose, and music enter your thoughts...It's no longer necessary to sit and stare at blank pages...Let sensations flow... Write what comes through the veil to you now."

Pausing, Jeanne adjusted the overhead lights, then said, "Open your eyes and write...You don't have to do anything, but some are writing rapidly...Go for the gold! Ignore the critic residing within your mind. Write what comes through the veil. Tell your mind to let everything flow...Don't stop to edit your writing. Your mind will take over later and delete what it doesn't like, but not now. Now is the time to let the flowers in your garden of verse bloom and grow forever."

After the seminar ended, Jeanne felt as though she was awakening from a deep trance. Her voice wavered as she spoke to Sandy now sitting quietly beside her on the stage. "After a session like today, I feel drained of creative joy, but the juices are still flowing. Everyone worked, but all I did was talk. I hate that!"

Bubbling over with heart-felt emotion, Sandy said, "Oh, Jeanne, you were wonderful. Everyone is thrilled!"

"Maybe yes, maybe no—some enjoy everything, and some were relaxed enough to write easily, but only one—if that, *wrote in Spirit*. I talked too much! In order to listen, they didn't work as hard."

"But you always say listening is hard work."

"Touché, right you are, Sandy. I tend to forget lessons others deliver through me. I have to remind myself that my classes are primarily meant for me...Let's go get a bite to eat. Maybe we can catch up on how you and your friend live in the same house, yet never do housework. I have to find out how you do that! This next year is going to be extremely busy—and I don't have a maid."

"Oh, that! Cleaning's not hard. It's easy, not like your work!"

Mimicking Sandy, Jeanne said, "'Oh, *that!! It's easy!'* Everything I do looks hard to you, but you think what you do isn't hard for others to do as well as you do it. When will you ever learn that everyone's life is as difficult, nerve-wracking, happy, and successful as yours?"

"Yours isn't! I never travel anywhere. I never go out once I go home—and I have only two really good friends."

"Only two *really* good friends? Is that living? You better believe it! Why would you think there should be more to life here?"

Looking forlorn and sad, Sandy said, "Your life is full of travel and adventure—and now a leading man who really is a leading man. Meanwhile, I sit at home reading and trying to write every other day or so. Really, I don't get to do anything!"

Struggling not to be annoyed, Jeanne said, "You should be ashamed of your mind, Sandy. You really should. That mind of yours is denigrating all you are and all you do—probably thinks it's being humble, but it's why you don't believe *your* work is equally worthwhile."

"I guess you're right, but I still envy you, Jeanne."

"Now that sounds more like the old you. Just be honest! It's easier to live in peace and find happiness when you are."

"I can't. We were honest as kids, but learned to lie, because the truth hurts people and causes trouble. I want to be loved more than anything else, but men hate women who talk about their problems or discuss serious issues. All men want to talk about is football, sports—and naked women. They aren't interested in spirituality or women who are beautiful on the inside."

Shrugging, Jeanne said, "It's your world, Sandy. You decide who is in it and who isn't. It's always your life and your dream. Normally I wouldn't mention this, but when we were kids you were never that honest. You faked it a lot. I remember teasing you, yet you never cried or said I was mean—until much later."

"That's because I liked it! Teasing and nicknames make me feel important. It means you like me better than others. When they saw you could tease me and I could take it, they thought I was like you. Now, no one teases me—because I'll cry. Anymore I'm extremely emotional. If someone interrupts me when I'm trying to make a point, I might even scream."

Under the scrutiny of departing attendees, Jeanne steered her old school chum to the coffee shop and an empty booth. Once seated, she said, "Sit and let it out—all of it. I don't have to be anywhere else for a while, and no one knows who we are."

Surprisingly, Sandy never noticed diners leaning toward them trying to catch their conversation. If she had, perhaps she would not have blurted, "Oh, Jeanne, I hate my life!"

Patting her hand, Jeanne lowered her voice and said, "Why? It looks good from here."

Sandy snapped back, "You have to know Jim and I aren't happy! We never talk when we're alone, and we aren't home together often—on purpose. Once a week we go over the big chores and finish them quickly. The house is clean because we don't do anything to dirty it, and we hardly ever sleep together anymore. When we're both home on workdays, we go to bed and put on reading lights so the other knows we're not mad—just not interested in sex. We never have sex! We sort of cuddle sometimes, ugh, but not very often."

"What's so bad about cuddling? I sleep alone, because I don't have a husband—and it gets cold, so cuddling sounds good to me." She spoke without conviction, but hoped it would discourage Sandy from revealing more intimate details.

Sandy whimpered, "It's a cold cuddle."

Feeling her heart melt, memories of recent events dimmed and Jeanne said, "A cold cuddle? That sounds serious. Tell me what's going on?"

"I think Jim has someone at the office he's more interested in than me, but he denies it. He cuts me off when I try to talk about it—usually turns on some game. If I try to get close or hug him, he automatically backs away. He doesn't listen anymore. He says I talk all the time, but I don't. He never talks—just sits and stares at the TV and acts like he's listening, but he isn't. I can tell."

"You're describing half the men in America—if comments on my blog are any indication."

Sandy shook her head, tossing her hair from one side to the other before saying, "No, Jim was different! He wasn't a jerk when we met. He was a really nice guy—sincere and jovial—even talked a little about serious things, but not anymore. Now he stares at porn sites and comments on how good other women look, but never talks about me or US."

"I see." Jeanne did not see, so she resorted to therapy babble in order to buy more time. "The way you see it, he doesn't see the real you anymore."

"I guess, but I'd settle for just talking about something other than the weather or the Braves or whatever team is visiting. I get so tired of sports, but he runs his life around them."

Easing a menu into Sandy's hands, so they might eat while taking up space, Jeanne said, "Why not? He doesn't have anything to do, so he hides behind the news and says he's busy. Perhaps he's tired of keeping up appearances and just wants to be by himself. I want you to try this: Sit down beside Jim and start reading a funny book, and whenever it's funny, laugh. Really let it out! If you can read a funny book and keep laughing, and he doesn't say anything, leave him!"

Sandy stammered, "What? Leave him! I can't do that. Where would I go? How would I live on what I make?"

"You're not going anywhere with him, so leave."

"I can't do that!"

"Why?"

Tears trickled down her cheeks as Sandy said, "You're hard, Jeanne. I'm not. You can walk away from men, but I'm sensitive. I have this thing about being alone. I need to be loved—you don't!"

Her voice rose as she stabbed a bloody red fingernail into Jeanne's arm and said, "You don't care if your man is fondling some woman three thousand miles away, but I'd die if Jim did that to me. I'd simply die!"

Stunned, Jeanne stared at her, trying to ignore the coughing and snickers from nearby tables. Now she had tears in her eyes, but was not about to make a bigger scene. Removing the too-long, false fingernail from her arm, Jeanne said just loud enough for Sandy to hear, "You really are a snake! You've made an art of hurting anyone who gets near you or befriends you, but you're not getting away with it this time."

Pausing to take a deep breath, Jeanne saw what was going on and what she had to do. "I'm not who you're mad at, Sandy. Save it for Jim! I won't let you dump on me now—or ever again."

Before she could say more, Sandy said, "I wasn't dumping on you. You asked me to tell you what was wrong, and I told you, but you don't understand or won't understand. It's not simple. It's complicated—and terrible, and I can't leave."

"Now you're telling the truth. YOU can't leave! You hate *his* behavior, but *you* can't leave. You don't like *his* actions, but *you* can't leave. You want attention and love, but *you* can't leave and risk not finding it again. You want him to notice you, so you don't have to leave. You're caught in your own trap—and his web of intrigue. Being discreet, Jim wants you where he can find you—when and if he ever wants you. Spiders don't always eat their prey right away."

"Now that's an awful thing to say! Jim isn't a spider."

It was obvious Sandy could not figure out where the next attack might come from or how to end it, so Jeanne said, "You bet your sweet bootie Jim isn't a spider. *Spider* is a revered totem, and Jim isn't even close to being wise or creative, but he is eating you alive."

"I don't believe you. I want to stop talking about him. I want to change the subject or go home."

Something drew Jeanne more deeply into the web. She could only watch as she said, "You can't go home, Sandy. You don't have one."

"Yes, I do. It might not be as grand as yours, but it's my home!"

"Now you're raving—and mad! We're not going to finish and have time for cheesecake."

"Oh, Jeanne, stop it. I have to laugh when you start all that superior attitude stuff, like this is the best time in your whole life. But it works—every time! I get so upset, meanwhile you stay super cool. I cry and you laugh. It's a wonder we're friends."

You're right about that, thought Jeanne.

Chapter Thirteen

Things Change, Time Remains

There is nothing wrong, but sometimes I feel lost and out of control. I want to be here, there, and everywhere—all because I'm in love. I was just fine before Steve came into my life, but now my life is in a constant state of chaos—because of Him! Maybe if I write it all out, it will improve somehow?

I get up in the morning and wait to see if there is going to be an early morning visit. When the phone isn't hooked up or I'm out, I wonder if he called, but didn't leave a message. Then I think maybe he doesn't want to call me anymore, and so on and on and on, ad nauseam. I get so silly at times. I wonder who I am and what I'm all about. I could scream at me—and will scream now.

'Feel any better? We do not. Please do not disrupt the universe with your mental equations based on sensations that make no sense to us.'

To anyone who tuned in when I screamed just now, Sorry. Like I was saying to my Guides, I'm going crazy and it's all over this guy.

'Why?'

Men surely aren't as stupid as we make them out to be, but some men really do need a brush-up course in thoughtfulness. I find that when a man is over a woman—doesn't want to see her anymore—he doesn't call her. He just stops calling. Finito! He doesn't say why or what happened or give a reason. He just stops calling or seeing you!

'That is dishonest, but it seems to be common in America.'

When He didn't call last week, I was so sure it was the end that I took down his picture and put it in the attic. I put it under a stack of pictures of all the men in my old life. It isn't exactly a stack, but there are a few pictures of old beaus there.

When I was young we went out more and did more than we do now, and I always took pictures. Now I keep only one picture—as a reminder. I think everyone goes through a phase of documenting everything you do together, but thankfully it doesn't last and you begin living instead of trying to 'capture the moment' in order to dream about it later.

When you have a main man who isn't the only man in your life, you can afford to be generous and give him a long leash and not be bothered if he doesn't call or see you every day or so. But if he is the only one (and with me that is the only way I operate), you don't have much patience to spare. You have to cut the line and hook another right away or forget men altogether.

'Cut the line and hook another right away—or forget men?'

You don't like how I describe this thing women have about love? It's obvious I'm not a romantic, but surely that doesn't come as a shock to you all? I hate being in love, but I expect it to happen every time I'm attracted to a man. What do you guys have to say to that?

'We are here to observe and learn how to manipulate your world, yet remain detached enough to help you live as you wish. That is why we live in this world rather than in a better one. We adopt this world's way of looking at love and life. It is absurd to be different, if we intend to learn why your world is the way it is, in order to help it or change you in some positive way.'

Hmmm, sounds like you all are missionaries of a kind...

When I was sure He wasn't going to call, I went out all day to make sure he couldn't reach me in case he did call. I was sure he wouldn't, so I took evasive action. As it turned out, he left three messages while I was out—sounded frantic, maybe a little jealous, because I wasn't where I was supposed to be—at home alone.

'Perhaps men are territorial by nature, but this business of women waiting to get the usual reports of a man's goings and comings is very strange.'

I have to go out and think this through. Do you all want to go with me?

I have to run around—or go crazy. Hmmm, no answer.

I'm going to let my thoughts fly then. Maybe I'll find the common denominator and figure out what is happening so I can leave the house on business and not be caught up worrying about Him.

Jeanne's voice rang out over the parking lot at the mall. "If you love someone, do you wait for his call or go out?"

No one took notice. She could have been talking to aliens or dogs for all anyone cared. Everyone else's energies were centered on a big sale at Macy's. At least that is where most were headed as they prayed for help and guidance. Jeanne's prayer was heard, too, but not answered immediately.

Eventually Jeanne's inner voice spoke—quite loudly. 'We should think more about this.'

Why? How would more thinking help? If you and I are in the same frame of mind—which we are, it doesn't matter when you think about it or how you do it and where you are. You can work with me here on Earth now or later—right?

'We are as one and will work on it together now. Do you dig it?'

"Dig it?" Sounds like someone has been spending too much time on Earth...

"Well, here we are, representing the universe as it is today. We love this human being who wishes to make her way to the altar and give her life to another. She does not understand this is what all priestesses do. They must honor their whole existence and sacrifice it to a god before moving on to the next step.'

Are you saying we are all priests or priestesses in one way or another, but may not see it that way now?

'Yes!'

But what about the 'real' priests, nuns, or whatever?

'We judge them harshly if they falter or fall, because they are professionals.'

Hmmm! Yes, they are paid to meditate, pray, and help others every day. I never thought much about it before.

'The clan from which they spring sees to it they are supported in their individual needs.'

If poverty is their vow, their clan raises the money or whatever so some can live without earning a living—so who is poor and who is rich?

'*Your world views romantic attachment as the preamble to marriage. If you are different, you are viewed as not much use to the world.*'

Except as a bad joke or a lesson on what happens to 'bad girls'.

'*If you try to change it, you will not end up in the front lines of society as a leader—even today.*'

I know. You're pushed back, never held up as a model to others—especially children.

'*That is wise.*'

But if you don't do it and someone else does, they change the way everyone looks at such romances, and the child in you is thrilled that someone dared buck society and got away with it.

'*But they do not get away with it.*'

Hmmm…Women in the theater are still valued primarily for their beauty, but a paid mistress isn't valued much by most men today. While women who are successful and can do whatever they want are more accepted by other women now

'*Too many men want to stone women who live happily without them.*'

Why? Hmmm, I see it more easily now. Men are afraid of such women, thus hate them, because they succeed in life without being a wife.

'*That is a very grievous sin against the world and yet to pass away.*'

Hmmm, you do realize I was raised in a paternalistic home by a matriarch of the highest order? Almost daily she insisted we honor father for his work. According to her, he supplied us with all our earthly needs. She maintained he had to drudge and slave so we could live free as the birds.

'*That was partially true, but he also loved his work and his assumed responsibilities for all of you.*'

He was a faithful and honest man—never asked for much, thus we denied he controlled us in a majestic way. For example, when he fell asleep before dinner, he would erupt from behind his newspaper fortress roaring, 'What's going on?' We would spring to our feet in terror and do whatever we thought he wanted. He was king of the house without doing much when there. Like the alpha male lion, he held the world at bay and protected us from it, so we could play and do whatever we wanted during the day. For that security, we reciprocated by working very, very hard to keep him well fed and his lair neat and clean, filled with happy, well-behaved children.

'You are making headway with your studies.'

Hmmm, when I marry I want a king, but not one who fights or philanders. I'm a queen now, but only Brian is subject to my tirades and charades. He doesn't notice my regal ways or escort me to balls, but he tries. I love playing princess to his prince, but being a princess is a drag—you have no time to be yourself.

'All your fairy tales extol the virtues of being a princess—not a queen.'

You can be a princess if you like, but for me being queen is as good as it gets. No other role is superior—not even being a mother.

'That sounds revolting, but we assume you are not going to leave this man because you are happy as is.'

"Revolting!?" Since Jeanne said this within earshot of the store manager, she was besieged by clerks who wished to please her. An interesting lesson on how to get better service, but it ended her reverie as she walked through the shops buying nothing. She had many errands which had to be completed, so she decided to wait until evening to continue this conversation with her guides and others who often appeared when she walked alone.

After putting Brian to bed, Jeanne opened her computer to a clean page, hoping to write in her journal whatever came to her. She often did this when she had no plans to go out or work with a client, but now she felt sad as her fingers hovered over the keys as if they, too, anticipated something unpleasant about to appear, something that would change her life as it existed now. Slowly at first and then more rapidly her mind expanded as words appeared on the screen in an archaic font asking her to define what she would like to write about. She had nothing to say, but her fingers tapped away anyway.

I was not ready to grow up, but it happened anyway. I went to high school one day as usual and my dad fell asleep as usual, but when I came home he was dead. He hadn't done a thing to make it happen. He just slept away his life that day in front of everyone. It was a wonderful way to go for him, but it left me in terror. I had no one left to tell me why I was me and what I should do. I was forced to be a woman. I was on my own.

My mother is gone now. My father is gone. My family is no longer a family. We have become a tribe of nomads living all over the United States, two live in Mexico. Siblings and their mates come and go, usually taking their possessions with them with perhaps one or two exceptions. When they do visit, they never intend to stay, just observe and add up what is going on 'at home' then try to manipulate me into doing whatever they want or feel is the 'proper thing to do' before disappearing into the sunset without leaving a dollar to cover changes they say need to be made to the homestead they expect to inherit one day.

I could smoke, drink, carry on with men, like other women, but my parents lived in that house and I was their child, so I could not. Everyone said I took after them, but it was just another way of denying I took care of my parents and still look after their interests long after they're gone.

I never thought about it then, but I am more loyal to my parents than any man has ever been true to me—but I digress.

When Jeff came into my life, I figured we would end up together one day. We would marry and have kids and later be grandparents, but he ruined that dream. He needed to own me. He wanted to buy a wife and mother who would stay home, do the cooking and cleaning, while he ran around. That was not for me, so I left him mad!

When I met Jack, he was just the opposite, but eventually reverted to the same old thing. Such men want to be free, while you are tied to a post. I want to be free of all the things in life that tie me in knots, especially the big noose hanging over us symbolizing the need to have a man around all the time.

'We started writing this way so you could become free of the earthly ties that bind, but instead it seems your spirit is freer than your mind.'

What if I announce to the world I need a raise? Would the world give me a best seller—just to keep me happy? I don't think so, but I never asked. I'll ask and see if it works!

'When you labor, do you ask for more money when you do a good job?'

I never think of money when I'm doing a good job. If you want more than you made in the past, you need to think it out and negotiate *before* you start a new project.

'If a good job isn't honored, and you are not paid properly, who gets that money?'

The wastrels, non-doers, non-believers, or whatever you call those who don't work and take credit for what others do.

'Managers!'

Ah, yes, managers! I existed about ten months in corporate America back in the '80s. About then I began to retreat into a world of my own. I decided to clean up the place, because our business was infested with rats and all sorts of pests gnawing away at company profits, as well as the gross national product. It was so revolting I had to rebel—and eventually left it all behind when I had done as much as could be done without the full cooperation of the executive staff.

Once I understood my position and what was expected, as opposed to what I could do and already knew, I eased off and did only what higher management wanted, which was the wrong thing to do. I ended up hating them and hating my work. The level of stress rose higher with every pat on the back and every raise until I wasn't well. I became sick—mentally upset. I had to resign. We shook hands and they gave me a bundle to stay quiet about what was going on there, and I took the payoff in cash— not stock. All of us eventually went on to other work, but today I'm busy and they're not. In fact, that company no longer exists.

'While you are in the midst of such a group, you think about people you know and their work. You seldom think about the total human being their work represents.'

I never saw them as vultures, if that is what you mean. I believed they were either extremely stupid or extremely dishonest. Either way, there was no place left for me to work without stress of the viral variety.

'When you leave any relationship, you believe you were the one who saw others as they were, but that is not true. Everyone is aware of what is happening, but it is not their time to leave.'

As I too often say, "If it hurts too much, don't leave."

'At times you wait until you are pushed out the door or thrown to the wolves before you release yourself from a situation.'

If it doesn't hurt—and they pay you to leave, it's time to go, regardless of whether or not you're talking about love or work.

When I went to work at Corporate Headquarters, I was extremely confident, because I had a defined assignment and knew how to complete all tasks and procedures entailed in doing a great job. I could see nothing wrong *then*. As a result, I'm now guarded when beginning any new work—making sure it will pay before I accept it. Without self-reproach, I learned the hard way that work has to flow both ways.

I can't afford to let people barge in and take up my time doing nothing more than commenting about my business or gossiping about others who also do their own thing. As an employee, gossip was a welcome diversion—better than watching over the daily production of waste and misspent money spiraling down the drain. When you work alone, as I do, you have to be alert—more about that another time. I have to answer the door now.

In this life there is nothing like love, but it can be a royal pain. While I was thinking of Him, flowers arrived. I was so in love with that serendipitous moment I never called to thank him for this totally unexpected gift. I know he's paid a lot to act charming and nice—and always does it with great style, but it isn't an act. He is loving and charming—and it pays dividends. He is paid to be himself, but everyone assumes it's an act because 'acting nice' is a dying art. I know he is a huge success because his work is a great fit, but I wish he wasn't quite so busy doing what he does best.

When He calls or writes, I stop everything I'm doing to think about him—constantly! He gets into my mind and I can't sleep or dream, because I have to talk to him or see him again!

We talk and talk, but say very little, yet I always remember it as being a great conversation. Wonder why? I guess my heart is satisfied, even though my brain is repelled by the inanity of what we talk about. We never talk about love and being together, but make love constantly when we're alone on the phone.

When I think of him with intensity, He says he feels it and sends me back a brain wave meant to wash over me like the tide. I wonder if it will get better, but worry that instead it will get worse and end in a fiasco. How can that happen if we stay in love? How do you stay in love? We are two people who have only this one life together. If it works for us, why care if no one else believes it will last?

My mind constantly prepares me for when He will drop out. I was so sure he would stop calling by the time he was in the third week of shooting his latest picture on location—far away from me, but he keeps calling—even more than before.

I'm beginning to pick up a pattern. When he is due to appear here, he calls a lot more than usual—like he's lining up his schedule. It's a pattern, but I don't know why he follows it.

When I'm so beside myself, wanting to call him, I wait until the urge subsides, because I know he won't like *that* desperate woman. If he calls me unexpectedly, I'm so taken back it's Him that I scream with delight—really makes my day and it shows—which he really likes. But if I call him unexpectedly, would he react the same way? I don't want to chance that he might get upset with me for bothering him while he's on set, so I wait for him to call. After all, he has the variable schedule and location, while I'm always here.

When you think about a man far away from you, you wonder if he is being honest and loyal, don't you? But you have to stop thinking about it. You can worry yourself into hating him or others equally innocent—and where would that lead?

'If you hate, it enters the atmosphere and blends with the neurons entering the collectiveness of all. We all then become angry and hateful for no good reason.'

I want to help the world—not hurt it, so I will love him and not let my insecurities cause trouble for others, but its sooo hard when He is a movie star!

When I was growing up—about 13 or 14—I fell in love with Marlon Brando who was already a proven star. My sister was positive I would turn into a 'Wild One' riding around on the back of a motorcycle, because his role in "The Wild Ones" apparently titillated her—not me. Can anyone imagine me on the back of a Harley? Absolutely ridiculous! She has a wild imagination and constantly projects her visions onto others, rather than accept them as her own. I believe that is why she told our mother I made a mess by hanging pictures of a man old enough to be our father in our room.

My father never cared about my sister's tantrums, while my mother took them seriously. But that time my mother ignored her whining. I was allowed to wallow in lovesick misery over Marlon Brando to 'get it out of my system,' as my mother called it. I was unaware it's one thing to chase after a movie star in your dreams, but totally different in real life. Because my mother let me run the course of my teenage love with a man I would never meet, I learned enough early enough not to hurt myself later—or so I thought.

While I was going through my self-imposed travail, spending my allowance on movie magazines and seeing Brando's movies, my sister heckled and jeckled me constantly. She wouldn't let it go! She became more and more vicious in her verbal attacks. Not being very smart and/or articulate back then, I got mad and did the unforgivable. I told on her! I told my mother what she said and what she did on the sly, and my sister fell from grace.

I quickly forgot I had revolted against her tyranny and won, but she never did. In fact, it separated us for good. Refusing to say I was sorry—for the first time ever, we never mended the rupture—and I lived ever so much more happily ever after. Even today my sister runs from woman-to-woman heckling and jeckling, hoping to find someone to hector as she did me, but peers drop her and never speak again. I haven't dropped her completely, but I don't have to see her. Do I?

'When you ask for love, you get what is available.'

What about me? I wasn't asking for anything. I wasn't even looking!

'Think back and remember what you prayed for—over and over again.'

Hmmm…I do remember when young wanting to marry a movie star. Is this the answer to that childhood prayer? Does it take that long to make a dream come true? Is this how I became involved with today's equivalent of Marlon Brando? If so, I bet some young ladies really hate me!

The gossip rags are saying our relationship is 'nothing serious' or 'nothing to take note of'. That isn't enough to crash my dreams, but it would have crushed my ego when young.

Steve hasn't exactly been told to deny our relationship, but his producers prefer he remain single and aloof in order to maintain intact his 'unattainable male' image. It makes him ever so much more in demand at the box office, and I don't care what they print as long as he keeps seeing me.

'*Honesty is a virtue best not forgotten.*'

Hmmm, yes, I do care, but I'm not his wife. He has his life and can do whatever he wants, but I have to live with the fact he is designed to be shared with millions of others—men and women who love to dream about him, too.

'*Are you competing with men again?*'

Oh, yes, he gets lots of letters from men. I never thought of that. He says he enjoys it because it annoys his manager. Marty wants his clients to be super-feminine and super-masculine—nothing in-between, but life isn't like that anymore. After all, what are movies for if not to entertain the brain?

My philosophy is: When I'm ready to marry, He will be ready. If he isn't, there will be someone waiting to get the okay from me. I know this is true, based on past history. I have never been without a man—when I needed one. Sometimes I place them on the other side of the world in order not to interfere with loving everyone else. Distance makes relationships easier to keep or break.

I find it hard to sustain elevated feelings—like loving the human race—when one man is getting under my skin—biting and picking at my bones to make me his alone. Funny, women always take the rap for wanting marriage, but men are the ones who propose—insist on it, and get things their way—even today.

'Is that a fact?'

Who do you think arranged all the laws, sacraments, and daily routines? Women didn't! But we love men so much we do what they want—or do we?

'What if women were just like male human beings?'

It would be a free-for-all. The testosterone would flow uncontrolled and ignite the Earth, erupting into war. Too many men are militant and eager to prove themselves that when they have no one to fight with, they pick on women and kids.

'If there were only men in the world, who would weak men pick on?'

I was talking to a group of men and women about my latest article, "The Power of The Press to Change the World," when it dawned on me neither sex sees things the same—so we couldn't initially discuss it in bi-sexual meetings—and make progress. Although our life is full of bi-sexual politics, few recognize it. I think most think 'bi-sexual' is a ruse for some kind of pseudo-vice when people unable to find preferred partners of their own sex seek someone of the opposite sex.

'What if your home life is limited to only one sex—the other sex is never around?'

You probably achieve a certain peace and lifestyle others don't understand. But you would lack balance—and balance is what makes this world hang together. In order to get ahead, we move forward only so far, then reach back and grab our rears and pull them up to where we are, going forward a step, reaching back and pulling forward, ad infinitum, until the whole world is immersed in a new work or new age or whatever.

If you want to include everyone, as a tribe does, it's a very slow, tedious process, but it can be done.

'Would you want to speed down the highway, letting the slow do whatever the slow do?'

You bet! But most of the time we're the snails, so we nix such ideas in favor of taking the middle path, or the road to reason, or the slow lane—whichever makes us feel better.

'When you are slow to learn, you realize others have an advantage, but not that great if you decide to catch up.'

Is that what you do as guides?

'No need to worry about it most of the time—or us.'

In other words, those who start out fast usually slack off and lose speed before their Guides rupture themselves trying to beat them.

'You can be almost perfect when slow—but you choose to hurry and not dawdle.'

But who is perfect?

'You are when you do your work and don't let others tell you who you are.'

That is so tough to do! I received a Letter to the Editor the other day saying my syndicated columns 'stink' and have no substance. The writer believes she can do a better job than me.

'Why would anyone want to write a column with no substance?'

Hmmm, I wouldn't normally write for the press, but I have to feed me and my child. When you write, you either tell it like it is or pretend to tell it like it is—either way, you end up dead meat when you get too close to the truth. People don't want real news! They want rosy-colored views of problems— not hard-headed solutions. They don't want to be bothered by conscience when they walk away rather than help others.

'*What is going on now?*'

To me, my column is about metaphysical happenings in the world. I spotlight the work of people who are unlike the mainstream, sharing how they compare to the rest of us.

'*What are you hiding, suppressing, or compromising to do this?*'

Actually, I write about what happens here in this town and the seven men who run it. It's a metaphysical exercise for me alone. I don't say much about local politics, but it got around that it's the gist of my column. When other towns discovered what happens here happens there, subscribers opted to read about our town instead. My column seems to be well received as a humorous commentary on the sad condition of urban America and suburbia wherever, but for some living here, I'm vindictive.

'*Apparently we have not kept up with your column. It got lost in this whirlwind of romance you have created.*'

Interesting! I thought someone above read everything I wrote.

Hmmm, this silence is embarrassing. I guess I got my answer!

Anyway, the way I see our town and write about it— most aren't comfortable about moving out of the city in order to escape their past. We blame foreigners, other races, whomever, for the decline in city life, but we want to forget our pasts—wallpaper over it and create the illusion we were born to the manor. We don't want others to quickly determine if we climbed or slipped relative to family ranking; so we moved out, hoping the homogenized working middle-class would transform into upper-middle class, even though sociologists claim you can't rise that much within a single generation.

This shifting movement not only upset families, it buried most of our arable soil ten feet below suburban lawns. In case of famine or draught, the 'unbuildable' land around here is the only land left, but I digress—again.

'So you are teaching sociology in your column?'

Maybe, but sometimes it's more about economics than anything else. At least that was my intention when I wrote about going to a school three blocks from home when I was a kid. The kids around here race two blocks to bus stops for transport to the furthest reaches of the school district to enforce a mediocre attempt to qualify for Federal aid to education.

I went further out on that limb and said we don't need Federal aid, that we have so much money that we overpay janitors. In fact, we overpay everyone in order to compensate for lack of interest or lack of respect for their contribution to our collective lives.

'Hmmm.'

Not only that, I wrote that we as individuals don't want to get involved in education or governing our community. Who is *really* interested in knowing where their property taxes go? We're the only ones who count when it comes to taxes collected here, but no one pays attention until they raise taxes again.

I wrote something like: 'Taxes are a pain if you're stuck or fall behind, but most people don't pay attention to them, as long as they're automatically deducted from their pay checks.' Since I have to send my taxes quarterly to the IRS, I check on what I get back from the Feds. I was sure it wasn't much, but discovered I got nothing from my Federal taxes for my personal use.

For making inquiries about my tax dollars at work, I got a letter saying I paid more than my share in taxes last year, but they're keeping it because I owe more this year. How do they know what I'm making now? Does any of this sound like me?

'Yes.'

Yes, I did slip in a couple of other gems here and there.

If I was going to move forward—or relocate, I would set aside enough money to move based on cost to move, as well as live in the new place for about a year....

That is not weird! Yet too many aren't prepared to even pay utility security deposits. You have to wonder how they find the time and money to move—but everyone does—sooner or later. We keep on moving—trying to release or relive the past, but no one really changes.

Here's another that got a lot of letters:

The loose change in the seat of your car isn't much, but it can help. I never tell anyone how much money is in my car, but I keep some in the glove compartment for tips, tolls, parking, plus a little extra for gas in an emergency.

I thought everyone did that, but no one writing in admitted to it. Am I the only one who figures I might get caught short at some point and need change? What's crazy is I never get caught in need of change—but everyone writing in did.

'Does worry make the difference?'

I think so. I once wrote about experimenting with worry. I decided to worry about Steve to see if he would back off his commitment to review a long story, then decided not to waste my energy—but it worked anyway. In fact, He is coming here next month for a long stay. At the beginning or end of it, we'll know what to do about us, but right now I'm stuck in the middle again. I have to decide if I want marriage or I'm merely working through another dream?

Chapter Fourteen

The Heart Will Win!

*F*eel silly, but Steve, do you want me or do you want me to leave?"

"Nothing silly about it! It's so serious I can't think."

"I feel sort of shy, but have to say this now or I'll be so upset later I won't be able to work—and Brian will think he's done something wrong. It's the hardest thing I've ever had to do, but if I don't speak up, our life will be miserable at best."

The man seated opposite Jeanne was wringing his hands, about to stand up and leave as he said, "I need time to think this over. You're so difficult to understand, and I'm accustomed to fragile egos and shallow minds that I can't think this deep. Before I can dissolve, I have to think more, if you know what I mean."

"Absolutely! I just can't believe you understand me."

"I don't."

"Yes, you do! Steve, you totally understand. I've been upset over the idea that you're too worldly to understand my spirituality—and here you are more spiritual than I am."

Steve didn't look happy, but his famous smile slowly emerged as he said, "Why is that so amazing?"

Embarrassed, Jeanne spoke with enough enthusiasm to almost compensate for her lack of tact. "Everyone assumes

Hollywood stars are demons that tempt ordinary mortals to move out of our safety zones into a decadent life that ends in the total collapse of humanity." Then in a final rush she added, "And if all media was eliminated, all the ills of this world would disappear with it."

"You're too brilliant to believe anything that stupid, but you're on target as far as what too many say about Hollywood. I hear it all the time, but we don't have time to go into all that now, but when I get back, we will. I promise. I have to hurry and get into my next role, but how 'bout you and Brian visiting me in Montana as soon as it's over? It would be great, and Brian could get a real look at my spread—not just the video version. I have it pretty near fixed up to where I want it, and we have four horses in need of a gentle rider to exercise them. They're old race horses, way over the hill—exploited and abandoned. We provide them with green pastures for the rest of their lives."

Eyes wide, Jeanne said, "Oh, no! I never knew you cared about abused racers, too. That's so wonderful! I love those horses!"

As she leaned toward him, tears welled up and threatened to ruin the mascara she had carefully applied to her lashes in preparation for this public scene.

"You don't know the half of it. We have so much in common, it's scary, but I have to go. There's the last call for boarding—and we are creating a bit of a scene, so we better kiss passionately or they'll say we broke up—again."

With that I fell into a well and arrived back in my mind only when I saw him waving as he was about to be swallowed up by the rush to board the plane. Only then did I realize I had my own lives to live. I had to let him go and try to forget—at least for now—what might happen in the future.

Tugging at my sleeve, Brian said, "Mummy, will Steve let me ride horseys?"

Thanks be to God that Brian was there. I couldn't hold back the tears any longer. He provided the perfect excuse to hide my face. Stooping to listen, I avoided curious, prying eyes and loud whispers that I didn't deserve Steve, which I already knew.

"Mummy, can I have an ice cream like that boy's?"

Without looking, she said, "Yes, no problem. You've been a good boy! Never complained or ran around while we were talking. You deserve a treat!"

With no curiosity about the people pushing closer, Brian said, "I like you to talk, Mummy. You talk nice."

Slowly withdrawing Brian's hand from her arm, she said, "Let me put on my sunglasses, sweetheart. My eyes hurt." No wonder people in the spotlight wear dark glasses. Nothing betrays your true feelings like red eyes. If I hurry, no one will know how I feel—only how I reacted to his leaving. Amazing that I rarely wore sunglasses before I met Steve!

Years ago I discovered most people don't believe you when you're open and honest—being your true self. Too many expect you to be devious and contrary. So if you're straightforward and honest, you make good time while they're slowed due to checking for loopholes, alibis, and lies they would use if they were you. Way too many don't listen or recognize truth, because they're consumed with playing games. I've consistently refused to play games, but maybe it's time to start—if I'm to have a life of my own?

It's easy to lose those who would follow you while walking through crowds in airports and large cities, but accompanying a young boy in no hurry to leave also rids you of stalkers. With this thought in mind I smiled as I escorted Brian to the nearest ice cream stand and waited while he chose the 'bestest flavor of all'.

"You can eat your cream in the car this time, Brian, but it's not to be a habit. I have to jot down a few things while they're fresh in my mind. They're for a future column or two."

"Otay, Mummy, but you better not cry." Brian looked at her with sorrowful eyes.

Smiling broadly to reassure him she had no intention of crying, Jeanne said, "So you've noticed I sometimes cry while writing?"

"Yeath, I see you cry lots of times, but it otay. I know you not mad at me."

She had to pull Brian to her and stroke his hair—in front of the few who continued to follow them. How can you better share how much you love a child?

Once in the car, Jeanne locked the doors and pulled out a notebook stored in the glove compartment. Since no one outside could see in, she felt instant relief, which surprised her. She realized she wasn't really dismayed—a bit afraid, but not dismayed.

What a day! I had so many things going through my mind—things that needed to be said and things I wanted to say, but what I did say was so important that nothing else matters. But what did I say? Something about wanting an answer now, but what else? My life isn't making sense!

If you were to film your life, would it be a neat and tidy movie? Probably not. Movies are edited, cut, revised, and worked over until they make sense and are cohesive.

Now and then I wonder who would star in the movie of my life if I abdicated and decided to write about myself rather than live to the fullest now.

What if I stop writing this column? Someone else will do it! It didn't exist before I created it, because no one wanted to write about local issues, but now it would be missed—so someone would fill the vacancy. That's life!

Finally, I can make a difference! But all I see are blights—not delights. If the column didn't make a difference, been controversial, it would've been forgotten in a day or two—and no one would want my job—and far fewer critics would be voicing their negative opinions on everything.

When your work is as fabulous as you are, you might claim to have done it all by yourself, but that would be a fabrication of your ego. *Fabulous* implies a fable or lie, and fables develop when people repeat a story over and over again—not you saying you're great. When you live a simple, direct, unassuming life, you're achieving your highest level of perfection, but who knows until it's over?

The life Brian and I share is perfect for us—and I don't think we can improve it. It's an idyll meant to take us from one point in time to another. We're not here to idle, but to move and grow, so off to work we go hi ho! hi ho!

After Charlton Heston played Moses, he never changed his delivery. He was Moses ever after, regardless of how diverse the roles. As he aged he grew to look like a patriarch, but it was his voice that made his fortune. He had little to say, but his thundering baritone filled people with images of power and glory. We imagined him to be a wise old god rather than a simple man reading a script.

How would Marlon Brando have played Moses? Probably mumble, since Moses needed his brother Aaron to speak for him back in the day. Would the role have changed Marlon's work?

But I digress.

If you say a brook has a voice, is a waterfall many brooks babbling or God speaking in the presence of angels—or what? Does God speak to us?

I'm really reaching here, fellas. You could help me out just a little.

'The Holy Spirit dwells in water.'

I know that! But how do I know that? If water or Spirit doesn't announce change, what does?

I never talk about God—that would be blasphemous, but when I speak *to* God, I immediately feel a presence and sense I'm changed in some fundamental way. Right now the sense of change is so profound I don't know what to write. Tears are about to flow—each a separate being made of water.

For a few minutes Jeanne stared straight ahead as if driving on the interstate, looking for an exit sign. Brian accepted her lapse into meditation, because she often sat this way. During such times he played with little cars he stowed in his pants pockets.

This isn't easy to accept, but I would like whoever is guiding me to help me select the best of all available paths in order to more easily assimilate life's lessons...so as to do the wisest thing for me and Brian! If my path leads to Hollywood or wherever, please point me in that direction now. If I have to exit and never share his life, let me do it now—not wait until I'm a total wreck.

Jeanne continued writing, but not as fast as previously.

What if God would suddenly emerge from a cloud and point at me? I'd die—literally. I'll be satisfied if an angel, or somebody like an angel, pushes my fingers to form letters. I'm not so foolish as to call out angels and ask them to work for me. God is God, and I know my place—and it isn't bossing around angels and saints.

What is a saint?

A few months ago I was writing about a saint, but it was so mind-altering I had to stop—without finishing the article—because somehow I became the saint. I really did! I felt the stir of all that is or was. A terrible humiliation left me with a burning sensation in my chest. Finally a burst of purifying energy washed over me and left me soaking wet—actually drenched in sweat. It was so dramatic! Too dramatic! I never finished the piece on martyrdom and I won't. I refuse to talk about my belief in God—let alone write about God in my life. Who can do that and continue to live as you did?

What if Jeff, Brian, Jack, Julius, and any other male I ever learned from were to all appear at once and present another life lesson? Would I recognize it? Probably not! More likely, I would be so overwhelmed by past feelings and fears that they couldn't enter this life. I wouldn't want them to enter my mind, either. I couldn't risk letting them change my mind now as I live in this state of euphoria.

Feeling euphoric because of Steve, but it isn't *all* about Him! Steve is human and happy to be alive, which makes him lovely and desirable to all who are depressed, upset, and otherwise out-of-touch with their own realities.

If the men who came before Steve were such jerks, maybe I wouldn't have waited for him and would have married one of them—and have had a child of my own? Instead, I held out for something better, even if it meant I would live alone a long time. Now I'm happy they were jerks and continue to be jerks! I hate to say it, but there is no better description available.

I may sound like a bitter old crone, but ask any woman to be honest and she'll tell you what she puts up with on a daily basis to stay married—*and it ain't pretty!* Remember, I've always been one to understate—not exaggerate problems.

You might think that by now men would be so accustomed to being in charge that they wouldn't feel threatened if you were Marlena Dietrich, Marilyn Monroe, Madame Curie, and Adele Simpson all rolled into one fantastic vamp, but way too many men hate outstanding women! If you need an example, watch how the insecure carry on about Hillary Clinton. Now there's a real role for Today's Woman!

Would any sane woman want to be Hillary? Apparently too many! Why else act out so negatively toward her and other women perceived to be powerful?

Men aren't the only ones insecure and jealous. Women are more prone to hide their thoughts than men—but jealousy makes the nicest woman mean. Too many turn mean when Hillary's name—among others, comes up. Their message is intended to warn women to avoid doing great things. When will women get beyond that kind of self-hatred?

Why do so many hate accomplished women? Is it because they don't bow down to men?? Maybe they make some women feel more enslaved, because they aren't doing what they want, too?

Yes, that's it. It fits! You know the truth when you feel it. I wonder if Hillary and her husband ever feel like chucking it all, too?

'Of course, they do. Who wouldn't in their shoes?'

Who wants to be the only one who knows what is happening, yet can't do anything to change it? Everyone! Just a little joke, forgive me...

I didn't consider myself in the vote when the election war was waged, but I did vote. Can't remember who I voted for, but it doesn't matter. The President is and the President will be, so get over it. It has nothing to do with you. If you can't accept a fact of life as simple as that, you really have a problem—and it's not in my mind.

When the next election comes up, will it matter? I was thinking about going into satirizing national politics, but it isn't funny. It's not even vaguely humorous. It's often dishonorable and downright mean. The word 'mean' is big today. I want to drop it, but it sticks to my pen.

When you write in Spirit, your mind flows and grows with the last thought, changing direction like a river meandering through pasture land. It nurtures the land and flows until it gives birth to the sea.

What about the sea compels us to sing about it, talk about it, vacation at its shores? I guess it's the majesty and might of its waves. No single wave will be remembered, but the continual movement and sound of many waves is. The tide comes unbidden and shares your space like faith, but you can't create it. It's evasive in its calming effect. Sometimes it inspires or retires your mind, as it goes on and on ceaselessly. You can't turn off the tide. It's raw power.

When I was a child, I was a child. Now I am no longer a child—right? Wrong, but right. You're a child if you think you are, and you're not a child if you realize you have learned the lessons of childhood. Even so, you may wonder if you learned them all. I wonder if I learned all about love and romance or am repeating the 'Marlon Brando syndrome' of my teens. I hope not.

If we could relive one phase of life, would anyone choose to relive their teens? The only people I know who enjoyed their teen years were jocks who never made it to college or have careers—yet too many tell me they're unhappy now, too.

'*When are you happy?*'

When I'm at home! When I'm home alone with Brian and know I'm thought of in a friendly way by others—including Steve.

It is such a wonderful time to be alive that I don't want it to end, but it is. Whenever I think about my life and how it was and how it might return to being that way again—and other depressing stuff that can easily come true when you're afraid…But why would I return to the past? I lived it! Did it all! So it stands to reason it's gone—but is it?

What a delightful day! Brian and I will go out for dinner tonight. We'll celebrate, because we might cry if we sit at home alone after so many nights with Steve. I have to call him later and see how his trip went. He'll say, 'It was great!' He always says, 'It was great!' I want the truth, but he always says 'It was great!' in that male kind of way that means he doesn't have a clue what went on around him, but he experienced no problems. Men can't stand too many problems, while women thrive on them.

When I went to school for a few months to study the foreign service and how it's organized, I was told we do so much for other countries who don't help the U.S. that it's amazing we have a country left. But is it amazing? We're not just a country. We are the universe. We have nothing that isn't available elsewhere on Earth. Although everything here exists elsewhere—all peoples live here—if only for a short time. Some struggle to get here, follow the rules and assimilate, while others fight to undermine everything and everyone….

Why fight? I guess if you have nothing to lose and want what others have, you might fight; but why fight when you can get it more easily by cooperating and working together?

When this is all over and I put my pen aside, Brian and I will drive out into the world and see it as it exists, but right now alone in this little car, we're totally isolated from every other human being—but are we ever alone?

Never would I say this world is covered with unseen beings, but maybe it is. Maybe I'm encrusted with other beings? Who's to know? Doctors know so little that anyone who thinks differently is drummed out of the corps. Obviously, only those who know—know they don't know. If you know you know, you don't care what others know.

Right?

Whatever became of the case where a woman was so mad at her family she left them and never returned? You hear about women doing that, but not about men who do it much more often. Why?

Men are jerks! They leave one woman for another and never worry about the one who gave up so much for them—so what then?

'To leave your children to the care of anyone and everyone is a serious way to lose this life and have to return.'

I never told anyone my childhood friend Julius was a wife beater, and had abandoned his child, but once he told me, I hated him as much as anyone could.

'He's better for having confessed, but will never say it again. Because he confessed, he can move on and clear up his mess.'

At some deep level I must have known Julius was a terrible person who abused his wife and child, but I never saw it. I had no proof, so I didn't condemn him. But once he confessed,

I dropped him immediately. You might ask why not simply ignore such people? Maybe I think I can help them.

There, it's out! I'm a terrible person! I think I am a god to such people—and I'm not. Now that I've confessed, I accept it. Will everyone shun me? I hope so. I'm tired of putting other people's lives back together. Let them find someone else to dump on—and leave me alone.

Wow! Where did that come from?

If I hadn't taken time during my hour of woe to sit in silence and write out my needs, wants, and whatever else, I wouldn't have received this healing. I'm now healed of the need to meddle. I can feel it!

At last I can go with Steve and live anywhere! I won't make alibis for those who are weird, stupid, ugly, vicious, or mean-spirited. I'll know them by the way they live, and won't say otherwise. I'm free of such guilt and need to apologize for what does not pertain to me!

I can sleep now, knowing anyone who has done me wrong will be repaid in curious ways over many days—never again worry about revenge. I'm me and can help Brian, but until now, Brian has been helping me.

Hopefully we will live to see the day when all people become aware their lives are mere movies in which they either star or abdicate their power. I live to be free of pain, suffering, despair—fully accepting responsibility for being me—but I have a long way to go and a lot of work to do first.

Chapter Fifteen

Turning Point

*R*uin isn't recognized until it stares you down. Success isn't believed either, so why are we so proud of our self-defined sanity and ability to be introspective?

As I left the house to put a few things in the car, Brian started screaming and crying. It felt like a sword—nothing so small as a dagger—plunging into my belly. I ran back and found him scattered about the kitchen. He was lying on his stomach and its contents were spewed over the floor, even the cabinets, but it was the blood seeping from his nose that scared me! What to do?

I ran to the phone and called a friend who is a nurse, but she wasn't home. I thought of calling 911, but rejected it since they would fly in with sirens blaring and without hesitation whisk him away to the hospital. People—even professionals, tend to overact when confronted with children like Brian. So I called out to the universe and asked God for help. No one wants to believe it, but an angel arrived immediately.

I didn't move Brian, but raised his head enough to wipe out his mouth. There was a big bump on his nose, looked like a bruise already in progress, and since he wasn't looking at me, I checked his eyes to see if he had had a seizure. No signs were present. That is when I noticed the step stool laying on its side a few feet away and surmised he had fallen—and as he fell, the shock caused him to throw up breakfast. He must have landed on his nose, may have broken it, thus all the blood.

As all this registered in my mind, the meter man knocked and asked if anything was wrong. This man in uniform was really an angel! He entered, surveyed the situation and proclaimed Brian had been scared and would be all right as soon as we cleaned him up, but I should check to see if his nose was broken. Turns out, this angel works for the ambulance service in town on his off-duty hours and has seen similar falls and their effects, but I hadn't—and certainly not involving Brian.

He carefully picked up my bleeding and bruised boy and laid him on the kitchen table to examine him with the gentleness of a nurse. We took off Brian's shirt to wash him, then the gentle giant wrapped him in a blanket and gave him a cup of herbal tea. By then I was emotionally drained, but Brian was radiant and happy.

Brian really was happy! No man had ever nursed him before. His pediatrician, the only other person who physically cares for him, is a woman, so this was a real novelty—just what the doctor ordered.

The ministering angel would accept nothing but our thanks, Brian's new pencil eraser, and a cup of healing tea. I intend to call his office and recommend him to his superiors. I can also see my next column writing itself, applauding his good deed. We take for granted these men and women who volunteer to protect our homes from fire and our bodies from trauma for little or no pay, and entirely too little public recognition. I wonder why?

'They are too much like parents!'

Parents are supposed to rescue you. Right?

Before Brian's tumble, I was sorting clothes I planned to take to Goodwill from those to be thrown away. I guess Brian was inspired to get into the act, too, and began throwing out food he doesn't like. He had disposed of rolled oats, a box of whole grain cereal, and a bag of rice, and was reaching for something else when the stool toppled and deposited him en masse on his head on the floor. Fortunately, he wasn't hurt badly, but what if he had been crippled or killed? I will never forget this accident!

'Let your mind absorb as much as it can from an accident, then erase it and do something new.'

Instead, I obsessed on it for hours—and nothing changed. It did not accomplish one thing to rectify the situation. After all, the kitchen stepstool is necessary to reach the high cupboards, and Brian enjoys perching on it while I cook, so it has to stay—but he isn't allowed to stand on the seat or climb anything for now. He will be allowed to climb whatever when he can run forever. I don't really mean it, just saying that because I don't want Brian to climb until he develops better motor skills and enough strength to support his weight when he loses his balance.

When Brian was a baby, friends assumed he would stay that way, but here he is going to school and doing good work. He does just about anything kids two years younger can do, and lately he seems to be making up some of that distance. I wonder why?

I suppose most doctors have little time for children diagnosed with Downs syndrome and other conditions too many nasty kids label as 'mongoloids'. It's their parents I have little patience with, so I and others are banding together to find doctors and support staff who care about our 'gifted' children—and have endless patience with us. I think that is why Brian and many others are doing better today than in the past. In fact, they are excelling to such a degree that some kids feel threatened by them! Brian isn't afraid of such challenges, but doesn't understand what 'just plain mean' means.

When you think of what all a child does at school, is it any wonder they want to relax when they get home? When Brian returns he wants to study and do his homework, and I want him to play outside until the sun passes over the back porch.

As you work, do you ever feel someone watching you? Brian does, based on his comments. Sometimes I feel that way, too. I have decided the face watching us belongs to the clock on the shelf—not someone or something else. I believe time is of the essence and irreplaceable, but no clue where I got that idea.

'We are not going to discuss time now.'

Okay, but I'm going to try to figure out why Brian is intellectually deeper than most folks around here.

Some of our neighbors don't seem to be aware life is marching onward. You can see it in their eyes when they look at Brian. They see him as a disabled child trying to be normal, while I see Brian as normal—experiencing a few more difficulties than the average boy trying to look and act like everyone else. His brain doesn't malfunction. He can do whatever it takes to survive. At times I think he is far more brilliant than he appears, but he doesn't want to manipulate me like everyone else, including the cat.

When we were finishing details on the house, the workers asked Brian if he had a special space he wanted built just for him. Of course, he had just the perfect spot in mind. Would a 'dumb' kid have a spot in mind just waiting to be asked where it is? They all chipped in and built a special room for him upstairs in the crawl space in the attic, using scraps from their trades. Brian can play there until he is about four feet ten or so, then he'll have to give it up—I imagine, but for now, it's his den. He goes there when he wants to be alone or senses something is wrong, and sometimes when he wants to share his world with someone he trusts. I've been invited there, but not often.

When you think of someone preferring their own space and living in their own world, do you assume they want you in it? Most people think a world apart from others is a great idea, per se, but feel they're special and should be allowed into your world, too, even if everyone else is excluded. What an ego system we have!

Quiet times come to us less frequently now. Fall is in the air and everyone is trying to help us get the house buttoned up for winter—a lot going on that will subside once bad weather hits. We're working mostly outside now. If no leaves, there is always trash blown in from the street. When I asked my neighbors why people throw out what can easily be pitched into trash bins, most said, "They're jealous."

My neighbors think others envy us our lovely homes, thus try to sabotage our hard work. I think it's more fundamental than that. I think people are lazy—and getting lazier. Wonder when lazy people stopped being scorned? Every home owner, even city dwellers, have more time and less work than previous generations due to labor-saving devices. Do we all feel guilty about it, thus no longer condemn those who flaunt idleness? Is it because we lie about not having enough time to work hard, too?

What if society restarted labeling people as lazy? In the old days, anyone branded 'lazy' was bullied into working harder. Everyone joined in nagging idlers to get a job and work. They didn't tolerate anyone sitting around doing little. Most labeled 'lazy' got jobs and learned to work hard, striving to keep up with others without being asked—and people forgot they were once considered lazy.

Today we often label idlers as being depressed or stoned! As such, they're permitted to lie around the house doing nothing, making no contribution to their upkeep; in the hopes they will spontaneously decide one day to join the human race. Once labeled 'sick', we don't have to nag them any longer to do something useful. Rather than training 'inactive-by-nature people' to do something useful and make a contribution to the family and society, we sedate or put them away. What if 'depressives' are just lazy? Perhaps too simplistic—but there may be merit in the theory!

Last month I was sure a girl in my chat circle was too depressed to continue working, that is, until I overheard her ripping apart another woman for succeeding at work. Apparently, she is not only jealous of those who work well with others, but too lazy to compete. She won't do anything unless told—and when she does, she wants paid more than everyone else. Worse, she resents anyone who helps others win. I know!

Recently Brian brought a friend home after school. When we took him home, his house stood in total darkness. The boy saw nothing strange about it, but I insisted on walking him to the door to meet his parents. The little guy had his own key to the backdoor and invited me in. We tramped through a mess in the kitchen to find his mother sitting in the family room watching television. She didn't even notice us! How can people sit—doing nothing but watch TV all day? They must be vacant-minded or insane.

'Perhaps they are in pain.'

Maybe, she is young and life probably isn't measuring up to her dreams—but whose dreams do? Anyway, she jumped at the sound of my voice, and without acknowledging either of us, babbled about losing track of time and needing to do something about dinner. She finished her soliloquy with something about fast food never hurting anyone—if you didn't eat it all the time. They would go to McDonald's again, maybe Wendy's, since they had a better kids menu. What a way to raise a child!

I wonder how many others with easy lifestyles do worse. I haven't figured it out, but doubt it matters what you do to pass time as long as it doesn't diminish what you brought to this world and promised to hold sacred—or harm another.

When kids are little, time passes so quickly you wonder why anyone would purposely miss any of it. After all, motherhood only entails about 10 years per child, if you do it right the first time, then you're more or less free to work at home on whatever or reenter the world around you once your kids go to high school.

Hmmm, if what you receive is what you sense and accept, I see nothing in this year's crop of movies and television shows that could tempt me to spend money on a huge TV set and order costly premium cable. I wonder if others analyze TV fare before subscribing—like they would if buying a magazine subscription.

When you make a commitment to read something and it doesn't hold your interest, you drop it and move to something else—unlike television, which is insidious. If it's boring or a rerun, you figure it'll soon be over and you'll wait for something better—which seldom happens, then you'll do chores. If you aren't disciplined, it can eat up your days and nights. You wake up and discover you accomplished little for weeks on end— even ignored relationships. Your ever-present alibi is 'I didn't have enough time.'

What if I sat and journaled while watching TV?

'Such entries would suffer for having shared your attention with strange, weird fallacies and false conclusions.'

The channel I watch most isn't great, but compared to the others, it offers some relief from stress. No murder, mayhem, and evil interjected for the sake of ratings. Serious subjects are set apart from everyday life and news—while we concentrate on the latest scandal or celebrity mishap. Deviant sex and violence have become the norm in all forms of media, even reading. I turn it off, but Brian can't, so I review the kids' shows and most are too violent for me, let alone a sensitive child. Are we the only ones offended by everyday exposure to the seamy side of life?

Too many young people around here appear listless and aimless—until we talk one-on-one. Usually I find them intelligent, engaging, gentle, even witty, but their outer persona is too often unattractive. Why dress like a Goth or act like a geek? Maybe to scare away intrusive people?

Everyone makes assumptions based on appearance, so in a weird way the grotesque escape close scrutiny because they all look alike. Childhood, teens, mid-life, old age—we are all the same!

While working a crossword puzzle I found a word used a lot years ago. A real gem, and I knew right away whoever created the puzzle was my age or older. That one word was a dead give-away. What is a 'dead give-away' anyway?

Ever listen to yourself and wonder how anyone can understand what you mean? I stopped using language that might sound elegant—because editors like the common tongue. In other words, talk down to the public in order to appeal to a broader audience. But when I address panels and peers, I can't use too many idioms for fear of alienating the educated among them, and so it goes. We've become boring and inarticulate attempting to harmonize or homogenize our community. Personally, I prefer diversity and contrast!

I thought kids wanted to be different, like I did. But its jeans, jeans, and more jeans! It's all most teens wear, as well as too many adults who haven't looked at their rear ends in a mirror lately. Have we succeeded in creating Stepford kids?

I offered to talk about journalism at the high school, but was told they stopped having assemblies and pep rallies because fights break out. Kids aren't allowed to gather anywhere now—unless there is an emergency. Wow! The kids lost a civil right, but who can blame the administration?

Rights aren't really rights, even though some choose to interpret Jefferson literally. He intended 'rights' to mean privileges. How do I know? I talk to him on a regular basis. He and Lincoln are still around.

'Jefferson and Lincoln aren't about to leave this country.'
Why?
'They invested too much of themselves in their work here. They refuse to give up on their creation.'

Lincoln isn't usually adamant, but Jefferson can be a tiger!

I want to revisit Washington, but Brian is too small to protect himself from harm. He has to be able to walk and run all day before we can attempt such a great adventure. In the meantime, we visit state capitols, but frankly, most look lost and forsaken. I wonder why?

'If a state is not governing citizens' lives, who is?'

I think most people see only the Federal government at work. I don't see DC people around here, but their cars scoot about town a lot. You see a lot of white license plates outside the deli at times, but who is a Federal agent and who is local is hard to know. My guess is most of the Feds are local, but who knows what they do?

My home emergency didn't involve local government, but the utility company provided an angel. He may have been trained under some government program, since utilities are as federal as a company can get, yet they move within our lives without our realizing they are quietly managing what belongs to us all. They're in our homes and work places 24 hours a day. Call a utility and complain and someone comes right out, but call the post office about a problem and see what happens.

On the other hand, I was going to make my home 'all electric', but the cost of bundled services was so condensed—and not explained, so I opted to be cautious and split up my utilities. Natural gas is cheaper to heat everything, but now I pay sky-high electric rates! The gas moguls charge too much, too, but it looks like they experience higher costs transporting Earth's bounty. But do they?

When did you dig up the pipe to your gas meter? Probably never! Maybe it needs replaced every 50-60 years, but your meter may need to be replaced and repaired more often. Obviously, we keep gas people working, but all they do is transmit what we own by birthright. Does the cost of transmitting gas justify such high rates? Supposedly we demand much service, but if you check out how they spend your money, you'll see why utility stocks pay high dividends year-in and year-out.

You can get upset and demand explanations, even withdraw participation, but not when it comes to utilities—especially phones. Utilities are more powerful and costly than the Federal Government; and when it comes to regulating them, DC politicians are mere window dressing.

When men and women traipse off to Washington to represent us, whose interests benefit their wallets? Not yours or mine! They favor those who support their reelection—every time, which may not favor their own district or state. Big business rules—but not many big corporations remain from the past. That leaves the utilities wielding the power behind all those thrones. We supposedly are they or them—and they us, but no one really believes it.

One of these days I'm going to write a column about monopoly—the real-life game. Unfortunately, 'utilities' spells *boring* to most readers—almost as boring as 'insurance'. The media never addresses insurance enough—especially in print. Editors visualize readers' eyes glazing over as soon as 'I N S U R A N C E' appears. A guaranteed snorer, but it's a domestic and business landfill with so many mines that we all avoid the subject even though somebody should expose them, but it's so much easier to expose greedy magistrates or naughty politicians.

What does the average person want?

'To be left alone—do nothing—and have it all!'

When everything goes great, I want to be left alone, but misery loves company. Too many Americans are in miserable shape—according to the news—but is it true? Everyone I know has no big, outstanding issue that politicians or statesmen can solve. We go on vacation and have enough of everything, so why be bothered by Washington's greed and graft. How bad can it be if we don't care what they do?

What if we all started sniffing around utilities, demanding transparency? Could we discover our money being wasted? They would tell us we have no right to make such demands of a private enterprise. Only the Public Utility Commissions can inform us about what goes on behind closed doors. You and I know they won't, but they're all we the people have. Does everyone want to do something about it? Nah! We have too much going on at home to worry about the world around us.

What if you and I sat around and never did anything?

'We cannot move—or do your work.'

Hmmm…I was going through a list of things I have to do to get Brian released from school for a week. It was so long and complicated I had to call his teacher. It was harder to get through to her than the President of General Motors. I know. I talked to him last week.

We're going to visit Steve at his ranch in Montana, but Brian's teacher insists he must study every day or I am denying him necessary education. What a crock! She was a person before turning into a bureaucrat who parrots the administration manual without understanding it—classic 'letter of the law' versus 'spirit of the law'. I tried to explain I don't expect Brian to work then, because he needs time to regroup, so she's holding *my* decision against *him*. I guess I'll have to stop Brian from observing and participating in real life to do her bits and pieces of busy work. No wonder we've degenerated into a nation of paper pushers—myself included.

What if we ran off and never reported back to school authorities? We could get away with it about a day before the truant officer arrived demanding redress, followed by a summons and legal threats in abundance. Since Brian is adopted and a 'Special Needs Child' he could foreseeably be taken from me, etc., etc. An army of bureaucrats with nothing to do but enforce rules meant to benefit kids, but more often than not are abusive and easily misconstrued. Can you blame kids for ignoring us and doing whatever they like in order to be whoever they need to be? I can see their point, but probably shouldn't. If you can't make your family happy, why worry about others?

Which, what, whom, and them are so over-used I intended to put them to bed and never write another sentence using them, but it's hard not to talk about '*them*' when I want to get personal. No one is personal anymore, but we hurt anyway. I was hurt when the local paper didn't assign me to interfere, I mean interview, the granddaddy of all local politicians, but after it came out in print, I knew why. They whitewashed his misdeeds, as though he and the editor were best friends— in another life, too. They're afraid of him, whereas I'm definitely not impressed, so my piece would have been totally unacceptable for whom?

'Them!'

Never again will I say I never got a good assignment, but this time I know the reason. Having been in the work, work, work world for far too long, I have the proper perspective to enjoy the rest of my life. Get it? The REST of my life!

I feel like I'm resting most of the time now, because I so enjoy my work. What if everybody enjoyed their work—didn't complain constantly about inane as well as necessary tasks and chores? Always blaming those working somewhere above them for whatever they didn't do well. If everyone pulled their own weight, we would have to restructure our entire economy! We wouldn't need specialists, therapists, economists—for starters, but how could we retrain them? Maybe specialized computer training—steelworkers did it, why can't professionals?

While looking at my old word processor I started wondering how long I should keep it, since it contains files that can't be transferred to a computer. I would totally abandon it if not for a novel, a cook book, a few hundred resumes, and a lot of correspondence, so I keep it.

See how the mind works? You don't want to give up things in order to grow or update. You sit on stuff until the house burns down—and when you tell the insurance company you had a fortune in sentimental things, they declare it to have no value, you then forget about it in a couple of days. If the insurance company can tell you it has no value and satisfy your mind, why can't you?

'Your mind doesn't think you are wise.'

Probably! I was trying to talk to my neighbor until she started complaining about her husband and kids never listening to her—especially when she knows she is right. I feel the same way, but what can you do?

'You could listen more—and so could your neighbor.'

What if all the old stuff was deleted from my mind and only new, fresh, wonderful thoughts entered, would I feel like I did when I left the corporate world? It took a while before what I did in the past grew stale, but it's of little use now—obsolete, yet I've done nothing to download or erase it.

The old word processor represents this period best—no need for the programs or files any more, but not quite ready to sell or give it away. Maybe I'm waiting for the appraiser to come and say it's worthless?

'If you don't believe in something, does it exist?'

Chapter Sixteen

Weak and Willing

*W*eeks go by and I'm fine, then fear strikes again. I feel weak and upset—and it's all about Him! I go for days daydreaming about Steve and beginning our new life together—then it all fades.

I want to be married, but I don't want to give up everything I created or earned. I know most successful women fear marriage, but we say we don't and would give up everything we have for a really great relationship, meaning marriage with a capital M, as though that is what we should say and what is expected of us. But really—why would we want marriage as it exists today?

If you have a life full of joy and good work, not necessarily in that order, and you're respected and well-liked, have money enough you earned, plus a great boy and a wonderful man—then told to choose to stay as is or give up all you have to marry—would you give it all up to be married? I don't think I can. I admit I've never given up much in the past, but it still hurts. Some say once you make that kind of commitment, you'll be as happy as before—but I seriously doubt it.

'You said you are happy now, but is it true? Why give up the boy?'

You might have a family, but the new man commands and demands to be the center of your universe and expects more than any child, so a child or children stand in line behind the man. Some women even give up their kids for a man. Just read the newspapers to see how many women do that. Apparently, you have to satisfy the intruder to make sure he doesn't do anything to your kids or chase after another woman.

When the man is as wonderful, handsome, and successful as Steve, you think: Why not get married? He is superior to all others, and I won't find anyone like him again this life. Right?

'But do you need him?'

No.

'You don't need him to be complete, but you want to act out the role of the perfect woman—and have everyone marvel at what a great life you have, especially other women. Why?'

I have a great life, but none of my friends acknowledge it or envy me much.

'Why?'

"Because I'm not married!" Jeanne shouted to the seemingly empty room.

If I was married to the worst ogre in the world, other women would obviously find fault with him, but believe I deserved him—perhaps worse! That is how messed up modern women are. I think I'll pass on this marriage bid and wait for another. But once he goes, I can't help wondering if I'll be able to live as well as I did before he entered my life?

Looking up from her computer as if speaking to someone in clear sight across the room, Jeanne shouted, "You want me to marry him—don't you?"

'Yes!' resounded in her head.

Angrily Jeanne nodded and spoke to those unseen. "You think it's the perfect ending of a woman's day to enter the bedroom and be swooped into the arms of a handsome lover with nothing to worry about. What planet are you living on?" Upon hearing no response, she tried to quiet her mind as thoughts bubbled to the surface and erupted:

Instead of having time to myself, I would have to go upstairs and prepare dinner as soon as I finished working. I would have to work out Brian's school assignments as I cooked dinner and put it on the table. I would have to be charming and happy as I presided over each meal—talking about both men's days, without comment about what I accomplished—unless asked, before cleaning up the kitchen and dining room to make space for the evening's festivities, which I previously arranged, so there would be something to do beside watch TV or read. Then off to bed to find him asleep because he has an early shoot. You don't see things clearly when you're in love, but even I can see that far.

I can see why men marry younger women, but those women mystify me. Why would they sell out for security or whatever—giving up their youth and beauty in trade? If they can't live happily on their own, enjoying the confidence and self-esteem of being true to self, do they think some guy twice their age will supply it or make it happen? I doubt it, but then I'm a cynic about younger women who choose older men—probably because when young I was never attracted to older men.

Once you round thirty, if you start thinking about having a man take care of you—BEWARE! You'll live to regret it. It never works! There's some old song that says: *"Every form of refuge has its price,"* and the price is way too high—because women can do anything they want now.

If a man is ten years older than you, you can age prematurely and look older, or he can work out—hoping to look a bit younger so others see you as compatible. But a man twenty years older can't work out that much! So, the woman dresses and acts older—becoming matronly long before she normally would—and she lives with a lot less sex. No problem if he has enough money.

Let's face it, women don't give up their youth for love. They do it for money or security and prestige. In the past some thought such women wanted big families, thus enjoying every blessing money can bestow on them, but no one bothers using kids as window dressing any more. Such women insist on diamonds, cars, furs—no hidden assets that might be missed when accountants go to work at divorce or premature death of their self-deluded lovers.

'Furs?'

Yes, fur is still an asset. When winter comes to us all, nothing beats the loss of heat like a fur—especially when the man seeks greener pastures or partners.

In my school days I knew a girl who was enamored with an older guy in the rackets—a junior mobster, because he drove a flashy car and threw money around. She married him a week after the senior prom and died about 3 years later of 'natural causes', but we all knew she died when she met him.

'*What if you died and never knew marriage?*'

You never had a chance to be a widow or divorcee! Look at it that way and the single life looks better. Right?

This is where Jeanne put away her private thoughts and began writing what she thought could be salvaged for her syndicated column about life in the middle lane from a woman's perspective. She started typing rapidly:

> *You have to agree that many men are too possessive and disrespectful of 'their' women, yet others envy such women! If you doubt me, watch a TV panel with several men and one woman—notice how the men dominate the woman unless she is exceptionally outspoken.*

You have to be alert to even notice, since it's always been that way—supposedly. Watch the local news when they announce a woman was raped—who believes the victim was totally innocent? If they announce a woman abandoned her kids, they echo: "Women are like that." If a woman does something wise or wonderful—use your imagination. Who is first to accuse her of trying to be a man or says she is a lesbian—and no one likes her? Yes, it still goes on in this 'enlightened age'. Pay attention—listen!

'*We do.*'

The only time I personally let my name appear in the press is as a by-line on my weekly column, but I don't use my picture. Perhaps that is why I get such insulting mail? Some attack me as a radical lesbian separatist or vacant-headed, idiotic girl. One said I had a political agenda bent on improving the status of women. Wow!

'*You are told to honor people who make the effort and take the time to write, but do others honor them, too?*'

I was so sore when Steve reneged on his promise to Brian. I had no choice but to break off our engagement of sorts! I was hurt that he thoughtlessly canceled at the last minute our trip to visit him at his ranch in Montana—because of a new movie.

No doubt about it, I did the right thing! I don't and won't call Him ever again!

So why is He calling me? He didn't care enough to cancel the shoot or postpone it to fulfill his commitment to Brian and me—as well as take a much needed holiday. Now he's sorry—beyond consolation, or so his agent said the other day. Why did he do it? Was it greed, ego, or need?

If I had done that to him, Steve would have bounced off the moon and never called me again. I know it. Would I ever do that to him? NO! That is why I'm mad! I never saw it coming until it hit me, but it doesn't mean I can't split and walk away with my life fairly intact—does it?

I have this thing about love, honesty, decency, respect, and doing what is best this life and next, so I don't tell people one thing then, careless of their feelings and plans, not follow through. I honor them—maybe too much to fit in today, but disappointment hurts—especially children. Too often in my life men didn't keep their promises, but Brian has no such experience. He's been so upset by all this that I can't regret breaking up with Steve—but it still hurts.

Brian is not a man in small clothes, but boys today are more mature than many men. I watch men act out like boys, playing games and collecting toys as if they were still ten? Why?

"Maybe they missed the 60s or had to grow up quickly."

Unable to stop smiling at the idea, Jeanne continued to grumble about men in general, while maintaining an open line to her intuitive side.

'But no one did.'

Obviously surprised, Jeanne said, "What do you mean?" She then listened intently for a response.

'You never miss what you need to experience, but are spared much grief at times when you think you missed a big event. Why go back over it again only to get more grief and less joy? Think it may bring back your youth? Why would well-adjusted adults wish to be young rather than healthy and happy? Why would happy, content lovers not want to marry?'

I think the best time for couples to marry is when there are no kids in the picture, since the purpose of marriage is to propagate the world, or so they say.

'That is what churchmen say, but what do they know about human emotions?'

Churchmen don't encourage marriage to flourish within the church itself. If a pastor can marry, he is expected to wed a paragon of virtue who will become a slave to the congregation— as opposed to churches who forbid women and men who lead them to have close contact with the opposite sex. So how do 'they' know so much about marriage?

As a Christian I was raised to believe women are subservient to their husbands. St. Paul was supposed to have ordered it. Wonder if he was ever married—or just wandered around and wondered about it? It's stated in nicer terms, but it gets back to the same thing, women are to be second-class citizens of the world according to this world's patriarchs. As they reinterpret the Bible every few years—I've noticed attitudes gradually being changed to reflect a different view of women, even elevating our status. How come?

'You do not change the status of slaves to freemen without proper approval from authorities, such as a deed or proclamation.'

Women received official sanction some time ago, but never noticed it. Why?

'What if someone called and questioned you about your sex life, would you oblige them by providing details they wanted to know?'

I wouldn't, but many women eagerly talk about it.

'Why?'

Who else asks for their opinion? Some women are so starved for companionship they talk on and on to a wrong number. Some men listen when women talk, but do they understand what we say? Too many men snort and walk away when a woman or child speaks, while others sit and stare into space when asked to help someone other than themselves. Why do so few men listen to their wives once they marry?

'Maybe they get enough sex then?'

Hmmm…I was at an all-day seminar last week and was excited to see many women having a great time with each other—even though they never met before.

'Why do people spontaneously react like that?'

Check out women prisoners released from solitary confinement and see how sociable they are! You really must start noticing such things.

Chuckling, Jeanne paused and said, "I'm only joking. I may seem weird, wise, scary, and sometimes not at all on the ball, but you don't worry and I do. Right?"

When no one in spirit responded, Jeanne continued plugging away at her column *"Thoughts for the Day."* After a few minutes, she closed that file and opened one titled *"My Diary"* and began writing in a different vein.

> *When my friends ask me about you, I say I have this friend in Tacoma I call up for advice and counsel. It cracks them up, because they aren't sure if I have a friend in Tacoma*

or not. I'm not sure, either. I write to you and about you, and you could hate my guts and never tell me. What is our relationship anyway?

'We're old friends.'

Women don't cut up old friends—at least not to their faces.

'We may never meet or go places together, but we are old friends.'

I knew it!

What if you had been with me when this latest relationship came apart and broke my heart? How would you have handled it? I bet you would have chased after him and begged him to take you with him on location.

No, that's too nasty to write, even in my diary. It sounds stupid, but way too many women do it. I want to be honest, but when I am, people get upset about what I write, so I water down my words to make them sound reasonable—if not logical.

'What sane mind would want a partner who has to be chased and changed before they are suitable to mate or work with or whatever?'

I know about the boring aspects of marriage—I've been down that road.

'When does marriage excite, stimulate, and lead a person to greater achievement than if single?'

Speaking aloud with more resignation than anger, Jeanne said, "Never if you're a woman!"

I think a male scientist is better off having a wife. He can go to the laboratory and stay there for days knowing his family

*unit is intact and his home runs better than when he is there.
But traveling salesmen away from their nests half as much
time are unlikely to enjoy a happy home.*

Want to know why? They aren't out of the reach of other
women, which is the problem with making movies. Steve is in
the clutches of a woman right now, which is why I'm so upset
I could spit!

*I watched TV the other night (I got in the habit of watching
all the silly tabloid shows to catch a glimpse of Him) and
there he was in a film clip rehearsing with this blond child,
hugging her and chatting away like he did with me. Not
a shade of difference! It was a terrible scene! I know she
believes he loves her. I believe it! Now I can see it's just his
way, but in the past I thought it was meant for me only.*

I used to cling to him when we danced, until I saw an old
movie where he was dancing belly-to-belly the same way with
some harlot-starlet. It totally turned me off on dancing with him
again! There was no difference whatsoever in the way he danced
with her on screen and how he danced with me in person.

He never stops acting. Our affair may resemble 'reel life'—
but I'm no walk-in. Well actually, I am a *walk-in*, but I'm not a
movie extra anymore.

You don't hear about people who change so completely
that everyone knows they're '*walk-ins*', but I ran into a woman
the other day who worked for a major corporation. She
discovered a huge sum of money being funneled into private
bank accounts of certain executives and was fired—given no
credit for uncovering the fraud. It will never come out, but she
walked away with a big settlement. She said she was lucky to

have survived and been able to walk away reasonably clean, but did she?

She said it was too tawdry to discuss, so now she works at the deli and delivers pizzas during the day—because "women can't deliver pizzas at night and risk being raped," according to her supervisor. Turns out she actually owns the shop, unbeknownst to her crew. She stopped serving corporate gods dedicated to the almighty dollar to run a prosperous enterprise of her own—and according to her she has it made now. She never looked better, and no one says anything about her past, so she is better off!

'Why doesn't anyone talk about the corporate theft?'

She isn't allowed to talk—part of the agreement she signed when she left. They don't want her to succeed, so they blackballed her—down-played her great reputation when others checked her references, and they can sue her if she tells anyone about the 'confidential work' she did there.

I know she is a *walk-in.* How else could she totally switch from one life to another—into another personality, too, and do everything so easily?

To survive, you do what you have to do, but it may not seem like enough until you're down the road a piece. I used to review my past every few months, but now I can't get away from it. It's depressing to dream and scheme to get the past back and ignore the present.

'You can't.'

But the mind tries—all the time.

> *During a televised interview the other night, I started reading a book by a famous author, trying to figure out how he can write so many best sellers. He claims he doesn't*

really write them. According to him, he just sits with pen in hand and the words spill out on the paper. When they don't, he sits for an hour or so thinking about nothing.

Sounds like meditation—just sitting and thinking of nothing. If something appears, great! If nothing, that's great, too. I have to begin meditating more.

'*When have I not said that?*'

"That I have to meditate more?" Jeanne's mumble stumbled, causing her to muse more than write.

Once you learn how to meditate, you can't imagine why everyone doesn't. I have a hard time figuring out how people make it through the day without it, but most Americans claim they don't meditate or pray.

Speaking to no one visible, Jeanne said, "What if you and I were to meditate every day around five o'clock your time and eight o'clock my time?"

'*Better make it later or I will always be out when you are in.*'

"Then how about eight o'clock your time and eleven mine?"

'*We can think and send messages, and see what comes through the veil.*'

Thinking, but not speaking, Jeanne sent a test message: '*Not long messages. I get tired.*'

Since this engagement/marriage fiasco, I have to concentrate much harder on my work. It takes me longer to calm my mind and still my thoughts, but I'll try. How about if we start with something easy? '*Send me white light and love instead of messages.*'

A beautiful disembodied voice replied, '*I'd love to do that, but you have enough. Although I include the whole human race in a meditation, I single out you and Brian, as well as two others—*'

plus Steve. I envision you all happy, smiling, and enfolded in God's love and light. But He is fading from view now.'

That is because I can't see his face any more without taking time to focus.

'You cannot retain a picture of another long. If you wish to retain a memory intact, you have to see the other often.'

Jeanne's fingers quickly slid over the keyboard as she wrote without thought:

> I intend to forget Him as fast as I can. A few weeks ago I decided to burn all my pictures of him and us together. It's the sort of thing I did when I was a kid, but it really hurt this time. I don't think I can ever do it again.
>
> I watch TV less, because it hurts to see him on camera acting like a shy guy fighting off women who help him get through barricades—then throw their underwear at him. No wonder he's spoiled!
>
> When a man or woman enters the unreal world of movies—even TV, I think another version of that person is created.
>
> Which image is closer to reality and which lives on after the game is over? I wonder if the personality on screen is better than the unreal one? It probably is. The words are rehearsed speeches. Someone else creates the illusion and others reproduce it.

I tried writing a few words about being in love with a famous movie star and how to blow it off casually afterwards, but it wasn't funny. I couldn't do it. I guess if you love deeply it stays inside You forever—but should it last that long?

'Drive over to the fair and see if you can find someone making apple butter.'

Funny! For the past week I've had this craving for apple butter, but the apples around here aren't good for making it from scratch. I found what I thought was a good substitute, but the finished product tasted strange or strained—not honest goodness like my mother's. But then what did I ever make that tasted as good as my mother's?

Hmmm…I haven't written about my mother lately. Maybe it's time to mention her, as well as a bit about the art of making love the old-fashioned way—through the stomach to the heart. Where did I put that file?

I wonder if someday Brian will talk about my cooking? Probably, but it won't match my admiration for Mum's cooking. She was divine. She lived in the kitchen and believed the kitchen to be the soul of a house and heart of the family. You only had to watch her cook once to fully enjoy her food and know it was better than anything served anywhere else at that moment in time.

To fully appreciate good food you need to see it being prepared, to witness how much effort and love goes into it— as well as time. Buying an expensive meal in a famous chef's restaurant isn't nearly as much fun as sitting at home and taking your time preparing a great meal. Expensive restaurants are meant to impress customers—not friends—maybe give your favorite cook a break.

'Who would you rather eat with—clients or friends?'

Too easy! I was trying out a new recipe yesterday and let Brian invite his boyfriend from next door. All of them (the boy's mother came, too) were ecstatic about the pizza I made and they decorated. You would have thought it was some exotic treat I invented on the spot—rather than something so ordinary that I worried it wasn't nice enough to serve company.

'She is getting a divorce and has not cooked in a week. Anything homemade would taste great.'

Long before a woman tells the world she intends to get a divorce or whatever, you can tell she is upset or moving in that direction, but not my neighbor. For years she covered up how much she hated giving up her old job, but it surfaced in her treatment of Brian. She took out her spleen on Brian, but it was her own son who was harmed—until Brian blew the whistle on her. Brian told me he felt sad for his friend, because his mother was always angry. That is when it all came together and we were able to get her on the road to recovery, hopefully for the rest of her life.

'You cannot contain hatred.'

Yesterday I was so energized I created a soup using different herbs and a bit of chicken with a lot of water. They thought it was canned soup—it was that good?!

'What now passes for excellence makes it easier to excel at cooking with very little effort.'

> *As a nation we accept shoddy workmanship without much comment, so nothing is lost by trying to make dinner yourself. You'll most likely do better with a couple of good ingredients than using whatever comes out of a box. It's ego-enhancing to cook your own food. It takes little practice and competence to cook better than local eateries. Just place a chicken in a pot along with onion, carrots, endive, celery, parsley, and a few bits of whatever herbs you like and it will turn out as good or better than Campbell's.*

'Does it cost more?'

"The bigger the group, the more you save."

I try to come up with things Brian has never eaten before and created a list of dishes based on his favorite foods. Thought he would like them, but he has trouble understanding what happens when you cook. He never saw anything made from scratch before he moved in with me.

Brian thought food wouldn't taste good when he saw it getting mixed together in ways he could not comprehend. Now he watches cooking shows on TV, but it's not the same as watching me. Their dishes always turn out perfect and on time, while in real life it's a series of tests and trials until it turns out great—and usually takes more time than implied by the media chef.

This reminded Jeanne of a decision she needed to make. She thought for a few minutes and then jotted down on paper:

Brian gets impatient as it is, so I think TV is off-limits from now on—except for the hottest shows. After all, he has to know what everyone is talking about at school if he is to fit in there.

Smiling with a sense of satisfaction, Jeanne returned to gathering ideas for a column about her mother, cooking, chefs, and whatever else popped up as she typed.

> *While watching a TV chef or 'chefess', you think about all the equipment needed to cook like they do—but what do you really need? Usually whatever you have is enough. Gadgets and tools designed to save time are available if you decide to cook on a regular basis, but don't fill your cupboards and empty your wallet buying them until you make the same dish three times and want to make it again.*

I don't even try making cheesecake anymore. Denise does such a great job and always has everything you need on hand. If she stuck to it long enough, she could easily claim a star for her door. Everyone praises her work excessively—and we willingly pay high prices for anything she decides to sell, but she doesn't see herself as a success baking cheesecakes. She wants to be a writer—not a baker. She doesn't respect her natural talent, assuming those who appreciate it aren't very bright. As for me, I think she needs to bake full-time to self-actualize and enjoy her best possible life.

'So do we!'

Enough talk about food, I'm getting hungry and haven't found the theme for this week's column—and deadline is tomorrow. What else can be said?

> *The other night at the school's open house, an event designed for the kids to introduce their parents or guardians to their teachers, I was surprised to see so many people skipping schoolwork to visit the gymnasium and cafeteria or walk around the campus admiring the landscaping. This worries me. Something is definitely wrong when the community is more interested in what the school looks like than the product produced—namely, a great education or whatever passes for it now. How do you get a community interested in their kids' education—as well as where and how they fit into our overall society?*

Jeanne diligently worked on this theme until the phone rang. Not having noticed the sun go down, or that Brian had come home from school, she suddenly realized it was almost suppertime. Thankful he was playing outside, dressed in his old clothes, working on his tree house that stands three feet off the ground. She had only a moment to wonder about when Brian had grown into such a competent person before picking up the phone.

After a brief greeting, Jeanne sat and listened to her friend talk non-stop many minutes before saying, "I want you to draw up a list of clothes for me to buy. I know I have too many things, so if you tell me what you think is absolutely necessary, I can more easily get rid of stuff cluttering my closet"....

"I was going to try on everything—but you're the greatest organizer of all time! Can you create a list of basics I need when traveling on book tours, PLUS things to wear around here and take on vacation? I'd like to hire you—instead of worrying about it"....

"I'll burn whatever isn't wanted"...

"Yes, I will. I'm into burning. We're not allowed to burn outside, so I'll put it in the fireplace"....

"Does that mean I'm harming the environment? I guess so. I better not burn any more, but if I put it in the trash, it fills up arable land. What to do?"....

"Not buy so much—what a concept!"...

"I have to go now and see what Brian is doing. He came in the house two minutes ago and is keeping busy, which can mean almost anything"....

"He's a good kid. I love to watch his hands. They're really flying now"...

"He doesn't move his arms much, but he's getting there. You have to build up"....

"I know. I was just watching him build a model of his school. He wants to always remember it, so decided to build a miniature. Imagine that!"....

"Well, he put the principal in the front office in a huge room with no books or papers around him and buried all the kids in paper. It's sort of funny"....

"Yeah, you have to admire that about men. They always make sure they're in the front office. In reality, women put them there and manage them—so who is at fault when things go wrong? Just one more thing, before I forget. I have this new look now"....

"Yes, I do! I went out a month ago and bought a new wardrobe from the old woman who runs the resale shop on Fifth Street. She set aside all the 60s stuff for me and I found a few things I wore back in the day. They look like it anyway, and I tried them on and felt like a kid again. Interesting experience—but expensive! That stuff costs more old than it did new. It's like dressing up for Halloween"....

"Yes, there is definitely a message in this...."

"Look over the new fashion books for me, but don't expect me to adopt anything too far out. I don't have the flair you have. I want to look as cool and crisp as possible, because I have to travel all over and meet all kinds of women in all sorts of get-ups. I can't be too over-dressed—and that's hard because only black women dress well anymore."

"I have to go now, but be sure to send pictures of the outfits and where you think I can find them around here. I'll have some made to help a few of the local women, but I don't want to spend more than $5,000 total. Have a ball and don't forget to send me a bill."

"You will? Cool!"

Chapter Seventeen
The Ruin of Man

ear Louise,
I would never tell others, but He is still on my mind. I can't seem to be by myself anymore. He is in my dreams, in my schemes, in my plots and plans, and in my house. I even see Him—a lot! What am I to do?

Would you call and then just walk out? I did, but I didn't. I was so sure he was dumping me that I dumped him—so now I don't know what I missed. I want to remain free, yet I want to marry Him and have a happy life. BUT can I ever be happy?

What if I marry Steve and he turns out to be a Hollywood tabloid nightmare? What if tabloids lie? What if stars have decent relationships until weasels start gossiping? We could all be victims of hack writers.

I have to go, but when I get back, I'll have a few new things to share with you. I feel the need for a massage and it really gets to me if I don't get one before my back crunches up.

I'm back. Sorry to leave you in the lurch, but letters are always better if you let them lie a while. Get it? You have to be an expert to attempt comedy, but you always know what I mean anyway.

As I was saying, I think about Him now and then—but mostly now, and it always gets me down. I feel like I have to say something to people when they ask about Him, yet I know nothing. Sometimes I take the easy way out and lie. I say he's doing fine, but haven't been in touch as much, etc., etc. I'm trying to wean their curiosity, but it isn't working! They want to know if it's over, and I just don't know if it is or not.

If you have anything to say about it, please write. I don't accept any more phone calls. I take time out to write my thoughts and instead of writing, you call and wipe it out. Gone in a flash! Afterwards, I can't remember a word you said.

I want to tell you about how Brian is handling all this, but I don't know. Do you? Maybe you can pick up on him? I've always relied on your intuition, because things you get on Brian are so on target it makes me wonder: Why are you able to know him so well? Is he more intuitive than me? BYW what is the real nature of Down syndrome?

When you write back—and you will write, I want you to talk about this thing I have going with Steve and why he is so important to me. I want you to talk about it like I don't have any vested interest in him—and if I should. I want you to advise me from the perspective of Guide and Counselor, not merely life-long friend. You have total freedom to say whatever you deem necessary. I want you to channel what you find to be worthy of the higher power's intrusion into your life for a purpose such as this, but I don't want you to call upon anyone to intercede just for me.

Is it possible for you to change me? Sometimes after listening to you, I feel I changed. Then I think: 'Why would I change if it wasn't the truth?' I know it's true, and truth is what rules me—most of the time.

I'll drop you a line when I discover what is going on at Brian's school. Right now they're still on the fence about all this testing.

I fear Brian is about to be exposed to the rude workings of the 'intellectual world' too soon. You can bet on it being a weird and worrisome world if kids have to listen to these women and men talk all day. However, I will not worry.

Love 'ya,
Jeanne

Dear Jeanne:

Hope you get this letter when you need it, but then you always do. That is life, but we seldom realize prayers are answered immediately. When it happens right away, we think it's a miracle, but our prayers are always answered quickly—unless the end result would harm you or others. I want to be sure you understand that what I am writing is not in my mind at the moment, but will be by the time it's down on paper.

I've ended my long disassociation with the printed word and am working on a computer twice a day—just like a boxer training for a big fight—except I don't skip rope. When you discover how easy it is to channel on a machine, you might decide to get one that is too much for you to handle in the hopes that it will increase your ability or whatever, but it only works as hard as you do. So you might as well admit you only need a very basic machine, like a pencil, to Write in Spirit—not a complete Mac system like I bought. LOL

I have never asked for any machine to help me in this work, but I do work hard to increase abilities and talents God has seen fit to give me, but the gifts of The Holy Spirit are what overwhelm me. I was reading your old columns, observing your growth, and suddenly it seemed you were channeling, too. I thought it started when Brian came to be, but it must have been before that or he would never have happened.

I want you to do spiritual work, because you have the talent to do more. You could write a book about it, but have too little time right now. When Brian is about 12 or 13, I think you should try to put aside time to let him really explore his early teens—maturate alone while you enjoy being an adult again.

Many parents forget to act adult. Some are too controlling for me to enjoy, but even they come to me seeking advice. I was sure you would never ask for such help. You have always been reluctant to understand why I chose such a wild and wonderful life. Knowing that this life is lived only one time, why not enjoy it and have fun? Know anyone working in a stuffy office with a bunch of greedy people having fun?

Originally I was sure you wanted Brian to succeed beyond his ability, but now I see it as my personal bias. I knew you would do whatever it took to make his life better, regardless of what anyone said, but I thought it too much to attempt at this time—Turns out you knew best. He is doing great!

This may surprise you, but I never studied developmental or child psychology. As a result, I'm better able to see the man inside the boy than so-called professionals who apply a label and feel no further need to probe to see what might be behind the façade of such an agreeable young man. These pseudo-scientists have said little over the past ten years about the syndrome, and it's a pity. So many are "growing out of it" that it makes you wonder why it was ever such a big deal. It was such a big deal that many parents in the past immediately placed children labeled with Down syndrome in homes and never visited them. What a tragedy! Thank God Brian, and others like him, were adopted by loving individuals who see them as capable human beings!

I was sure you knew a lot about his condition before you met him, but since you have only one child and think a single case history is anecdotal and can't be applied to others, you and many like you haven't spoken out about your work. Why has that denial of your wisdom been accepted? Professional jealousy, I suspect. We are all alike, and one is as much the same as the other if much of the physical and cultural make-up is the same. Downs is not a physical ailment, but has physical complications.

I have not drawn up any conclusive evidence on the matter at hand, but I see Brian as capable of dancing and singing and doing things few others can do, but he will settle for less than his best. He isn't driven like you, but he is better for being with you and observing how you prepare him for life out there. He won't be the typical teenager, but who is? You have to see him as he is, then see him off to college. He will go! It's in his mind now, which is okay. He will teach and do a better job than teachers he has now—which is no real tribute to his ability—but Brian will be greatly influenced by a teacher yet to be. He has not had many people interested in him, but having a mother like you compensates for the entire world being naive.

You will find others in his peer group no longer see him as an oddity. He is not odd! He is full of fun and happy, but won't always be that way if he doesn't stop interfering with others. He tries to take care of the boy next door, and tries to baby babies and others less fit or able than he is, but we can see that as an offshoot of having been helped much by you and others. In time he will learn otherwise.

When he is about 18, we need to check in and see what his future will be, but right now all we know is he will go further in school—but not very fast. You have to grow along with him, so it will take a bit longer for him than it otherwise might. You must be able to tutor him in math. He is going to need it. The days of mathematics by rote are gone and hand-held computers are allowed in class, so he doesn't get enough practice calculating. Fractions and percentages will be the hardest things he ever learns, but he will learn. You will also learn by teaching him much more math and less reading. He knows how to read, and you're forcing him to do too much. Let him do what he wants when it comes to reading.

We will never have to tell you to discipline him or do his work over for him. He will work well because he has a lot of self-esteem. Actually, he has more than any of his friends.

When you see how much effort it takes him to get to school as opposed to others he knows, can you see why he feels confident he can get home and back alone? He still needs to know you will be there most of the time, if his confidence is to remain intact and he learns how to warn others not to take advantage of his good nature.

Maybe Brian has many admirers now, but doesn't know yet who is for him, which is good preparation for life,. You can't see him in class, but I envisioned him there this morning. He is definitely not a lady's man, but ladies dislike that sort of man anyway. I know he will marry, but not too young. He likes to help those who have less than he does—even if it is technically not true, so he will find someone who is a bit less intelligent to marry.

At first when you talked about Him, I thought you wanted to know if you should marry Steve or not, now I think differently. You have become who He is. You are more concerned that what happens to him in public will happen to you—but maybe I'm way off target? I'm asking for guidance and counsel now so you can see why the world is tough on those who make it to the proverbial top—yet everyone wants to reach the top—including you and Brian.

When you discovered He was the one for you, you had just accomplished a major goal and had only begun to sample life's many offerings. His arrival ended your search. You saw him as someone who could take care of you and sweep away all your lonesome times—help you with Brian. Meanwhile you would remain free of work attributed to average wives, but it all returned with the next tide.

You have to decide now if you have enough love to share or you're merely experimenting and will move on without Steve. I was sure you were here to experience everything this life had to offer, but years ago you surprised me and settled for a job in a stationary world of static achievement and dubious pleasure called 'corporate America.' Since you no longer dream about that, I can see life as full of pleasure, with encounters of the strangest kinds—and you deserve it!

When He was young—not even thinking about love, he had a friend who was much like you, but a man to be. He was his buddy, and ever since he has searched everywhere for such a friend. You were the first woman he ever met who could fill that role. You can have him if you want—but don't expect a lot of amorous attention. Buddies don't behave that way. He is not the buddy type, you say? You have no idea how compatible you are and how many want you to end up together. Some are even fans of you both now—which says a lot!

When your hands are tied in knots and your heart is at war with your mind, let your heart take over. That is what I would do. That is my advice!

I have no intelligence or experience to draw upon when making that recommendation, but I have a lot of friends in High Places who can teach you about love and how it exists.

You have to do what you want to do now in order to say when you cross over to the next life that you lived as you wished and not as you were told. When you decide to let your old self die, you merely let go of it; but you want to reinvent that old self and imagine yourself as a suburban-kind of housewife doing things in the traditional middle-class way. Those days are over.

If you decide to marry, and you're the only one stopping you, you will do it differently than everyone else, because you can! You have always been a trailblazer—even in your youth. All you have to do is sit and stare at crowds of women lunging at him, trying to tear off his clothes, and intuitively ask them to settle down and behave. They will. How?

Your will is stronger than their combined desire consisting of single-minded thoughts. They wish to have a single piece of his entire being, so they act a part. You don't! You really love Him— and not because he is a movie star. Oh, yes, He will always support you—in every sense of the word.

We know He isn't going to be in movies forever, but will always be in the limelight. He is definitely going to arouse animosity among the wealthy, but is wealthy enough to outshine the worst of them. I know for sure he will support the wolves being moved back East to thin the deer herds, and he will help with water purification rights, but he will try particularly hard to get equal pay for women. You'll do your part, but he is the one women will listen to when you appear together. Men can get women to change, but no woman can get another woman to change if she isn't ready.

What you have to do now is sit tall and straight and beam a brilliant piece of news to Steve. Once he can see you clearly in his thoughts, he will never let the vision die. He does a lot of deep meditation, so all you have to do is continue doing whatever— and he will never stray. We mean it! Men are not all dogs in heat seeking mates. You have to blame women for a great deal of the *philandering that goes on. You are more woman than any woman I know, but if you ever find someone dumb enough to take you on—run them off the spread.*

You've heard nothing from me you don't already know, but you never know how much you know until someone tries to tell you what to do.

I love you and can tell the world (if you like) that you will marry, but it's your decision—always! We are only here for this life, then gone—if we do it right. I want to be around to see you walk down the aisle, but know it won't be easy. You have a very tough mind!

Love, Louise

I could write a book about Louise, but it would never describe her properly. What about her is most admirable? Who is she? What does she do? Why is she doing it? Who does she love? Where is she now? Why do I bother to guess?

Louise does crazy things to me. I keep telling myself she is the one who is crazy, but more and more I know she is the wisest of all my friends. We had a sorority of sorts growing up in the city. A few oddballs in the group dropped out along the way, but Louise was the one who kept us together longest. Once she tired of the group, it fell apart in a week. You see, we never really liked one another, she did.

What a life Louise has had! When you think of all the people she could have been, you would never have thought she would become a nun—then leave the convent. She was the least likely to be a nun, but the most brilliant. I can't imagine her leaving the convent forever.

I love Louise for her words and common sense, but it's her wisdom and love that stuns me most. I'm sure she writes one thing and does another, but then it's like me to wonder about her like I did when she left the convent. I still wonder if she will return, because Louise is still a nun. She just doesn't have any old habits.

When you see one of your own after a long absence, you think about it, then wonder why you aren't like you once were, but who is? I love this man, but would he always want to be with me? I love to be with him, but would it be as much fun if it was just the two of us all day and all night—every day and every night?

I want Brian to be full of ambition, but Louise says he does a lot just to please me. What if she is wrong? She may be. Louise is only human—or is she an angel?

Angels are all the rage now—or so they say. But angels are warriors and known to rage, so I don't write about them in my columns or personal correspondence, but see them. I can tell when they're around, but they never reveal why they're near or here.

Jeanne put her friend's letter in the middle drawer of her huge desk and said aloud to whoever might listen, "What do you think of angels?" It took less than a second for a disembodied voice to say:

'When you think of angels, you think of winged women and men. Why on Earth would angels be created that way?'

All thought stopped as her mind rewound, then slowly proceeded to think haphazardly:

Here we have two sexes, but would beings elsewhere have sex? I mean, be a particular gender. You have to be sure of your gender before you say someone else isn't the same as you, but half the human race isn't the same sex. When I was young, I thought being a boy was better and raised myself to think that way. I raised me and so did thee…I don't know why I use 'thee' so much, but it's in my blood.

What if you were predestined to be one sort of person but decided to be another? I think you would have to be crazy to actually alter your body, but some people do. Flat-chested men and women get silicone injections and pads inserted in order to be super-male or female, but who else cares?

I was born with a body that is okay by me, but at times when young I criticized it—but never now. I'm appreciative of this body. It's all I have, and if I play it right, I may be able to work and walk all my life, but not if it decides to go on strike.

Why would any body refuse to work? Unfair labor practices, unfit food and sleeping arrangements, lack of air and light—nothing beautiful to look at or listen to, any number of things that create a blight. I want to last, so I try to treat my mind and body equally well, but this body is the best gift of all. Unlike my mind, it seldom complains—unless I eat junk food and drink a lot of diet soda.

Smile lines crept from Jeanne's mouth to her eyes as she thought of Brian. He dreaded going to the dentist, but his teeth needed a good cleaning. Whenever his appointment drew near he became eerily unsteady—a real bear, but afterwards he was happier than usual. What a guy!

Chapter Eighteen

The Ruin of Women

*T*he phone's ringing, Mummy."

"I know, honey. I'll answer it—in the other room."

The nerve of telemarketing freaks! I'm sick of them calling whenever we sit down to eat dinner. I've been ready to boil over all day for whatever reason, so whoever this is will get the full blast of my anger. I'm not sorry or regretful for anything—forget it! If they can be rude and ignorant, so can I.

Thus, Jeanne barked into the phone. "Hello?"

"Is that you, Jeanne?"

Taken aback by the softness of a woman's voice, Jeanne immediately lowered her voice. "Why, yes. Is this Charlene?"

"No, it's Cheryl—next door, Justin's mother. I'm sorry to call you at dinnertime, but I wanted to let you know 'He' was on Entertainment Express tonight!"

Puzzled by her neighbor's sudden interest, Jeanne thought she sounded out of breath and excited. She wondered: What's the big deal? He's on TV every other night, but before she could speak, Cheryl said, "Did you see it?"

"No, Cheryl. I've weaned myself away from that stuff. It was starting to overtake my life."

"Oh, I understand. But you should have seen it! Or maybe you already know?"

Something's up. Her voice is different—concerned? No, she doesn't care about anyone but her son and soon-to-be-ex-husband. Classic case—she is feeling smug about something, no mistaking she believes she has something on me. Smiling so her words would not sound as bitter as she felt, Jeanne said, "Brian and I were out and I had to rush around to make dinner. We're eating now."

"Oh, I'm sorry, Jeanne. I thought you would be done by now. I just had to let you know before everyone starts descending on your house again."

What is she talking about? I could feel the gnawing aggravation that had been simmering below the surface all day was about to erupt, scalding Cheryl with a few choice words.

Hoping to control herself long enough to get off the phone and sit alone, Jeanne spoke very slowly. "I don't know what you're talking about, Cheryl. No one's called, and I haven't turned on the TV. What's up?" A disturbing vision rose into view as Jeanne struggled to stay cool.

Bristling with importance or whatever takes over mousy women when they get the scoop on something ugly, Cheryl shouted, "Steve's retiring—from the movies!"

"What?"

"Yes, 'HE' is retiring from the movies—and He's leaving them stranded in the middle of filming this last movie, *Red Skies over Wildflowers*—or Wild Fires, or whatever it is. He's refusing to do a nude love scene with that starlet, Jennifer McNeil! Everyone says it's because of YOU!"

Unable to conceal her shock, Jeanne managed to squeak, "Oh, no!"

Quickly regaining enough composure to keep most of her thoughts under control, she remained worried. How can they link me to this? We haven't talked in weeks. We haven't said a word to each other—except in bitter frustration. Maybe it was his anger I felt today—not my own? After all, I had no reason to be mad. In fact, I had every reason to be happy, having received a big check. Instead, I was churning with bitterness—ready to quit my job—and I don't have a boss!

When she said nothing, Cheryl filled in the gaps, hoping to get something to tell all who depended on her to dig deep into Jeanne's affairs. Jeanne could hear her talking, as through from a great distance.

"If you and Brian want to come over here to make it look like you're out of town—again, I'd be happy to have you both. It's always so exciting to hide you!"

Annoyed and no longer loathe to shield Cheryl from her implosion, Jeanne said, "I know you love to play at intrigue, Cheryl, but this is serious."

Ignoring the shift in Jeanne's mood, possibly unaware, Cheryl said, "I know it isn't. But you better get your stuff packed and come right over before the TV news crews arrive. All the local media will be out in no time to interview you."

Something snapped into place and Jeanne erased whatever she planned to say and reacted in true Spirit as she spoke to her meddlesome neighbor. "Okay, Cheryl, you're right. Brian can't be put through all this uproar again, but I'm in the mood to take on the world tonight. I'll get his things together and bring him right over. I'll tell him Justin wants him to sleep over—and he doesn't have to go to school tomorrow."

Excitedly Cheryl said, "Good! It won't matter if Justin stays home from kindergarten. That way we can all sit and watch the media circus together."

Without thinking Jeanne mumbled, "There may not be a media circus when I finish with them. Hopefully, by dawn only a few wounded hyenas will be left to howl."

"Oh, Jeanne, no one can chase the media away once they're on to something or on to someone like you."

"Well, they never saw me mad before. I'm not someone to mess with or take lightly when I'm angry."

Although Jeanne thought she sounded tough, Cheryl laughed merrily. "Oh, Jeanne, you couldn't insult a fly. You're always so polite and diplomatic! You're straight out of the South."

Shaking her head, Jeanne said, "Not this time. This time I'm mad! And when I get mad, I stay mad!"

Perhaps Cheryl realized the need to back away, hearing Jeanne was prepared to end the farce for good, because she spoke as though rocking a child to sleep. "I know that, but you can't beat back these people. They control the world with their cameras and their pens. If you make them mad, they'll get even with you—eventually."

Defiant and determined not to back down, Jeanne snapped at the hapless woman. "So what, I've had enough garbage written about me to sell a million books. Who can possibly believe such trash? If they report to *my* readers what I'm about to say, my family, friends and fans won't believe it and will lash out at them!"

"Oh, Jeanne, I can't wait to hear what you'll tell them. It will be so much fun!"

Disgusted, Jeanne said, "Never mind, Cheryl, I'll bring Brian over in a few minutes—with his nightclothes and a change for tomorrow. He should be done eating by now. So I'll bring enough dessert to share with you and Jason—I mean Justin."

"Oh, Jeanne, what is it?"

What is it? This woman is impossible. Is she talking about what I think she is talking about? Yes, she is! "It's raspberry marble cheesecake from Denise's Delight."

"Oh, Jeanne, to die for! Her stuff is absolutely the best!"

Shaking her head, Jeanne tried to keep the frost out of her voice as she said, "Good, I'm glad you like it. We'll be over in twenty minutes or less."

"See you then," chirped her neighbor as she slammed the receiver down.

Jeanne hung up grumbling and mumbling, "It really burns me up how the public supports tabloid trash. Think of all the people fueling that garbage, plus the trees slain to publish rot—and wasting the talent of people producing it. It's sickening, but I'm going to have my day—TODAY! Maybe I'll throw up on them."

My ADRENALINE is flowing so fast and furious I'm thinking in upper case and can't calm down. As soon as Brian is settled in, I'm going to set up an ambush. I'll let them stumble to the porch in the dark and set off the siren alarm, the flood lights, the loud speakers with the barking Dobermans, and call the police. That should create a big enough scene!

But what if no one comes? No, someone has to make a point or a buck on what's talked about on TV, and a big-name star dropping out of a huge project—who happens to be slightly acquainted with someone anywhere near your station is the ideal way to promote yourself to the national media. How can anyone resist?

Brian's safe, so I can get into my best looking casual outfit, as though that is how I lounge around the house. Put on my public makeup and comb out the curl from my hair—if that's possible. That way I'll look like I always look my best even when I have no company—or this is me at my worst, which is what they really want to see.

Jeanne's down mood shattered at the sound of tires slowly crunching over her front lawn. She leaped off the couch to stand beside the front window so she could check out what was happening outside. Mumbling unladylike thoughts, she watched the first van download several cameras and a lot of cable as an antennae rose from its roof.

"I knew it! The last time they ripped up the lawn in ten different places. I sent them the bill because I thought $3,250 for new sod and shrubs would sober up their eager-beaver editor enough that he wouldn't do it again, but maybe this is another station?"

Jeanne could not stop thinking, but stopped talking. There, I heard another door slam. They're all getting their antennas in place—and that little blond from Channel 2 will be fluffing her hair right about now. I don't intend to do anything until I see the whites of their eyes, but the suspense is getting to me.

"Hmmm, what if my plan backfires?" No, it won't. One of them should cross the motion detector just about now.

As if on cue, the entire front yard erupted into sound, light, and barked warnings. Bang! Barking dogs, lights, camera, action! Jeanne waited in anticipation of hearing police sirens descending rapidly into her cloistered neighborhood.

This is what I call a big deal! I'll have to throw a party for everyone for putting up with all this mess—and invite the police as well. The noise was terrific, but the police quickly had them in tow before anyone reached the front door.

"The police think I'm not at home."

Hiding behind the potted plants, Jeanne watched the vans in the caravan change direction and leave. She wanted to shout, but settled for saying, "I know someone is hiding in the shrubbery! I can't see him, but I can feel it! There is a man out there among the bushes by my neighbor's utility shed. Yes, there he is!"

I'll act like I'm Becky and report a prowler. After all, it's her yard and she'd call if she knew someone was lurking there. "All's fair in love—and especially war with the media and weirdoes who send hate mail, making threats on Brian's life and mine."

After placing the call to Community Services, Jeanne mused about what she had naively thought success and stardom would be like. A lot of great stuff immediately flooded her mind, so she opened her computer intent on writing off her frustration.

> *When you say you want to be rich and famous, do you imagine what it's really like? If you do, you immediately stop all attempts to be noticed. If you ever experienced what happens when suddenly plunged into the public spotlight, you run and hide.*
>
> *The rich can't afford to be idle—let alone those who work for every bone. The famous have to work hard to keep people away—spending huge sums on security, but it doesn't prevent outsiders from destroying their peace of mind. Telephoto lenses and high range microphones force you to travel in chauffeured armored cars to visit close friends or go out to dinner. Your vehicles are often monitored so they can follow you. The paparazzi have gone too far!*

When I watch interviews claiming to provide the inside scoop or real life of a celebrity, I want to shriek! In Today's World, people do and say almost anything about anyone in order to be invited on bizarre talk shows. I wonder about their sanity. So hungry for recognition and fame, they feed media's greed without realizing how it devastates careers and lives—like courting a rattlesnake, only rattlers warn you they have lethal fangs.

What if the public refused to listen to or read trash? It would go away eventually—to a certain degree. Could it be influenced by a boycott? We'd have to organize one to find out, but I bet the worst TV hosts of absurd free-for-alls dubbed entertainment would disappear overnight. Would their replacements be worse? Not likely!

In the past, sending the bill for the replacement of my sod to a low-level executive was more effective than suing corporate headquarters. It came out of his budget since he made the assignment and gave the order to overthrow my privacy.

If shooting blanks at the heads of giants doesn't scare them, maybe knocking out their knees will catch their attention. If we aim high enough, we might even hit them in the groin. I always thought media machines were male, but everyone says women in media are equally responsible when it comes to major network decisions.

That is the hardest thing to swallow. Women finally getting to the top and they don't change anything. There is no discernible difference in how things are run. The old boys may have been fired and retired, but from where I sit the new girls are no better.

I want to make an impact on this area, but the whole country is on my back now. I don't know what happened! I don't want to turn on TV and listen to their garbage, but I guess I need to find out what is happening to Steve—and by extension happening to me.

If it's all a publicity stunt, and it smells like one, no one will be back tomorrow. But if it turns out to be true, I won't have any peace for weeks. Someone has been driving by or checking out the house ever since Steve and I parted company— just in case he shows up unannounced.

There's something slimy about people who peep into windows or private lives, intending to tear you apart, but the people who buy it are just as bad. Gossip sells only if it sizzles. It doesn't have to be true. So who is worse, the prostitute or the John? Hint: Greed is the seed.

If I stop talking about me and you stop wishing to be someone else or stop hating others for living the life you wish you had, would the paparazzi disappear? I bet they would! Who would pay them to snoop? At times I wonder if we are all crazy?

If we weren't sick, we wouldn't read such trash. The dash to stores when trucks deliver the latest edition of whatever mudslinging rag would end. I would be out of a job, too, because I write about modern mores and culture. I'd have nothing to complain about! If women didn't want to know about others, I'd be poor again, but in time I'd get another job and a better life for me and Brian. That is Life!

You lose a job and openings appear—opportunities you never noticed when absorbed, exhausted, or seriously deranged about the importance of your career. It's simply a matter of concentration. Most people are so frightened by the prospect of losing steady income that they stay on jobs they hate—and will work for ANYONE!

I once had a job best described as grueling. How grueling? I can't remember. It was tough—and rotten at the core, so I don't wish to remember it. You forget bad jobs and such things once you get far enough away, but it takes time to escape such traps—so avoid entering them in the first place.

Work on my life is such that once it's done I intend to cash in my chips and leave quietly, but I do want to hang around long enough to see how Brian makes out. He's a good kid and destined to be a fine man, but the world isn't going to change direction. It will take a miracle to inspire others to reach higher.

I believe in miracles, so why am I without hope for this world? It's too big for my mind to comprehend, but if we cut it up into bite-size pieces, and many more people assume as much responsibility as I do, we could redo this depraved world in a very short time. Wonder why no one is trying to renew it now?

Maybe it's because we all hate to be told what to do to improve. Improvement usually means we have to change old habits and no one takes to that easily. I hate being told to do something new or unpleasant, but try not to show it, preferring instead to chase down sources and create more work.

Why can't we do something to improve this world right now? We're either scared or nervous about our image or place in the world—maybe too lazy. It can't be any more complex than that, but as a huge organism we can't diversify easily.

I have a need to be liked, too. We all have similar goals, but if everyone is to gain, we're going about it all wrong. I think I'll spend tomorrow in bed and reorganize the world. That should be enough to keep me busy for a day or two.

Climbing into bed, Jeanne reached over to her bedside cabinet and pulled out her now-shabby diary and prepared to write.

Her yawns subsided, but she appeared to be exhausted. With eyes closed, her fingers began to trace letters across a page.

I hate sleeping in late. If I want to do nothing, why tie myself down—bedclothes are too restrictive.

Think about teenagers who sleep all day and half the night. It's hard for most adults to remember those turbulent times, so we excuse teens as growing or developing while they dream. Did we really sleep as much as they do?

Children have lots of dreams! Lying in bed, they think about growing up and how to be different from everyone else or how to fit in or how to be admired.

Suddenly Jeanne awoke with a start and mumbled, "I need to get Brian, but better wait until Cheryl calls. If I call, she'll think there is a crisis." She immediately began writing again—only this time it was as though she were reading someone else's thoughts.

Never sit by the phone waiting for someone to call. It wracks your mind with something like pain. It makes your eyes water—you automatically feel sad. It doesn't make sense!

I don't know what's going on, because I haven't watched TV. If Steve is out of work, what is he going to do? I can't stand sitting around not knowing what is going on with Steve. I have to do something, but I can't write. My mind is too foggy and worried.

I must be confused. My journal entries are confusing, and I'm thinking about little things Brian likes to do, even though he isn't here. I wonder if the guy lurking in the neighborhood was nabbed last night?

Maybe I can run out and get the mail? No, that would extend my territory beyond the limits of my control—and that's when I get in trouble. Better keep the blinds closed and

stick to walking around inside. I can always do housework—
Nah. That is the worst thing I could do, but it may come to
that if I'm confined for a day.

From her vantage point behind the shades, hidden among
the houseplants, Jeanne could see a lot going on outside. "I can
see a car that doesn't belong in the neighborhood. Wonder if
I should call the police? Maybe it is the police? Maybe they're
using an unmarked car? Funny how I hate the very idea of
a police state, but when trouble comes, I want the police to
protect me and my estate."

Lapsing into deep thought, Jeanne decided to write out
what she was seeing and feeling, hoping to make a quantum
leap into time.

*You should be in my feet! They're itching to travel, but Brian is
stuck where he is. My toes are crunched up and don't want to talk.
They're hiding. You see, they think for me. If you let someone touch
your feet, you know your toes will rat on you. I had a foot massage
once and the guy too quickly knew everything about me!*

*My toes refuse to cooperate now. They're hiding. They're
crunching up as I try to sneak around. Why? Maybe they're trying
to tell me to wise up and live—forget about what might happen if
I go outside.*

"Why not go out? I'm free! This is my house, but I'm
letting them reduce me to being a prisoner, letting my son be
taken from me. This is absurd! I refuse to hide any longer. I
won't be afraid of the press or whoever! I can see now I was
afraid—and had no need to be. I've done nothing wrong! I'm
right to assert my rights and ignore what others say. Gossip
can't stand up to truth!"

What is the biggest lesson in all this? That I'm afraid of people—as in The Public!

If it wasn't written for me to read, I wouldn't believe it. There is no public, just a lot of people I haven't met yet. Singularly, I'm not afraid of any of them, but I fear them in a crowd. This has to end!

I'm going to live! I refuse to hide, stoop, cringe, or get angry about Him, me, our relationship—together or severed. They can hound me until they're tired of getting nothing they can publish. I will win this battle if it takes the rest of my life.

Fearing publicity and nosy people must be how agoraphobia begins. You begin to think your private life is interesting to others and start hiding from strangers. You retract more intensely with each exposure to crowds until you never want to leave your home.

Thinking about her response to unwanted publicity, Jeanne heard herself say, "I was going to leave, but talked myself out of it. I was going to live, but talked myself out of it. I was going to face them all and get it off my chest, but I talked myself out of it. I do entirely too much talking to myself. I better get out of here right now!"

Chapter Nineteen

End of the Trip

As the dawn peeked through the rear window, Jeanne lazed about in bed and thought—a lot. She often did this when deeply concerned about the future or what she had to do next. The sky brightened as she moved to the table near her bed and picked up a pen and the three sheets of stationery she had laid out to write to Louise.

In her estimation Louise was endowed with major psychic ability, as well as experience in psychiatric counseling. Because of that, Jeanne never thought about the absurdity of asking a nun of many lives for advice about marriage. She wrote seamlessly across the pages without bothering to edit her thoughts.

Dear Louise,

There are several different people within me today—and one is enough to drive me over the edge and never return. Do you know who You really is, if you don't know who <u>you</u> are?

As Jeanne read what effortlessly slipped off her pen onto the page, she mumbled. "I was sure I had it all—knew all I had to know to get ahead and stay there—until I fell madly in love with a stranger half the adult population of this world is infatuated with—based on his image. I'm not sure if I can handle being married to a man who populates the dreams of so many women and men." Her thoughts continued to drift until her pen started writing again:

You have to admire that the mind is all there is to those who believe in sanity, but falling in love presents a case for temporary insanity—which may cause a divorce from your true self. I want to be free, but I also want to be married. I go back and forth over it again and again, but can't find the answer. What to do? Where to move?

If I marry Him and he truly doesn't want to be married, we won't be married long before he finds another woman or three of them to run to now or again. If he wants to marry more than I do, will I want another man in time? Probably not—but why not?

Think of all the people who marry and cheat on their spouses a week or so later, and you have to wonder why they went into the relationship to begin with—but it's never that simple. Is it? You have to want to be married, and you have to want to give up your present life for another or it won't work in the future of either.

If you resent your spouse in any way, you'll find your love gone before you can say, 'Have a nice day.' You can't love someone who isn't rooting for you or doesn't care about what interests you, or can't sense when you're upset—yet everyone does it at least once. Why? I think I know, but I may be wrong.

Pausing, unable to put her concerns into words, Jeanne floated within her mind for a moment before letting her thoughts take shape. In a clear voice, she said, "If you touch and the other jumps, you feel the tension in your relationship. But if you love and the other notices little or doesn't care, does that mean you're through or incompatible? I think it might, but I could be wrong."

A disembodied voice rose from the direction of the foot of her bed and said, *"Although you never said it, you were wrong to think every man and woman should marry. You once assumed if a man or woman remained single it was because no one had asked them to marry—which is just as absurd. Almost every human being has at some point been on the verge of marriage or could have married. Most people are not in love with their mate when they marry—which you fail to grasp. You have to love and trust another much to give them all that is you."*

Was this her Higher Self talking or what?

"Many women rush to form a relationship with the first person they are attracted to—then wait for others to show up who may be more perfect—jumping out of one relationship into another without returning to heart center. They may believe the perfect solution is to leave one lover for another, but that destroys the home, any children, the extended family, and the ego of the one abandoned."

Wondering if she might hear more, Jeanne sat still before returning to where she was when Spirit descended. Within minutes her hand began to move of its own accord as she resumed writing to Louise.

You can see my dilemma, Louise. Can't you? I have no one to blame if I marry Steve and he turns out to be a womanizer of the highest order or turns to another woman shortly after we mate. That is why I have to know for sure if he is ready to marry for love and forsake all others. I have to be sure, but can you know someone you never knew. If I really tried, I could figure out what he intends, but would it be ethical?

After a few moments a different, softer voice spoke to Jeanne. *"You may discover you know how to change water into wine, and do whatever you wish, but such power is abused more* often than used as intended. For that reason, you are watched by the hour whenever you use power from within You. If you slip or use it unwisely, you could be burned to the bone. If this life is to be lived for 'You' alone—or not, let others know your intentions immediately upon meeting—before you get romantically involved—even though it is hard for people to take things seriously then."

Jeanne listened intently for more, before her hand resumed writing to Louise.

No one wants to talk. Everyone wants to watch others live or play, rather than talk to each other—all action and no thought.

Watching as her hand put aside the pen, Jeanne's mind deserted her.

I saw a television show last night about women like me who seek the perfect man. It was so depressing I had to turn it off or cry alone. We were portrayed as totally pathetic! Seen by most as being desperate for attention—exhibitionists! Eager to display what we should conceal in order to be noticed— thus proving we don't deserve good men, let alone someone like Him. It was the worst piece of crap I've watched in a long time, but everyone is talking about it today. Why?

Shaking her head, Jeanne noticed her hand writing as if totally disconnected from her thoughts.

Why marry anyone who can't see us as we are? We may not know who we are, or see who we could be if we waited until we got it together, but to buy into marriage in hopes of finding peace of mind, a home of your own, or the mythic 'happiness of security' is the worst kind of human bondage—and it's all self-imposed!

Why do you want me to marry Him, Louise? You don't? You sit and stare at men, then shake them off, never explaining why.

You never cut up anyone, but you're not impressed by men, either. Could you write out why you think I should marry while you remain single, solitary, and uninvolved?

When you figure it out, write and include hard evidence of my being better off married to Him and happier than I am living alone as I do now—And do not say Brian needs a father! That isn't a necessity—even I know that much.

'Til next time, girlfriend,
Jeanne

When Louise's reply arrived by mail, Jeanne was not disappointed—nor was she happy with its contents; therefore, it required several rereads. Her advice and thoughts were organized into columns with lines of conclusions filled in at the bottom of each page, like an accountant might compile. Jeanne thought for a long time before sending an e-mail to the convent Louise recently reentered:

Wow, Louise, you really know how to line up your facts, but I don't see how they apply to me—and not to thee.

I never saw you jump from one subject to another with such abandon, like when you wrote: Were you drinking? Just kidding! Your flow of ideas never stopped. The ink trailed from one word to another like someone else writing for you, but it had to be you. Right?

When you said this wasn't your life to be a wife, I thought you were referring to this time on Earth, but now I see that within this framework of life on Earth you have a life within another life, and in this particular life you're not meant to be a wife, which is hard to digest. In fact, I need an anti-acid tablet right about now. LOL

When you tell others how to live, you adopt a patient, pedantic attitude, then wait for them to get worked up before revealing what is really going on, but this time I refuse to follow through and get upset. I won't react as I usually do!

When you get this, please refer to my last letter—the one I sent through snail mail, and rephrase my questions. If you still feel the same about these conclusions after reading it, please rephrase your answers and provide more instances where it would benefit me to remain single and less instances of why I need to develop a love relationship now.

Almost instantly a reply from Louise appeared in her inbox, but it took some time before Jeanne responded.

Wow, Louise, you write fast! I barely got my note off before you replied. Can I have some extra time to analyze what you added? I need to sit and study your thoughts—let your words work on my heart.

Your last letter was difficult to read, while this one is almost too easy to understand—even though dense with facts.

You replied so quickly! How do you know so much? The size of your 'brief' indicates you created a huge thesis. I need to study it more closely, so I will wait 'til later to answer.

When Louise and I started this daily e-mail correspondence, we thought it would help us write a book together. Along the way it pushed our friendship beyond where it had been, but we couldn't write together as co-authors. Instead, we helped each other figure out why we are as we are—especially when we disagree.

I love to write and Louise is a wordsmith. She is terse and uses extenuating circumstances with a precision I can't match or mean to compete against, but it happens now and then. She is influencing my style by accepting my faults and teaching me patience, while I contribute joys of everyday living she has never explored.

What if you and your best friend's life story were the same? Could you be sure others understood you both? Once in a while Louise can and does adopt and adapt to my life, but usually she can't. For example, when Justin threw a rock and almost brained Brian, Louise got so mad at Justin she called and told me to hang a sign on him saying he was a dangerous animal.

I smile because she is unaware Brian is a terror at times, too. He is a tease. He does something one minute and the next pretends he can't comprehend it—but he does. In this instance Brian got frustrated and acted up after playing the dunce two days—unable to do anything right. He started running his mouth and Justin couldn't take it. He threw a rock at what he perceived to be the source of aggravation—Brian's mouth.

While throwing something you may not be fully aware of the consequences, but some are calculating and cold enough they force you to throw a punch or a dish and are never blamed for instigating it. The dupe doesn't see the strings being pulled behind the scene. Brian, Steve, Louise, and several others know how to manipulate me, but no one else is going to yank my strings again.

You can bet everyone's busy now! I threw the challenge out to the universe to see if anyone would call and start pulling me down or yanking me around and, sure enough, the phone rang as if on cue.

It took Jeanne a second to realize it was Brian whispering. He obviously did not expect to find her mind wide open and mouth clamped shut as she listened to his whine. Keeping her voice level, revealing nothing until she heard the entire story, Jeanne said, "Why can't you come home now?"

"I can't find my glove. I lost it. I was playing with Justin and it got in the dryer—but it's not there anymore."

Suspicious, Jeanne spoke slowly. "You were playing with the dryer?"

Quick to read her tone if not her words, Brian scrambled to cover any damage. "Well, we were playing by the dryer and Mrs. Friend must have picked it up and put it in the dryer."

"Why?"

"She didn't see it."

"You don't have your glove now, but you know she lost it?"

In over his head, Brian resorted to wheedling his way out of whatever. "I didn't do it."

Amused, but not admitting it, Jeanne repeated his plight in a flat, quiet tone: "You lost your glove, but someone else may know where it is—So ask."

"I did, but no one knows."

Without further ado, Jeanne said, "Post a note and come home immediately."

"Aw, Mummy, I was watching cartoons and we ate some stuff that isn't going good. I want to wait until I feel better."

Annoyed at this new ploy her boy was trying out on her, Jeanne spoke slowly and softly. "So now you're sick?"

"Yeah."

"You better come home right away before you throw up. I don't want Mrs. Friend having to clean up after you."

"Aw, Mummy, we were just getting to the good part, and I need my glove, and I don't see very well since the outside light burned up."

Jeanne's voice rose as she spoke with haste. "The light isn't the only thing burned up. You better get over here now!"

As she hung up the phone, she suddenly felt very alone. Her thoughts turned to the future and what she would do when Brian was no longer willing to listen to her—just because. When your son tries to abuse your patience, you may not believe he realizes what he is doing, but he knows.

You have to train people not to abuse you—especially your children. If you don't, you either let them run over you and knock you down or stand aside and let them brush against you as they leave. In the past, I was the one who let others leave—not now. Now I have too much invested in Brian, and Steve, to let go without a fight, but they must respect what I believe to be right, too.

It feels strange being unable to understand what Louise means, but she is a strange woman, too. She never married, but is sure she married once. Maybe when raised in a home where you take responsibility for everyone at an early age you think of it as being like marriage, which could turn anyone against such relationships for life. I've never heard Louise complain about her lost childhood. She wasn't that old when her mother remarried and no longer needed her to hold them together, but her step-father isn't like her. He treats Louise better than her mother ever did.

I want Brian to have a childhood he can draw wisdom from when he is old and gray and talking to kids—use it as an example. He's drawn to the arts now, but I know he will be a teacher. I can see it clearly, but he won't become one right away and may not teach in the usual way.

When you train people, you explain various applications of what you are trying to get across. If you could eliminate all who learn differently, you could use just one theory or method—but it better be good!

What if Justin is Brian's student? I think he may be! Justin is younger and not as socially adept as Brian—even though some around here consistently describe Brian as 'Mongoloid'. Justin isn't talkative, probably because Cheryl doesn't have time for him when she is busy talking on the phone trying to ease her pangs of loneliness and discontent. I sometimes wonder about Cheryl, but many women talk a lot to people who won't be around long, meanwhile ignoring their kids who are on their tab forever and a day.

Someone said when Cheryl was young she was so beautiful her family gave her whatever she wanted. She wanted very little then and wasn't hard to please, but she married a man who was very demanding—whenever he was home, so she began more and more demanding, too. She became so demanding that few could stand her more than an hour before remembering they had errands to run. I think she enjoyed being difficult, but also think it was due to a bad marriage. Cheryl needed help and direction then, but since her husband left, she does everything without complaint.

Sometimes Cheryl looks beautiful, but the bloom of youth is gone. She gets her hair cut every three weeks in the same style she wore ten years ago and does a few unnecessary tricks whenever she remembers to smile. But on those rare occasions when she drops her guard and enjoys life, Cheryl is radiant!

Too bad she is so seldom happy. Which ruined her: the failed marriage or lack of faith? Why depress yourself?

As if awakening from a dream, Jeanne snapped her fingers and looked at the clock. Realizing five minutes had passed and there was no sign or sound to indicate Brian was on his way home—an annoying buzz erupted in the back of her brain. She felt strange. Her first thought was to go over and talk to Cheryl, but Brian would listen. To talk as adults, she would have to call rather than visit, thus giving up intimacy to achieve privacy.

Trying to control her waning patience, Jeanne sat down at the kitchen table and thought of nothing for a minute or two. Even with such a brief meditation, she felt release from whatever loomed over her. Sitting still, her mind accepted what it gathered from visions and flashes of intuition. When the last flash disappeared, she picked up a pen and wrote on an envelope what she had seen or heard.

When Justin is old and gray, he will be an insurance executive. How do I know? He isn't very inventive—extremely conservative. Even as a child, he never says what isn't in his own best interests. He never smiles—like his mother and father. Insurance executives are not responsive to moods and trends, but rally when money enters the picture.

As Jeanne scratched out Justin's name and inserted the name of another boy, she heard, *"I want you to do something for me."*

Without thought, she responded. "But I have to email Louise."

The voice persisted in the same tone as Jeanne used when Brian was determined not to listen.

"Would you do this for us? Make a list of all the people you hate and all the people you love. Thanks."

It took Jeanne less than a minute to get to her office and start another email to Louise.

Dear Louise:

You must know by now that I'm not unduly influenced by your poor attempts to persuade me to do what you would never do, but I am going to get married. I just don't know to whom or when.

Are you surprised? You should be. You don't care if I marry Him or someone else as long as I end up in a loving, lasting relationship which will teach me to give and take better than living alone with Brian. I'm off to find a relationship that won't harm my ego or spirit.

You want me to expect a miracle now, but don't offer useful suggestions. You will have to do a lot better if you want to keep me talking. I read your latest memo and find it generic—It generalizes too much. Doesn't go directly to the point—and your notations are deplorably deplete of humor.

Which reminds me, when will I do all these things you believe must be done a.s.a.p.? For example: You say women must not expect much from men—but not to accept little. What does that mean?

You say women are not loved initially, but if men really like them, they will love them eventually. What are you saying?

Here's another: "If you can get him to do just one thing different from the way he always did it, he will be a great husband." That is about as inane or insane as anything you've counseled so far, but you seem so sure of it. Why?

You never said what you wanted out of your one and only relationship, but said your only love wasn't satisfactory and caused you to express so much anger and frustration that you don't want to repeat it. When did all this happen? Are you secretly involved with someone now—or just thinking? If so, I bet it's the guy who repairs whatever is always malfunctioning on your computer!

You also told me: "You have to decide what you want out of life, and then go after it!"

Do you really have to go after it? I believe you never went after anything until I began working with you this way. Now you work, work, work, but no one else is aware of it.

You're sharp—and proud of it, but you're stupid to think I can't see through you and what you're up to now. LOL (Just seeing if you're still with me.)

When you get to the part describing your life's work—where it gets really tough and you can't figure out how to end it, do you stop, go back and reread—or pray? I do all three, but prayer helps and the others seldom do.

Jeanne sat entranced. Nothing moved, not even her hands until an Instant Message flash across the screen. It was from Louise. Instead of laughing, Jeanne screamed.

When I can see the light of day, I know the night is over, but the darkness lingers if I wait to see it end. Do you watch light more and more, yet continue to linger in the shadows? Please walk outside and jump high and yell: "I'm a free woman and I'm in love!"

Once you do that, watch to see if someone new comes into your life or reappears. I bet three would-be lovers arrive in a very short time, but you may refuse to accept one or all of them, because you are so stubborn.

Jeanne's fingers danced across the keyboard as she flashed a message back to Louise.

How about you marrying first and I'll follow you down the aisle? You think if I get married we'll continue writing daily—and I'll tell you all about marriage so you don't have to do it yourself. That could only happen on TV. You have to live to be alive! You can't watch someone else love and lose or whatever. You have to do it yourself! Shirk work and you lose. Believe me!

Jeanne waited a few minutes before she resumed typing.

When you came back from Italy I was shocked you were disappointed because you never got pinched, but now I realize you're a romantic at heart. You wanted some mad Italian Romeo to caress your butt! Why not walk like you want it? I don't invite attention, but get it anyway. Most men need to be encouraged, but some arrogant pigs take what isn't offered. I won't mention it again, but I'm encouraging you to swing a bit now and then. LOL

Just as her message entered the internet stream of consciousness, a response arrived from Louise.

When you work and work and never go out at night or even during the day, do you see your work as a life in itself? I did once! Now I see it as me—but I'm not exactly my work. I live to work, and work hard, but it never gets done. I always have something left over to do the next day, even though I don't want to leave today's work for tomorrow. Do you read me?

Jeanne hurriedly replied:

I'm still fuming over your earlier remarks, so this isn't as sweet as usual, but you'll find once this whole mess is straightened out that I will be married—but it may not be to Him. Stay tuned for the next episode....

Suddenly realizing Brian still had not returned, Jeanne stood and pushed her chair under the desk with undue force. What was she to do with Brian and his stories? Louise had no idea how inventive he could be.

I want Brian to learn from being around others, but it appears they learn more from him. He isn't above teaching how to avoid issues and use disability or whatever to gain greater patience, understanding, and love from others—meanwhile he doesn't grow more virtuous.

Brian had more spunk when younger, but now he is gaining stature with others. Maybe it's a trade-off that will pay big dividends someday. I hope so, but when he disappears into the lives of his friends, I watch him go with tears in my eyes more often than not.

An image accompanied by a nagging whine entered Jeanne's mind. She heard old, old tapes playing at high speed: *You have to watch men…Men are lazy and shiftless!* Who said that? My aunt—the one who never married. Why?

Her father's voice joined the chorus. *"You have to work hard and earn a decent living."* He wasn't referring to women. Wonder why?

Her old high school Civics teacher crooned, *"You have to take a lot of guff from men if you want one."* She must have been taking lots of guff—and not just from her then-husband.

Jeanne's reverie ceased when the phone rang. Cheryl chirped a few words before Jeanne recognized her voice. Immediately, she wondered if her thoughts had projected into her neighbor's mind.

Nodding, she smiled as Cheryl said, "When we get together, would you list the reasons you haven't married. I've forgotten them. I want to be sure they're still valid—not just a ruse to talk only about you."

Shaking her head, Jeanne smiled at her neighbor's lack of comprehension and consideration before saying, "What if I drop over for tea tomorrow morning? Could you stand company?…I'll be over about nine or so. I have a new source of unwanted calories—raspberry scones. They're sooo scrumptious that if you can't have tea with me, I'll eat them all myself…Take care and don't be upset."

When writing to Louise, I never forget how very particular she is about words—never resorts to exaggerations when one good word sums it up, but I live, love, and express everything in larger terms in order to survive in the 'reel' world. When writing in my journal, it helps to let the pen flow, but with Cheryl you never know what she might remember, so I carefully monitor the flow to her.

Back at her computer, Jeanne moved the mouse to chase away her screen saver and discovered another message from Louise.

What you do now isn't important, but what you do determines who you are. Is that how you see it?

Smiling, Jeanne wrote: *What to do?*

Almost immediately Louise's ideas came into view.

Sit at the computer and let your mind run wild. I'll let mine fly. Maybe we can combine our work, figure out a plan, or do something together or in tandem, but it has to be good or why collaborate?

I think marriage is like that, but not good to imagine. You never come close to seeing what you don't know. We're surprised, shocked, disappointed, or harried when we think something should go one way and it turns out different, so don't be upset if my plan backfires. Let's give it a try! I'll write my way, and you write as always.

Jeanne wrote back: *We can help the world, but only if the world is ready to accept help—and accept us.*

Chapter Twenty

What Work?

No longer hidden behind dark clouds, the sun shed beams of brilliant hues, mostly red and orange. Ignoring the light, Jeanne huddled over her computer. Worry lines etched across her brow, tears dribbling down her cheeks, erasing any pretense of having slept well and now awake in a state of grace. Rapidly tapping out her views and dreams to someone unseen, her mood began to lift.

What if I tell everyone I'm married? If you asked me and I said, 'I'm married,' would it be true? Why not? If you say something, it doesn't mean it's true. Doing something doesn't make it true, either.

What if you and I, and a few others, decided to live together in a fine, old house and told everyone we had a great life, would it necessarily be true? No, but if we all lived in harmony and had a great life, most would be unaware of us and few would want to hear about it. You have to know you and your friends before you can open up about who you are as a group, but it can be done.

I live in a fine, old-fashioned house. It's very pretty, but isn't warm and gentle the way a house filled with people would be. There should be scars and dents in the kitchen table as reminders of those who made them, but there are none. I crave a home filled with love—and people devoted to each other. But how to make it happen now?

If I marry Steve, there will be two boys—HE and Brian, plus a girl from his past who is now unloved by her mother—perhaps never was, and a dog and three cats. Does that make us a family? I doubt it.

Some of us aren't that attached to another. We might float around—no central theme uniting us in a common cause—unless we work together doing something for others, or perhaps pursuing a craft or project that takes years to complete—possibly have a pay-off when done.

That is how most utopian villages worked in the past—and they did work! I want to work at something worthwhile, but have so much to do now that I doubt I can find time to do something new with others, too.

Crouching, Jeanne scanned what her cyber friend wrote in response. Smiling, she sat down again and began to write.

What a day! What a year! What a life!

I left friends in one city to rejoin enemies in my hometown and became so overwhelmed by the negativity of this experiment that I turned to the positive joys of work, but my job isn't as easy as it used to be.

I have to do something! I can't sit and do little but thinking and stewing all day over what may or may not happen. If I sit and stare at whatever, it grows, but if I do something about it, it shrinks. So I can't let this image of being married get so big that it frightens me—like it is now.

When I'm with you and Friends on The E, I think of all the great times we've had together. It makes me want to write and write and write and never see anyone in person again. Can you believe I'm saying that—again?

What if we turn into computer hackers or yakkers who never see anyone in 'real life' continually dwelling in a little 'reel world'? Would it be any different from this? So many don't talk much to friends anymore—except occasionally by phone.

When I worked in corporate, two men phoned me almost constantly. We had such lively times talking, but when I met the 'funniest man alive'—or so I thought him to be—he stood mutely behind his boss staring at me, but never spoke!

The other guy was such a sucker for hardline women that when I met him, I couldn't keep up the pretense. What was fun on the phone was stupid in person! Maybe he wasn't himself, either. It was more like a four-party conversation going on since both of us were alter-egos of our real selves.

I had to be myself, but they weren't interested in that me. They preferred the pseudo-personality I developed while talking to them on the phone. Hope I'm making myself clear....

Now sitting in full sunlight, yawning at the screen which in turn gaped at her, Jeanne poked at the keyboard.

What if you turn off the lights and look into the dark and never see yourself? That can happen. You can look and never see anything but your skin, etc., or you can see your mind working as well as Spirit moving.

Jeanne paused to read an Instant Message flashing on the screen. Beaming, her fingers flew over the keys fitting words together with lightening speed.

I love to watch my eyes, too, but they say nothing about me—really. I see them, but they don't see me. What if you write a line, then I write a line, going back and forth like in a chat room? We could write a book instead of Instant Messaging ourselves to death. Okay?

OKAY!

Great! With you writing in all caps and me writing in italics, it should be easy to follow. In the future, if we want to re-read or publish, voila! Just have to remember who started it—or changed sides as we do when arguing. I'll start...

What are you—really?

REALLY? YOU MUST KNOW BY NOW A FILM IS NOT A MOVIE OF LIFE AND DEATH, BUT A PIECE OF CELLULOID ENHANCED AND PLACED IN A MACHINE, PROJECTED TO ENTERTAIN AND AMUSE, BUT TOO OFTEN FRIGHTENS THE AUDIENCE WHILE CHANGING THEIR HEADS FOREVER.

Enough already! Get back to you. Who are you?

IF I HAD KNOWN YOU WOULD BE SO CRABBY I WOULD NEVER HAVE FALLEN IN LOVE WITH YOU. THAT WAS REALLY A SHOCK, YOU KNOW, AND WOULD HAVE NEVER HAPPENED TO THE OLD ME. I'M A NEW MAN—AS I KEEP TELLING YOU—BUT YOU HAVE TO KNOW THAT BY NOW. YOU READ ME SO EASILY. I'M LIKE AN OPEN BOOK.

Quit running me around and get to the point.

I AM. I'M JUST NOT SURE YOU ACCEPT THE FACT THAT I AM THE SAME AS YOU ARE.

Now you're making sense. I believe you—maybe.

WOW! I NEVER MADE A POINT SO EASILY—AND I HAD A FULL CAST BEHIND ME—AND A MILLION-DOLLAR-A-SCRIPT WRITER MAKING UP THE WORDS. YOU ARE REALLY SOMETHING!

Meanwhile, back at the ranch—what is it you're hiding from me?

ME? HIDE SOMETHING FROM YOU? YOU'RE THE ONE WHO IS NEVER SEEN AND NO ONE KNOWS ANYTHING ABOUT. MY LIFE IS REPORTED FROM ONE END OF THE WORLD TO THE NEXT—DAILY! YOU ARE NEVER SEEN OR HEARD FROM EXCEPT IN PRINT, USUALLY RELATED TO MY LATEST 'AFFAIR.'

The print reveals the soul, but not the mind—That should be the other way around. Actors don't reveal who they really are, and I want to know the basics about you—now!

LIKE WHAT?

Tell me why you select roles you will spend your life working on, or are they selected by your agent? Who tells you what to do and what is best for your career? I want to know why you don't do more for the world. You could. You have the ability to read lines, add expressions that reinforce good and downplay evil—instead of reading lines as if evil is about to take over the world.

EVIL IS THE WORLD! I'M NOT TRYING TO CHANGE THE WORLD. I ACT, AND I LET OTHERS ACT. WE DO WHAT WE ARE PAID TO DO, BUT I THINK WE ALL BELIEVE EACH MOVIE WE INVEST IN IS GOING TO DO SOMETHING FINE AND GOOD FOR THE WORLD. REALLY! WE WOULD NOT MAKE MOVIES AND TV SHOWS WE THOUGHT WOULD HARM YOU OR CAUSE THE WORLD TO CRACK. IF WE DO THAT, IT IS DONE UNWITTINGLY. IT'S WRITERS WHO ARE OUT TO CHANGE THE WORLD!!!

I think you may be right, but producers and directors are responsible for the final product. They are the ones who cave in and deliver shoddy goods for quick profit. I did one little stint on a pilot for a TV thriller—never again! I couldn't stand constantly rewriting to suit everyone who thought they had a better line or wanted to drop a star or add another character. It was bedlam! Most of the cast lost any sense of what was worthwhile by the time it was done. I hated it because it wasn't writing!

NOW YOU KNOW WHY NO ONE WANTS TO WRITE FOR US. ACTORS WRITE ALL THE TIME AND ASK DIRECTORS TO CHANGE A FEW LINES OR MAKE CHANGES—SNEAKING IN AS MUCH AS WE CAN TO INFLUENCE CHARACTER PORTRAYAL. IF THE INITIAL PLOT'S NOT WORKING, WE GET NERVOUS AND FRUSTRATED, THEN GET IT WRONG AND CALL FOR NEW LINES. LIFE IS LIKE THAT, TOO.

What if you said: "I'm a man and I love acting?"

THAT WOULD SAY NOTHING. WHY STATE THE OBVIOUS? I'M OBVIOUSLY MALE AND HAVE CERTAIN CHARACTERISTICS NOT LIKELY TO BE FOUND IN FEMALES, AND I HAVE A GOOD MEMORY AND ABILITY TO EMPATHIZE (IS THAT A WORD??) WITH FEMALES—EVEN PLAYED ONE— BUT ONLY ONCE! I AM NOT THE IDEAL MALE, NOR WILL I EVER BE THE 'QUINTESSENTIAL MALE' WHO SEEMS TO ALWAYS BE RIGHT. I HAVE PLAYED SUCH MEN, BUT THEY DON'T EXIST IN REAL LIFE.

I'M NOT ACTING WHEN ON SCREEN! I'M EITHER WORKING OR PLAYING—BUT NEVER ACTING. ACTING IMPLIES YOU HAVE NOTHING AND ARE PUTTING OUT WHAT YOU THINK OTHERS WANT TO SEE. I NEVER DO THAT! IT INSULTS THE

AUDIENCE. HOW CAN YOU RISE TO STARDOM BY ACTING?

Well, I think you act pretty good, but now you're saying it isn't acting, that it's actually you! That definitely changes how I think about you.

REALLY?? BUT YOU KNOW ME! YOU ALWAYS TALK TO MY INNER SELF, NEVER WASTE TIME WITH SILLY PRATTLE ABOUT APPEARANCE, ULTERIOR MOTIVES, HIDDEN ATTRIBUTES, ETC, SO I THOUGHT YOU SAW THE REAL ME.

Maybe I do, but don't know it—but doubt that very much.

HUH?

I feel like I know more about you now than I knew when I saw and talked to you face-to-face almost every day, but that has to be ridiculous.

WHY? YOU HAVE TO ADVANCE TO THE NEXT MOVIE OR SCENE AND SEE WHAT IT WILL BE BEFORE YOU DECIDE HOW TO HANDLE IT. IF YOU DON'T LOOK AHEAD, JUST SIT STARING AT WHATEVER, YOU MELT INTO A LUMP OF LARD.

I USED TO JUMP INTO PARTS AND ONLY LATER FIGURE OUT IF THEY WERE GOOD FOR ME OR NOT. AS I AGE, I THINK AND PLAN MORE. I MEDITATE MORE ABOUT A ROLE. I DREAM OF LIFE AS IT WILL BE ONCE IT'S OVER—BEFORE I COMMIT TO DOING IT OR NOT. EVERY ROLE AFFECTED ME DEEPLY, BUT MEETING YOU CHANGED ME MOST!

There is something about you that really gets me! For example, I thought you were superficial. A man who had it made and knew it— then you wrote deep, meaningful stuff—hate that word—so I can't stop admiring you now—AND I don't normally admire pretty men.

I GENERALLY DON'T CARE MUCH FOR BEAUTIFUL WOMEN, BUT YOU'RE THE EXCEPTION TO THAT RULE!

Enough already, we're not talking about me. Do you follow?

I KNOW WHAT YOU MEAN, BUT MOST PEOPLE DON'T SEE IT THAT WAY. THE PUBLIC IS INTERESTED PRIMARILY IN YOUR LOOKS AND WEIRDLY ENOUGH, YOUR AGE, THEN THEY ARE IN MY SEEMING ABILITY TO SOLVE THE WORLD'S PROBLEMS IN TWO HOURS. THEY ARE WHAT ACTORS CREATE AND EXPECT. WE SEEK THEM OUT AT NO COST TO OURSELVES, MAKING THEM PAY TO SEE US.

What if we stopped computer yakking and met again? Would you continue being this interesting?

NO, I WOULD ADMIRE YOU AND SAY WHATEVER TO GET YOU TO DO THINGS FOR ME. I WOULDN'T SAY MUCH OF DEPTH, BECAUSE WE WOULD COMMUNICATE WHAT WE WANT WITHOUT WORDS. I KNOW YOU THINK IT SHALLOW, BUT THINKING AND TALKING ARE TWO THINGS NO ONE DOES WELL AT THE SAME TIME. WHEN I'M WITH YOU, I CAN'T DO MUCH DREAMING—BECAUSE YOU ASK A LOT OF QUESTIONS AND I HAVE TO CONSTANTLY THINK UP ANSWERS.

We could sit in silence and simply look into each other's eyes.

HA! YOU WOULD HAVE TO TALK.

What? You do most of the talking. Men always say women talk too much, because they're peeved that they're not talking instead.

I've been told all my life that I talk too much—never by women—always by men. Why? Because men love to talk and talk and talk, but watch when a woman chimes in. Men don't like to talk about others, they prefer to spar off and argue about stuff they can never change—and women want to change others. When a woman and man talk, usually she believes she has a problem, and he's sure he doesn't. You can laugh, but it's true.

YOU ARE SO FUNNY! I NEVER SEE THINGS THE SAME AFTER TALKING WITH YOU—OR IS IT THAT I TALK TO YOU?

We usually talk at one another, but writing like this we let the other complete a thought. It's teaching us to share—maybe that's a good thing.

SHARING IS EASY, BUT BLAMING OTHERS IS WHY WE KEEP THEM AROUND. I NEVER DO ANYTHING WRONG BECAUSE I HAVE A WHOLE CAST TO TAKE THE BLAME, BUT IF WE GET MARRIED AND THERE ARE NO KIDS AROUND, WHO WILL WE BLAME FOR OUR PROBLEMS?

You can handle it—you have broad, broad shoulders. However, I might not be able to accept the blame for what you do. I do my own thing, and usually it doesn't involve blaming others, but I do hate to be told by idlers that I did something wrong. You think you're blaming someone else, but you can't get away with it, because you know the truth.

I'M GETTING FRUSTRATED WITH ALL THIS BACK AND FORTH STUFF.

Let me write a while, then you write—about anything—like a short essay. It won't be as tiring as switching back and forth.

IT'S YOUR GAME. YOU WROTE THE RULES, BUT I
HAVE A BETTER ONE TO PLAY WHEN WE'RE DONE.
Just like a man!
WHEN DO WE BEGIN THIS ESSAY THING?
*Right now...I'll get back to you with mine in a few minutes.
Meanwhile you write your stuff.*

*Women often say sexist things like 'just like a man!' even though
we never see ourselves as sexist. I guess that makes me sexist, too.
My friends talk all day about men doing—whatever, and then
they do the same. Sexism and its twin—racism—are motivated
by jealousy or envy. That kind of mind assumes it can take what
others create by discrediting or degrading them.*

*I hate myself when jealousy erupts! I discovered that if I assume
'my idol' is not as good as I am at a lot of things I do well, it helps
erase jealousy. Is this a healthy mind? I think so, because it keeps
me healthy and reasonably free of jealousy and envy now.*

*What if one country is so jealous of another it overlooks all
the great and wonderful things it does, instead describing the
other country as illogical, demonic, or worthless? My take is they
could not be true allies. Isn't that the same with individuals? Am I
making any sense? Probably not, so maybe a change of venue will
serve me better....*

*What if you and I travel together? Would you want to spend all
your time in tents and caverns and places where you "rough it" or
always prefer everything be First Class? I love to rough it, if it is not too
rough, but I hate it if First Class turns out to be second or third class.*

*Another pet peeve of mine is: When you advertise something is
rustic or needs tender loving care, everyone knows it's an inferior
product and you don't intend to improve it. But if you advertise you
are great and wonderful, very careful, and do the best you can with*

what you have, everyone expects you to have done it already—even though they never do it. Why advertise anyway?

Jeanne hesitated to send her 'essay' to Steve, but in the end sent it out as is and waited for his reply. She was surprised to see his reply hit her inbox within a few minutes.

YOU SENT QUITE A CONGLOMERATION FOR ME TO THINK ABOUT! I WAS BACK AND FORTH AND AROUND AND OUT OF MY MIND WHILE YOU WERE WRITING. NOW I CAN'T REMEMBER WHAT I THOUGHT.

FIRST, I DON'T LIKE TO ROUGH IT! I HATE TO LIVE IN LESSER ACCOMMODATIONS THAN MY HOMES, NONE OF WHICH ARE LUXURIOUS—BUT ALL ARE COMFORTABLE.

SECOND, I DON'T LIKE PEOPLE WHO SAY ONE THING AND DO SOMETHING ENTIRELY DIFFERENT, BUT IT IS VERY HUMAN, AND SINCE HUMANS ARE ALL WE ARE—AS FAR AS I KNOW— GIVE ME A BREAK ON THIS ONE.

Jeanne could not wait to read more and quickly dashed off a note:

Well, you apparently don't know much about our planet or you could easily see several hundred different kinds of humans living here, and several different kinds of species within that range who are not of Earth, but it necessitates you see them easily. Whereas I find it hard to imagine we are the only beings on Earth, you find it hard to believe we are not. We are definitely ill-matched if not ill-suited to one another, or so it seems to me, if we base our relationship on our philosophies.

BUT WE AREN'T! YOU HAVE ADDED A NEW VISTA TO MY LIFE. I NEVER SERIOUSLY TALKED ABOUT

LIFE ON EARTH BEFORE, AND YOU APPARENTLY HAVE, SO YOU HAVE ME AT A DISADVANTAGE. JUST BECAUSE I NEVER BOTHERED TO CONCERN MYSELF WITH IT BEFORE, DOESN'T MEAN I CAN'T SEE WHAT YOU MEAN.

YOU SAY THINGS TO GET ME TO THINK, WHICH I LIKE. IN OTHER WORDS, YOU ARE VERY GOOD FOR ME—AND GIVEN SOME ADVANCE NOTICE ABOUT WHAT YOU WANT TO WORK ON IN LIFE, I THINK IT WILL WORK OUT WELL FOR US. AFTER ALL, A RICH, POWERFUL WOMAN WHO HAS IT ALL HAS TO HAVE AT LEAST ONE PET PROJECT TO PERFECT—AND IT MAY AS WELL BE ME!

You are too gracious. I was being a bore—and a conceited one at that! You are right—we do complement each other. I see things on a different level than you now, but you're way beyond me in other ways. I couldn't soar with you as I do without all this wind under my wings at liftoff. Obviously, you can't thrust much if you have no energy, just joking, but we do develop such electricity using all this wind to increase our energy—to synergize and produce a new kind of being. But why would we want to do that?

I WANT TO BE THE MAN I AM WHEN I AM WITH YOU—ALWAYS.

And I want to be the woman I am when I am with you.

THEN LET'S GET MARRIED!

Don't you see it yet? If we get married, it will mess up everything between us. I'd become the stereotypical woman afraid of losing her handsome, movie-star husband, and you would become the man who eventually loses interest in what he has at home, because I am always on your case about something or other—you know what I mean. I watch so many marry, totally forgetting themselves and what they came to do. In fact, I have friends who actually committed a kind of suicide when they married—not physically but spiritually.

NOW YOU'RE TALKING ABOUT OTHER PEOPLE AGAIN! WE ARE NOT LIKE ANY OTHER PEOPLE WE HAVE EVER KNOWN AND NEVER WILL BE EVEN REMOTELY CLOSE TO BEING LIKE ANYONE ELSE, SO WHY COMPARE?

Studying others can show you how it will probably turn out—if you're normal.

NOT REALLY! I ACT ALL DAY, AS YOU SAY, SHOWING PEOPLE WHAT TO DO IN CRITICAL TIMES WE MAY SHARE, BUT I'M NOT 'THERE FOR THEM', DOING WHAT HAS TO BE DONE WHENEVER SOMETHING DOES COME UP. I'M NEVER AVAILABLE FOR THEM TO DRAW FROM ME WHAT THEY NEED. YOU DO A BETTER JOB OF WRITING THAN I DO OF ACTING, BUT YOU CAN'T MAKE PEOPLE BEHAVE OR THINK DIFFERENTLY, EITHER.

Your point is a good one, BUT you forget we are all systematic in how we act as a race and body of people during our stay on Earth. We don't really want to be like others, but forced to act like people who had similar lives or lived such lives before.

We each have roles we need to play in order to keep this present world in its place. If we stop and refuse to obey the standards of people who are around us, we will be cast out as misfits and have to form another world, or we may be egotistical enough to believe we can cast out the world—which never works. One dictator is the same as another, only the hands taking the money change.

What if I ask you to go for long drives, and help taking out the trash, and do things I don't like to do alone or do at all? If you marry and the other person is not willing to cooperate or pick up any slack, what happens then?

I WON'T TAKE OUT THE GARBAGE UNLESS I MAKE IT. I HAVE A RULE THAT IF YOU MAKE IT, YOU TAKE IT. I FIND IT HARD TO MAKE A MESS IF YOU HAVE TO BE THE ONE TO CLEAN IT UP, BUT YOUR AIM IS IN THE RIGHT DIRECTION. WE WILL HAVE TO MAKE SOME ALTERATIONS IN THE WAY WE LOOK AT EACH OTHER, AND OUR FRIENDS, IF WE ARE TO SHARE MUCH, BUT IT CAN'T BE THAT HARD—MILLIONS DO IT EVERY DAY.

Who for instance does it well?

YOU ARE SOOO CYNICAL!!! I SEE PEOPLE HERE AND THERE LIVING IN QUIET HAPPINESS, NOT DISTURBED BY ANYTHING OR ANYONE AROUND THEM, WHILE OTHERS ARE SO NOISY THERE CAN BE LITTLE PEACE AND HARMONY, BUT IT STILL EXISTS—BETWEEN THEM. IT IS WHAT IT IS. YOU ARE WHO MAKES IT WORK—OR NOT.

I feel harmonious now, but will I feel that way tomorrow?

WHY WOULD TOMORROW BE DIFFERENT FROM TODAY?

You are too rational. I have to regroup. Can we continue this another time?

YOU'RE A LADY, AND LADIES CALL THE SHOTS.

Thanks, but I prefer being in the background.

SEE, WE MAKE A PAIR—I LOVE TO BE OUT FRONT.

Chapter Twenty-One
The End

*H*uddled over the computer keyboard, her face hidden, Jeanne worked feverishly to release the pressure behind her eyes. She was at the library when the fit began and could not sense if it was due to her mind being scattered in time or the thought of becoming a wife.

In a way, she felt fine and said so to the Librarian and friends she passed along the way, but once at home, Jeanne rushed to the phone. She felt terribly alone when she saw no message waiting there. Her next step was to race to see if any email had arrived while she was out. Her search produced only obscene ads and a few bankruptcy and foreclosure notes. She resented their capacity to annoy others so casually. Collapsing onto the soft leather chair in her office, Jeanne cried. As time moved forward she sat in the sunlight, turning her back to the winter scene outside.

Meanwhile Brian raced in and around the room before returning outside to resume peering at her through the window. It was as if he could see into her mind and knew she was upset with someone and feared he was the one. But what had he done?

Unaware of Brian's concerns or thoughts, Jeanne relaxed deeper into the chair as she reviewed what she wrote earlier for the daily papers about disharmony in the nation. Nothing came together, nor did it end with a flourish, as it usually did. She decided to open Instant Messaging and try to contact Louise. At times Jeanne wondered how it was that her friend was invariably available when she needed her. Were they so in tune with each other that Louise knew when to be there?

Waiting for a response, Jeanne shivered for no good reason. Usually when this happened she could soulfully connect with whatever she was writing, letting the world fall away, but not today. She could not ignore what came through the computer as if by magic then. It was becoming her sole or soul way to approach problems and communicate with others.

At such times Jeanne believed she was channeling or scribing what lived and developed deep within her body and mind—or maybe it was Spirit. Fortunately Louise was not averse to her practicing this gift or art on her. Wishing to initiate such a sitting now, she was disappointed when Louise did not respond.

Pulling up a new page, with no real thought about what she would tell Louise, apparently on the fly with convent business, Jeanne decided to test this new way of writing on others. Maybe it was time to move into the world. She would decide later who was to receive whatever came forward. Fingers flying, head high, mind elsewhere, Jeanne wrote:

Once again I find myself in a dilemma that has no real meaning, yet occupies my entire being and thoughts. Why do I do it? Why do I worry about things already done? When will I grow too old to wonder why anyone would want to marry me?

Leaning back, Jeanne intended to stretch and straighten her back when words written in a strange font appeared right below hers.

You do it in order to figure out why you are here...

The message just appeared. Does that ever happen to you? Perhaps I'm going over the edge and can't see it yet?

Interesting thought, but once you figure out why you are here—and don't need anyone...

That's running ahead of my story...

Let me write now and see what happens:

You have to find out things for yourself. No one, but no one, can tell you what is best for you except You—your Higher Self.

If your life is full of futuristic thoughts and belief systems, and you wanted to live in the 21st Century before it arrived, you probably went to fairs and expositions, looked at what others thought the future would bring—even though you knew what would happen—because the 21st Century already existed within You.

Since no one else can be YOU, and you can't change You enough to make any difference from who you are, why bother to wonder about the future anyway? Why care?

In this reality I became so frustrated by my inability to calculate when, where, and what kind of life I wanted I didn't live for quite some time. I merely survived on the hope that someday someone would come along and react so romantically toward me that it would sweep away mental cobwebs and elevate my social status enough that all would believe I inherited it, but it never happened—which goes to show there is a God! If I had been swept away by some knight of yore and been ensconced in a temple of love long ago, would I have found my way to live this way today?

No! You must be honest, and admit this is true. You have to know love is not the same as life. If your life is so full of romantic thoughts you can't see your true self, you're not happy and you're suffocating your spirit. If your struggle with self-love is so all encompassing no one can enter your thoughts, you have a terrible life—even if you refuse to admit it. But if your love and life are bound together and you learn more about you and your roles, due to a relationship, you can have a great time while here.

I was having a really great time—until I got sidetracked in a media blitz. I became enamored with the possibility of making movies. I even thought I might be a star one day, too. I was excited enough to think I was in love!

When you get into the ego phase of development, you think you are evolving beyond who you were—forgetting that you remain the same. It's necessary to gather all your strength and attack the ego, time and time again, so you can evolve beyond its strong limitations on love and life as it appears to exist in this time.

I was so sure of Steve that I decided to take a chance and marry again, but it so happens he wasn't ready. He was sure I was there for him, but I knew I wasn't. I have much work of my own to do first. I have to take care of Brian, who is a hand-full at times, and I have to *really* know I am who I say I am. He thought I could freeze-dry myself and remain as is forever—lost in his many charms, willing to disarm myself to the point I would no longer protect who I must be and wish to become.

When you think of all the people you love and those who love you, you may never know how many there are, yet believe you can group them and shell out exactly the amount of love needed to keep each happy with you, but you can't.

It's impossible to love everyone equally, so you spread your joy and love around and hope for the best, like I did.

When you are happy, you reside within the core of your being, which you refer to as You. If you are sad and downhearted, You may be there, too.

I know I was. I never left my core being for Steve, but He did. He let his heart direct him away from movies where he always starred to sharing the lead with me and Brian—and he didn't like it!

When you discover you can't share You with others, you must bear the wrath of those who believe you have no right to keep You to yourself.

I never expected anything like what I encountered with Steve, but it was an expurgatory experience and ended our relationship quickly, if not neatly. We will not be talking in person or over the phone much longer, but will continue to e-mail—at least for now. I want to do things he has already done, and he wants to tell me about them, so we can do new things instead—not necessarily with Brian.

Sharing another's views and experience is not the same as living them yourself. You have to do what your mind wants to do—plus you need to evolve. How can you evolve if your spirit is not in it?

I was sure Steve had evolved beyond acting out a scene if things did not go his way, but he surprised me. I was sure he would never cut me up if I left him, but he did—a lot. I was sure he loved Brian, but he didn't. I was sure he cared about us as we are, but it isn't in his nature—He's not that mature.

When it comes to being a friend in the future, Steve may be. But if he is not, it will not hurt as much if I drop him forever in a few weeks.

Hmmm, now who should I send this to?

I was sure you would know when it happened, but you don't. I wonder why? We were always so close....

As the sun cast a rosy glow across the western sky, Jeanne was awakened by the phone ringing. She had drifted off to sleep on the couch in the family room while Brian napped in his room—or so she assumed.

Jennifer's voice boomed over the phone, "What a day! I just got back from grocery shopping and saw your e-mail. I want to tell you that what you said about Steve is so hypocritical I want to throw up! And I want to give up on you while I'm at it. You're not done with Him! Let me be the first to tell you—and to yell about it, too!"

Blinking from the onslaught of her friend's tirade, as well as the glare from the table lamp, Jeanne barely managed to say, "What?" before Jennifer continued to bawl her out.

"You're not done! I had to grab the phone out of Julia's hand and force her to submit to being without it for a few minutes so I could tell you—You're still in love!"

Fully awake and unhappy about it, Jeanne said, "No! I'm not! I'm going to say this just once, so listen carefully—and listen to what I'm not saying. It's over, Jennifer! He's out of my life—for good!"

"You might feel out of it, but your heart's engaged or you wouldn't be enraged. I admit I was a bit stumped, but Steve's the one. He just moved too fast, if you ask me. The butterfly saw the net and got scared—flitted out of his reach for now, but he's not going to give up the chase. Don't worry! You're not going to be caught. It's going to be your choice."

Bristling, Jeanne responded with subdued bitterness. "Just what about this conversation is weird?"

Jennifer at her end flung her long mane of hair around as she said, "You being told what to do by me is weird, because I'm always the one who needs your 'great' wisdom, but not today. That's what friends are for. One day you're the giver and the next you're the 'givee'. When it comes to matters of this world, I know a heck of a lot more than you! I'm definitely street-wise and you're not."

"Okay, so you've been married twice as many times as me, but how many times do you have to be involved with someone to know you're not going to make it to the altar?"

"So what if you visited the altar once and tripped, you're definitely ready to visit again, but don't want to admit it."

Unsuccessful in her attempts to maintain control of her feelings, Jeanne said, "Me? I know as much as I need to know about marriage—so stop the phony baloney about love."

Jennifer screamed, "Exactly! You don't have any experience, but I do! I know men! I was raised with two handsome brothers and have had six marriages."

"Six?" Jeanne gasped at that revelation.

"Yes! I was engaged twice, then lived with two men, married twice, and dumped who knows how many others along the way and how many more in the future, but I know why I left every single one of them—because I did the leaving every time—even if some say they left me."

Resigned to being harangued by her friend, Jeanne said, "Well, I can see your point, but no man is willing to change a woman, because there's too much work involved. They would rather add a new line of fillies to their entourage than get too deeply involved. I've wondered about that in the past—but not anymore."

Sputtering, Jennifer said, "They need protection—from women. Men love us, but we use them!"

Stunned, Jeanne said, "What are you saying?"

"You know what I'm saying—and you don't need what He has to offer, either. That's why your relationship is stuck in second gear."

Wincing, Jeanne tried to snap back, but could only manage to say, "I'm not driving him to get married. I'm out of the race to the altar."

Crowing as if she was showing off her trump card, Jennifer said, "Not true if you're writing him almost every day. Even *you* have to know love is going to flourish if you want to know more about him than press releases twice a week. He's aware he has it made, but doesn't have you—and because he doesn't have you, he wants you, so he'll continue to hang loose. I know men like him! You have a powerful, persuasive personal charm that controls him—may even be changing him. Believe me, Steve is in hell now, but he's not going to tell you!"

Smiling for no apparent reason, Jeanne spoke softly into her friend's ear, "I love you, too, but your line of reasoning is empty. It doesn't make sense. I've learned a lot about myself from Steve—picked up a lot going on around us when he was with me, so if we were soul mates or whatever, I'd be the first to know."

"Soul mates? Now what are you talking about? I hope not more of that New Age crap! People are souls—and they have mates, and everyone has many things in communion—I mean common—with everyone else, so you can't compare or describe another as being the only mate for your soul. Your soul is eternal—and love here on Earth is fleeting and dies in time!

Obviously, you can't believe in such things and not be in love. I know you, Jeanne! You love and never stop loving anyone you trust, but this is different. This is about sex, and sex isn't the same as love. It has the power to shut down all reason."

Jeanne nodded. Picking lint off her sweater, she said, "You may be on to something, Jennifer, but whatever it is escapes me. Anyway, I have to go and see what Brian is up to. If you care to continue this conversation—rather lecture—call back after nine."

Not dismayed, Jennifer laughed and said, "Okay, but be sure the Big YOU isn't involved—that this is all about little *you* and is coming from You. Remember, I'm being used by the Holy Spirit, too."

As if stunned by an electrical charge, Jeanne said, "What did you say?"

"You heard me. I'm channeling what you already know, but refuse to accept. If you need help, get it yourself. I'm going to get off this stool and finish cleaning out the refrigerator. It's time to cool off."

"You are very sweet, Jennifer, and I do appreciate your thoughts, but your wisdom isn't apparent to me. I don't see how you can look at what has happened and say, 'It's meant to be.' But I'll let it go for now. Enjoy yourself and think about all of us shoveling snow tomorrow."

In conclusion, Jennifer said, "See you later—and don't forget to find Brian."

"Smart aleck, of course I'll find him. He's in the next room."

Forty minutes later Jeanne was chewing out Brian. "Whatever possessed you to sleep under the bed? I looked everywhere! I was worried sick."

Whimpering as he rubbed his eyes, Brian looked at her and said, "I was going to sleep, but heard someone talking. I wanted to listen, but fell asleep."

"Brian, you know better than to listen to other people's conversations. Why would you do that?"

"I heard my name. If someone talks about me, I am okay to listen. I'm the one being heard."

Jeanne shook her head, wondering, wherever does this boy learn such things? Aloud she said, "What are you trying to say?"

"You were talking to Junie's mom—and I heard my name, so I was trying to find out what I did wrong."

Hoping to reassure him she smiled and said, "You should know by now that I never say anything negative about you to others. We're family. I don't run anyone else down, do I?"

"No, but sometimes you tell someone what I did wrong that I didn't know I did wrong—so I listen to find out when I'm bad."

Jeanne's head dropped as she thought: He really is an all-together guy, and I have to admit he is highly regarded by many, but I never realized he was the one handing out the discipline—not me. He seems so sure of himself now—it's just his way, but it makes me wonder who he was last time around.

Not to be forgotten, Brian said, "I was going to go over and see Justin, but he said I wasn't welcome. His mom isn't home. She left with some man—and Justin is mad."

"Oh, and you were surprised she went out with a man? Why? You know Justin and his mom have a lovely house, and visiting other pretty places is fun to do. Lots of people love her, so why shouldn't she go out without Justin sometimes?"

Blushing a bit, Brian said, "You know, she out with a man!"

Wanting to laugh as she checked his face, Jeanne thought: He's so disgusted with my lack of understanding I could hug him to bits. However, she did not make a move, wishing to continue their conversation a bit longer.

"Isn't it nice for her to have a fun day away?"

A brooding mood descended as Brian said, "No! Justin's daddy is still his daddy. She won't be his mother if she marries this man. Justin said so."

Caught off guard, Jeanne said, "What did Justin say?"

"He's afraid of him. He's taking his mother away."

Sensing Brian was talking more about himself than Justin, she lowered her voice and said, "That will never happen. His mother loves him and will never leave him—ever."

His expression softened as he said, "Well, you might not leave me, but his mom isn't like you. She likes this guy and doesn't do anything if he's stopping by or gonna' call her. She sits and stares into air—and gets really mad if we make any noise."

Oh, oh, she is in deep, thought Jeanne. Improvising, she said, "I was wondering if you and me, with Justin and his mom, might go to the movies tomorrow. Want to ask him now?"

Without hesitation Brian said, "He said his mother's gone all weekend."

Stunned, Jeanne thought, She really has flipped out this time! What a way to get over a bad marriage. She can't be serious. I thought she had sense, but she has abandoned her son for the first man to come along.

Unsure of what to do, Jeanne said, "I guess you and I can still go to the movies—and maybe Justin would like to go, too. What do you think?"

"Oh, goody, Mommy. Now he'll be glad I told you."

All Jeanne could think was, but will his mother be happy that I know what's going on? I doubt she's ready to reveal to anyone—especially me that she's head over heels in the dumpster now.

Unaware he was headed for the phone, Jeanne said, "Why not call Justin and get his baby-sitter on the line? She might need a break—or she can go with us if she isn't allowed to leave him alone."

Brian scrunched up his nose as he spoke, enunciating each word as if she were hard of hearing. "It isn't a lady. It's Billy from over the other street."

"Billy Shields?"

All Brian said was "Yes," but it created a tornado in Jeanne's mind. Billy Shields, the kid who tried to burn down his mother's house? Is she crazy?

Reining in her thoughts, she said, "Well, then, let's see what Billy and Justin are doing tonight. Maybe we should go over there now?"

Brian put down the phone and said, "That's great, Mommy! I love to see you smile. You look sooo beautiful when you smile."

She wondered why Brian said it, but kept quiet as he reached up to hug her.

"You sad since Steve left. Did he leave 'cause he mad at me? I think he saw me crying."

Filled with remorse for not saying enough about the relationship ending, Jeanne's thoughts lashed her mind. How terrible! I didn't try hard enough to explain what happened. It looks like he knows what happened, but how could he?

Stooping to accept his hug, Jeanne said, "We aren't as close as we were. We had a lot of fun though, didn't we? But now Steve's busy—and I have lots of work to do. You were never any trouble to him—or me."

Smiling brightly, Brian said, "Okay."

'Okay? That's it!' Jeanne never ceased to be amazed at his sudden shifts in mood. She wondered, will he always be this way?

"I afraid you marry him and move away, but he isn't marrying us, is he?"

Jeanne smiled and said, "No, you and I are a team. I'd lose my mind before I'd let anything or anyone split us up. You know I'm very, very sensible."

To her amazement, he said. "No, you aren't,"

"What? What are you saying? You know, Brian, you're an impossible imp. Why would you say such a thing?"

"Cause I like Steve. He was okay for us, but you didn't want him."

"I love you, too, Brian, but Steve isn't the only one I like. He happened to be the only man you met."

Someday she would tell him about men who hang around single women. She would never casually bring men into their home—to baby-sit or whatever. Her thoughts veered in a different direction then. Brian's safe, but what about Justin being alone with Bobby Shields?

Just a bit too quickly, Jeanne said, "Brian, I think you should ask Justin to sleep over here tonight—that way Billy can go home and come back tomorrow."

Eyes wide, Brian replied, "Billy can't go home. His mother's gone."

"What?"

"His mother left his daddy. She isn't there anymore. Billy's not welcome at home. That's what his daddy said."

Stunned, Jeanne mumbled, "Why, that is impossible. He's only 15 years old. You can't just up and abandon a child."

Nodding like an old man, Brian said, "He said he's never going home."

"When did he say that?"

Looking surprised, Brian said, "When we ask him."

"When was that?"

"Yesterday."

When Jeanne said nothing, Brian added, "He told us he could watch us—and other kids—make lots of money and never go home. Now I don't think I like him."

Jeanne thought, oh, oh, I don't like this, but said, "Why?"

Wrinkling his nose, Brian said, "He smells."

Totally taken aback, Jeanne said, "What?"

"He smells funny. Sort a sick smell, sort a sweet—not nice. I get sorta sick when he comes close to me."

It had to be marijuana. Jeanne's thoughts settled into a downward trough. I knew it! This kid is lost and no one is going to tell me otherwise. What am I going to do to get this out in the open—right now?

After a moment or so, Jeanne said, "Did you see him smoking?"

"Yeah, he smokes funny cigarettes. He never smokes in the house. Brian's mother doesn't know."

Incensed, but trying to keep a lid on it, Jeanne said, "Kids around here are smoking when they should be experiencing life, but I know you won't do that."

Nodding, Brian said, "Smokin' causes cancer, and I don't want to die."

Trying to figure out how much Brian knew about drugs, Jeanne said, "It costs a lot of money and causes you to see yourself different from what you really are. That kind of cigarette is bad. It makes boys lazy. I don't think Billy can baby-sit anyone, and I don't want you to be alone with him. Whenever he arrives at Justin's, I want you to come home immediately."

Brian looked confused as he said, "Aww, Mommy, Billy's not bad. He just smells funny."

"Billy is too old to play with you and too immature to baby-sit young boys. He doesn't live by the same rules as we do. You have to be in bed early and he stays up late. I see him standing on the corner whenever I work late."

"But he's afraid of the dark!"

This stopped Jeanne. "How do you know that?"

Brian nodded and said, "You know."

"How do you know he's afraid of the dark?"

With what appeared to be infinite patience, Brian said, "He wets the bed."

Impressed with his line of thought, Jeanne nodded and said, "Oh, I see what you mean. You used to do that, when you first married me, but it wasn't because you were afraid of the dark. It was because you slept too deeply—didn't wake up when you felt the need, and you often dreamt you were on the toilet."

"Is that why I did it?" Brian's face was moving in several different directions, and Jeanne realized he had worried about this for a long time, but it never came up until now.

"Yes, it happens a lot, but you outgrew it. Now you sleep and dream and get up when you have to go. It's just something that happens to some kids."

Apparently excited, Brian asked, "Why don't we let Billy sleep here and bring Justin with him?"

Rapidly backpedaling, Jeanne said, "You only have one bed and Justin is too big to sleep with you—and Billy is too old."

"Why don't we have more beds?"

Totally unprepared and frankly tired of the subject, Jeanne said, "We don't need people sleeping over here. Our company always goes home. We don't entertain people without a home."

"I saw a homeless man. He had a stocking over his head."

"That's too bad, but it's his choice."

Brian appeared perplexed—and unwilling to drop the subject. "I don't understand. Why would he want to do that?"

"When you are older, you could decide to do that, too, if you were that kind of person—but you're not. You're not the type of person who expects others to rescue you when you're doing what you want to do. Besides, you don't trust others that much. You don't let people walk all over you, either."

Warming up to the subject, Jeanne added, "Poverty is a state of mind *you* can prevent. You're settled—and have it all, but that man can't see he's not here forever and has to get it together—so he can move beyond it—but he will. Some people endure a lot of misery before they realize they aren't the only ones with problems. It'll happen to him. He'll be able to do something he admires." Once again Jeanne wondered if she was a fit mother for such a brilliant mind.

If Brian didn't understand, his words did not reveal it. "We have this kid at school who can't sleep at night, but comes to class and sleeps all day."

Feeling her lethargy slink off into the night, Jeanne said, "What?"

"His daddy's gone and his mother can't get work, so she stays at the YWCA, but he can't sleep there."

"Oh, my, that's terrible!" Jeanne was stricken with remorse.

"But Mommy, you just said it was that man's fault he was homeless. Why isn't it her fault?"

Thinking: Brian is so astute. No way can he follow my sophistry. I have to explain it better, if I can.

Stooping to look into his eyes as she spoke, Jeanne said, "I mean she was abandoned by her husband—the father of her child and she has no money because she totally trusted someone she loved. She believed him when he said he would always take care of them. Many people think men are supposed to provide their families with the means to live well—and some women believe that. In fact, many still want it to be true—and it's true as often as not—yet some women can't imagine things ever changing. They try to do it all. They want to be on their own— independent, but when it comes too fast, they aren't ready for the break—anyway, it's a crime to abandon those who care for your children."

Brian looked into her eyes with deep understanding before saying, "You were all alone, but I'm with you now—for always. Right? I have a nice bed and the boy at school has none, is it my right or his wrong?"

Stroking his head lightly, Jeanne managed a smile as she said, "I think you mean—am I lucky and he isn't?"

"Yeah."

Letting her mind flow into time, Jeanne spoke without editing her thoughts. "Luck is not a word I use lightly. It can't be ascribed to me, but it happens to others—sometimes. I found you, but 'luck' didn't bring us together. It was ordained or prophesied long ago. It didn't just happen. I was looking for treasure and spotted you. You were waiting and knew me immediately. We both saw each other at the exact same time it came to be, but it wasn't luck. This boy isn't waiting. He isn't watching, but he will one day. When he discovers this life isn't for him, he'll create the life he craves inside himself, not out there somewhere. He'll be a strong man or deceitful, but the lessons he learns now are soon over. He can't be held responsible for his mother's plight, even if he contributed to it."

Unsure about what just happened or what she had said, Jeanne looked at Brian and tousled his hair. "Let's call the Y and see if anyone wants to go to the movies with us."

Brian blinked and said with some consternation, "Oh, gee, I don't think he'd go, Mommy. His mother isn't pretty."

"What?"

"You know. She looks sort of old—and her clothes aren't nice. She always comes to school and looks in the window, but we act like we don't see her, 'cause she's not all right."

Shocked, Jeanne almost screamed, "Is that any way to talk about another human being?"

Not backing down, Brian said, "You know how people talk about me. I'm okay! Some kids used to say I wasn't okay—I was crazy. Now I know what they mean, 'cause she's not right. She looks sort of haggy-baggy and doesn't smell too good, but she's nice to me."

Shaking her head, Jeanne said, "I think we'll call the Y and see if we can take them to the movies tomorrow."

"Okay, but I told you."

Jeanne thought: Brian is aware I get edgy when I cold-call people. No one else suspects I'm shy, but I am—especially when it comes to calling strangers or lovers. It gets the job done quicker than anything else—except telepathy. If it's for business, I'm okay, so people think I'm outgoing—not realizing I hate to talk to strangers.

When Jeanne finished the call she looked at Brian and said, "We'll stop by the Y and pick up your friend and his mother at seven—tonight, but first I have to do a few things. Can you watch this pot and make sure it doesn't boil?"

Rushing to put on his apron, Brian said, "I know how to cook. Water is my specialty."

"Okay, master chef. You're on."

A few minutes later, beyond his reach, Jeanne thought: When someone calls and asks you to go out and tackily asks if you would like some clothes to wear, you have to be desperate to accept such an invitation, but I'm glad she did. I love to help those who are accepting by nature, but it scares me that this woman doesn't even know me and immediately accepted my offer. She seemed unsure about going to the movie, so it must be the clothes she wants. I'll give her a business suit, too. I feel certain she needs it. How do I know that? Oh, dear, I forgot about asking Justin and Billy Shields to go to the movies. Oh, well, as Scarlett would say, I'll worry about that tomorrow.

Instead of worrying about her next-door neighbor's baby-sitter, Jeanne started pulling clothes off hangers, deciding whether or not to include them with the love offerings she placed on Brian's bed. She had ample time to think about how other women lived without men until suddenly remembering a time when she was younger and less wise and had joked that she would never be a *bag lady*.

"I guess I never trusted anyone enough to let them take care of me. I always saw myself as doing a better job of caring for me than others could or would. I never believed I would end up a bag lady—not part of my belief system—like not believing in demons and vampires. This woman's story is far too familiar, and it's not being told right! If it was, there wouldn't be so many waiting to join her. Perhaps she was selfish, never thought about what would happen if he wasn't there to take care of them." With a start Jeanne realized she had been talking under her breath while sorting through one closet after another—but wasn't embarrassed.

"When you have a child and give everyone the impression you'll always be that man's wife, I think you have a better chance of making it, but this woman is obviously more of a mother than a lover or wife. Once her child was born, she didn't love the man as much."

I do need to curb this tendency to talk to myself. "Why am I so sure I know so much about this woman?'

Realizing she was talking aloud again, Jeanne shivered and clamped her lips shut, but continued thinking about it. When I get all this figured out, I'm going to write a book about women like her—but not now. Today isn't a day for writing. Now is the time to gather what needs to be said in another way on another day.

Shivering, Jeanne whispered, "I feel strange. What's going on?"

Stopping to look into her bedroom full-length mirror, she spoke to her image. "I don't want just anyone. I don't need you! I want Steve."

Frowning, Jeanne whispered, "What's wrong? Why am I talking all the time about Him? Please don't tell me I'm still in love!"

Chapter Twenty-Two

Many Endings...
But Only One
Beginning

I was trying to end my life as a wife and resume being a writer and mother—not a lover, but my life was so disrupted I had to go back and sort through all the reasons I can't be a wife and why I refuse to even consider it. Can you follow me?

I feel quite sure 'You' would understand, since you're my Higher Self, but my little *me* is the one causing all the trouble. I think I can explain it better in writing. Let's see if You can explain what isn't adding up.

Why is it that when I sit and muse about what is happening on the news I suddenly become aware my mind is out-of-line with the times I live in now? This is true! How can I think about things remotely connected to what others might do or would like to read? I'm long overdue for an internal data review—an audit or reboot of my life program, so I can accomplish more than before—or not, but at least be aware of what I've done to deserve my lot in this life.

Tapping out a few more lines, Jeanne stopped and let her thoughts take over. *I was going to move into the next life without being a real wife this time, but now I feel this life isn't complete. Maybe being a wife is what is missing? I have to do more, but it isn't in me to do it alone. I'm constantly massaging my mind, hoping to squeeze some sense into it. But it comes back to knowing I could do everything I came to Earth to do—if I married a man who would willingly back me up and help me at times. That's how I'm thinking. I have to change or rearrange my ideas if I'm to stay happily unmarried!* As if in response to her thoughts, Jeanne's fingers began to type.

Is it not terrible that the mind tells you how to live and controls your spiritual and creative work? The mind! You have your entire life on Earth to live, yet you let the mind run you—though you seldom recognize it. You think, then you act—or so you believe. You pray and God moves mountains of energy to be there, yet you doubt a miracle happened. What a waste of the Divine—and time!

Staring as the message arrived from somewhere in time, Jeanne said under her breath, "I was going to go to the store, but remembered all the stuff stored in the freezer and fridge. Can't fit another thing in either, but only then did I cancel shopping. What if we all live with pantries crammed with food that can spoil—and do no one any good? That's happening to me now!" As if in response, Jeanne's fingers moved across the keys again.

I believe it is possible to visualize everything—but seeing YOU is extremely difficult.

Letting out a sigh, Jeanne spoke to the empty room, "I know! I try to imagine doing things ahead of time to insure it will happen, but I never imagined I wouldn't want to be married—

so now I have to contend with that idea." Immediately an unseen correspondent's message appeared on the screen:

You have to do what you think and know is good for you and others, but it must also agree with what is right for the entire being that is YOU.

Jeanne greeted this message with, "Now where did that come from?" She felt immense energy flowing up and down her spine in a double helix as she typed:

I am.

I am who I am.

You are me and we are one, but you see only who you are.

We work, we dally, we sit, we're silly, but we are one.

You in the ego state have no one—you are only you.

You cannot possess, meet, marry, or be anyone but who you are.

You must rid your mind of fear before it can fill with love.

Once fear disappears, love remains forever.

Realizing she was having a dialogue with those who guide her from within her mind, body, and spiritual life, Jeanne intuitively posed a question and waited for the answer. When she heard nothing, she wrote:

What to do about HIM?

Her expression remained sober and serious as awe flooded her mind with an answer that echoed through her mind: He is YOU!

Hesitantly, she wrote:

What? I don't understand.

Typing questions she expected to be answered intuitively, Jeanne was startled to watch as she wrote out in bold type the answers, as if a spiritual scribe.

You think you are in love with a man who is a movie star, and if you marry him, others will try to separate you, thus causing much trouble. Havoc will reign! That is not fact! You made it up and believe it. It is your mind creating lies. It is not grounded in what is called reality. It exists only in your imagination. Do not visualize that way! If you believe, it will be as your will directs—not as it really is.

What if I sit and relax—looking at pictures of Him and asking what I should do?

You could do that. It is possible, but it is better to question others in person.

Are you saying photos reflect more than the image of a person?

When you look at a picture, you are not in it—yet you are. Seeing the image, your mind can create the being—but not easily if the being is not known in your reality. You can conjure within your mind and emotions a state of disharmony or harmony capable of harming or helping those pictured. If you do that type of visualization, you disarrange your mind and cause it to ebb and flow from you into the world.

Are you saying 'spells' work like that?

We never spell out 'spells' and don't intend to start. We mention it now because you have been under one.

You're saying someone cast a spell over me?

Actually, your ego created it—and only your Higher Self can remove it. Your world thinks it rules and causes you to fall, fail, or succeed, but it does not. You alone are in charge of what you are— or you have given your power to others. If you give your power to others, you lose your identity and live under what is commonly called a 'spell.' There is no magic involved—magic is not for humans. Magic is not for demons, either! It is for the heavens to use as needed.

When you go here and there, seeing yourself as demonstrably ignorant or fearful, you are demonic—not being true to your true self. You cannot bedevil anyone else—only yourself. Since you have to be You, and it is within you to do so, you remain attuned to You even though you may not realize it now.

How very interesting. What if I just sit here like this and stare at the wall and visualize Him? Would it be held against me or increase my spiritual being?

You can see whatever you dream or want to see, but it is a waste of energy. You need only call, write, or place your path within his to see him.

Why not imagine it? What's wrong with that?

You need to use your power to materialize and decipher the writings of the wise. You have to do that! You have enough power to live, grow in wisdom and grace, and destroy evil, but you do not have enough to waste on demonstrations of your power over love. Love flows or it goes! You have to let your mind know you are in charge—so do it now! Another day wondering this way, refusing to take full responsibility for your life decisions, is a wasted effort— although not a loss of time.

Wow! You say I'm not in charge of me—yet I think I am. In fact, I know I am! Why are you saying I'm not in charge of me and my thoughts?

If you were in full power, you would not be contacting us like this. You would be active, happy, successful, and dynamic. You are not a scribe. You are not paid to write like this, so you sit doing this to avoid working on your present life. You have work to do! If we can make it happen, we will, but you have enough power to stop us.

Wow! God is in You, yet You can be stopped?

You are of God and stop 'You' every time you see yourself as someone else—but we digress. You are not to be interfered with by anyone! If any being, entity, or soul tries to interfere with another, there is punishment so great it cannot be erased in one life. You would have to come back again and again—but we digress—again.

This is absolutely fascinating. I'm all eyes! Please go to whatever lengths it takes to explain everything to me. I have all day to read and write like this.

'you' have no time to sit and work like this and accomplish nothing, and 'You' has no time to waste, either. You must work out your present life first. Realize it is not the life of a wealthy woman and handsome man getting together, rather the life of a woman who will change the world once she gets her act together. You have the means and the man to do it—but you are afraid to move.

Jeanne became so excited she yelled, "Wow!"

Yes, now you are fascinated, but why did it take so long?

I don't see myself as wealthy. I never imagined that.

No imagination required. It is a fact—you are wealthy! The money you make is not used to pay for daily expenses. You have far more than you need. What else can you say about wealth that makes better sense?

I do have enough to be comfortable, but I think I have to work constantly or I'll end up without money, and in the end will have to rely on the good will of others to get by the rest of my life.

That is not a fate to fear. You have done your share. God of All will never let you fall—because you have more work to do here. You are not wasting time sitting alone, but you waste time writing what is never going to be published. You have to afford yourself more time to think, dream, and sit in silence.

338

Why?

You were born to be a scribe and must write if your livelihood depends upon it, but you do not have to write if your life does not depend upon it. Your life no longer needs such money! Now you need someone who will acknowledge you are You, one who has a life plan, too. You do not need anyone to work for you. You only need a shot of adrenaline from time-to-time to encourage the body to do more, since it does the physical work and does not complain about your neglect of it—yet.

Why not let my mind do this work, while I do whatever God wants?

Finally you get the message! Finally you understand meditation.

Hoping her child was nowhere close by listening, Jeanne said, "Meditation? Is this all about meditation? I can't believe it! Why is it we always get back to meditation?"

You either meditate and know what 'You' does—or play dumb and waste time. 'you' knows that—and we know you know that—so we leave now.

"Wait! I need more answers."

You have the answers to all your questions—written out. You have the solution to all your problems, too. Now you need to meditate and find out where you filed the wisdom away—when you refused to obey.

Where do I start?

Anywhere!

Give me a hint—please.

'I was' and 'I am not' are not ways to think of yourself, but how you think now. Work on cleansing your mind. Get issues out and away from you. Drop the gate, stay out of range of high-and-wide enemy shots and you will remain unscathed by others' wars. If you linger or stray far from your fortress, you will die alone—probably in pain.

Why would God let me suffer?

You are asking God of All that?

Yes.

We flee before it is heard above. We are not so selfish and self-centered as to believe we can demand answers of God. It is your life—and you decide when you want to die.

Die—just because I asked a simple question?

You have been told. You should listen! You have no knowledge you cannot use. If you have knowledge and do not use it, do not ask for more. You must seek. You have no need to ask, but if you do, be sure to meditate and accept the response.

When I meditate, I usually pray and ask for a number of things, but only one is really concrete.

You can concentrate on only one thing at a time. Do not flow over or block the stream of consciousness with extraneous matter. If you do, your bloom will wilt too soon.

I was going to ask you more questions, but I guess I shouldn't.

We are not God of All. We work within the realm of God. We are of YOU, so you can in a generic sense ask god, through us, for all you need and wish to know—but do not question God of All.

I don't understand.

Just believe us!

I believe you! It's funny, but I know God is in this writing—always. I know I connect, but with who or whom is my question.

You can only know what you know.

With a loud sigh, Jeanne said, "I guess I better go now."

Instantly, she heard someone within her say: "*You have all day to think or meditate—which one always pays?*"

"I know, I know—meditation!"

"Then do it!"

Chapter Twenty-Three

Run For the Door

Hey Louise,
Want to flash some random thoughts by you that I discovered while cleaning my office the other day. I can't use any of it in my columns. It isn't suitable for business—and highly unlikely to work in any book I might write, but I thought it would help you or someone working on my stuff understand me better—what I went through to reach the point where everyone else believes I'm a fairy tale come true. LOL If you don't have time to go through all of it, or it's too stupid or confused, scrap it—just don't tell me.

Jeanne

Checking out old computer discs, Jeanne examined one that stuck to her hand as if glued to it. Opening to the first stored entry, she read:

When this day is over and done with, I think I'll just cry and get onto the next work I came to do. I have so much to do I don't know where to begin, but I have to end everything and get going again.

I tried to end a romance, but love bloomed and held its own. I tried to raise a 'handicapped' child by myself and got harassment and resentment from women who wanted little to do with raising their own 'normal' children, but had plenty to say about how I raised Brian.

I tired of writing about trivialities and how we whine all the time, but had a huge following by then. I had to continue in that vein to please them—until I grew weary of constantly being upset. It all came together anyway and here I am.

Jeanne mumbled as she searched through the loose threads of her journal hoping to find a central theme or motif. Thinking: What to do with all of this? She selected highlighted entries and began reading what she had written long ago. Her thoughts wandered over the material until she settled on:

Once before I tried to end this work and do something different, but it stayed. I came back to it later and found everything was much better.

I wonder if that could happen again. What if I write the ending to this book and begin another—will anyone want to read either? I've given my readers plenty of work to judge me by—told them a lot about my personal life, but no one really knows me. Maybe I should say more, but then, why should I?

What if we met on a plane and I told you everything you know about me—would you want to know more? I doubt it. If I told you I was traveling into the future to marry a handsome movie star, it's likely you would want to keep in touch—maybe even get to know me as a person. Is that the epitome of hope or not?

Right then the wireless mouse moved of its own accord to another page, stopping at one point to indicate a text should be included. Is it the mouse or my mind sorting through my work?

When you dream, you don't look at what went into producing the dream, but see what will be or what you hope will happen.

I was never a dreamer until I met Brian—then HE immediately appeared! It was no mere exercise in wonderment, but it shows that if you open to love and give all you have, the greatest things then happen—as if by chance.

In a state of abstraction, Jeanne easily related to what she had cut and pasted on the pages addressed to Louise, but wondered what others might think if they spotted how often she worried about Him and what she had actually done.

You can do whatever you want!

Since you can do whatever you want, why not strive to be great? I always try to complete every detail. It takes time to be clever and eager to explain whatever. It's the way I am—including the fussing and fuming. You may not nitpick, because it can take you places you don't need or want to re-view or do again. If you do everything, there is nothing left to redo or finish. If you don't complete something— even one little thing, it appears again and again until you do it.

Puzzled by this last entry, Jeanne said, "What am I really saying?" She decided not to change it. The mouse continued to scroll down the page and selected:

You think living is leaving? You may have a point, but it isn't about leaving others or things behind. It's the letting go!

I was going to let go and leave behind the man I had admired, then loved, and finally rejected, but it was not to be. Some of life is predestined, but most of it is not.

I want people to know that if you ever find yourself like me, in a quandary over a man or woman, to just let go. Let it subside. Then if emotion stirs your pride, you know your heart is telling you what to do. But if you hate, end it right away!

If you continue to yearn for someone, go to them once again, but don't be foolish and ask them to return to you—just talk and speak your truth. If you can't talk easily, it's time to drop them.

Removing that disc and inserting another, Jeanne watched with growing fascination how her fingers rapidly selected items to be shared with Louise and members of her dream team.

What a time to care and share with Brian! He is so thrilled to move. He was happy living here, but anticipates being happier there. He has not learned the lesson of life that you are 'there' here, but he will.

That was the only selection from that journal entry before her hands moved to recoup other files.

What helps most is to sit and write out your problems—then let them sit. I was sure I had none until I met Him and his friends. I couldn't absorb it all then. I discussed them ad nauseum with my friends—going over every detail, everything they said, instead of praying about it as I did before.

Back then it felt like I was being watched by the entire universe, so I wrote about me and them every day. I think I should dump these journals now to insure that no one gets hurt by things I said back then.

Some may think words don't hurt, but they are the only things you create that really hurt others. Hands, fists, stuff picked up and hurled don't hurt the essence of a being. People may damage your body, but the mind is what hurts when you cry. If you do hurt me, then I want to hurt you and have to talk myself out of it.

You can't hurt me if I don't like you or listen to you!

When you're sarcastic and rude, you may think you annoy or hurt others' feelings, but you don't. You're the only one aware of the damage you intended. If you make fun of others in an attempt to diffuse a situation, you may end up being attacked for lack of tact. It's always easier to say nothing rude or weird about others.

It took years to learn that simple wisdom, but once it became a part of me, I've had all the friends I could ever want.

What attracted this handsome man to me had little to do with how I was dressed or what I was doing that day, but everything to do with my usual behavior. I was extremely comfortable—on top of my form. It wasn't a self-conscious display of beauty or style I created as my public image, but my everyday ways that caught his attention. If someone is vain, silly, weird, or just plain showing off, you know she is genuine—plastic! Does anyone prefer a zircon to a diamond?

I wasn't trying to be anyone but me, and he liked what he saw. Since I never knew anyone like him, and was enamored with his persona, I was the one who had to discover the man living behind the image. I was afraid he would turn out to be totally different from my dream. He was different, but not because of anything he did in real life. I just couldn't believe he was the same in person as he was on the screen.

Weird to admit, but He really is the same as the characters he portrays. The various roles show off different aspects of his personality. He developed and evolved with them. It's like everyone's life here on Earth, but we don't see ourselves as actors. I wonder why?

What if you staged a play and no one showed up? No matter, because the play would still go on. You do whatever and then let it go. If you're great, careful and diligent, some may think your work is fair to good, while others never notice you. If you're 'knowing'— really know people, you can stage an act and make more want to know you better.

What you decide to be is what you are, but you can't see that easily if you don't succeed. Wrong and right are the same, but those most likely to use such words are on the wrong track—off their beam.

In a dream I was watching myself as a leading lady be upstaged by a young starlet. I immediately tried to write myself out of the play, but the director shouted, 'I want that woman! She must remain.' I asked myself if the play was fun and decided it was, so I reentered the scene. No big deal, but it can be when it's your life.

Fumbling with a cup of tea, Jeanne's mind returned to the present. Her conscious mind had not directed the collecting of thoughts and images, only the cutting and pasting, so she continued grasping at threads seemingly lost in limbo. Does she know what her gift is?

A voice erupted and commanded Jeanne to stop what she was doing and focus on what she must do now and in the future.

"I want you to sit and stare at what is called 'your life' and identify what you like about it. Do not cry or laugh. Examine it as if a museum piece considered priceless—and you cannot understand why it is so highly prized. If you stare at anything long enough, it moves and assumes other positions or shapes, yet remains the same. Your life is like that, but it moves much faster and never returns to the original shape."

Drifting back to the center of her mind, Jeanne whispered, "You can see I'm different. I lost my career, but I can return to it. Will I?"

The voice from within said, *"You decide."*

Right then Jeanne realized her mind wasn't working, but her fingers were. They moved rapidly across the keys.

Exhausting your energy to work at something isn't bad, but it isn't an accurate description of what happens. You can't exhaust energy or destroy it. It is! It just is! God is energy and God just is. Never idle and debate issues you can't conceive or understand. It's truly a waste of time—which is another way of looking at energy.

As if echoing through a tunnel in time, a voice spoke to Jeanne and she scribed it.

Time and energy, love and war, whatever else comes to mind are elements of a time that can and will transcend it and grow into you. You have to decide which way to go and when. It is determined that you will leave this place and time at some point and proceed to another—when that happens is your decision. Either take advantage of all opportunities to grow and ascend or sit still and let everyone else end their lives here and take you there. Life happens!

With a start, Jeanne saved and filed the message in a special file. Then she spotted a CD with a bright red logo she had designed when a bit muddled about what to do with her art, as well as home-schooling Brian.

Without hesitation she inserted the disc and let the mouse seemingly decide which entries to explore.

I never intended to fuss about Brian's schooling. But when it came time to relocate, I had no choice but to move him from his carefully planned home-school life to a private school where he could adjust to being the only 'special' boy in the midst of seventy so-called 'normal' kids. I decided to do this so I could more easily introduce him later into public school, where he will have to survive with twice as many students who think they're perfect.

Why do it? To help Brian! It is neither wise nor unwise, merely a decision that can be renewed or revised over time. What to do now?

I haven't prepared Brian for Montana! I intuitively know it won't be hard for him at first, but have to check it out before I actually believe it. I have to see for myself that Brian can make it in a different sort of world than he experienced here.

In my vision Brian is fine. No one really notices him. All sorts of people see him as he is—immediately. After the first few minutes of meeting Brian, no one thinks much about him again. He isn't their worry—they're worried about drugs.

Only a few things in this life require a warning label. Most think evil is people or places—ideas. Today's youth seek out and use drugs like nicotine and alcohol to create an image of maturity, which looks pathetic to adults.

Why do teens risk so much? Why do the young want to be old? Because they know it's not wonderful to be young—especially now.

So many things happening at school and play that are bad for youth—But who is to blame? While growing up I was sure Today's World would be so much better than it turned out to be. I dread seeing visions of its deterioration: people growing courser, less social, more cynical—seldom beautiful and serene. What caused this?

Concerned with what she had copied and pasted to Louise's file, Jeanne felt compelled to write an explanation:

I want this day of moving from one place to another to be easy—complications reduced to a minimum, so I won't root around in deep, dark places.

Please forgive me for reminiscing a bit before I throw away relics from my past. I'm going through so many bags and boxes—not digging deep enough to figure them out, but I do know what I'm doing, where I'm going, and what I will need. Peeking inside boxes I instantly decide to dump or save.

Even if you're not moving, you need to examine what you've collected so far—and reach clear conclusions about it now. Don't wait for a big move like I did!

Your junk and my junk are the same, but different. We want to salvage something from what we previously saved, perhaps still unable to understand why we cling to it. The reason lies deep within the subconscious and doesn't really matter—but our stuff does matter to us! If we are to help heal this world, we must rise up and end the tyranny of musty, messy things that prevent us from living in the light of cleanliness!

I was sure when I married (always knew I would) that I would live near a major city, but here I am—moving to a ranch and enjoying the prospect. Why? I lived here long enough! Got all the enjoyment I could out of a sojourn in a foreign house in a beloved city. It was over and done before I met Him.

I got to experience sharing life with another before committing to marriage, even though Brian will be in my life only a short time before growing beyond me. So what? Life happens!

When Brian leaves our home to become his own person around age 25, it will end nothing but his dependence on me. I will always love him, and he will always honor my role as his mother. It will be easy, because we are good friends already. We will always be friends.

I wasn't going to talk to Brian and Steve about any of this, but I can see its necessary and must be done soon.

Louise, I know you want to know how we're going to resolve issues pertaining to family and children—If Brian and I will act in tandem or compete against Steve and his child. We're not like that! We will live and grow into a combined family.

No need to force it. It's already done—before the ceremony. Brian and I have always been a family and Steve and his child aren't one yet, but when we add love, as well as attention to detail, we'll have a pretty nice life not too unlike the lives of those born into an integral family.

There is nothing left to recite, repeat, or retaliate against. I know I can leave and move forward easily now. I've figured it all out!

You and I need time to circulate and center our attention and intentions and decide who will remain in the closest circles within the outer reaches of my home life. We don't have to make quick decisions now. The time for rapid movement is over.

We are settling into a routine that ends only with death. I welcome this time. It's the overture—not the finale.

As a family I think we'll want to know everyone and be a friend to most. Each of us has learned much and once we're together we can make short work of the grueling details. We're not children who don't know who we are and have no understanding of others. When it comes to love, we're just as callow and naïve as any youth, because we never loved others more than we do now. We're only now admitting we never learned that lesson—but have plenty of time to learn it now.

As for joint life experiences, 'I will or want to do whatever, and Steve has already done it' sums up where we are.

I was unsure you would continue working on line and stay to the end, so I want you to know that our lives—yours and mine, are even more entwined then before—in some strange and amazing way. It's like we live as a single entity outside the framework called life or this world. I can't view the energy you have exerted in my life, but I know it's there. I feel it moving me to do more than I or we ever did before.

I would like you to teach this lesson for me: Work hard to live your life story. If your present life gets boring, make it more exciting and thrilling. But once you create a steady, comfortable life, let it stand. Don't tinker with it! Don't add exciting leading ladies and men to the plot. If you tire of another, don't stall in a muddle of indecision. Do what you have to do to finish whatever you set out to do—or don't start it!

I meant to stop here, but have to say one more thing. Louise, I want you to be all you are and can be—today! I know it isn't easy to be true to You—even in a convent. At one time I thought I was perfect as I was, and it turned out to be the most miserable time in my life. Why? Because I didn't believe it! If you think you have it all, know self-doubt is waiting around the corner to destroy your peace of mind. I know. I've been there—done that!

Since you have this annoying capacity to see deeper into what is going on around you than most—notice how weird things happen to you, and not others, and let others go blindly into time. They aren't going to be any happier if you relate what you see, know, or experience.

You have learned how to cope alone. However, learning to cope alone doesn't insure you can always cope. I have to cope with people more than ever, but fortunately I learned the basics so long ago I don't worry about it now. If I hadn't paid attention to my work then, it would be tough now.

Put your brand of psychology to work for you. Publish your books and believe what you write! It's all happening now! These are the times that will end men's souls.

Your friend—again and again,
Jeanne

Chapter Twenty-Four

The End is Never When You Expect It

*W*hile ending my career, it flared up again. We never have as much knowledge of the future as we think we have—fortunately. If I could reach out and give you my best advice, it would be this: Don't think for one minute you are not You (your Higher Self). If you ever doubt You, you will regret it. No time left to dawdle and do little about this life. I must tell you that once you move and do whatever it is you most fear, the whole universe greets you with open arms.

The time to end the life you came here to live doesn't happen when you think your work is done. It happens when God of All recalls you. If no call comes through to do something new, continue doing what you usually do. Trust me on that one! One last piece of advice before I retire to other things: Do what you want, but if you do something that helps everyone, the universe will help you free of charge.

I love helping anyone who does good things for the Earth, so out here in Montana where shepherds and cattlemen, along with men of strong hatreds, are always fighting about grass, land, and water—that doesn't belong to any of them, I'm real busy. I get up early and go to bed after our family time—and I'm flying all day!

For a change of pace I got a horse as big and strong as he can possibly be. I ride him every morning and let him work all afternoon. He loves to walk and takes me along for the ride, but loves working more. He was made for hard labor and standing around all day is hard for him to endure, which he did until I discovered how much he wanted to work. He is so happy now!

Yes, we talk. You probably know horses and people have about the same intelligence, but horses are more sensible. They don't like to walk over culverts or hollow things if they can avoid it, but men will force them to do it anyway. Why do they fear culverts? They intuitively know their weight can cause hollow things to collapse and break their legs. They know they're top heavy. They know what is dangerous, but men goad and prod them to do what is unwise for all involved. See what I mean by sensible?

What you learn now and again in the city isn't as big a deal as what you learn in one day out here on the ranch. I learn so much some days I can't absorb it all. In order to figure out what is going on, some days I stay in bed as late as possible—maybe 6:30 or 7:00 AM. Meanwhile everyone else is up and out and going strong, which leads me to work harder than I otherwise might. Men want me up and about doing things that don't necessarily benefit me, so I know why horses do what they do. We let men take over because it's easier.

Another thing, I love Brian so very much, but he isn't the same. He is entirely different! Brian is a man now and doesn't bother much with me. He goes down to the corral after school instead of coming in the house and doing his homework first. He thinks math is more important than literature, so he studies with a guest staying here—a renowned physicist, and doesn't care what we do. He usually waits to talk with me in the kitchen when he eats and before going to bed—when he wants or needs something.

Whatever, it appears I thrive on being with men, but not because I love them. They're selfish, sometimes brutish, and not very communicative, but all are basically honest. That is more than I can say about many women I've known.

I sleep less and less in order to absorb this ever-changing life. When weary, I sit and meditate. The boys tease me about it being woo-woo, but they all meditate, too, while in the saddle or driving across the plains.

Wheat and oats are being plowed under in order to build sod, but we don't plant much. We let the cows trample the same acreage over and over hoping to imitate how the old herds of buffalo created the old prairie. Buffalo are most suited to this land. It is always those who can adjust who survive. Buffalo will restore the Earth's plains—not cows or well-intentioned men. Remember that, but don't rush out and get one. It just happens!

Whatever happens, I let grain grow and rain fall, but the wind is too mysterious to ignore. I know God—God is the wind, but this wind isn't like the God I knew. To know God, it's necessary to be compassionate. If you can't manage it on your own, don't worry—mercy and love comes to us all in the end.

What I want now is to rest and digest all that is our lives together, because this journal isn't going into the fire. I want it to have a life of its own—to get out and about, maybe be published abroad. I want to share my news and views with a select circle of friends—not just anyone, but once anything gets out into the world, all is beyond our control.

Streets teeming with life and death cannot know who we are and why we came to this star. Only God above knows you, me, and all we are, but I want you to know my story and what I've learned so far. I don't want to jeopardize your work, so don't speak too loudly of our differences.

We're not here to end all suffering, but to advance without harming others. Let the love of God shine in your work so no one can say you caused pain. I will write again when I can, but today I feel the need to sit and meditate.

It's always hard to say good-bye to an old friend, but I am.

At 23

A Poem by Jeanne Beck

At 23, you never ask.
You dislike facts.
If asked, you say you are okay.

What you want is a face
That creates a state of grace
And makes men want you
—over and over again.

When 23, you see nothing
In anyone
And want no one
To say a magazine life is unwise.

You hate women with lives unlike yours,
Yet envy and strive to be more like they are.

I was laughing at my dad.
I saw him as he was—never sad.

I left college and he got mad.
Never again did my dad laugh
And praise me to my face.

"What a disgrace!"
Is what he said.
Why?
I'm just like my mother.
Right?

When a woman works and earns
Nothing more than a purse or two
To pay for treasures to display,
She never thinks
She could be working herself
Into a depressive state.

At 23 she has great expectations
Sure a man will enable her to spend again.

When life goes,
And a full-day's wages
Can't pay for burial expenses,
She sees no such needs at 23.
Why?
Her defense is not offensive.
She believes she will never die.

She had everything.
Her life was that of a princess
Planning to be a bride.

She would one day
Buy whatever was advertised.
Her domain a store,
Not doing chores,
Able to eat whatever she craved.

At 24, she left her mind and entered time.
No man had arrived to rescue her
From the boredom of an idle life.
She was upset and thought:
When did this happen?
Where did it begin?

You left your family
For a year of fun.
You went to college
On the largesse of others
To get drunk and do drugs.
You never thought
It would do any harm.

At home,
Your mother's latest is alarmed.
He did not intend to educate anyone.
You and he—a team since 18—split.

Mother said I was not to blame.
My father had been the same.
Father of me was a success,
So I would be one, too,
Or so she said.

My mother's man decided to leave his job.
To work out in gyms,
Rather than listen to her talk about others.
This change ended with mother seeking another man.

I was blind-sided.
Secure in my life
As a woman of beauty and style,
I would go far.

When my stepfather
Refused to advance more tuition,
Due to too many F's,
I left him.

Went to my father.
Said I was ready to work.
He took that as his cue to
Demand I leave my mother's clan
To stand with him and his new family then.

It was not to be.
He expected me to do work
I had never done before.
He expected immediate results,
And was not happy about my way of life.

I left his plan and ran.
I shocked them all!

My attitude and careless views
Produced nothing new.

A friend said I needed to get a man
That would make everyone happy or mad again.

It was a plan that was not to be.
I only knew how to be a princess then.

All the guys wanted a wife
Who was a mother in disguise.

At the date of submission,
Grad school entrance was denied.
I changed my mind.
Dropped-out until 25.
Not knowing how
I had harmed my mind.

At 25 I came alive,
And learned to survive!

Afterword

This *is* Jeanne's Story—but it's not over! When it ends years from now, Jeanne and her son will have traveled to the edge of our world and back again. Much more remains to be discovered about this amazing woman who sets out to explore the lives of modern women and succeeds in creating an amazing life of her own.

Jeanne's Story continues in the sprawling epic novel, **Angel of The Maya.** Within its pages she promised to share her past life prior to her arrival in Mayaland and taking up residence with other stars in the realms of art and spirituality. Perhaps Jeanne's most amazing friend within these further adventures is the amazing shamana, Mandy Sheridan aka Mandy Brown. Her backstory is already available in **Within the Veil:** *An Adventure in Time.*

There is more to come relative to Jeanne's progress in life and spiritual development, so check back to see what Ruth Lee scribes in the future.

WRITING
IN
SPIRIT

Jeanne's Story

READER'S GUIDE

A Conversation with Ruth Lee

Question: Is Jeanne the same character who transformed into a Spiritual Scribe in Angel of The Maya? While living that life Jeanne promised to write the backstory of the gifted women who work with Mandy in Mayaland. Is this Jeanne's backstory?

Ruth Lee: Simply stated, yes, this reveals a bit of Jeanne's background as promised in **Angel of The Maya**. This is my third book teaching in a 'novel' way, and you may be surprised to learn it arrived right after I finished writing **Within the Veil:** *An Adventure in Time*—many years before I wrote **Angel of The Maya.**

In 1995, when I wrote what I thought would be a sequel to Mandy's amazing adventures in Mayaland (**Within the Veil**), my hands raced ahead of my mind to create a story totally unlike the sequel I expected. That story became **Writing in Spirit ~** *Jeanne's Story.*

As years flew by I continued to write about successful women of different lifestyles. Their lives appeared to stand apart from others—until **Angel of The Maya** arrived on the scene and pieced together their amazing tales in a beautiful tapestry depicting a wonderful life of peace and harmony achieved communally in the Land of The Maya.

Question: Can you tell us a bit about your process when you create intriguing books whose far-reaching esoteric messages weave and merge in new and intriguing patterns. Do your writings reveal arcane knowledge or merely your imagination at work?

Ruth Lee: Like many other authors, I write in an altered state of mind. Sitting before my computer, I watch my fingers fly over the keyboard much the same as Jeanne describes in **Writing in Spirit.** Each session is identified as a chapter, with no conscious thought or plan in mind about what will happen next or where the novel is headed.

Question: Many authors say their art follows or imitates their lives, thus they write about what they know and experience. Is this true of you? Does your life precede your art and you share your life experiences in 'novel' ways with readers?

Ruth Lee: That's an excellent point! What truly sets my work apart from others is that *my life imitates my art.* It is not planned by my conscious mind, yet over time I seemingly follow some adventures described in my books. Since 'channeling' the first novel (**Within the Veil**) in the mid-90s, I have lived much of the book in piecemeal style.

Originally, I smiled when people tried to define me by that book, assuming it to be autobiographical. It was not—then, but today I cannot state that as confidently as I once did, because many things described in that novel have come to be and exist in my life now.

Question: Could you provide an example from **Within the Veil ~ An Adventure in Time** that came to be later and is present in your life now?

Ruth Lee: There are so many instances that I have to go to the book to see what jumps out as something I do now or experienced since creating mystical Mandy.

Just now I opened **Within the Veil** ~ *An Adventure in Time* to page 59 where the discovery is made of a dead tourist in the jungle. I actually laughed when I wrote it, because nothing like that would ever happen—Right?

That scenario was written in 1994. Five years later I was riding in a second-class bus enroute to view the Feathered Serpent descend the staircase at the great pyramid in Chichen Itza, along with a few of 'Mandy's Friends'. A well-dressed Mexican boarded late and sat beside a large Chicago cop on vacation. I did not notice much at first because they were seated off to my side.

One of our crowd had been unwise in diet and caused us to continually stop the bus full of Mayan men and women—who offered prayers and herbs as he repeatedly exited and returned to the bus. His untimely sickness turned out to be timely. It caused our bus trip to be delayed about an hour, providing enough time to discover the American tourist slumped in his seat—struggling to stay awake. He had made friends with a couple from Ecuador who called his name and when he did not respond, sounded the alarm. Turned out the Mexican had slipped a needle into the tourist's arm in preparation to rob and leave him for dead. Yes, it actually happened!

Question: What happened then? Was the would-be murderer/thief caught, did the tourist survive?

Ruth Lee: Oh, yes, it was all wrapped up with such style that no one would believe it, if in a novel. It actually was miraculous!

Our Guide, who had been recommended by scholars at Yale, turned out to be a federal cop. Few noticed his behavior throughout the trip, taking for granted his skill getting us whatever we wanted—regardless of how improbable it might be. He had objected to going to Chichen Itza on the equinox because such occasions bring out thieves. Turned out he was delighted to be involved in the excitement that preceded us to Chichen Itza.

On the bus when I told him something was very wrong, he took action. The would-be thief ran out of the bus into the surrounding fields. My seatmate, Jeanne, yes, Jeanne, took charge of the victim. We got him to the front of the bus where he collapsed on the steps just as our guide hailed a taxi holding up his badge and demanding the passengers exit so he could use the cab as an ambulance.

That is when it gets really amazing. The two passengers were doctors! The woman spotted a pin hole in Bill's arm and assessed it as a powerful drug used by thugs. She administered an antidote right there and then. With the doctors, our guide, and the bus driver all struggling to carry the big gringo to the cab, it was all over in a few minutes. Meanwhile, our sick amigo was so preoccupied with his problems he managed to relieve himself twice while the bus was stopped. I'm sorry to smile at the memory—as I said, nothing like that ever happened to me before I met Mandy in **Within the Veil ~ *An Adventure in Time!***

Question: That is truly amazing! Since writing **Writing in Spirit ~ *Jeanne's Story*** years ago, has anything happened to you that resembles Jeanne's work or life?

Ruth Lee: I started to say 'not that I've noticed,' but realize that is far from the truth. Since scribing **Writing in Spirit,** I relocated and produced a number of retreats and seminars similar to Jeanne's work. Fortunately, I have not become involved with a movie star or the paparazzi.

Question: One last thing, does a common thread/theme run through **Writing in Spirit ~ *Jeanne's Story?***

Ruth Lee: The theme running through **Writing in Spirit** is relationships most women encounter personally or vicariously throughout their lives: Ending old or worn-out friendships, relocating and establishing new friendships, parenthood, and romance. Along the way fame and wealth are also explored as capable of enhancing or destroying one's dreams.

Study Group Questions

*I*f you are fortunate enough to know others of like mind who enjoy discussing books you have all read, you may want to offer opinions on some of the topics suggested below:

1. What was your first impression of Jeanne? Did your initial appraisal of her character and status hold up over the course of the book or did it change dramatically or systematically by the end? Explain.

2. Throughout the story you meet women who are initially important to Jeanne, but their influence wanes over time. Why do you think these relationships change? Do you maintain good ties with friends and neighbors from long ago or have you changed so much that such relationships no longer fit? What do we owe neighbors?

3. Jeanne is successful, wealthy and seems to have it all. However, for much of the book she worries about finding a lasting love relationship. Do you know other successful women who are unhappy in their romantic relationships? Why do you think that happens?

4. Do you have a greater appreciation or understanding of women who adopt "special needs children"? Would you consider adopting such a child yourself?

5. Do you enjoy reading about celebrities? If so, what attracts you to their lives? How do you feel about Jeanne's reaction to celebrities and fans?

6. How much wealth and fame do you believe Jeanne amassed during the period explored in this book? If your views differ, are you surprised everyone has a different idea of what wealth means or represents—or are you all in agreement? Discuss and possibly identify what you need to be satisfied and happy with your life.

7. Does anyone in the group 'Write in Spirit' as described by Jeanne? Do you have enough information and guidance to try it, or does it already provide greater understanding of your spiritual work?

8. Do you feel comfortable discussing spirituality? What does it mean to each member of your group—or do you assume others would not understand it if you were to bring up the subject?

9. What do you suppose Jeanne's underlying belief system may be? Do you agree that she operates with a highly evolved ethical structure in place—or not? Discuss how much you would share of your personal feelings and beliefs if you wrote a book of this type.

10. Jeanne frequently remarks about the negative moods of friends and others. Do you think she exaggerates such moods in women today? If so, what do you think causes

women who possess much to display negative states of mind rather than confidence and success?

11. Imagine you are about to attend one of Jeanne's events. Why did you sign up to attend and what do you expect her lessons to cover?

12. Does the image of Jeanne making her way in the world using only her talents and gifts to create her own business appeal to you or not?

13. Have you ever dreamed of having a relationship with a movie star? If so, name your idol. What about the unattainable idol appeals most to you or others?

14. Where do you think the next chapter in Jeanne's Story takes place and do you think she will be happier then or about the same as now? Why do you think that?

15. It is often said that Ruth Lee's books of this genre teach lessons about life or provide different views on everyday interactions in a 'novel' way. Do you agree or fail to see how that applies to **Writing in Spirit ~ *Jeanne's Story?***

If you doubt that you can write in Spirit, release the doubt immediately. Know that you, too, can grow in Spirit as described in **Writing in Spirit ~ *Jeanne's Story.***

About the Author

*R*uth Lee, Scribe began writing in Spirit shortly after leaving a long, successful career with two of the world's largest corporations. Stunning everyone, she walked away and never returned to such work in order to pursue a life of contemplation, writing, art, teaching, and traveling the world.

During the years following her departure from corporate America, she came out of the closet and finally admitted to being exceptionally gifted spiritually. No one is more amazed by her unusual ability to help others live more perfect lives than Ruth Lee.

Scribing The Teachers of the Higher Planes' six **Books of Wisdom** earned Ruth Lee a place among the highest level of esoteric writers published today. It took years to publish all materials scribed prior to writing books that teach in 'novel' ways, including **Within the Veil ~ *An Adventure in Time*** and **Angel of The Maya,** but the wait was worth it to the growing legion of fans of Mandy and her friends.

www.ingramcontent.com/pod-product-compliance
Lightning Source LLC
Chambersburg PA
CBHW071507260626
47170CB00002B/287